He was tempted. So tempted.

How many times over the years had his thoughts strayed to Bree and where she was and what she was doing? And then to have her practically dropped into his lap by a weird twist of fate and weather…

She looked almost exactly the way she had when she was his. It was hard for his brain and his body to recognize that was no longer the case. When his fingertips brushed across her pink mouth, her lips had parted seductively, nearly begging him to kiss her. And he'd wanted to. Man, he'd wanted to.

Which was why he walked away. Why he had to stay away from Bree Harper.

* * *

Snowed in with Her Ex
is part of the Brides and Belles series—
Wedding planning is their business…
and th~~eir pleasure~~

D0795085

SNOWED IN WITH HER EX

BY
ANDREA LAURENCE

MILLS &
BOON

Published in Great Britain 2015
by Mills & Boon, an imprint of Harlequin (UK) Limited,
Eton House, 18-24 Paradise Road, Richmond, Surrey, TW9 1SR

© 2015 Andrea Laurence

ISBN: 978-0-263-25245-3

51-0115

Harlequin (UK) Limited's policy is to use papers that are natural, renewable and recyclable products and made from wood grown in sustainable forests. The logging and manufacturing processes conform to the legal environmental regulations of the country of origin.

Printed and bound in Spain
by CPI Barcelona

Andrea Laurence is an award-winning contemporary romance author who has loved books and has been writing stories since she learned to read and write. She always dreamed of seeing her work in print and is thrilled to be able to share her books with the world. A dedicated West Coast girl transplanted into the Deep South, she's working on her own happily-ever-after with her boyfriend and five fur-babies. You can contact Andrea at her website, www.andrealaurence.com.

To My Mountain Companions—
Linda Howard, Linda Jones, Marilyn Baxter,
Kimberly Lang, Kira Sinclair & Dani Wade

This book, quite literally, would not be possible without all the great trips we've taken to the mountains together. (Some of the settings might sound a little familiar!) Linda, thank you for generously allowing us to have this experience with you. I have a lot of great memories of our trips, including rowdy games of Cranium and Cards Against Humanity, midnight Walmart runs to make foil hats, and watching Kim pull silverware out of her purse at Dixie Stampede. With you guys, I laugh until my face hurts and my throat is raw. Those trips are one of my favourite times of year.

Prologue

"I'm sorry." Briana Harper interrupted her business partner in the middle of their weekly meeting. "Did you just say we've booked the Missy Kline and Ian Lawson wedding? *The* Missy Kline and Ian Lawson?"

Natalie, the wedding planner and office manager, looked up from her tablet, her brow furrowing in mild irritation at Bree breaking her flow. "Yes," she said with a heavy sigh. "What's the big deal with that? We have plenty of celebrity weddings."

Bree shook her head and returned to tapping absently at her own tablet. "I'm just surprised, that's all." That wasn't all, but she wasn't going to tell her best friends and business partners that. One of the most important rules at From This Moment was to remain professional at all times. It didn't matter if the ring bearer knocked over the wedding cake, a guest spoke up during the dreaded "if anyone has any reason why these two should not be wed" moment or the groom was your ex-boyfriend. So Bree kept her mouth shut.

"They're all over the magazine covers at the grocery store checkout lines," Gretchen added. "I don't know how you could've missed it. Apparently she's pregnant, too."

"I guess I've been eating too much takeout," Bree muttered. Pregnant. The bare-midriff pop queen was going to have Ian's baby. For some reason that bothered her. A lot. How could she have missed this news?

Natalie flung her dark brown hair over her shoulder and continued on with her Monday morning briefing. When Natalie was focused on the job, there was no room for joking around or unnecessary drama.

Each Monday, the four owners of From This Moment met to discuss new clients, business issues and the previous weekend's wedding.

From This Moment was a one-stop wedding venue that catered to the discriminating Nashville bride. Anybody who was anybody got married at their facility. In just six short years, college friends Natalie, Amelia, Gretchen and Bree had gone from being nobodies with a dream to members of the Nashville business elite.

Together, they were a powerhouse of wedding perfection. If they couldn't do it, they knew someone who could. Anything the bridal couple wanted, they made it happen. No request was too complex, and they built a reputation on that. That, and a policy of strict confidentiality.

Natalie was right; they did have their fair share of celebrities marry here. Missy Kline was just one more star they could add to their roster of famous clients, but Bree couldn't care less about her. She was far more interested in Missy's groom—Nashville music producer and owner of SpinTrax Records, Ian Lawson.

Once upon a time, Ian had been the center of Bree's universe. They had met as freshmen at Belmont University in Nashville and for more than a year, they had been inseparable. He had been the sexy coffee shop musician with the long hair in his sleepy eyes and the smile that could charm her panties off. When he'd played his guitar and sang to her, all was right in the world. And then he had stopped playing and everything went wrong.

"Bree?"

Bree's head snapped up. The other three ladies were looking at her. She'd obviously missed something. "Yes?"

"I said," Natalie repeated, "will you be able to do the engagement portraits this Thursday and still be back in time to cover the rehearsal dinner for the Conner wedding on Friday?"

Now it was Bree's turn to frown. "Why wouldn't I be back in time? It only takes a couple hours for an engagement shoot."

"The bride wants to do the photo shoot at the groom's cabin in Gatlinburg." Amelia repeated the detail Bree had missed.

"That should be fine."

"Okay, good." Natalie made a note. "I'll get you the address of the cabin. Plan to arrive around noon."

That was that. Once Natalie noted something in her tablet, it was virtually signed in blood. There was no getting out of it now. Bree would finally come face-to-face with the man who had haunted her thoughts and dreams for the past nine years.

And his new bride.

One

"This is not good."

As though the universe had heard Ian's words, the tires on his Cadillac Escalade skidded on a patch of ice. He corrected the truck's erratic movement and steered it back into the lane and away from the deep ditch on the side of the road. Gripping the leather steering wheel with white-knuckled tension, he cursed and silently thanked his assistant for making sure he left first thing this morning. Any later and he might not have made it.

The snowflakes were growing increasingly difficult to see through and were collecting along the side of the road. On the freeway from Nashville toward Gatlinburg, the weather had changed from rain to sleet to an icy slush. Now, in the heart of the Smoky Mountains, it was one hundred percent snow.

And a lot of it.

At the bottom of the hill that led to his mountainside

community, he backed up slightly, put his SUV into a lower gear and started accelerating up the incline. Slow and steady, he made it up and around the long, winding curve to his driveway at the very top, then pulled into the garage.

Ian grabbed his bag from the passenger's seat and stepped out. He walked to the door to his cabin, pushed a button and watched the snow continue to fall until the garage door closed and blocked out the inclement weather he hadn't planned for.

He should've known this would happen. It was just one more thing in a string of screwups that had plagued his life the past few months. He knew that he should think of them as happy accidents, but he couldn't help but feel trapped by his circumstances. This weather was no exception.

Ian never came to the mountains in January or February. The weather was always too unpredictable this time of year. Living at the top of a mountain was luxurious and the view was incredible, but you could only benefit from it if you could get up there. He wouldn't be here now except that his fiancée, Missy, had insisted they take their engagement photos at the mountain house. Against his better judgment, he'd agreed.

Ian set his bag on the granite countertop and glanced out the bay window to the valley below him. It was a sea of white out there. At this rate, the few inches on the ground would easily reach half a foot or more. "No accumulation of note." He snorted after mimicking what the man on the news had said last night. Missy had left from Atlanta, so maybe the weather was better from the south, but likely it wasn't. He was pretty sure Missy wouldn't be able to make it up the mountain in her little Jaguar.

And the photographer… Who knew what kind of car he or she would be driving. If this storm had surprised him, it had probably surprised everyone.

Thank goodness he'd had the cabin stocked with supplies. Ian walked around the kitchen, opening the cabinets and the refrigerator to inspect the contents. There was enough to feed them for several days, as requested. His caretakers were a married couple who lived down the hill. They kept the grounds tidy and the cabin clean and well maintained. Before he made a trip to the house, he would give Rick and Patty a list of food and supplies and they would see to it that everything was there.

Sometimes Patty would even do a little extra to welcome Ian home. Today there was a bottle of champagne chilling in the refrigerator door and a pair of flutes sitting on the counter by a vase of fresh flowers. Neither had been on his list, so that was Patty's way of congratulating him and his new fiancée on their engagement.

She must have somehow missed the announcement that Missy was eight weeks pregnant. Missy had gushed about their newly forming family to anyone who would listen—from her two million Facebook fans to the journalist at some tabloid magazine. Ian didn't think there was a person left in the United States who didn't know about his personal business.

They would wed in March at a venue in Nashville that Missy had chosen. Ian had not been involved with the details. He had told himself, and Missy, that he was busy with work so she could plan whatever she liked. It was her big day, after all. The truth was that he was still coming to terms with all the new developments in his life. But he was hoping to turn that around.

He wanted this baby to be welcomed into a happy, loving family and he was willing to make the effort to turn that into a reality in the next seven months. It would take work on both their parts. Missy wasn't the easiest woman to be with. She was demanding, spoiled and used to people constantly telling her how wonderful she was.

They weren't a love match by any stretch of the imagination, but Ian was beginning to think love and the trappings that went with it were just a myth, anyway. Any marriage took work. Their situation might not be ideal, but she was going to have his baby and they were getting married.

He should make the most of a complicated situation. A romantic weekend together was just what they needed to stoke the fires. After all, plenty of men would love to marry Missy Kline. Her sultry voice and hard body had been a staple in Top 40 radio for the past few years. She was the star of Ian's record label.

At least she had been. Her most recent record hadn't done that well, but Missy wasn't worried. She had the wedding and baby to keep her relevant. Her manager had arranged to sell the exclusive story and pictures from their wedding to some magazine. They were working on making their upcoming ceremony into some television special. It was going to be invasive, and Ian hated the idea of the whole thing, but Missy was pretty business savvy. They couldn't pay for this kind of publicity. The day their engagement was announced and photos of her ring hit the gossip blogs, her latest song hit the top ten on iTunes. As her label, he couldn't complain. As her fiancé, he wasn't as thrilled.

This weekend they would take their engagement portraits and project the image of the happy power couple to the world. Then they would spend the next few days together trying to make it into a reality. A crackling fire, a stunning view, hot cocoa on the deck while snuggled under a blanket together... It would be a romantic music video come to life. He hoped.

Right now, he couldn't guarantee that any of it was going to happen. Missy had said the snow would be romantic. He had no doubt she'd changed her mind by now.

Frowning, Ian walked to the front door, opened it and stepped out onto the front porch. The snow was sticking in earnest now, piling on the grass and creating a solid blanket across the road. You couldn't even see the pavement. Or the layer of ice likely forming beneath it. In the South, it was rarely snow that was the problem. It was the ice that sent you skidding into ditches and sliding backward down hills.

As he watched the snow fall, a little white SUV rounded the corner and headed in his direction. His house was the last on the winding path, so once the car passed his closest neighbor he knew it had to be the photographer. If the photographer could make it from Nashville despite the weather, maybe Missy would make it in from Atlanta. At the very least, he knew the roads hadn't closed yet.

The SUV pulled up by the steps to the front porch. Ian pasted on his smile, readying himself for a day of Academy Award–winning acting. He took careful steps down the stacked stone stairs to greet the photographer and help bring in any equipment.

A woman in a tight pair of jeans and a fitted turtleneck with a fleece jacket over it got out. She was dressed for a January day in Nashville, not the mountains. The snow had obviously been a surprise for her, too. She had no heavy coat, no gloves and no scarf, and her red Converse sneakers would offer about as much traction on ice as baby oil.

At least she had a hat. Her long blond hair peeked out beneath the knitted cap pulled down over her head. She was wearing wide, dark sunglasses, so he could see very little of her face, but for some reason, she seemed familiar to him.

The woman slammed her car door shut and slipped off her sunglasses. "Hi, Ian."

In an instant, the face, the voice and the memories slammed together and socked him in the gut. It was Bree. Briana Harper. His freshman romance. The one who distracted him from his classes with her young, firm body and adventurous spirit. The one who dumped him at the lowest point in his life.

Ian swallowed the lump in his throat. "Bree? Wow. I had no idea you were, uh, that you would be…"

Bree winced and nodded. He could tell from the visible tension in her neck and shoulders that this was equally awkward for her. She was strung tight as a drum, and the familiarity of their past urged him to reach out and massage her neck the way he used to. But that was just nostalgia talking. He sincerely doubted touching Bree would help this situation.

"You didn't know I was coming?"

"No, I…left all the details to Missy. She didn't mention who the photographer would be."

"I knew that I should've said something," she began, "or given you some kind of warning in case you didn't know, but I'd hoped not to make a big deal of it. My business partners didn't know you and I were acquainted."

Acquainted. That was one word for it. Touched every inch of each other's bodies was another way to phrase it. Once the shock of her arrival faded, Ian let his curious gaze run over the rest of her once-familiar curves. There were more than he remembered, but they'd practically been kids then, still teenagers. Now she was a full-grown woman in a pair of jeans that looked painted-on.

"Is this going to be a problem for you?" she asked. "It's not for me. I intend to keep this very professional. Your fiancée doesn't even need to know we've met previously, if that's what you prefer."

"Yes, that's probably for the best." Although Missy claimed she had little competition, she was at the same time insanely jealous. She had made headlines for starting catfights in night clubs and industry parties. She'd snatched the extensions out of her supposed rival's hair for just *talking* to her ex-boyfriend at a promoted event in Las Vegas.

Ian hadn't given Missy any reason to be jealous, but he knew how easily that switch could flip in her. The last thing he needed was Missy throwing a fit about the photographer. They needed these pictures done and released to the magazine for the scheduled issue. They couldn't wait for someone else to come up here and replace Bree.

That is, if anyone else could even make it up the mountain. The snow was falling faster than ever now. "We'd better get your things inside," he suggested.

Bree nodded. When she turned to head toward the back of her car, her shoe skidded on the slick pavement. Her eyes widened and her arms shot out for something to steady her, but it was Ian's lightning-fast reflexes that saved her. He reached out, his arms encircling her waist and tugging her up and against his body.

Ian instantly knew he'd made a mistake. The whole length of her was pressed into him. The scent of her favorite lotion mingled with the baby shampoo she'd always used. The familiar combination rushed to his nose, bringing back flashes of hot nights in his dorm room and in the back of his car. His entire body tensed, the cold unable to dampen the sudden arousal that being near Bree had so easily caused.

Bree clung to him, her ivory cheeks flushed pink from the cold and a hint of embarrassment. Her baby-blue eyes met his for a moment and the connection between them snapped like a current flowing freely through a copper wire. It had always been like this. Even minutes after he'd had her, he'd want her again. Back then, if she wasn't in his arms, she was all he could think about.

He tore his gaze from hers, letting his eyes settle on the pink pucker of her mouth. That wasn't much better. Her lips had been the softest, most welcoming lips he'd ever encountered, before college or since. Kissing Bree had been one of the divine pleasures of his life. Losing that had been almost as hard as losing his music.

That thought brought him back to reality. Ian steadied her on her feet and then disentangled himself from her before he did something stupid like kiss her. Bree reached a hand out for the side mirror of her car, taking a solid step back from him.

"Thank you," she said, her cheeks now crimson. "That was really embarrassing."

"That was nothing," he said, more to himself than to her, but he followed it up. "Embarrassing would've been bruising your hind end on the driveway and getting your pants soaking wet and muddy."

"True," she said, looking around, apparently unwilling to meet his gaze again.

"Are your things in the trunk?" he asked.

"Yes." Bree perked up, seemingly happy to focus on her work again. With one hand on her car she stepped cautiously to the back and opened the hatch on her Honda. She slung a green backpack over her shoulder and then pulled out a few black bags and a tripod.

Ian took as much as he could from her and escorted her up the stairs into the cabin. He let her focus on setting up her equipment and turned to his phone as a distraction. Hopefully reading a couple emails would help dull the raging arousal that still pumped through his veins and clouded his mind.

He hadn't had a reaction to a woman like that since… He thought back and frowned. Since the last time he'd held Bree in his arms. Not even the belly-baring diva of his record label could match the need Bree built in him right now. He didn't want that to be the case—life would be so much easier if things were reversed—but there was no denying it.

Missy would have a glass-breaking fit if she knew.

Bree focused on setting up her equipment even though she knew it was a pointless exercise. An hour had gone by without any sign of his fiancée. If she didn't show up in the next half hour, the odds were that she wasn't coming. One glance out the window made it perfectly obvious that the drive in would be next to impossible.

She had barely made it up the mountainside herself. Her tires had spun a time or two, lodging her heart in her throat. But that was nothing, nothing compared to the collision she'd just had with Ian.

It had been nine years since they'd been together. She should be over him by now. Long over him. Yet, when she was pressed against the hard wall of his chest and staring up into the dark green eyes she'd once lost herself in, the years apart seemed to vanish in an instant. All the reasons she walked away, all the heartache and the doubts, gone.

She thought he felt it, too. For a moment, she sensed a connection between them. An instant of attraction and longing had flickered in his eyes, a soft smile curling his lips. And then he'd looked away. A hard glint had shone in his eyes as he gently pushed her out of his arms.

And just as quickly, she'd realized she was a fool.

She hadn't been able to get to her equipment fast enough. Bree needed the safety and security of her camera. It was like a barrier between her and the world. As long as she only looked at Ian through the lens, she would be okay.

At least that's what she told herself.

That didn't keep her from sneaking peeks of Ian now as she worked. As much as she tried to focus, her gaze would lift and she would take in a few seconds of his broad shoulders clad in black cashmere. His strong hands gripping his cell phone and typing madly at his laptop computer. The firm curve of his rear, highlighted by the custom fit of his gray wool pants…

Groaning, Bree focused her attention back on her equipment. The work is what would get her through this. It was just stupid, misplaced attraction mixed with nostalgia and jealousy. It wasn't like things between them had ended well. There were plenty of good reasons why they didn't work as a couple, and she had broken up with him. No sense in pining for something she had given up.

Not that it had been much to give up near the end. During the last two months of their relationship, Ian had completely changed as a person. Part of what had initially attracted Bree to Ian was that he was as different from her father as a man could get.

Doug Harper was a certified workaholic. He was successful and driven, spending nearly every waking hour of his life managing his construction company. He'd helped build half of Nashville and had made a fortune doing it. Her mother had filled the empty hours by traveling around the world and spending her husband's earnings. That had left Bree alone at home with the housekeeper each night.

It had been a miserably lonely existence she didn't intend to repeat as an adult. She'd always told herself she wanted a man who came home at night. One who was more interested in living than working. Who would put more importance on family and love than money and business. A soulful musician fit the bill nicely.

Ian had been everything she wanted and he'd really had a shot of doing well with his music. Until he'd stopped playing music and dropped out of school to work at a record company. Suddenly, he'd always been working.

It seemed like overnight she had lost her musician and in his place stood a clone of her dad. It had broken her heart to watch it happen, but in the end, things had turned out for the best. Ian had become extremely successful and was marrying his pop star. She had a career she was proud of and hopefully would one day find the perfect person for her, too. The photo session shouldn't be awkward at all. At all.

So why did she have butterflies fluttering in her stomach?

Her thoughts were interrupted by Ian's voice. He was talking loudly to someone on the phone. He didn't sound happy, but she was relieved to hear it was the weather and Missy's tardiness that concerned him. For a moment, she'd thought he might ring up Natalie and demand another photographer. That would be so embarrassing. She couldn't go back to Nashville and face her friends after something like that.

"What?" Ian's sharp voice cut through the cabin, echoing in the large open space of the living room where she was unpacking. "Are you sure? No. No, of course I don't blame you. I want you and the baby to be safe. That's the most important thing. We can reschedule."

Bree froze, waiting to hear the rest of the story. She was thankful she'd opted to have Amelia book her a hotel room nearby. Making it back to Nashville in this weather was a dangerous prospect. She glanced out the large bay window that looked over the valley below. She couldn't see anything but white. No cars, no roads, no trees. Just white.

A loud curse followed by a hollow thunk startled her. She straightened up and turned back toward the kitchen. Ian blew through the archway a moment later, his jaw tight and the edges of his ears red with anger. He looked at Bree, about to speak, then he stopped himself. He shoved his hands into his pockets and took a deep breath. "She's not coming."

Bree had gathered that much. "What happened?"

"The roads are all closed unless you have snow chains and even then, some roads are impassable. Missy was coming from Atlanta. She made it as far as Maryville, but then they started sending cars back. There's no way to get here." He shook his head. "I should've waited to do this until we could drive up together."

Bree bit her lip, not quite sure what to say to that.

"I guess we can reschedule the session in Nashville, if that's easier."

He nodded, his gaze dropping to the polished wooden floors. "That's probably the best plan."

Bree nodded. There was a confusing pang of emotions in her stomach as she turned back to her equipment to pack up.

She was relieved that she didn't have to face his beautiful and successful fiancée today. She didn't really feel like snapping pictures while they posed together intimately and smiled at her camera. She'd dodged the bullet. When she got back to Nashville, she needed to confess the truth to Natalie. It was probably for the best that someone else handle their engagement portraits and maybe the wedding itself. There was being a professional and there was being a masochist. She recognized the difference now.

At the same time, she didn't want to leave. Walking out the door meant she might never see Ian again. When he'd held her outside, she'd felt a heat in her belly that hadn't burned that strongly in a long time. She wanted him to hold her again. To kiss her the way she hadn't been kissed in years.

She groaned inwardly and zipped her bag. Maybe she *was* a masochist. She was fantasizing about her ex. Her engaged, soon-to-be-a-daddy ex. The ex she'd broken up with because she couldn't take the sudden change in everything about him. Overnight, he'd gone from a music major to a record label toadie working eighty hours a week. Bree was certain none of that had changed. He ran a successful record label. Just because he took a weekend off to pose for engagement pictures didn't mean he was cured of his affliction.

Bree stood up and slung her camera bag over her

shoulder. She was about to grab another bag when she heard a loud knock at the door.

Ian looked at her and frowned before turning, walking over and opening the front door. An older man in a heavy jacket and cap was standing there.

Bree couldn't hear their conversation so she moved closer.

"I've been walking around to all the cabins in the subdivision while I can. Everything's shut down. During Superstorm Sandy we got a bunch of snow and it took a few days before they could get the roads cleared. They can't really start, though, until the snow stops falling. There's already ten inches on the ground and they're expecting upward of another fifteen or so before it's done. I've lived here twenty years and I haven't seen it fall this hard and fast."

"So we're stuck here, Rick?"

The older man nodded. "For a few days at least. That incline is too dangerous for the plows. Patty stocked the kitchen and I added half a cord of firewood to the pile. It should keep you until it's safe to head back to Nashville."

Bree heard the man's words, but part of her didn't quite process it at first. It wasn't until Ian closed the door and turned to look at her with an expression of pure agony that it clicked. It wasn't as simple as Missy not being able to get here. They also couldn't leave. They couldn't even get down the mountain so she could sleep in her reserved hotel room.

Bree immediately reached for the remote control and turned the television to the weather station. Hopefully the National Weather Service knew better than the caretaker. The map of the country finally came up and the woman in the nice suit pointed out the weather trouble spots. When she got to the Smoky Mountains, Bree gasped.

"…An unexpected barrage of snow in the area after two smaller storm cells merged into the newly dubbed Winter Storm Shana. Blizzard-like conditions are expected overnight with up to forty inches of snow. Roads are closed and the highway patrol is asking people to stay in their homes. Do not try to travel as emergency crews are having difficulty getting to distress calls."

At that, Bree's knees gave out and she plopped down into the armchair behind her. She was stuck here. With Ian. For an undetermined amount of time.

And Ian looked anything but pleased about it.

TWO

Days. Days! Trapped in this house with Briana Harper. What, exactly, had he done to deserve this? He must have done something because if the past few months weren't karma coming back to bite him, he didn't know what it was.

Ian scowled at his phone as appointment change notice after appointment change notice came through. After finding out they were snowed in, he'd called his administrative assistant and asked her to clear his calendar through Tuesday, just in case. Each meeting on his packed schedule generated another email as it shifted ahead into an already overcrowded week.

On the plus side, he had his laptop and cell phone, and the cabin had DSL internet service, so the wheels of progress could still spin to a point. He might be stuck here with Bree, but it was a big house and he was a busy man. Certainly with three stories and twelve different rooms to choose from, they wouldn't have to cross paths very often.

He leaned to the side on his stool to peek into the living room. Bree was camped out there with her own computer and equipment. She'd been on the phone on and off, too. He'd tried not to listen, but it was hard not to. She'd called a woman named Natalie, then Amelia. The talk had been all about work and covering the weekend wedding festivities, but a part of him kept waiting to hear his own name.

Bree had mentioned that she'd kept their past together a secret, but surely now that she was trapped here with him, that information would be shared with her coworkers. In the scheme of things, it seemed noteworthy. Unless, of course, he was as distant a memory in her mind as his music was in his own. If that was the case, good for her. He hadn't been as lucky. Thoughts of Bree still plagued him, angered him. He'd be happier now if he could've forgotten about her. Sometimes the intricacies of his work would push the thoughts away, but a quiet moment always brought them screaming back into his head.

She'd called her mother and left a message so she wouldn't worry. One call she didn't make, however, was to a boyfriend or spouse. He'd thought for sure that a man would've met Bree's requirements by now. There were plenty of hopeful artists in the world for her to choose from. Or maybe she'd grown up and realized that it wasn't practical for an adult who needed to support a family. Not that he was bitter.

Finally, she'd called a lady named Julia at the Whitman Gallery and said she'd have to reschedule her final appointment before the showing.

Ian had been to the Whitman Gallery on several

occasions. They did a lot of special art showings and liked to feature local Nashville artists. Perhaps Bree was planning a show there. That would be a big step for her photography. Back in school she'd been big on nature and architectural photography. She took snapshots of people but almost never posed portraits. She'd told him once that she liked to capture genuine moments.

How things had changed! His engagement portraits were about as disingenuous as moments could come. But as he well understood, sometimes art had to give way to paying the bills, and wedding photography was a high-dollar business. The wedding industry as a whole was a racket. The paperwork Missy had brought home after she'd reserved the venue and put down the deposit nearly made him choke. The floral bill alone was running him nearly six figures.

Bree stood up and Ian quickly shifted his gaze back to his computer screen. He tried not to give her much notice as she came into the kitchen and opened the pantry doors. She pulled out a bag of coffee. "It's freezing in that big room. Do you mind if I make a pot of coffee? Will you drink some?"

"That's a good idea. I'll drink it." The thermos he'd demolished on the drive up here had burned off a long time ago.

Bree filled the coffeepot and went about setting the controls and adding grounds to the filter. "When it's cold like this, I need something warm to drink."

"I think we'll be drinking a lot of coffee, then."

"I noticed some decaffeinated herbal tea in the pantry, too. I'll probably switch to that in the evenings. Otherwise I'll be up all night."

Ian's brain instantly went to the nights he had kept her up without the assistance of caffeine. How many times had he missed his 8:00 a.m. English lecture because he'd lost track of time in Bree's arms?

His eyes focused in on the curious expression on Bree's face. "What?" he asked.

"I asked if you take cream and sugar," she said with a smile.

"Yeah, two sugars. I like it sweet."

Bree got down the mugs and turned to him while she waited for the coffee to finish brewing. "Still got a sweet tooth, huh?"

He nodded, remembering all the junk he used to eat back in college. Like any college student, he'd consumed his fair share of pizza and Chinese food, but more often than not, he could be found with a candy bar, a cookie or a can of soda in his hand. Sometimes a combination of the three. "This machine runs on sugar and caffeine most of the time. I have tried to scale back a little. I have a one-candy-bar-a-day limit my assistant enforces by keeping snacks in a locked drawer in her desk."

The warm scent of hazelnut coffee filled the air. Bree turned to pour two cups and doctored them appropriately. She set a mug down next to his laptop and crawled onto the barstool at the opposite side of the kitchen island.

"I guess I always envisioned you marrying a pastry chef. Or a chocolatier. I'm going to take a wild guess and say that Missy doesn't bake."

"Lord, no." Ian chuckled. "I don't think Missy has so much as turned on an oven in her entire life. She was singing on mall tours at fourteen and was an opening act for a world tour at seventeen. I signed her with Spin-Trax when she was twenty. She knows how to work an audience, but that's about it."

Bree took a sip of her coffee. "I suppose she doesn't eat that stuff, either."

"Missy doesn't eat much of anything."

Food was a constant point of contention in their relationship. Missy's personal trainer had convinced her that greens and fish were all she needed. Anything else and she'd blow up like a pop star has-been. When she'd announced her pregnancy, he'd expected her to add some foods back into her repertoire, but the opposite happened. Since she knew there were certain kinds of fish she couldn't eat, she'd gone fully vegetarian instead of taking the time to figure out what she could and couldn't have. She insisted that was why her belly was still as flat as it was on her last album cover. He wasn't sure how well she was going to take it when she hit the third trimester and even a strict diet wouldn't keep her from putting on a few pounds.

"I guess I'll never be a rock star, then. I like food too much," Bree said with a smile. "Of course, I've got the junk in the trunk to show for it."

One of Ian's eyebrows shot up. He'd tried not to look, but he'd noted Bree's trunk was nicely full. "I don't know what you're talking about," he said, trying to sound sincere without seeming too interested in her body. "You look great."

Bree smiled, a blush rising to her cheeks. She tucked a stray strand of blond hair behind her ears. "Thanks, but we both know this isn't the same body I had back in college."

"Thank goodness. I don't think I was skilled enough to handle curves that dangerous back in school."

Bree wrinkled her nose. "Were you always this big a flatterer?"

"I think so. I just did it with a song then. Now I have

to be more direct. I don't have time to beat around the bush."

Bree's bright blue gaze met his for a moment, and he felt the familiar heat rush through his veins once again. What was he doing flirting with Bree? He was engaged. He was going to be a father. He needed to focus on his relationship with Missy, not his past with Bree. How could he forget the fact that Bree had kicked him when he was down? That she had offered him the closest thing to a real relationship he'd ever had, then snatched it away?

Ian needed more space between them if he was going to get through the next few days. He couldn't decide if he wanted to kiss her or give her a piece of his mind. Neither was helpful. He remembered the feeling from school. She knew just how to push all his buttons and make him unsteady on his feet. Back then, it had brought on a rush of excitement. Now, it just frustrated him.

He had to give Missy credit in that department. He knew exactly where he stood with her: she was using him to salvage her career. There was no great love between them, at least when the cameras were off. It wasn't where he envisioned he would be with the mother of his child, but at least he understood the terms of the relationship. Bree was a wild card.

He looked back to his computer screen and closed his laptop. "I, uh, guess I'd better give you the tour so you can get settled in."

Bree slid down from the stool, carrying her mug with her as she followed him into the living room.

"This is the main floor. My bedroom is over there under the stairs." He gestured up to the loft overhead, then they headed up the steps. "You'll see there are two bedrooms and baths up here, and two more bedrooms and baths on the lower level. If I were you, I'd sleep up here, though. Because of the vaulted ceilings, upstairs stays a little warmer."

He led Bree back to the main level, past his bedroom door and down the staircase. At the bottom of the stairs was a spacious room with a big-screen television, a poker table, a pool table and a stone fireplace. "This is the game room. There's also a hot tub out that door on the deck."

He watched Bree roam around his vacation home, taking in every detail. She investigated both bedrooms, and then she looked out onto the deck. The direction of the snow was blowing such that it wasn't piling on the patio at all. That meant the front of the house would be waist-high in drifts by morning.

"This is really a beautiful place you have, Ian." Bree turned her back to the window and looked at him. "Do you get to spend much time here?"

Of course not. She had to have known the answer to that question before she asked it. It had been months since he'd last been here. Mid-September. Before his moment of weakness with Missy derailed his life. "Not as often as I'd like," he answered instead. "My mother and stepfather come up here from time to time. So does my stepbrother and his wife and kids."

"So your mom ended up marrying Ned?"

Ian's father had split nearly the moment he'd been conceived. When he was in high school, his mother had started a fairly serious relationship with Ned. Ned had one son of his own, a few years younger than Ian. "Yeah, they got engaged not long after you…" His voice trailed off. He was about to say "not long after you dumped me," but they were stuck here together. There wasn't much point in antagonizing one another, at least on the first day.

Bree's mouth tightened a bit, knowing what he'd been about to say. After a moment, she pasted back on her cheery smile. "How is everyone doing? I think about your family sometimes and wonder what they're up to."

Did that mean she thought about him, too? Ian knew he shouldn't care, but a part of him wondered. She'd certainly been on his mind over the years. Sometimes he was angry and bitter. Most times he just felt disappointed.

"Ned is getting ready to retire and my mother is trying to figure out what she'll do when she has to look at him all day. His son, Jay, and his wife just had their second child. They're all great. I actually haven't seen them in a while. Work has been pretty hectic."

Bree nodded and turned back toward the stairs. "You sound like my dad."

Ian noted the flat tone of displeasure in her voice. Bree and her father still had their issues, he could see. The man had been chained to his desk twenty hours a day when they were in college, and he blamed Mr. Harper in part for their relationship's demise. "How are your parents?" he asked.

Bree reached the top of the stairs and turned back to look at him. "Dad's recovering from bypass surgery after his second heart attack in five years."

Ian felt his own chest tighten in response. Bree had accused him of turning into a workhorse like her father. He tried not to work longer than eighteen-hour days, but that probably wasn't enough of a distinction in her eyes. Or the eyes of a cardiologist. "Is he okay?"

"Yes. He's too driven to die. But the doctors want him to scale back his hours and pass the running of the company on to his partner. That—" she laughed "—might actually kill him. That and the diet his doctors tried to put him on."

Ian nervously pulled at the suddenly tight collar of his sweater. He imagined the candy, coffee and liquor he consistently consumed was not on the doctor's recommended eating plan. "I'm glad he's doing okay. Is he back to work yet?"

"Yes," Bree said. "He returned to the office the day his doctor released him, although I suspect he'd been sneaking in some and checking his email from home. My mother divorced him last year, and he said it was hard for him to sit at home alone with the housekeeper. I find that kind of ironic considering that's how I'd spent most of my time. But his business is important to him. He's already sacrificed his family and his health for his job. It'd be a shame to lose his company, too. It's all he has left. You'd be wise to learn from his mistakes."

Bree had no idea why she'd said that last part, but the words left her mouth before she could stop them. It wasn't helpful. Or polite. Or any of her damned business. But a part of her just had to do it. If he was going to start a family, he should know what the price of his workaholic lifestyle would be. He should know what it would be like for his child.

Ian frowned at her and put his mug down on the side table. "What's that supposed to mean?"

Bree took a deep breath and shrugged. "You know what kind of hours you keep, Ian. They're probably worse than they were back in school when you forgot my birthday and left me alone night after night."

Ian widened his stance and crossed his arms over his

chest. "Are you still mad that I missed your birthday? I apologized twenty times."

"So did my dad, Ian. He apologized and bought me something expensive to make up for it, just to do it again. That's the point. You can work yourself to death, like my dad does. That's his choice. That's your choice now. But not when you have a family. Things are about to change for you. You can't work as hard as you do when you have a child at home who doesn't understand why you're never there."

"Since when do you know anything about me and what I do, Bree? You walked out of my life nine years ago."

That was an interesting way to look at how their relationship had ended. Her interpretation of the past was quite different. Bree planted her hands on her hips and prepared for battle. The minute she'd found out she was coming up here, she'd worried this moment might come. The presence of his fiancée would've kept the old feelings and hot tempers in check, but stuck alone? It was time to have the fight they'd never really had.

"How long did it take you to notice I was gone? A week? Two weeks?"

Ian clenched his jaw, fighting to hold back words he'd obviously suppressed all this time. "I noticed, Bree. I noticed that the woman I thought loved me just turned her back on me when I was at one of the lowest points in my life."

Bree scoffed at his cold assessment of her actions. "I didn't turn my back on you. You're the one who made this huge lifestyle shift and shut me out. Suddenly, you were all about working at that record company and you had no time for me anymore. You missed my birthday. You stood me up for that dance. You left me sitting alone at a restaurant waiting for you, twice. I did you a favor by easing your guilty conscience. You didn't have to feel bad about ignoring me if I was already gone."

"Thanks so much. I'm sure you were only thinking of me when you walked away. I made that huge 'life-style shift' because I was struggling to find my place in the world, Bree. You never realized how lucky you were. You were a talented photographer and you knew that your work could become a successful career for you. I had to face the ugly truth that my music wasn't good enough. *I* wasn't good enough. Do you know how much it hurt when my advisor told me that?"

Bree snuggled deeper into her fleece jacket, trying to disappear. She had assumed that time was hard on him, but he'd never talked about it. He had been like a steam locomotive that switched onto another track—he'd just kept on going. He'd started working at the record label, dropped out of school and charged ahead at full speed.

"How could I know anything, Ian, when you wouldn't talk to me about it? You never talked about anything important with me. You never shared your feelings. You saved it all for your songs. And when you lost that, you just clammed up and worked even harder."

She saw a touch of the anger ease out of his posture. His tense shoulders relaxed and his jaw unclenched. Ian shook his head sadly. "I never intended to shut you out, Bree. I just didn't know how to talk to you about it. I didn't know how to handle everything that was happening."

"I felt like I was losing you, little by little, like sand slipping through my fingers. At first I thought that job at the record label would help, but it just took over your life. You dropped out of school, moved off campus and wouldn't return my calls. What was left of the Ian I'd loved vanished. You were distracted, dismissive… I felt like I didn't matter to you anymore."

Ian ran his hand through the short, dark strands of his hair, the pain of that time in his life suddenly fresh in his eyes again. "Yeah," he admitted, "I threw myself into that job. But I was trying to find something I could do with my life. My dream of being a musician was dead, but at least working at that label let me keep my connection to the music industry.

"It's not an easy business, you know. Yeah, I worked long hours, but that's what they demanded. One of my professors got that gig for me. I couldn't disappoint him, especially when there was a line of other kids just waiting for me to screw up so they could take my place. So I fought for it. I put every ounce of energy that had once gone into my music into this work instead. And I succeeded. I climbed the ladder. I went out on my own and started my own label at twenty-five."

"You should be very proud of yourself."

Ian shrugged. "I guess. It wasn't an easy road, but I did it. It sure would've been a hell of a lot easier with you by my side."

"I know you think that, but it's probably not true. I would've been a distraction. You never would've gotten where you are now with a relationship making demands on your time. Besides," she said cheerfully, "things worked out for the best, right? You have your company, your fiancée, a baby on the way… Life turned out the way it was meant to."

Ian narrowed his green gaze and took a step toward her. "Do you honestly believe that? You haven't regretted the way things ended between us?"

Bree frowned and took a slight step backward, feeling her shoulder blades meet with one of the rustic wooden columns that supported the loft. "Of course I mean it. I mean, breakups happen and they're sometimes ugly, but you're happy with your life now, right?"

"If you believe what you read in the magazines, I guess so. I know I should be. I'm marrying one of the sexiest women on Earth. We're going to have a beautiful baby. My business is better than ever."

Bree's eyes focused on the slight downturn of his mouth as he spoke. He wasn't happy. Not at all. And she hated that. No matter what had happened between them, she wanted to see Ian happy. "So what's the problem?" she asked.

He took another step toward her, his height towering over her as he came nearer. "The problem?" A bitter chuckle escaped his lips. "Well, first, I'm not in love with Missy. Hell, I'm not even attracted to her. It's a long, sordid story I won't bore you with, but the punch line is that she's selfish and spoiled and doesn't give a damn about me unless there's a camera nearby. Second, she's the worst possible woman I could've chosen to start a family with. I'm already interviewing nannies because I know that's the person who's going to raise our child."

Ian leaned in, planting his palm on the polished wooden post over her head. "And to make matters worse, on top of all that, I find myself here. Trapped in a cabin with you. A woman who did love me once. One who would've made an excellent wife and mother. One who had the power to set my blood boiling with just a touch."

Bree drew in a ragged breath as Ian's hand brushed over her forehead and moved a strand of her hair from her face. Her entire body was tense, her stomach knotting tighter with every word he spoke.

"One who still has the power to make my entire body ache with the memory of making love to her," he whispered.

His gaze was focused on her lips as he spoke. He ran his fingers along her cheek and Bree's eyes instantly fluttered closed to savor the touch. The warm heat of his caress against her skin made her pulse pound harder than it had in a very long time. She took a deep breath and forced her eyes back open in time for his thumb to graze gently across her lips.

Was he about to kiss her? It would be wrong. So wrong. Yet, in that moment it was all she could think of. All she wanted.

"And I can't do a damn thing about it." He pulled away, taking several steps back as though her touch had nearly burned him.

Bree felt her knees weaken beneath her once he pulled away. It was as if he had yanked the rug out from under her. She righted herself and fidgeted, tugging anxiously at her pullover and tossing her hair over her shoulder.

What the hell was she thinking? She had very nearly melted into the arms of another woman's fiancée. She was their wedding photographer! Past or no past, that was all kinds of wrong. Natalie would kill her if she knew.

Bree took a deep breath and pulled herself together. Reacting to Ian didn't help either of them. "I'm sorry to hear your relationship is less than ideal," she said in her most formal, detached voice.

Ian's gaze ran over her face for a moment before he spoke. "Yeah. Me, too," he said, turning on his heel and disappearing into the other room.

Three

"Gretchen, I've made a big mistake."

Bree had made a quick getaway to her bedroom after her encounter with Ian. She'd needed some personal space to clear her head and purge her lungs of his scent. She'd hauled her bags up the stairs and selected the room with a wall of windows overlooking the valley below. The queen-size four-poster bed had a gray velvet brocade comforter and navy silk curtains to enclose the bed if she chose.

That wasn't a bad idea. The room was luxurious and spacious. Perhaps she should just wrap herself up in a silk cocoon and stay here until the snow melted. She could forage for food in the night while Ian slept and maybe squirrel away a box of crackers or something to keep up here. Maybe then they could stop antagonizing each other.

After closing the door, she'd grabbed her phone

and dialed one of her friends and business partners, Gretchen. Natalie would be horrified by the entire situation. Amelia would want to talk about Bree's feelings. But she just wanted to vent to someone who would listen, then tell her to put on her big-girl panties. That was Gretchen—their calligrapher, invitation and program designer and wedding day jack-of-all-trades.

"I hear you're snowed into a million-dollar mountain house. I really feel bad for you."

That was one way of looking at it, but it was getting harder and harder to remember that fact. The house *was* beautiful; every inch was filled with expensive furniture, detailed stone craftsmanship and state-of-the-art electronics. Her bedroom was nicer than some five-star hotels. "Did Amelia leave out the part where I'm stuck alone with the groom?"

"No, she mentioned that. Why does it matter? Is he creepy? Or a jerk?"

Bree hesitated. "No, he isn't creepy. But he is my… uh…*ex* from college."

"What?" Gretchen's sharp voice nearly climbed through the phone to smack her upside the head.

"Shh!" Bree insisted. She had no doubt that Gretchen was in the office and she didn't need her shouting to draw the others. "No one can know, okay? Especially not Natalie. She'll flip out."

"It sounds like *you're* flipping out. Is that what the thing Monday was about? Why you were so interested in the Missy Kline wedding?"

Bree frowned. "Maybe. It caught me off guard to find out he was getting married. And to her, of all people."

"So now you two are trapped together. What's going on that you're not telling me? You sound really wound up. The guy is getting married. And to Missy Kline! There shouldn't be an issue, even with your past together. Wait…you haven't tempted him away with your worn-out Converse and your messy ponytail, have you?"

"You hush," Bree snapped. She felt bad enough comparing herself to Missy; she didn't need Gretchen's help. "It's a proximity problem. We didn't exactly part well and being together after all this time…"

"Don't pick at the scabs, Bree."

"What is that supposed to mean?"

"I don't know what happened between you two, but considering I've known you for eight years and have never heard of you dating this guy, I figure you're picking at an old wound that should've healed a long time ago. You need to leave it alone or you'll reopen it. That's not the best idea when you're trapped in a house together. What good will it do to stir all that stuff up again, anyway?"

She was right. Nothing Bree said or did this weekend was going to change anything. When the snow melted, she would drive back to Nashville and resume her work. Ian would do the same. He might not be rushing home to reunite with the love of his life, but he would still go home to Missy and the baby. She had no doubt of that.

In college it had taken months to get Ian to open up to her about his family. He hadn't been much for talking about his personal life. It had been easier for him to communicate through song lyrics, but that had left no room for questions. That was probably how he'd liked it. But eventually, Bree had worn him down. He'd told her about how his father had bailed when his mother got pregnant. As he spoke she'd seen a haunting look of rejection in his eyes that Bree would never forget. Even though it really had nothing to do with him, he'd said he thought, deep inside, he wasn't good enough for his father to want to stay.

His college advisor echoing the same sentiment about Ian's musical abilities had been like a knife to his soft underbelly. He'd been defenseless to the attack and when it had come down to it, Ian had believed the man's words because he'd believed he wasn't good enough. Nothing Bree could say or do would've changed nearly twenty years of feeling inferior.

And nothing that happened this weekend would change the course Ian was on. He wouldn't do the same thing to his own child, even when the thought of being with Missy made him frustrated and desperate.

"It will do no good whatsoever," Bree answered Gretchen.

"Then steer your ship like you're in iceberg-filled waters. Stay diligent, keep your eyes open and avoid a collision. Eventually, you'll make it to port in one piece."

"Yeah," Bree said, her voice not sounding particularly confident.

Gretchen sighed. "Are you still attracted to him?"

The pointed question instantly flustered Bree. "What? Attracted? I mean, no, but then again, he's still… Yes," she spat out at last. "Because I'm an idiot."

She *was* still attracted to him. And she shouldn't be. It was so ridiculous. Her libido had flamed on like the Human Torch the minute she'd laid eyes on him again. The same libido that had been mostly ho-hum for the men she'd dated over the years. It was incredibly frustrating to find her body betraying her, especially over someone so unobtainable.

It was like her body remembered him. Nine years had done little to erase the claim he'd left on her. Just one touch and she was nearly putty in his hands again. Begging him to kiss her with pouty lips. Ignoring the fiancée unable to make it up the mountain…

"You're not an idiot. You just need to get laid."

Bree nearly choked. "Pardon?"

"You've just been working too hard with the gallery showing and all those post-Christmas engagement photo sessions. No time to play. And you haven't mentioned going on a date in forever. Maybe you should look into doing some online dating. It could help take the edge off."

That wasn't an entirely bad idea. Walking into Ian's house after months of celibacy had left her at a distinct disadvantage.

"Maybe you're right. If I keep my head down, I can make it through this." Even as she said the words, she didn't really believe them. She was a mess and it had only been… Bree looked down at her watch. Six hours. Only six hours with Ian had put her every nerve on edge. What would a few days do?

"Just remember," Gretchen said in a tone mocking the ever-proper Natalie, "keep it professional and keep it classy."

"Yeah." Bree snorted with contempt. "I'll do that. I'll call you later." She hung up and flopped back onto the bed. She closed her eyes, startling herself when the image of Ian hovering over her, midthrust, popped into her mind.

She shot up with a start. That settled it. She was going to lock herself in the bedroom. Bree pulled a book from her bag and set it by the bed. Investigating the large, marble, brass and glass tile bathroom, she decided that tonight she would crawl into her large whirlpool tub for a long, hot soak and read a book. She always lost herself in stories, so it would be an excellent distraction from Ian.

A disgruntled rumble sounded from Bree's belly.

So much for locking herself in the bedroom. She'd been up here a half hour and the rumblings of hunger pangs had already begun. She'd stopped for a quick bite on the road to follow up the granola bar she'd scarfed down before she left her apartment, but that had burned off. She could distract herself by unpacking her things and assembling her toiletries in the bathroom, but that would buy her minutes, not hours.

She needed to eat. And more important, she needed to desensitize herself to Ian. Perhaps the more they were together, the easier it would be. Either way, she couldn't ignore the inevitable. Eventually, Bree would have to go back downstairs and face him.

"Okay, I'm officially starving."

Ian looked up from his laptop to see Bree in the kitchen, searching the cabinets. He'd spent an hour or so staying as far as possible from her and focusing on work. After what had happened this afternoon, that seemed like the best idea. He wasn't entirely sure what had gotten into him. He'd been angry with Bree only moments before, and then suddenly, he had needed to touch her.

Relationships weren't exactly Ian's strong suit. He'd actually had very few that he'd even characterize as "relationships." He'd only been in love once, with Bree, and that whole thing had bitten him in the ass. From then on, dating had taken a backseat to work, and emotions usually had no role in the process. But he'd never been unfaithful to a woman. That just wasn't in his blood.

Besides, he was usually too busy with work to make one woman happy, much less two or three.

But here, now, for the first time, he was tempted. So tempted. How many times over the years had his thoughts strayed to Bree and where she was and what she was doing? And then to have her practically dropped into his lap by a weird twist of fate and weather…

Time had been good to Bree. He watched as she opened every single cabinet door, making thoughtful sounds as she moved around the gourmet, U-shaped kitchen. She was just as beautiful as he remembered, giving Missy a run for her money—and without three hours in the hair and makeup chairs to get there. She still had long honey-gold hair, which at some point today she'd pulled it into a messy knot at the back of her head. Her baby-blue eyes were just as bright. The freckles across her nose had faded, but she still had the same charming smile.

She looked almost exactly the way she had when she'd been his. It was hard for his brain and his body to recognize that was no longer the case. When his fingertips had brushed across her pink lips, they'd parted seductively, nearly begging him to kiss her. And he'd wanted to. Man, he'd wanted to.

Which was why he'd walked away. Why he had to stay away from Bree Harper.

Shaking away the unproductive thoughts, he looked down at his watch. It was after five. Food was probably a good idea. Bree had ended her quest at the refrigerator.

"Champagne, strawberries, spinach, brie…fancy stuff. Perfect if you're having acquaintances over for a wine soiree." Her blond head popped up over the door to look at him. "You don't happen to have makings for a cheeseburger tucked away in here, do you?"

He shook his head. "No, sorry. Missy doesn't eat red meat and she says that since she got pregnant, watching me eat it makes her ill."

Bree's lips twisted in thought. She eyeballed a loaf of sourdough bread on the counter and looked back inside the refrigerator. "How about grilled cheese and tomato soup?"

Ian's brow went up with curiosity. "Are you offering to cook us dinner?" The Bree he knew from college wasn't much of a culinary wizard. Of course, living in a dorm didn't exactly lend itself to cooking.

She shrugged, tossing a block of gruyere onto the counter. "One of us has to do it unless you have a personal chef hidden away somewhere."

"No." He chuckled. "I like to keep things more casual here, so I don't keep any staff."

"You have staff at home?" she asked while slicing the cheese on a wooden cutting board.

"I just have Winnie. She's… Well…I pretty much pay her to be my wife."

At that, the cutting stopped and Bree looked up. "Care to clarify that?"

"She takes care of everything at home so I can focus on work. Winnie cleans the house and does the grocery shopping. She cooks. She does my laundry and picks up my dry cleaning. Winnie pretty much does everything a wife who works in the home would do. I don't know how I'd survive without her."

Bree retrieved a skillet and a pot from the cabinet and put them on the blue flames of the stove. "Sounds handy."

"She is. I'm going to miss her when Missy moves in."

"Why is she leaving?"

That was a damn good question. "Missy is…particular. She has her own staff, which includes a housekeeper, a chef, a personal trainer and a personal assistant. She insisted there was no need to keep Winnie on when she moved in with her entourage. Once we add the nanny, that's just way too many people, although I hate to do it. I'm giving Winnie a huge severance package and I'm trying to find a new position for her."

Ian didn't mention that Winnie was relieved to be laid off. He got the distinct impression that she had no interest in looking after the pop princess. He didn't blame her. Missy was a handful.

He watched Bree at the stove. She had the tomato soup simmering and the sandwiches were turning perfectly golden and toasty in the skillet. He watched her give them an expert flip and then slip them onto a plate. The Gruyère cheese was oozing out the sides with crispy burned edges. She ladled the soup into big soup mugs and put them beside the sandwich.

"It may not be the gourmet meal a kitchen this grand calls for, but I can't think of anything else more perfect for a cold day in the mountains."

Ian picked up both plates and carried them into the dining room. "I agree. It smells great. I don't think I've had tomato soup since I was a kid."

"Really? Why was it in the pantry?"

He shrugged and put the plates down at two of the place settings near the fireplace. "It's probably left over from the last time my stepbrother came with the kids. They were here at Christmas."

They sat down together, the large stone hearth roaring with flames beside them and the picture window overlooking the valley opposite it. Ian found it unnerving that he couldn't see anything except the bare branches of the trees in his yard below. The snow was still falling as hard as before.

With a shake of his head, he took a bite of his sandwich and groaned aloud. It was probably the best grilled cheese sandwich he'd ever had. The gruyere reminded him of a *croque monsieur* he'd enjoyed so much in France. "This tastes wonderful."

"Thanks," she said before tentatively sipping a spoonful of the hot soup. "I'm not much of a cook. It'll probably be all downhill from here. Amelia won't even let me help in the kitchen when she's slammed."

"Who is Amelia?"

"One of my business partners at From This Moment. She's the caterer. You'd much rather be snowed in with her, I assure you. First-class cuisine all the way."

Ian sincerely doubted that. He'd take Bree's company and grilled cheese any day. "Does the wedding business take up all your time, or do you still have the opportunity to do the artistic photography you did back in school?"

A soft smile curled Bree's lips. "I do. This year, I've done a black-and-white series called 'The Other Side of Nashville.' I wanted to show the parts that most people don't think of. There's no country music, no cowboy boots. Just a collection of places I love and people who look less like Grand Ole Opry stars and more like middle America."

That was the Bree he remembered. The one who hated posed pictures. "Are you doing a show? I thought I heard you talking on the phone to someone at the Whitman Gallery earlier today."

"Yes." She brushed a stray stand of blond hair behind her ear. "It's the Sunday after next. I was supposed to have my last meeting with the curator tomorrow, but I obviously had to cancel. I'm going to meet with her as soon as I can get back to Nashville."

"Is this your first show at the Whitman Gallery?"

"It's my first show anywhere since college. And those hardly counted. I couldn't really focus on my art the first few years after we started From This Moment. Even though we all had our specialties, we had to roll up our sleeves and do everything from setting up chairs to sweeping floors. We couldn't afford to hire anyone to help us for a while. If I wasn't taking pictures, there were a million other things to be done. The last year or so, that changed. That's when I started my new collection."

Ian appreciated her work ethic. As fresh meat at the record studio, he'd sorted mail, emptied trash, fetched sparkling water for the singers…anything and everything they asked of him. That was just what you had to do.

"So tell me about the business you guys have going. Judging by what you've said and the estimate I received, you all are doing quite well now."

Bree chuckled. "Not all our weddings are on the same scale as yours. We have everything from week-long million-dollar extravaganzas to couples that elope in the garden with only their parents. Whatever a bride wants, we can make it happen."

"How did you start all this?"

"I met the others when I transferred to UT. During our senior year, while we were trying to think of what we wanted to do with our lives, one of us came up with the idea of a wedding facility. A friend had gotten engaged and complained that it was hard to find the right kind of venue that wasn't at a church or wasn't a tacky, in-and-out kind of chapel. We spent months putting together our grand plan and trying to round up investors."

"I can imagine it wasn't cheap to get off the ground."

"Oh, no. Even with some startup investments and money from my dad, we're mortgaged to our eyeballs. The initial costs were astronomical, but that's because you have to buy all the things you'll use repeatedly over the years like chairs and tables and stemware. Once you've got it, though, you've got it, and our expenses have gone down over time. Like I said, it took several years of hard work, but we've managed to make a profit every year. The facility itself will take a long time to pay off, but that's the nature of the business."

"Did you buy a place and renovate it?"

"No. We bought land and built everything exactly the way we wanted it. Natalie had a vision of how it should be laid out, and there was nothing even close on the market. Having a dad in the construction business certainly helped there. I probably saw him more that year than I did all the years before it."

Ian noticed the faint bitterness in her voice when she spoke. He knew her words earlier hadn't been solely intended to antagonize him. She'd meant them. She knew what it was like to be the child of a busy, driven man. He never wanted to do that to a child, which is why he'd deliberately not married or started a family. Missy getting pregnant was a mistake. Until he held his child in his arms, it would be hard to think otherwise.

"So…care to tell me what's going on with you and your pop star? It doesn't exactly sound like you two are living the fairy tale the magazines are reporting."

Ian sighed. "Can't we talk more about your photography? It's far less depressing."

Bree set down her spoon and crossed her arms over

her chest. "Come on, Ian. From what you told me earlier, seems like you need someone to talk to."

He popped the last of his sandwich into his mouth and stood up. "Wine first," he said, carrying his plate back into the kitchen. He opened the small wine chiller and perused the collection. A nice 1993 chardonnay ought to do the trick. "You want some?"

"Sure," she said, following him in and putting her dishes into the dishwasher. By the time she turned around, he'd poured two generous glasses and had one held out to her.

"So, Missy and I…" he began as he took a sip and walked into the living room. Ian settled into the large leather chair by the fireplace. "Were never really Missy and I. I signed her to my label three years ago. She was one of my first. She was on the brink of hitting it big and I signed her just in time. I've made a fortune on her, don't get me wrong, but she's been a handful from the start."

He paused to look at Bree. She was curled up in the chair on the other side of the hearth, listening intently. It was easy talking to her. It always had been. He didn't realize how much he'd missed that until this moment. He hadn't had any long, meaningful conversations that weren't about the business in quite a while.

"Her contract ended with this last album. It didn't do well. Her single barely cracked the Top 40. I wasn't happy with her, but she wasn't interested in anyone's opinion. It wasn't until I told her manager I wasn't going to renew her contract that she came around. Suddenly, she was all rainbows and sunshine."

That should've been his first clue. "One night she came in after hours. No one was there but me by then. It was nearly nine. She brought a sack of hand-rolled sushi and a bottle of premium sake. Missy said it was a peace offering. While we ate, she apologized for the way she'd acted. She was attentive, she was sweet and, before I knew it, the bottle of sake was empty and she was in my arms."

"She's smarter than she looks," Bree said.

"She definitely has a head for business, and I'm pretty sure our relationship is just business to her. She's certainly sold every moment to the press. To me, it was just a mistake I couldn't quite untangle myself from. I asked her over for dinner one night, fully intending to break it off. It had only been a few weeks, but it just wasn't working for me. She'd gone back to her old diva ways and nothing made up for that. The words were on the tip of my tongue when she told me she wanted to give me a present. Wrapped in a box with a shiny bow was the positive pregnancy test."

"Wow" was Bree's only response.

"I don't know how it happened. I'd taken every precaution. You remember how militant I was about using protection. But as Missy says, it must be meant to be. So we're getting married."

Bree studied him, the flickering flames of the fireplace dancing light and shadow across her face. "You know you don't have to marry her. You can still be a part of your child's life without marrying his or her mother."

At that, Ian vehemently shook his head. "You know that's not an option, Bree. Even if I financially supported our child and spent every moment I could with him or her, it wouldn't be the same. I want to do what's right for my child. I'm not going to be like my father and walk away from my responsibilities."

"How happy of a family will you be if you don't love his mother?"

Ian slammed back the rest of his wine. "Missy is having my child. We're getting married. End of story."

Four

"The internet isn't working."

Bree was admiring the wooden beams of the vaulted ceiling when Ian made his announcement. When the sun went down, she decided she was done worrying about work and their awkward circumstances. She was going to make the best of this situation. She'd gotten her camera out of her bag and started taking pictures of the beautiful details in the cabin. The craftsmanship that had gone into building this place was unbelievable. Ian had come a long, long way from the small, run-down apartment he'd grown up in.

She turned to find Ian checking the router and growling at it. From across the room she could see the lights weren't flashing like they should. "It isn't? It was working a little while ago."

She watched him get up and walk over to the phone. He picked it up, listened for a moment and then put it down with a curse. "That's why. The phones are out. I have DSL out here."

"At least we still have our cell phones," Bree said brightly. "And power." With this storm and the low temperatures, power was critical. She was going to recommend they bring in some wood for the fireplace just in case the electricity went out in the night.

Ian eyed her, significantly less optimistic about their circumstances than she was. He walked back to his computer, grumbling the whole way. Bree returned to taking pictures of the hand-carved mantel around the fireplace and the painting she thought might be an actual Rembrandt mounted over it.

"You have got to be kidding me!" she heard him shout after a few seconds.

"What's the matter?"

He took a deep breath and tossed his phone onto the granite countertop. "I've got no bars, no data. Nothing. It hasn't rung for over an hour, but I thought maybe things were just quiet at the office tonight. I hope the storm didn't take out the cell tower. Is your phone working?"

Bree went to her purse and pulled out her phone. "No bars," she confirmed, looking at the grainy black and gray screen.

"What about data?"

She shook her head. "I have a dumb phone. Top of the line circa 2003. No games, no apps, no internet. I'm lucky it has a camera, although I wouldn't dare take a picture with it. The quality is terrible."

Ian looked at her as though she had sprouted a second head. "Are you serious?"

"Yes. I only have this one, really, because Natalie insisted she be able to get in touch with me for work. It's her old Motorola RAZR. I like it. It's pink."

"You have a flip phone with no internet. Hell, that thing doesn't even have a keypad, does it?"

"No. But that's okay because I don't text."

Ian ran his fingers through his hair. "What planet are you from? Seriously, I think you're the only person I know under the age of *seventy* that doesn't at least have a phone with the *ability* to get on the internet."

Bree frowned at him, defensively slipping her maligned phone back into her purse. "It might be able to get on, but I really don't care. I like the peace and quiet of unplugging. I like that people can't get ahold of me every second of every day. Sometimes, I actually turn my phone off and forget to turn it back on for days!"

She watched Ian's eyes widen in horror. "Listen," she explained, "when I go out into the woods to take pictures, I want to hear birds chirping and water rushing over the rocks, not some cheesy symphonic ringtone of an old eighties tune."

"If you had a cell phone from this decade, you could have ringtones made of real songs."

She shook her head. This wasn't the first time she'd fought this battle. As it was, Natalie made everyone in the office use laptops that detached from the keyboard as a tablet. Natalie was very plugged in, as were Gretchen and Amelia. Like most people were anymore. Bree was just resistant to the constant barrage of technology and information.

"No way. I've seen people and their phones these days. It's like an addiction. They've constantly got to check it, even if they're on a date or have all their friends with them. Who ignores their real friends to post stupid messages to people who are only their friends in cyberspace? *Everyone*, that's who. I work on computers because I have to, but I prefer to unplug and get away from all that when I can."

Ian crossed his arms over his chest and shook his head in bewilderment. "Well, congratulations. You've stumbled into the perfect storm. I, however, feel like my right arm has been amputated. How am I supposed to get anything done without phone or internet service?"

Bree set her camera down on the coffee table and walked over to him. He was tense and twitchy; the type A personality he'd evolved into over the years paced inside of him like a caged tiger. She put her hands on his shoulders to hold him still, ignoring the heat of his body radiating through his shirt. "Relax. Turn off your laptop. It's after nine on a weeknight. You don't need to be working, anyway."

She felt his muscles loosen under her fingertips. He looked around the house, seemingly at a loss. "What will I do, then?"

Bree shrugged. "Do whatever you like. Watch your big-screen television. Listen to music. Read a book. Talk to me. Play billiards downstairs. Enjoy this incredible home that you've obviously paid a fortune to own." He didn't seem convinced.

"Personally," she said, "I was thinking about taking a luxurious bubble bath in my garden tub and reading a paperback I picked up last week."

Ian chuckled. "Don't tell me, you don't have an e-reader, either!"

"No!" she said with a laugh, pulling her hands away from him. Touching him for too long was more comfortable than it should have been. When he smiled down at her, it would've been easy to lean in and rest her head on his chest. Not an option. Why did she have to keep reminding herself that *she* had broken up with *him*? And for a good reason. A reason that was still very applicable, given how sore he was over losing internet access.

"Maybe I'm just old-fashioned, but I like the smell of the pages and the ink. I like the weight of a book in my hands and the texture of the paper between my fingertips."

"You're a Luddite."

"I have a digital camera!" she countered. She'd only had it three months and she still preferred her old-school SLR camera, but she was getting used to it. She liked being able to take as many shots as she wanted and not worry about wasting the expensive, and getting hard to find, film. "Trust me, that's progress for me."

The banter between them seemed pointless, but it had served a purpose. Ian had finally relaxed a little. Making fun of her was apparently a soothing activity for him. Well, whatever helped them pass the time the next few days. If he was mocking her, maybe she wouldn't notice the full lips doing it or the way his emerald-green eyes watched her when he thought she wasn't looking.

"You're just going to read your paperback book and leave me here twiddling my thumbs?"

He looked pretty pathetic, like a lonely child. She supposed the book could wait. "Do you have games or something? Cards, maybe?"

Ian shrugged. "I have no idea. My family might have brought some games up here. I'm usually here alone, so I don't play games aside from the ones on my iPad."

Bree walked over to the closet by the stairs. "Let's see what we can find. A rowdy game of Scrabble or Sorry! could help pass the time." She opened the door and flipped on the light, which illuminated a stash of cleaning supplies and a bookshelf filled with assorted games, puzzles and crafts. "Yep, here we go. You've got Monopoly, Life, Clue, Sorry!, Scrabble and a couple decks of cards."

"Pick whatever you want. I really don't care."

Bree reached out for one of the games and noticed a familiar shape sticking out from behind the shelf. A dusty, old acoustic guitar was propped in the corner. Bypassing the games she'd come in search of, she reached down and picked it up.

After pulling the strap over her shoulder, she made a poor attempt at strumming it. "What have we here?"

"Did you—?" He stopped speaking when he saw her come out of the closet with the guitar. "That's not Scrabble," he noted.

"Nope, but I found something better," she said in a singsong voice, continuing to fumble at the strings. She had zero musical ability. She had an eye for beauty, not an ear for it. That didn't mean she didn't appreciate it in others. Few things had ever been as soothing to her as the sound of Ian strumming his guitar and singing to her.

Wouldn't it be wonderful if she could get him to play for her again? It would be amazing to hear him after all these years. Then, maybe, for a short time, she could be reminded of the man he'd been *before*. She missed that Ian.

Ian took a few steps back from her as she came closer with it. Apparently, the idea was not as intriguing to him. "I thought I threw that out," he noted with a look of distaste.

"I don't know much about musical instruments," Bree said, "but I can tell this is a high-quality guitar. Don't you dare throw it out."

"It's old. The same one I had in college, actually."

"That's like saying a Stradivarius is an old violin so it should be thrown away. Is it really the same one you used to play at the Coffee Bean?"

"Yes. Flip it over, you'll see."

Bree lifted it off her shoulder to examine the back. There, carved ever so carefully was "IL & BH Forever." It was the same guitar. She ran her fingers over it, the sight of the familiar carving forming a lump in her throat. She remembered the night he'd put that there with his pocketknife. The memory and the emotions hit her all at once. "That was the night…" she said, her voice drifting off.

"I told you I loved you for the first time." A faint smile curved his lips as he remembered it, too. "We sat on the lawn outside the quad and looked up at the stars while I played the new song I wrote for you."

Bree felt the prickle of tears in her eyes. The blanket under the stars, the sweet melody of a love song, the strong arms of a man who loved her… When he'd carved their initials into the guitar, it had felt as if they were sealing their future together. It was the most romantic night of her life. Nothing before or since had ever come close to that moment. How many women had had a man write a song for them? It was a sentimental, romantic tune that had made her eighteen-year-old heart thump like a jackhammer in her chest when she'd heard it.

"'I'll Love You Forever, And Then Some,'" she said. Ian had been such a talented artist. He was gifted with an ear for melody and a perfect lyric. His stuff was better than most of what she heard on the radio these days. "I might be partial to it, but I always thought that was your best song."

Ian nodded. "I thought it was, too." He reached out

and took the guitar from her. Her breath stilled in her lungs for a moment, thinking he might play a song or two for old time's sake. She longed to see him play again, to sing the way he used to. To feel that flutter of excitement and desire curling in her belly. Ian was a handsome man, but she was never as attracted to him as she was when he played.

Instead, he held it by the neck at a distance, as though it might contaminate him if it got too close. "It's a shame my advisor disagreed."

He brushed past her to the closet and unceremoniously flung the guitar back inside. With a slam of the door, he turned back to her with a pained expression lining his brow. "But he was right," he said. "After years in the music industry, I know better now. He wasn't being cruel—he was being kind. Someone had to tell me I wasn't good enough."

At that, Ian turned and disappeared into his bedroom, shutting the door behind him.

With a disappointed sigh, Bree made her way to the staircase. Maybe it was just as well. She couldn't afford to lose control and act on her building need for Ian. With that guitar in the closet, her desire could also stay firmly locked away.

Damn that stupid guitar.

What the hell was it doing here, anyway? Ian paced around his bedroom, irritation surging through his veins. He'd paid movers to bring furniture and some personal items to the house after it had been built. They must have grabbed it by mistake. He certainly hadn't brought it, and his mother knew better than to bring a musical instrument into the house.

How many times had he been up here and never

known it was hidden away? And of all the people to find it—it had to be Bree!

With a sigh, he flopped down onto his bed and dropped his head into his hands. That stupid guitar had flooded his brain with memories he didn't need right now. Good ones of loving Bree and bad ones about losing his musical career. Either way, he had no use for the thoughts and images that haunted him. He was going after that guitar with an ax first thing in the morning. It would make good kindling for the fire.

Not long after he went into his room, he heard the water running upstairs. He assumed that it was Bree taking the bath she'd mentioned. That didn't help matters. The sound brought to mind unwelcome images of her creamy, naked skin, slick with soap and glistening in the steaming, hot water.

Maybe he could break the guitar by repeatedly bashing it against his skull until every thought about Bree was driven from his mind.

He loathed himself in that moment. Ian wasn't his own biggest fan to begin with, but he'd really taken the crappy cake this time. He was not allowed to be attracted to Bree. He was engaged to Missy. He was determined to be a good father, better than his own. That meant marrying the mother of his child and being a part of his life, whether it made him happy or not. He knew what it was like to not feel important enough to matter. Ian might not be happy about the turn his life had taken, but he would never, ever let his child feel that way. His son or daughter would feel loved, special, important… He would see to that.

Being attracted to someone else while the future mother of his child was miles away was an epically bad start.

Ian needed a distraction. He picked up a random book from his bookshelf and forced himself to read it for nearly an hour. By then, he thought perhaps the phone gods had smiled on his pathetic situation and brought back his connection to the world. As he slipped from his room, the house was quiet. Bree was probably asleep by now. He ventured back out into the living room and found that all the lights were off on the ground floor. Only the small light over the kitchen sink was burning. His phone was on the counter where he'd left it. There was still no connection, making it just as useless as before, except now it also needed charging. He dug the cord out of his bag and plugged it in by the coffeepot.

He picked up the house phone. No dial tone.

With a sigh, he went back into the living room and flopped down on the couch. It was nearly midnight now, but he couldn't sleep. His brain was spinning and there was nothing to soothe it.

When he was younger, the music had helped. The doctors had diagnosed him with a hyperactivity disorder when he was a child, but his mother had refused the medicine. She had been determined to find a way for him to channel his energy. He'd played soccer for a while, but the real change had come with a chance encounter at a pawn shop.

He and his mother had gone there to pay off a debt she had against her mother's wedding ring. They'd needed the money for rent. While they were there, a guitar had caught Ian's eye. It had been way more expensive than he could afford. He had been only thirteen at the time. The man who ran the shop had offered to trade Ian the guitar for help on the weekends cleaning up the stockroom. He'd snapped up the opportunity and continued to work there after it was paid off to fund guitar lessons.

Music had changed Ian's life. It had given him focus. It had helped him in school. Writing songs had come easier to him than any homework assignment. When he'd gotten to high school, he had joined the jazz ensemble. Some of the happiest days of his teen years had been spent holding the very same guitar that was in the closet right now.

Ian felt a pang of guilt for handling it the way he had. It wasn't the guitar's fault that the person playing it wasn't any good. He sprung up from the couch, walked to the closet and turned on the light. The guitar was haphazardly lying on the ground, a flutter of loose Monopoly money on top of it. Apparently, he'd knocked the game off the shelf when he'd flung the guitar inside.

Reaching down, he picked up the instrument and carried it back into the living room. A quick inspection proved he hadn't damaged it, thankfully. Ian sat down on the couch and cradled the weight of the guitar in his lap. It seemed like forever since he'd touched a guitar. He'd quit his music cold turkey. If he didn't have what it took to succeed, he hadn't wanted to waste another minute of his life on it.

Now his fingers itched to brush the strings. What could it hurt? Bree was asleep upstairs. If he played quietly enough, just one song to soothe his curiosity, no one needed to know.

He turned the guitar and gripped it. The first few notes were off, so he took a moment to adjust and tune it. His first solid chord sent a shiver down his spine. It was like his soul had reconnected with its true passion again. He began a quiet, mellow song—one of his coffee-shop favorites—to test himself. He wasn't as rusty as he thought he'd be. The music flowed smoothly, the chord changes, second nature.

When that song was done, he tried another, this time singing along. That song seemed to fly by. He remembered how easily the time would pass when he played. The same happened with his work now; he lost himself in it. This was a lot more enjoyable, though.

With a happy sigh, he looked down at the guitar and the carving on the back. One last song.

He started playing his acoustic cover of "Hello" by Lionel Richie. He remembered that he'd serenaded Bree in the coffee shop with that song the first night they'd met. He'd noticed her earlier watching him play and he'd found himself looking up at her again and again. She had looked beautiful and so intense in the way she studied him. When he'd gotten to this song in his set, he'd stood up, walked through the shop and sang the last chorus directly to her. Then he'd asked her out. When she accepted, the audience cheered.

Playing this wasn't the smartest thing to do considering he was trapped in this house with her, but he was going to finish what he started. Closing his eyes, he let the music flow from him. He easily connected with the emotion of the song and the memory of the first moment he'd laid eyes on Bree. As he reached the last few notes, sadness washed over him.

It was done. Both his music and his time with Bree. The guitar and the memories needed to go back into the closet.

"That was always one of my favorites."

Ian leaped off the couch, his heart shooting into his throat. He spun to find Bree at the bottom of the stairs. How long had she been listening? He felt an uncharacteristic flush of embarrassment rise to his face.

"I'm sorry," he said. "Did I wake you up?"

"No. I couldn't sleep so I was reading my book. I was coming downstairs for a drink when I heard the music. I didn't dare interrupt you."

Ian shrugged. "You should have. I let it go on too long."

Bree walked across the room to stand beside him. Her long blond hair was pulled up into a messy knot on the top of her head. She was wearing a pair of flannel pajama pants and a long-sleeved shirt. On anyone else, he imagined it would be like a splash of cold water on his libido, but on Bree it was anything but.

The plaid pants rode low on her hips, showing a scant inch of skin when she moved and her shirt rode up. She wasn't wearing a bra. He could make out the full, round curves of her breasts and the tantalizing result the cold air had on them. He had to shift the guitar down a touch to save himself additional embarrassment.

"Play another one. Play *my* song."

Ian stiffened. He wasn't sure he could do that. Or that he should. There were way too many emotions wrapped up in the song he'd written for her. "I don't know, Bree."

"Please." She took his hand and led him back to the couch. Her wide blue eyes pleaded with him in a way he knew he wouldn't be able to resist.

He followed her because he couldn't help himself. Her touch was magnetic, the tingling draw of positive and negative coming together and refusing to part. Before he knew it, he was back on the couch again and Bree was beside him, waiting with nervous anticipation to hear him play her song.

There was no getting out of it without being rude. No matter what, he didn't want to be unnecessarily mean to Bree. He could play the song. It was just one song. It didn't have to mean anything. He just had to make sure he focused one hundred percent on the guitar and the song and not on her. Sitting this close, he could smell the scented lotion she'd always put on before bed. Touching her hand was enough for him to know how smooth and soft every inch of her skin would be.

Closing his eyes to block out those thoughts, he concentrated on the music and the lyrics he'd gone so long without bringing to life. About halfway through, he opened his eyes again. It was so quiet in the room he wondered for a moment if she had left.

But she hadn't. She was there, listening intently with glassy tears shimmering in her pale blue eyes.

Without meaning to, he stopped playing. The sight of her tears had made his chest suddenly too tight to keep singing. "Are you okay? I—"

In an instant, Bree leaned in and kissed him. Her lips met his with the force and emotion that only nine years apart could create. Ian was startled by the sudden attack, but he couldn't pull away from it. Right or wrong, he still wanted Bree. His brain and his body refused to get on the same page when she was touching him.

It was a mistake, but he was going to enjoy every moment while he could. Bree's kisses were an experience to cherish. Her lips were soft and tasted like the peppermint tea she'd drank earlier. She made soft noises against his mouth, her hands caressing the stubble of his jaw. It aroused a primal instinct deep inside Ian.

The surge of need shot down his spine. Every nerve ending awakened with a desire he hadn't felt in a really long time. He cursed the guitar between them. He wanted to wrap his arms around her and pull her tight to his body until those full, perky breasts crushed against his chest.

"Bree," he whispered in a half groan against her lips.

The sudden sound seemed to snap her out of the haze. In a flash, Bree had flattened her back against the other side of the couch. Her wide eyes flickered with emotions that Ian couldn't interpret. Then her hand flew to her mouth and smothered an *"ohmygod"* before she leaped to her feet and ran up the stairs to her room.

Five

Normally, Ian popped out of bed at six in the morning. It didn't matter if he was at the office or working on his laptop into the wee hours of the morning. Every day his eyes would open to a room dimly lit by early-morning sun, and he would immediately check his phone.

This morning, Ian rolled over and reached for the phone, but it was nowhere to be found. Then he remembered. It was charging in the kitchen. Opening his eyes, he was surprised to see how bright the light was coming in the windows. It must be the sun reflecting off all that snow.

Ian sat up and looked at the clock on the bedside stand. It was nine-fifty in the morning. He rubbed his eyes, expecting the digits to shift, but they remained stubbornly in place. He'd slept until nearly ten.

He threw back the blankets and slipped out of the bed. The wooden floors were cold against his bare feet, but he didn't care. He needed to get his phone.

His phone without service.

His fuzzy morning brain finally put the pieces together. He could go out there and check it, but considering he was wearing only boxer shorts, that was probably a bad idea. At this late morning hour, Bree was no doubt awake and roaming around the house. Last night, she had fled the room like her hair was on fire. Parading around half-naked wouldn't make matters better for either of them.

A shower, he decided. That way he could go out dressed and presentable, and his phone would have thirty minutes or so more time to get back to functionality.

Climbing into the large tile enclosure, he turned the knobs that activated the multiple showerheads and body sprays. The scalding-hot shower felt wonderful as it pummeled his body from all angles. Ian was warm-blooded, always flinging back the blankets and going without a coat, but even he was getting chilly with all this snow. He dried off quickly and slipped into casual clothes. A pair of jeans and a sweater seemed appropriate attire for being snowed in at a mountain cabin.

He laced up his boots so he could go outside later. He needed to bring in more firewood and, if he could, shovel a path to the road.

Finally, he emerged from his room and found the house still and quiet. A pot of coffee had been brewed, so he poured a cup and glanced out the window over the sink.

The snow had stopped and the sun was out. That wasn't saying much. The massive piles of white fluff were hip high in some places. He couldn't tell his front porch from his driveway from the road. It was just white in every direction. Maybe shoveling was a pointless venture.

A soft chirp distracted him from his investigation. He ignored it for a moment, then realized the significance of the sound. It was his cell phone. It was working!

Lunging across the countertop, he snatched up his phone and hit the button to activate the screen. Five beautiful bars and 4G data. He had never been quite so happy to see these old friends.

He had missed a lot. His screen was crowded with pop-ups about missed calls and texts and a hundred unread emails. That was more than even he had been expecting. What the hell happened last night?

A noise from behind him in the dining room forced Ian to look up from his phone. Bree was coming in through the glass door that led out to the covered, wraparound porch. She was bundled up in a quilted blue coat that must have been in her luggage. It was almost the same color as her eyes. Her long blond hair was in a thick braid over her shoulder, a knit cap tugged over her head. She was red-cheeked from the cold but smiling. She had her camera with her. She must have gone outside to take pictures.

"You're up," she noted. "I was beginning to worry that old guitar had sucked out your soul. That, or I'd made such an ass of myself last night, you were afraid to come out of your room for fear I might throw myself at you."

"Neither," he said. Truthfully, if he thought she would throw herself at him again, he'd have slept on the couch to catch her the minute she woke up. But they were both adults and knew the kiss they'd shared last night was a mistake. He wouldn't even have mentioned it happened if she hadn't. Ian didn't want things to be more uncomfortable than they already were.

"I guess without my phone chirping and beeping at me, I slept later than usual. It's working again," he added cheerfully, holding it up with a triumphant smile.

"Oh, good. The balance is restored to the Force."

Ian chuckled. "I think so. But it seems that everything went crazy while it was down. I have twenty-five missed calls, ten voice mail messages, fifteen missed texts and a hundred emails."

Bree set her camera on the granite bar and walked over to make herself a cup of coffee. "You're more important than I gave you credit for."

"Not really. Most of it is from Missy. That's weird. She's not the best at keeping in touch. Besides, she knows I'm stuck up here in bad weather. I'm not sure what she expects me to do about whatever is happening."

"You don't think she found out you're up here with me, do you?"

Ian shook his head. "No. She wouldn't know who you were, anyway."

Bree pouted. "You mean you've never told her about your college romance?"

He shrugged. "We don't really talk about me."

Bree's eyes widened at him for a moment, but she didn't respond. She just turned back to sweetening her coffee. Ian was relieved. He didn't really want to explore that topic so early today.

Thumbing through his screen, he saw a phone message from his label's talent manager, Keith. He would listen to that first. Business before Missy's drama.

"Ian! Call me the instant you get this message. I've got press crawling all over the studio. I had to hire some private security to patrol the parking lot. This mess has totally blown up. I wish to God you weren't trapped in the mountains."

Ian's heart started racing. His fingers fumbled for a moment as he tried to hit the buttons to call Keith back, but he finally connected and it starting ringing.

"Is everything okay?" Bree looked concerned.

He shook his head. "I don't know yet." Keith finally answered. "Keith! What the hell is going on? My phone has been out since yesterday afternoon so I've been out of touch."

There was a painfully long silence. Ian expected Keith to start spilling the information, so the quiet was even more disconcerting. "Have you spoken to anyone?" Keith finally asked.

"No. You're the first person I called. I have a million messages, though."

"Oh, Christ." Keith sighed on the phone.

"What is it? Is everything okay?"

In an instant, the worst possible scenario popped into his mind. The frantic calls and texts from Missy. The press swarming the studio. Keith's dismayed tone. Something had happened to the baby. The dull ache of dread pooled in his stomach and tears welled up in his eyes. Not that. Anything but that. He could barely form the words to ask. "Is the baby okay, Keith?"

Keith groaned. "Ian, I swear to you that no one is dead or injured. Your mom, your stepdad, everyone is okay. But there's something I've got to tell you, man. Are you sitting down?"

"Yes," Ian lied. He took bad news better standing up so he could pace across the floor and burn off all the nervous energy. At the very least he knew his family was okay. The baby was okay. He could deal with anything else.

"A story about Missy hit the tabloids yesterday. It's all over the place—television, magazines, blogs. Apparently a woman in Nashville has come forward claiming that she sold Missy a positive pregnancy test on Craigslist."

With only a few sips of coffee under his belt, it took a moment for Ian to process what his friend was telling him. Missy had bought a used pregnancy test. A *positive* one. That meant...

"There is no baby, Ian. There never was."

"So she's not really pregnant? It was all just a ruse to..." To what? Mess with his head? Trick him into marrying her? Keep him from dropping her from his label?

Yes, yes and yes.

He'd always known Missy was ruthless when it came to getting what she wanted. But he'd never thought even someone like Missy would stoop *that* low.

"That's what they're saying. The evidence is pretty damning. The woman who sold it to Missy was no fool. When she realized who she was talking to, she knew there was a bigger payday than just the hundred bucks she'd make selling the test. She kept screenshots of her email conversations with Missy and took a photo of her Jaguar leaving the parking lot where they met. Personalized plates and all. It's all online if you want to look."

Ian wished he had taken Keith's advice and sat down. He stumbled over to one of the tall bar stools and leaned against it with one hip to steady himself. Missy wasn't pregnant. *Not pregnant.* Could it really be true? It sounded like a pretty credible case against his fiancée, but Ian wouldn't let himself completely

believe the story until he spoke with Missy directly.
More convincing lies had been printed in the tabloids.

Yet, it *felt* true.

He'd been meticulous in protecting himself over the
years. There hadn't been so much as a late period scare
with a girl he'd dated since he lost his virginity. He
never wanted to make the same mistake his father had
made by creating a child he had no interest in. If and
when he had a child, he was going to be dedicated to
it, no matter what.

Missy showing up with that pregnancy test had
thrown him for a loop, but he'd recovered. He'd tried to
make the best of it and stay involved, but Missy seemed
determined to keep the baby stuff at arm's length from
him. She had refused to let him come to the doctor's
appointment with her. He'd wanted to hear the heart-
beat, but she'd said it was too early. When she hadn't
come home with one of those grainy pictures, she'd told
him the sonogram machine was broken. Her flat belly
hadn't budged. No morning sickness. No sign whatsoever that she was having his child.

She'd lied to him about the whole thing. He felt
sick. Lightheaded. Foolish. But the strongest feeling
sweeping over him was that of utter and complete relief. A moment ago, he'd been devastated that he might
have lost his unborn child. Now, the child had never
existed, was nothing but the manipulative imaginings
of its would-be mother. He felt a bubble of hysterical
laughter rising in his chest that he absolutely couldn't
let out. Keith and Bree would confuse the sound for one
of happiness, and that wasn't an accurate description of
the maelstrom swirling inside him.

"Ian? Are you okay?" Keith's voice had more concern in it than Ian had ever heard before.

Ian cleared his throat, swallowing the emotions inside of him before his manager panicked. "Yeah. Thanks for telling me, Keith. It's better I heard it from you."

"What shall I do about the reporters?"

"Tell them that SpinTrax does not comment on the personal lives of their artists or employees. Then send them to Missy's house."

Bree was afraid to speak. Afraid to move. She was trapped in the kitchen, bearing witness to an uncomfortable situation she had no business in. She had only heard one side of the phone conversation, but that was enough. Judging by Ian's suddenly pale complexion and unsteadiness, she knew whatever Keith told him was bad.

She waited patiently for Ian to turn off his phone so she could see if he needed anything. In a moment like this, there wasn't much she could do, but she knew enough to offer. It was the sentiment that was important. If he preferred to be alone, she would go downstairs to give him some privacy. There, she could turn on the television so she couldn't hear his voice upstairs. "Ian?"

He looked up from the phone. He seemed shaken but, at the same time, eerily calm. She knew from experience that wasn't good. He was thinking. Processing. Preparing. Fighting with Ian had always been frustrating for her because the majority of the fight seemed to go on silently in his head. She would say something and just sit back and watch the wheels turn in his mind while, outwardly, it appeared he was ignoring her. Eventually, she would just stomp away and he would throw himself into his music. Or his work. This wasn't a problem he could ignore, though.

"Yes?" he answered softly.

"Can I do anything? Get you anything?"

"No," he said with a slow shake of his head. It made Bree wonder if maybe he was in shock over the whole thing. She supposed that whether the baby was ever real or not, it had been real to him. He was still losing the idea of a child and the future he was planning with it.

"I need to call Missy here in a minute. You might not…" His voice trailed off.

Bree nodded. She wouldn't want anyone else around when she had a hard conversation like that, either. "I'll give you your privacy. Let me know if you need me." Bree reached out and put her hand over his. She gave him a reassuring squeeze and a weak smile before heading downstairs.

When she reached the lower level of the cabin, she walked over to the leather couch and scooped up the remote. She put the television on a loud action movie with lots of gunfire and explosions. But even that couldn't muffle everything.

The calm from a moment before was gone. She couldn't make out exactly what he was saying, but Ian was yelling. Bree turned up the volume and wished she had packed some earplugs in her bag. She considered taking a shower. Or a walk. Or crawling under some blankets and covering her head with a pillow.

She felt awful for Ian. She knew he wasn't happy, but he had been making the best of things for the child's sake. He had always told her how important being a good father was to him. In her young, girlish fantasies, she'd imagined what Ian would be like with their children. She'd thought he would be a hands-on dad. She'd had fantasies of him singing them to sleep with lullabies he wrote especially for them.

To think that Missy had taken that loyalty and dedication in Ian and used it against him… It made Bree feel sick.

Despite the fact that Bree had broken up with Ian in college, she'd never wanted to hurt him. She'd tried to help him, but when that had failed, she had to err on the side of self-preservation. She couldn't have sat back and watched his downward spiral any longer. Not when she'd loved him so much.

And she still cared about him now. She didn't want that to be the case, but seeing Ian again had brought all those old feelings to the surface. In only a few short hours together, she'd been bombarded by her attraction to him and wrestled to keep herself at a physical distance. At the same time, her disappointment in his workaholic lifestyle was just as present. He was just as dedicated to the job now as he had been back then. But she couldn't ignore her fierce protectiveness where he was concerned. Missy was lucky she'd never made it to the house last night. If all this had come to light with her here, Ian would have had to separate the women before someone had gotten hurt. And by "someone," Bree meant Missy.

She entertained herself with fantasies of winning rowdy catfights. Eventually, she noticed the yelling had stopped. Bree didn't know if he had hung up the phone or if his anger had finally run its course. Either way, she wasn't going upstairs anytime soon. She flipped the television to a documentary on Pompeii and let her mind get lost in history instead of the eruption taking place upstairs.

About twenty minutes later, the dull thud of footsteps coming down the stairs roused her from the show. She turned down the volume and looked up in time to see Ian in the doorway. His face was stony and emotionless as he came over and dropped down onto the couch beside her.

Bree sat quietly and waited. He would talk when he was ready. She knew better than anyone that he didn't like talking about his emotions. It might take him a while to be able to voice his feelings about what had just happened. Even Bree wasn't sure she could find the words if faced with a betrayal of this magnitude.

"It's true," he said at last. His voice was steady and even. The yelling was done and now he was back to the even-keeled Ian she knew. "Missy is not having my baby."

At least now he knew for certain. "I'm sorry, Ian. Is there anything I can do?"

"No," he said dismissively. "Missy has done enough."

"I'm surprised she admitted to it."

Ian chuckled bitterly. "She didn't want to, I'm sure, but it's the kind of lie where you'll get found out eventually. I'd done my part by rationalizing away all my doubts, but eventually she would have had to start showing. Eventually, she'd have had to give birth to this baby."

That was a hell of a lie to pull off. Had she really thought it through? "Did she tell you what she intended to do? If the story hadn't hit the press, she couldn't have kept the lie going on much longer."

"She said she was hoping that we would stop using protection and she would actually get pregnant. If that didn't work, she was going to pretend to miscarry after the wedding."

Bree shook her head. "With so many women suffering through the reality of losing a child, I can't imagine her faking something that terrible."

"That's because you don't know the real Missy Kline.

All anyone sees is the sexy blonde in music videos and on album covers. I'm sure people think she might be spoiled or a diva. But the truth is that she's ruthless, especially when it comes to her career. She learned it from her viper of a stage mom."

"Is that why she did it? For her career?" Bree's career meant everything to her, but she had a limit of how far she would go to be successful. Most people did.

"That's not what she said at first. When I confronted her, she cried and wailed that she thought she was losing me. She said she did what she had to do to keep us together because she loved me too much."

Ian looked down at his hands folded in his lap. "That was absolute crap. I know what it feels like to have a woman love me and it was nothing like that. She barely knew me. She certainly didn't love me. Missy has never been interested in anyone but herself. The truth was that her last album tanked and she was scrambling. I had no intention of renewing her contract and she'd burned too many bridges to jump to another label easily. That's when her whole demeanor changed. She was buttering me up, using sex to get her way. I knew that much. What I didn't know was that she'd realized it wasn't working. Before I could end it, she'd cooked up the fake pregnancy to keep it going.

"That just turned into a publicity gold mine for her. Celebrity weddings and babies are big news. She started this whole charade to save her career, and it worked better than she'd ever imagined. The publicity about the engagement and the pregnancy boosted her mediocre songs to the tops of the charts. She'd sold the exclusive rights to our engagement and ceremony photos to *Celebrity Magazine*. The wedding was even going to be televised. Did you know that?"

She didn't. Natalie might have mentioned it, but Bree had spent last Monday in a daze after finding out about Ian getting married. "Sounds romantic."

"Doesn't it? Every step she took was cold and calculated. She was going to revive her career so I would resign her. And if not me, she would see to it that she made enough headlines to get some other label to do it."

"The whole thing sure backfired on her, though. Who's going to sign her now?"

"I don't care," Ian admitted. "It sure as hell won't be my label. The wedding is off and the minute she's fulfilled the final obligations of her contract, I never want to see her pinched face again. If anyone else is dumb enough to offer her a record deal after all this, they deserve what they get."

They sat in silence for a few moments, absorbing everything that had happened in the past hour. Apparently being held hostage by a blizzard was just the beginning. Finally, Bree spoke. "Well, I'm sorry about all this. There's nothing I can really say or do to make it better, but I wish that I could."

Before she could stop herself, she reached out and clasped his hand in her own. She expected him to accept the brief gesture of comfort and pull away, but he didn't. He tightened his grip on her fingers, sending a surge of emotions through her. She probably wasn't the best person to help Ian through a moment like this, but she was the only one here. She wanted to hug him. Comfort him. But was that dangerous with their biggest barrier suddenly removed?

"Thanks, Bree," he said, running the pad of his thumb over her skin. "I guess I should be happy the snow kept Missy from getting here. Can you imagine the three of us trapped in the house when this happened?"

She shuddered, but she wasn't sure if it was his words or his touch. "I would've had to cut a bitch," she said with a sly smile to help lighten up the situation. "Seriously, I know how important being a good father is to you."

Ian nodded. "I keep telling myself that everything works out for the best. A part of me is relieved. A part of me is so giddy to break things off with Missy that I want to skip through the house. At the same time," he added, a sadness creeping into the green depths of his eyes, "even though I didn't want Missy to be the mother of my child, I wanted that child just the same. Even though he or she was never real, it felt real."

"Of course it did. And you should give yourself the time and space to grieve for the baby, imaginary or not. You can't just blink and have the whole situation suddenly not matter anymore."

"Thanks for understanding. You're right, and that's how I need to think about it. I'm glad I'm here instead of back in Nashville. I think some people there would just pat me on the back and say to get over it because none of it was real."

"It was to you. So take the time you need. Do what you have to do. I think you should take advantage of the peace and solitude here to deal with all this. That way when you return home, you're ready to face the fallout."

Ian looked at her with a furrowed brow. "Peace and solitude? I don't even know what that is, much less how to take advantage of it."

"I'll tell you what it is. And how to get it. You made fun of me last night, but unplugging is the best thing you can do right now. You start by turning off your computer and your phone. Forward your business calls to your assistant if you have to, but you don't want the press and well-meaning friends pestering you about all this. Give yourself pure radio silence."

"Turn it off," he repeated, although he didn't sound convinced.

"Yep," Bree said with an encouraging smile. "It's easy. I'll show you how."

Six

Silence wasn't all it was cracked up to be.

Bree had sold the idea to him like it was the greatest thing in the world. Not true. Without technology to distract him, Ian found he was uncomfortable with his own thoughts. Bree had given him his space and he was drowning in it.

Less than an hour after unplugging from the world, he was suiting up for the cold and heading outside. He had too much nervous energy and too many thoughts swirling around in his head. When he was younger and had the same problem, his mother would give him a physical task.

Then, and now, there was nothing that some hard labor couldn't fix.

In the garage, he grabbed the snow shovel and a plastic tarp, then headed through the house to the front door. He opened it carefully, leaving a preserved wall of

snow going about three feet up the doorway. He spread
the tarp down on the wood floor to protect it from snow
that might fall inside and melt.

This was as good a place to start as any. From inside, he thrust the shovel into the top few inches of
snow and hurled them to the side of the porch. Then
he grabbed a second scoop and flung it to the opposite
side. Again and again he shoveled until he was able to
step out onto the porch and close the door behind him.
From there, he lost himself in the physicality and mo-
notony of the work.

It took more than an hour to make a good path down
the front steps to the road. It took another hour to clear
in front of the garage doors and excavate Bree's SUV.
They wouldn't be driving anywhere anytime soon, but
if the snow started to melt then refroze in the night, it
could turn to an icy shell around her car and damage
the paint job. Maybe even crack her windshield.

The work had done wonders for his outlook. His
arms and shoulders ached, but he had powered through
the stages of grief in a rapid-fire assault on the snow in
his driveway. The anger, the disbelief, the disappointment, the relief and the associated guilt came and went
with every shovelful of snow. Two hours and three blis-
ters later, Ian finally felt the mysterious sense of peace
that Bree had mentioned earlier.

Resting his arms on his shovel, he admired Mother
Nature's handiwork. He normally didn't come up here
when there could be snow, so the sight of the familiar
landscape transformed into a winter wonderland was
stunning. The sun made the piles of snow sparkle like
they were coated in a dusting of glitter. Icicles hung
precariously from tree branches and the rooflines of

houses in the distance. The chimneys of his neighbors puffed towers of gray smoke against the bright blue sky.

It was perfectly silent. No cars driving down the road in the valley below them. No people talking or walking around. Even the animals were deep inside their dens staying warm. He felt a sense of inner calm being out here that he'd never expected to find, especially after this morning.

When it was all said and done, he couldn't be angry anymore because he'd been given a second chance. A chance to marry a woman he really loved. To start a family with someone he cared about. It was a life he really hadn't given much thought to until Missy had reeled him into it. And now that he was free of her deception, the idea of a family—one the way he imagined— brought on an overwhelming feeling of hope.

That sense of hope was shattered as he felt something cold and soft slam into the back of his head.

Ian turned around to the sound of a feminine giggle and discovered Bree on the patio. She was armed with several snowballs and ready to go to battle. An innocent grin spread across Bree's face, but there was a wicked glint in her eyes. "It's a snow day," she argued.

"Aren't we a little old for a snow day? I don't recall hearing school was canceled."

She wasn't deterred. He recognized that determined lift of her chin. She had strong-armed him into turning off his gadgets and now she was going to bait him into having some fun.

"You need something fun to distract you from all this crap. It doesn't matter if we're eight or twenty-eight, we're going to play in the snow." She chucked another snowball at him and this one landed squarely on his chest.

"Oh, it is *so* on!" he shouted. He used his shovel to fling a huge lump of snow at Bree. It sent her scattering off the porch, giving him time to make a few snowballs to defend himself. He took a defensive position behind her SUV. She hunkered down behind a tall drift by the porch.

They lobbed attacks back and forth. Bree got him in the head once, but he fired back and nailed her in the rear end when she bent over to make more snowballs. She squealed in mock rage, kicking off another round of assaults. Ian was getting frustrated, though. They could go like this for hours. It was time for some hand-to-hand combat to make things more interesting.

With a commando-like roar that would've made John Rambo proud, Ian charged through the snow and tackled Bree into a drift. With a cry, they sank a good foot into the snow. Once she recovered, Bree playfully fought beneath him. They rolled around, burying themselves in a dusting of white powder and making the most distorted snow angels ever conceived.

At one point, she was able to push Ian off of her and he fell backward into more snow. She started frantically burying him as though they were on the beach, until he rose up, ruining all her hard work and tackling her into fresh powder beside them.

Laughing and exhausted, they finally stopped fighting. Ian couldn't help smiling as he looked down at Bree, pink-cheeked and grinning with the snow at her back. She looked so beautiful in that moment with her messy blond braid dusted in white powder. Not the perfectly airbrushed and digitally altered perfection of his former fiancée, but *real* beauty. Flawed and lovely.

He wanted to kiss her again. Last night had whet his appetite without giving him enough to feel satisfied.

And he realized at that moment, he could. Without guilt. He wasn't engaged. The mother of his "child" was nothing but a manipulative liar. Missy would probably keep the six-figure engagement ring he'd bought her, but it was a small price to pay for freedom. All the thoughts about Bree that he'd beaten himself up over in the past twenty-four hours were no longer off-limits.

Bree looked up at him, her bright blue eyes wide and inviting. Her lips were parted softly, her frozen breath escaping her lungs into the cold. He watched intently as her tongue snaked across them. She wanted him just as much as he wanted her. It could happen. He could have everything he'd fantasized about since she'd stepped out of her car yesterday. He just had to careful. He'd learned not to give anything more than his body to a woman. Because this was the woman who had taught him that lesson, he had to be doubly careful. He could make love to Bree while they were in the mountains as long as he remembered they would never work in the real world.

"I'm not engaged anymore," he said, stating the obvious.

"I know," she said, her voice breathy.

"Last night we had a million reasons why kissing was a bad idea. I hated to let you go, but I knew it was the right thing to do. Today, I can't think of a single reason why I can't kiss you again."

This was her chance. If she didn't want him—if she still believed he was just a thoughtless, self-destructive workaholic—she just needed to say no and he would respect that. But damn, he didn't want her to say no. He wanted her to say that she wanted him *despite* the fact that he was a thoughtless, self-destructive workaholic. That she couldn't focus on anything but how much she desired him. In the here and now, none of that other stuff mattered.

"Neither can I," she said with a soft smile.

Barely a second after the words escaped her lips, his mouth was pressed against hers. Bree wrapped her arms around his neck, tugging him closer. He reacquainted himself with her, letting his tongue and his hands roam across the familiar yet different territory.

Bree made soft sounds, her fingertips gently pressing into him and urging him on. The noises she made were such a turn-on. They reminded him of heated nights on an uncomfortable twin dorm mattress. Of nights when school, his music, food…nothing was more important than making love to Bree. There was no day so stressful that losing himself in her couldn't fix it.

He longed for that comfort again. Ian hadn't had a day this bad in a long time. He wanted nothing more than to find relief from the worries in his mind by forgetting everything but how Bree liked to be touched.

His body stretched along the length of hers, every hard inch of his desire very obviously pressing into the soft curve of her belly. Her body undulated beneath him, the tight fabric of her jeans creating a delicious friction. An aching throb of need was growing more and more intense. If they didn't go inside right now, he was going to make love to her in the snow.

He had no interest in getting frostbite on sensitive parts he might want to use again later.

Bree broke the kiss. "I'm getting cold," she said, nearly reading his mind.

"That's funny. I'm burning up." And he was. Every inch of his skin felt as if it was doused in kerosene and set ablaze by the heat of her touch. Of course, he wasn't the one lying against the snow.

Bree leaned up to kiss him again, a smile curling her lips. "Well, then take me inside so we can strip out of these wet clothes and you can warm me up."

Bree had lied when she'd said she couldn't think of a reason why Ian couldn't kiss her. Well, at least physically there were no barriers to him doing whatever he liked, kissing included. It was more like reasons why he *shouldn't* kiss her. There were plenty of those, starting with the most recent and obvious one—that he was emotionally rebounding—and ending with all the reasons they broke up in the first place.

Until this morning, she hadn't had to give the idea of her and Ian much consideration. There was an attraction there—their chemistry had always been off the charts—but nothing would come of it. He was engaged and starting a family, and she was a professional photographer who didn't intend on making a habit of sleeping with clients.

With his relationship with Missy imploding this morning, the major barrier to their physical impulses was gone. But that didn't solve everything.

Handsome or not, Ian was still a workaholic. He still had his business to preoccupy his time. Being trapped here in the mountains had put his impulses on hold, but it wouldn't last beyond the blizzard. None of this would. The minute they returned to Nashville, everything would fall apart. At best, she would get two, maybe three days with Ian. And she knew that.

But in that moment, when he looked at her with eyes blazing with desire, she didn't care. None of those reasons mattered anymore. She would deal with the ending of their relationship when they got to the end. But she wasn't going to let herself ruin the beginning worrying about it.

Not when she was standing in Ian's bedroom, each of them slowly slipping out of their cold, wet snow gear. His dark green eyes never left hers as he tossed his gloves on the bathroom floor and shrugged out of his coat. Bree did the same, only Ian reached out to take her clothes from her.

They'd left their boots on the porch, so it was easy to take off her socks and then peel the wet jeans from her body. It was at that point that Ian froze in place, watching her undress. Despite how much she wanted out of those cold clothes, she was going to take her time. She turned around, giving him a full view of her rear end as the denim peeled away and exposed the pink satin bikini-cut panties she wore beneath them.

Ian groaned aloud as she bent over and stepped out of the pants. She followed it with her long-sleeved shirt. When she turned back around wearing nothing but her bra and panties, Ian was standing exactly as she'd left him.

Walking over to him, she pulled his sweater up and over his head. He cooperated with a smile until she reached for the button of his jeans. Then his hand came to hers, covering her fingers and keeping her from going any further.

"You get into bed and under those covers," he said. "Your skin is like ice. I'll start a fire."

Bree pouted for a moment but had to admit that was an excellent idea. She sauntered over to the bed, slipping off the last of her underthings and crawling beneath the heavy down comforter. It was like slipping into a warm bath. She sighed as she snuggled down into the luxury linens.

Ian quickly went to work building a fire. In only a few minutes the fireplace just beyond the foot of the bed roared with flames. That done, he finished undressing and disappeared into the bathroom. Bree waited patiently, unbraiding her hair and combing her fingers through the blond waves left behind. He returned a moment later with a handful of foil packets.

Bree was surprised to see the physique he hid beneath those bulky sweaters he wore. Back in college, he'd been tall and lean but not particularly athletic in build because he spent most of his time playing guitar. Given that for the past ten years he'd mainly sat at a desk, she'd expected him to have a head start on middle-age spread.

Instead, she was rewarded with a hard, lean body with thick muscles twitching beneath his skin. He had more chest hair now; the dark sprinkle across his pecs narrowed to a trail down his belly. At that point, her cheeks flushed. His desire for her was no secret. Her palms tingled with the need to touch him, but he was just out of her reach.

He paused at the edge of the bed, holding up one of the condoms. "I'm trying to fight the urge to wear three of these at once. I'm feeling a little paranoid. Please don't take it personally."

"One is perfectly effective," Bree said, "as long as the woman in question isn't after anything but your body."

Ian's dark brows went up. "Bree, are you just using me for my body?"

"No," she said with a sweet shake of her head. "I fully intend to, of course, but at the moment you're out of reach."

Ian laughed and tossed the condoms onto the nightstand. "I feel so cheap." He eased back the blankets and slipped in beside her. His skin was blazing hot as he brushed against her. How was it possible that the man could produce so much body heat?

Bree groaned and pressed the length of her body against him like a nuzzling cat. Ian hissed for a moment when her ice-cold skin touched his, but he was gentlemanly enough not to pull away.

"You're freezing, Bree."

She ran her palm over the hard muscles of his chest and leaned in to give him a kiss. "Then warm me up."

"If you insist." Smiling, Ian rolled over, pressing her back against the mattress and covering her body with his.

The heat and the weight of him were soothing. When he dipped his head to kiss her, she forgot all about being cold. His touch heated the very blood in her veins, the spreading warmth awakening her long-ignored body's desires. She relished the slide of his tongue along hers. His every caress was expertly targeted to her most sensitive parts as though the almost decade apart had been just a blink of an eye.

When his thumb brushed over the hard peak of her nipple, Bree gasped. When he sucked it into the warm heat of his mouth, her back arched up off the bed. He was relentless in his assault, teasing her with his teeth and tongue as his hands glided down her hip and dipped between her thighs.

"Ian!" she cried as he made contact with her feminine center. He smothered any other sounds when he kissed her again. His tongue mimicked the movements of his hand, slowly sliding in and out of her mouth. She squirmed beneath him, panting as he drew her ever closer to the edge of her release, again and again, always backing away before she shattered.

Then he reached for the nightstand. Ian sat up to roll the latex sheath over himself, then slipped back between her thighs. He tugged the blankets up over his bare shoulders to keep them in the warm cocoon and then lowered onto his elbows. His mouth found hers again and with a subtle shift of his weight, he was pressing against her entrance. Teasing her. Toying with her despite the need he was responsible for building inside her.

But she'd already waited too long for this moment. Now, she would have it. Bree cradled Ian's hips between her thighs. Impatiently, she drew up her knees, gripping his hips and drawing him forward. He moved with her and before she knew it, she got what she wanted. Every inch of Ian was buried deep inside of her. The moment was familiar, pleasurable, memorable…perfect. It shouldn't have been. This wasn't a reunion. They weren't getting back together. They were just venting pent-up desires and emotions and frustrations on each other while the snow kept the rest of the world from existing.

But what would happen when the snow melted?

Bree closed her eyes and bit her bottom lip. It didn't matter. None of it mattered. In this moment she didn't want to let all those worries creep in. She just wanted to enjoy being in Ian's arms again. Watching him play his guitar and sing last night had built a need in her that only he could soothe.

Ian eased forward and thrust into her a second time with a sharp hiss. Bree rolled her hips, taking in all that she could. Her body strained and flexed around him, her muscles clamping down until he groaned.

"Nice trick," he said. "But we're not finishing that quickly."

Leaning down, he kissed her and started moving

at a quicker pace. Eventually, Bree had to tear her lips from his so she could cry out with each pleasurable drive into her.

They fell into an easy rhythm, her hips rising off the bed to meet his every advance. The pleasure easily built up inside her again, this time with more intensity than before. He had toyed with her so much earlier that this release might be one for the record books. She clawed futilely with her short manicured nails at the taut skin stretching across his shoulders. She was trying to find something to hold on to, something to keep her anchored when her orgasm hit like a tsunami.

It was coming. Her whole body tensed, and her mouth fell open into a soft "O."

"Yes," Ian coaxed, recognizing the telltale signs of her impending release. "That's what I want to see. Don't hold back, Bree. Come apart for me, baby."

He increased his pace and she hardly had a choice in the matter. In an instant, the dam broke and the waves of pleasure crashed in on her. She gasped, she cried, she thrashed and writhed beneath him. And when it all subsided, her eyes fluttered open to find he'd watched every moment of it.

"You're so beautiful," he said, looking down at her.

She didn't feel beautiful. At that moment she felt flushed and sweaty. Her hair was damp and plastered to her skin. Her lips were swollen from kisses and her core was throbbing from good use for the first time in a long time. She wrinkled her nose, smirking dismissively.

"No," he argued, dipping down to kiss her. "It's not up for debate. You're beautiful. Perhaps the most beautiful woman I've ever seen up close."

At that, Bree laughed and pushed her hair out of her face. "You work in the record industry, Ian. There's got to be a steady stream of *Tiger Beat* princesses and sultry songstresses in your social circles."

"I know. And?"

Bree's eyes widened and she swallowed hard. How could it be possible that she ranked up there with all the music stars at the Grammys? It was sweet but impossible. She reached up to his face and ran a fingertip down the bridge of his nose. "I think we need to get you some glasses, Ian."

With a growl, he flipped, rolling onto his back with Bree sitting astride him. Bree squealed with the sudden reversal, their bodies never disconnecting. "I don't need glasses and I'm going to prove it."

His hands gripped her hips and he started thrusting into her from underneath. Bree braced her hands on the padded leather headboard and moved with him. His eyes never left her face and in mere seconds, his jaw was tight and his fingertips were pressing insistently into the flesh of her hips.

If he wanted to watch her, she'd give him something to watch. Bree arched her back, running her fingers through her hair and thrusting her breasts out.

"Just watching you move like that…" He half spoke, half groaned, his words interrupted by the powerful rush of his release. She rode out the storm, finally collapsing onto the mattress beside him in a state of physical, mental and emotional exhaustion.

Ian scooped her into his arms and pulled her back against the hard wall of his chest. "Beautiful," he whispered, planting a kiss on her bare shoulder as they both drifted off to sleep.

Seven

"Aha!"

Ian poked his head out of the closet, the Monopoly game clutched under his arm. "Aha?"

Bree was in the kitchen, her back to him. She turned toward him and held up a handful of full-size candy bars. "You've been holding out on me, Ian Lawson. I found your secret stash!"

He laughed, shut the closet door and carried the game into the living room. "It's not a *secret* stash. It's an emergency stockpile. Are you telling me you don't have a kitchen drawer filled with candy at your house?"

Bree planted a hand on her hip. "Uh, no. I use my drawers for utensils and towels. Normal stuff."

"That's because you don't have Patty grocery shopping for you. She makes it her personal mission to keep me happy by buying me treats even when I don't ask. She may have gone overboard this time considering

I'd requested a bunch of healthy food this weekend for Missy. She probably thought I'd starve up here."

"Well, we might with what I've found in the fridge." Bree turned back to the drawer and opened another. "Oh. Here's a bag of mini candy bars in this one."

"Bring them. We can use candy bars instead of money for the game. It will make things more interesting."

"What?" Bree's nose was wrinkled in confusion, an expression that he'd always found undeniably cute and, at the same time, sexy.

Back in school, he would kiss the tip of her nose when she made that face. Now, he turned away and started unpacking the pieces of the game instead. They were far from that level of intimacy, despite having slept together.

"Each piece of candy can have a dollar value. Plain chocolate is worth five dollars. If it has peanuts, it's a twenty-dollar bill. Crispy pieces are a fifty. Dark chocolate is a hundred. And the five-hundred is…one of the full-size bars. How's that?"

"Gambling with chocolate. I like it. I get to be the banker." Bree came into the room with her arms full of candy. "You'll steal from the bank."

Ian frowned. "What if I get hungry?"

"It will cost you some of your winnings."

He loudly groaned in complaint but happily continued setting out the cards. "I'll manage the properties, then." He started laying them out on the coffee table by color. "Do we want to play the quick version?"

Bree looked up at him with an arched brow. "Why? What else do we have to do?"

A sly smile curled Ian's lips. He could think of quite

a few things they could do, none of which involved dice and paper money, but Bree had wanted to play a game.

She noted his devious expression and shook her head. "I hate to break it to you, but we are *not* going to lie around and do nothing but have sex until the snow melts."

Ian knew that much. Despite how easily Bree had fallen into his arms today, she'd practically launched right out of them when it was over. He'd fallen asleep spooning her, the drama of the morning feeling as though it were a million miles away. Then he awoke a short time later to an empty space beside him in bed. By the time he stumbled back out into the living room, Bree was showered, dressed and suggesting they play a game. Like their encounter had never even happened.

He decided to go along with it. For now. He wasn't entirely sure where they should go from here. He'd simply acted on instinct, claiming what he'd desired. There hadn't been much thought or discussion put into the decision. All he knew was that he was aching to touch her again. He didn't know if voicing that need would send Bree running into his arms or out into the snow.

"It's either marathon sex or I'll get back on my laptop," he threatened. It was a hollow threat, however. Ian didn't really want to get onto his computer. He would never admit to anyone, especially Bree, that he was enjoying his time away from technology. His calls were forwarded to his assistant. His out-of-office message directed people to contact Keith in his absence. General business operations at the studio were under control. That only left his personal accounts. Considering everything going on, he had zero interest in wading into those waters.

Before he'd shut everything off, he'd texted his mother

and told her he would be out of touch for a few days and not to worry. No one else mattered.

That left nothing but a rowdy board game to distract him from his thoughts about Bree. And that worked for a while. An hour passed quickly as they collected real estate. It was something easy and fun to do. Ian couldn't even remember the last time he did something as simple as play a game. It was nicer than he expected it to be, almost like stopping and taking a deep breath after running a marathon. And he had been running a marathon since he was nineteen.

Bree rolled the dice, then moved her piece to one of his green properties with a hotel. She groaned. "What's the damage?"

Ian picked up his card. "That will be fourteen hundred dollars. Or, if you prefer, your Snickers, your Butterfinger and four of the mini special dark bars."

"You've nearly bankrupted me." Bree handed over the candy with a frown. "All I've got left is this crispy rice bar. And you know what?" She looked up at him and popped it into her mouth. "I'm hungry. Game over. You win."

"Good. I'm hungry, too." Ian unwrapped a piece of candy and ate it. The day had passed in a blur of drama, snow shoveling, lovemaking and board games, but now it was time for dinner. "Let's see what we can come up with tonight."

He climbed to his feet with his winnings and dumped them back into the kitchen drawer to eat later. He opened the pantry door and looked inside. He didn't typically keep much there, but nonperishables would carry over from trip to trip, and as he'd mentioned, Patty sometimes went off script.

"Check the freezer," he said.

Bree opened the door. "Hmm. Popsicles, a bag of frozen biscuit dough and…" She stopped to reach inside and pull out something. "Two rib eye steaks. They look pretty new. There's no freezer burn."

Ian took the package from her. It was definitely only a few days frozen with a packaged date stamp of the previous Tuesday. "God bless Patty." A wire basket on the counter held a mix of potatoes and onions, and she'd bought some fresh vegetables. Together, they could manage an excellent meal. "Tonight, we eat like kings."

Neither of them were experts in the kitchen, but things worked out pretty well. They thawed the steaks in the microwave while the potatoes baked in the oven. While they grilled the steaks, they steamed delicate haricot vert. An hour later, they had dinner on the table, complete with a bottle of merlot from his stash.

The logs in the fireplace were crackling beside them as a fire warmed the dining room. The food was good and so was the company. Ian had hoped for a romantic weekend, but this wasn't what he'd had in mind. It was even better.

"I feel so guilty," Bree said after a few moments eating quietly.

"Why?"

"It's Friday night and I'm in the mountains eating a nice steak and drinking wine that didn't come out of a box."

At that, Ian had to laugh. "What's so wrong with that?"

"I haven't had a Friday night off in six years. Friday night is rehearsal dinner night. As we speak, the soon-to-be Mr. and Mrs. Conner are just wrapping up their rehearsal at our facility. In a few minutes, they'll be loading into a limo and heading downtown to have their rehearsal dinner at a fondue restaurant. I should be there for all of it."

"Who's taking pictures instead? Is the caterer pinch hitting?"

Bree laughed. "No. Amelia is doing prep work for tomorrow and finishing up the wedding cake. Natalie and Gretchen are decorating and coordinating with contractors like the florist and the DJ. We have a contract photographer we call for larger weddings or emergencies, like today. Willie is covering the rehearsal dinner and, thankfully, the ceremony tomorrow."

"So when was the last time you had a whole weekend off?" he asked.

"Uh…" She hesitated, looking up at the ceiling as she tried to calculate it. "Not since college, I'd guess. I might've gotten a weekend over Christmas when people don't want to get married, but that's about it. The first few years after we opened, we worked nearly every day. Now, I get Tuesdays and Wednesdays off. That's my weekend."

Ian understood how it went. Starting from nothing took years of hard work, jumping in the ring to do anything and everything that needed to be done. "Considering all the grief you've given me about working too hard over the years, it sounds like the pot is calling the kettle black."

Bree avoided immediately responding to his observation by taking a large sip of her wine. "Perhaps," she said at last, "but I love what I do. When you love what you do, you don't work a single day, right?"

He nodded. That was the difference, he supposed. Ian was working himself into an early grave because he had nothing else to do. He didn't have a passion for record producing urging him on. "What about your personal life? Do you leave yourself time for relationships?"

"If you're asking if I'm seeing anyone, no, I'm not." She gave him a crooked smile. "A question that might've been better asked this afternoon before…" Her voice trailed off, her cheeks flushing red. "But no," she said, clearing her throat. "I haven't had a serious relationship in several years."

Ian was relieved to hear that. He wanted Bree, but he didn't want either of them to feel guilty about what they did. Especially because he wanted to do it again. "Me, neither. I mean, the Missy thing aside. Before everything happened with her, I hadn't dated anyone for more than a few months at a time. And I wouldn't have bothered dating her if she hadn't dangled herself right in front of me where it was easy to grab."

"Well, you know what they say about low-hanging fruit. It isn't nearly as good or sweet as the fruit up high. You just have to be willing to work to reach it."

Ian chuckled. "Yeah, I've certainly been going for the low-hanging fruit. I haven't had time to work any harder at a relationship. It's a shame, though. If I got one thing out of this whole mess with Missy, it was that the idea of starting a family really appealed to me. I just didn't want to start it with her."

"I don't blame you."

Ian sighed and sat back from his plate. Despite their discussion, he'd managed to demolish everything they'd cooked and still had a hankering for something sweet. He might have to go claim some of his Monopoly winnings before too long.

He looked up and watched Bree as she chewed her food and looked out the window. She was as beautiful as always, but their conversation seemed to have brought her energy down a little. He couldn't tell if she was overworked, or if the lack of love life was bothering her.

"It sounds like we could both use a vacation," he noted, trying to perk up the discussion.

The sadness slipped away from her expression, her thoughts returning to the present. Bree smiled and looked around at the cabin. "What would you call all this?"

This might be the closest thing he'd had to a vacation in a very long time, but that didn't mean it qualified. It just proved to him that it took a blizzard to get him to relax. "I call it captivity. When I say the word *vacation*, I mean beaches, warm breezes and suntan lotion." He looked at her with a raised eyebrow. "Bikinis. Frothy drinks. Skinny dipping in a private splash pool at midnight."

Bree's eyes grew wider as he spoke until they were like giant blue marbles watching him. Her cheeks were tinged pink, her lips moist and open slightly. He could tell her mind had followed him to a tropical location with the two of them mostly nude. Then, in an instant, she stiffened up and regained her composure. "That sounds like a nice idea. You should go when you find a new lady friend."

"What if I've already found a new lady friend?" he asked boldly.

Bree took a deep breath, her shoulders shrugging slightly. "I think we need to survive this trip before we start worrying about another one."

"May I take your picture?"

Ian looked up at Bree with a frown. They'd loaded the dishwasher and cleaned up together, then he'd carried his glass of wine into the living room to relax.

Bree had picked her camera up off the coffee table and started tinkering with it. Their dinnertime conversation had sent her brain spinning. A vacation? Together? Yes, they'd had sex, but she knew this wasn't going to go anywhere. Did he? It didn't sound like it.

When life got problematic, Bree preferred the buffer of her camera between her and the world. Because there was only so far she could go from the temptation and complication of Ian, the camera was her best bet.

Judging by the look on his face, he wasn't expecting Bree to spring this on him. Especially after she'd awkwardly rebuffed his offer of a holiday in the Caribbean. "Why would you want to take my picture?"

She shrugged. She couldn't exactly tell him her initial motivation. At the same time, as big a mess as this weekend was, she wanted the photos to commemorate it. "It's what I do." Bree reached for her nearby camera bag and pulled out a different lens filter. She held the camera up to look at him through the lens, snapping a quick photo to test the light in the room.

Looking at the shot, she was reminded how photogenic Ian was. He was a handsome man in person, with penetrating green eyes and a square jaw covered in evening stubble. His features were masculine but refined. His dark hair was thick and wavy, yet kept short enough to stay under control. Photographing him, however, brought out an aura of confidence and power. There was an edgy male energy in his photo. And if she looked closely…signs of long-term exhaustion and stress. She recognized that look from her father. It was the kind of bone-weariness that came from weeks and months of working at an insane pace. Success at all costs.

And that was why she couldn't go to the beach with

him. Once they got out of here, things would be just like they were before and she'd be pushed aside for his work again. If she was going to make time in her own schedule for a relationship, she wanted it to be with someone who was willing to do the same.

"Do you want me just sitting here like I am? Or would you prefer me nude?" he added with a wicked grin.

Bree sighed. Of course he would turn her request into a sexual innuendo. He might be nearly thirty now, but she was coming to learn that most men's sense of humor stopped developing around fourteen. At least it got her mind off her worries for a while. "Clothes on, please. I haven't taken nude portraits since my college project on the human form. It's not really my thing."

"I mean, I don't mind," he continued, ignoring her protests. "I couldn't help but notice you admiring my stunning male form earlier today. If you want to blow up a photo of me and hang it over your fireplace or something, I totally get it."

"No nudes. And no huge egos, either. I need to be able to get your whole, inflated head in the frame." At that, she hesitated. What she would really like was a shot of him with his guitar. In her old scrapbooks, Bree had pages of photographs with Ian playing. At the coffee shops. On a park bench. In his dorm room. Even on stage during one of his only school performances before he'd quit. She'd really loved photographing him while he worked, and adding another picture to the collection seemed appropriate. "I would really like to take your picture while you play, actually."

At her suggestion, Ian frowned, just as she'd expected him to. "Last night was a one-night limited engagement. I don't intend to do it again."

Bree dropped the camera to her lap, a pout threatening to force out her bottom lip. She tried to hold it in. "Please, Ian. You can play whatever you want. Just let me take a few pictures."

He sighed, then leaned forward to rest his elbows on his knees and look at her. "Bree, I know that you still think of me as the Ian you knew in school. I do the same thing. I see you and think about spotting you in the crowd at the coffee shop or when you helped me study for my algebra finals. But we're not those people anymore. It's been a long time and we've both grown up. That person you remember—the charming musician with the guitar—is long gone."

"But last night…"

"Last night," he interrupted, "was just for old time's sake. Nothing has changed. I'm not suddenly going to grab that guitar and pick up my music career where I left off nine years ago. Those were just the dreams of a teenaged kid who didn't know any better."

And those were the words of a grown man made bitter by having those same dreams crushed. It made her sad to think that one person had the power to make him throw everything away. He'd disengaged himself so much from his music that he wouldn't even pick up a guitar. Certainly he could at least play for fun without thinking he was going to be a rock star one day. Bree enjoyed her photography and had moderate success, but she never expected to shoot for *Vanity Fair*. She did it because she liked to do it. Wasn't that enough?

"Will you answer me one question, then, Ian?"

She could tell he didn't want to, but he would for fear she might not let the subject drop. "One question. And then we let the subject go and you will photograph me nude."

Bree twisted her lips, holding back her irritation. "Why does having a successful record label keep you from playing guitar? Why can't you have both?"

His dark green gaze narrowed at her. "That was two questions," he noted, dodging them both.

"Damn it, Ian. Come on. I know you still love to play."

"Of course I still love to play. Picking up that guitar last night was like being reunited with a long-lost brother. Like coming home. If you have music in your soul, you can't just lock the door and throw away the key. It's always going to be there. I try to channel it into my artists, but it never really goes away."

"Then why do you torture yourself? Why don't you play if you want to?"

"Because it still hurts, Bree!" He shouted the answer, almost as though he might not get the words out if he didn't. His face contorted with surprise and irritation before he shook his head and wiped his palm over his face. "I'm sorry, I didn't mean to yell. I just… It's easier for me not to play at all. If I don't play, I can try to forget about all the plans I had that never came to fruition. I can tell myself it was just a phase I grew out of. That I wasn't that good so I didn't lose out on my big chance. That no amount of practicing—" his voice trailed off "—would've kept me from losing the most important person in my life."

Bree opened her mouth to argue with him, but then she stopped. Her eyes met his and there was no doubt in her mind that he was talking about her. She swallowed hard, trying to choose her words wisely. "You didn't lose me because I thought you weren't a good musician, Ian. I thought you were a great musician."

"Then I lost you because I gave up." He shrugged. "No one likes a quitter."

Bree placed her camera on the coffee table and settled next to him on the couch. She took both his hands and covered them in her own. "No. Not even close. I loved *you*, Ian. You happened to play guitar. But that wasn't all that you were any more than me taking photographs was all that I was or am. I loved your spirit. Your thoughtfulness. I loved that you always held the door for me and would help me haul my camera equipment no matter how far off into the middle of nowhere I wanted to go. I loved your smile. I loved the way you loved animals and how excited you would get about the idea of getting a dog once you graduated. I remember you had the breed already picked out and the name to go with it."

"Gibson," he said, the surprised expression on his face making it clear that he'd forgotten until that moment.

"There were a million things I loved about you that had nothing to do with your music."

His green eyes were nearly boring into her by the time she finished. It made her chest feel tight, like he was squeezing her rib cage in his fists. "Then why did you leave me?"

Bree swallowed hard. "I didn't leave you, Ian. You left me. You didn't do it on purpose, but losing your music changed you. Day by day, the Ian I knew disappeared and there was nothing I could say or do to get you back."

"I'm still here, Bree. I always have been."

"Then prove it to me. Show me that inside the CEO of SpinTrax is the man I used to love. The one who would do anything to make me smile." Bree pulled away from him, walking over to the closet where the guitar was stored. She carried it back to him, holding it out.

Ian hesitated. His jaw was tight, the muscles in his neck and shoulders like stone. His gaze flicked over the guitar, but he didn't reach for it. She could tell he wanted to, but it was an internal struggle she couldn't understand.

"Then don't do it for me, Ian. We haven't been in love for a long time and you don't owe me anything. But you owe yourself a lot. Do it for yourself. Play your guitar. Write some new songs. You might find that keeping your music alive isn't nearly as painful as holding it inside."

That was what it took for him to reach out and take the guitar from her. He slipped the strap over his head and held it for a moment. "What do you want me to play?"

"Play whatever you want to, Ian. I just want to capture the moment." Bree took a few steps back and picked her camera back up from the table. As she turned it on and adjusted some of the settings, she heard the familiar notes of a Kansas song begin. This had been one of his staples.

As he began to sing, his heavenly baritone filled the large room.

Bree moved back, crouching down to take her first shot. Framing Ian perfectly, she stopped short of hitting the button. Instead, she just watched. His eyes were closed, his fingers moving deftly across the strings. He sang with such emotion, the melancholy lyrics touched her as strongly as if he'd written those words himself.

She only took a couple pictures. Four at the most. She couldn't bear for the sound of the camera interrupting his song. Ironic, considering her desire to photograph him playing had driven this entire, emotional discussion. About halfway through the song, she dropped the camera into her lap and just listened to him sing.

The final notes carried through the room, followed by a resounding silence. The house suddenly felt empty without his music filling it. Bree expected him to immediately set the guitar aside, having appeased her, but he continued to hold it. His fingers flexed around the neck, his palm caressing the smooth wood.

"Thank you," he said at last.

Eight

Bree awoke the next morning to a familiar sound. At first she thought she was dreaming it, then she heard it again and knew it was real. Lying facedown on the mattress, she rolled over and tentatively opened one eye to see Ian standing beside the bed with her camera. Taking her picture.

She immediately shot up, feeling an unnerving cold breeze on her skin. She looked down and realized she was naked. She quickly tugged the sheets up to cover her bare breasts and prayed Ian hadn't gotten a shot of that. They'd spent the night together and her clothes were currently scattered around the room. Ian, of course, was fully dressed, putting her at a distinct disadvantage. Last night it hadn't seemed that important, but she hadn't expected to be the subject of a photo shoot first thing in the morning.

"What are you doing?"

Ian twisted his lips in irritation and lowered the camera from his face. "I was taking pictures of a beautiful woman while she slept, but the moment has passed."

Bree leaned over the side of the bed, scooping up her shirt from the floor. She pulled it on. "Why would you want to take pictures of me?"

"Why would you want to take pictures of other people?" he countered.

Bree frowned, an expression that brought the opposite reaction to Ian's face. "You don't like having your picture taken," he said.

She wrinkled her nose. "No, I don't."

"A photographer who hates having her picture taken. How is that possible?" he wondered aloud.

Bree smoothed out the wild strands of her hair and tugged the blankets even higher under her arms. The fabric of the shirt was thin and did little to make her feel covered. "I prefer to be behind the camera, if you must know."

Ian raised the camera again and snapped another picture before she could turn away. "Now that you mention it, I seem to remember you were always the one taking pictures in college. I didn't think much of it at the time because that was your thing. But I remember going through old pictures after you transferred to UT and being frustrated because you weren't in any of them. I guess this is a lifelong aversion. I just didn't notice it before."

It was hard for Bree to imagine Ian poring through old pictures, looking for her after she was gone. She thought he'd already forgotten her, even before she'd left. "I've been avoiding photos of myself since my parents bought me a camera for my tenth birthday."

"That's a shame. You're more beautiful than most

of the women I see in magazines. You should spend more time in front of the camera for a change. For the benefit of society."

She shook her head, ignoring his attempts at flattery. Instead, her thoughts drifted to last night's discussion of nude portraits. "Before these pictures...*benefit society*...you didn't take any shots of me naked, did you?"

"You were naked in all of them, but you were sleeping on your stomach. There's nothing to see."

Bree's mouth tightened. "If I see so much as a nip slip when I go over those images, Ian..."

He held up his hands defensively. "You won't, I promise. There's nothing on this camera but images of a golden angel sleeping in my bed."

She'd believe it when she saw it. Her glance shifted over to the bright streams of sunlight coming in the window. "What time is it?"

"About eight-thirty. I woke up at six today like I usually do. Yesterday was a fluke. I showered, dressed, made coffee and watched a little of the weather forecast. I've got some good news for you."

Good news? "You've made me breakfast in bed?" she guessed.

"No," he said, twisting his lips in thought, "but that isn't a bad idea. I should've thought of that."

Bree flopped back against the pillows. It was too early for a guessing game. "Then what is it?"

"The weather station is reporting it should get to almost fifty degrees today. I heard the snowplows going by this morning. They're expecting most of the snow on the plowed roads to melt. With any luck, we should be able to head home tomorrow morning."

Bree smiled because she knew she should, but for some reason, the news didn't make her happy. Somehow, being trapped in the snow was the ideal environment for the two of them. They'd spent so much time talking, getting to know one another again. It felt like old times, except that it wasn't. And that fact would be crystal clear the moment they arrived back in Nashville.

"That's great," she said, feigning excitement. "I guess we should make the most of our last day here then."

"You're right," he said, setting her camera on the nightstand. "Stay put. I'll be right back."

Bree sat patiently waiting for Ian to return a few minutes later. He had a tray with some fruit, toast, jam and coffee. Ian carried it over to the bed, setting it down between them and kicking off his shoes before sliding under the covers.

"Breakfast in bed!" he announced.

Bree leaned in to kiss him and he captured her, pulling her closer. She wanted to melt into him, to make the most of these fleeting moments, but she knew she shouldn't. The closer she let herself get to Ian, the more she would be disappointed when it all fell apart. "Be careful," she said as she pulled away. "You don't want to spill the coffee."

Ian reluctantly sat back and they both started to eat. Bree slathered her toast with butter and strawberry jam before taking a bite. It was sourdough bread from the loaf they'd used to make grilled cheese the first night. It had a bite to it that mixed nicely with the creamy butter and sweet jam.

"Can I ask you something?"

Bree hesitated, her toast hanging midair. What could he ask that needed an introduction like that? She'd been awake less than ten minutes and had had two sips of coffee. "Sure. What?"

"Well, Thursday night I have this industry thing to go to. Cocktails, schmoozing, maybe a little dancing. It's the kind of shindig that makes me completely miserable, but I'm expected to be there. I'm also expected to bring a date."

Bree's breath caught in her throat. Was he asking her to go on a date once they were back in Nashville? That was a big deal. It was as if he was acknowledging that the two of them might be viable outside of this cabin. He'd hinted at it with their talk about fantasy vacations, but this was real. Concrete plans. Bree wasn't nearly as certain of their longevity as he was. Sure, he'd played the guitar a couple of times. He was trying, but he was still a far cry from being the carefree Ian she remembered. Right now, she was just a distraction from his laptop. Could there really be more? She both craved and feared finding out the answer.

"I RSVP'd last week to go to this thing with Missy," he continued, unaware of the tension that had leaked into her muscles. "Obviously, that's no longer an option. I could go by myself, but I really don't want to face all those people on my own. Since I've unplugged, I have no idea how the fake pregnancy scandal is all going down, but I'm sure everyone will be whispering behind my back or feeling sorry for me. I thought if I showed up with a blonde bombshell on my arm, it might shut them up. It might also be a lot of fun having you there. What do you think? Would you like to go with me?"

Bree hesitated. She wanted to go, yet she was afraid to say yes. If Ian was trying to have a life outside work, she needed to support that, or she had no room to criticize. She didn't have to work Thursday night. She could go. She wanted to go. She just didn't know if she *should* go. A glamorous night out, champagne with important people, bodies pressed close together while dancing across polished marble floors… Was her heart strong enough to withstand a romantic assault of that caliber?

"Okay," she said at last.

A wide smile broke out across Ian's face. "Really? Awesome. I think you'll enjoy yourself. I can introduce you to some musicians. Quite a few will be there. Do you like Jack Wheeler's music?"

Bree's eyes got big. Jack Wheeler had once been a member of one of the biggest bands in rock. He was an icon. A member of the Rock and Roll Hall of Fame. He was also a photographer who had put out several books in addition to gallery showings and magazine spreads. Yeah, she wanted to meet him. That would be amazing. "Sure," she said, trying not to sound too eager.

That just brought the worry back into her mind, this time of a more frivolous nature. She was going to a party with rock stars. What was she going to wear? She felt her chest tighten with panic. She didn't dress up very often. For weddings where she was shooting, she wore black pants and a black blouse so she could move almost invisibly through the party. She wanted to get great shots but not at the expense of the people at the wedding. She might have a cocktail dress. Maybe. Perhaps Amelia did. They were close to the same size, although Amelia was doubly blessed when it came to "the girls." She'd have to go shopping. She didn't want to embarrass Ian in front of his peers.

"What's wrong?" he asked. "You don't look very enthused. You don't have to go if you don't want to."

"No, no," she argued. "I want to go. I'm just not sure what I'm going to wear."

"Judging by the women I've seen at events like this, something chic and sparkly. And if I can inject my personal preference into the equation, something on the shorter, tighter side so I can spend all night imagining you taking it off when we get home."

That brought a smile to Bree's lips. "I suppose I can manage that. I'll go shopping when I get back to Nashville. Or I'll raid Amelia's closet. She will know just what to do. She's the fashionista. I'm just the photographer."

"Always behind the camera," he noted, referencing their earlier conversation.

"That's how I prefer it."

"And *I*," Ian began, "prefer *you* without that top on." He lifted the empty breakfast tray and moved it to the nightstand before snuggling up beside her. "Here's to making the most of our last day here," he said before pulling her into a deep, passionate kiss.

The moment his lips touched hers, all her worries vanished. There were no parties, no rock stars, no fancy dresses and no painful past. Just him and her together, cherishing their last day in the safe haven of the cabin. Tomorrow, they would return to the real world. And despite how carefully she had tried to hold back with Ian, she knew she couldn't last much longer. Soon she would give in and be his, no matter what the consequences. She'd tried to be strong, but his touch and his words made her weak.

Resistance was futile.

Ian stepped out onto the front porch the next morning and took one of his last lungfuls of fresh mountain air. The roads were clear and finally open. Their time here was at an end.

For some reason that bothered him. He didn't know why. He should be happy to get home and return to work and life as usual, but suddenly his everyday life didn't seem that appealing anymore. It felt empty, like he was just a robot going through the motions each day.

It was just like Bree to be able to sow seeds of doubt into his life in only a few short days. He'd gone nine years without playing a guitar or picking up a pen to write a song. As long as he kept those thoughts from his mind, he was okay. Now, his fingers were achy and restless to get back to playing. That wasn't what he needed to be spending his time and energy on. He was a four-hour drive from Nashville and the personal and professional cluster that awaited him in the wake of the fake pregnancy scandal.

He wasn't looking forward to dealing with any of that, most especially dealing with Missy. She might not be his fiancée any longer, but she was still one of his artists. Until the final terms of her contract were met, he'd have to work with her, but it would not be much longer. In maybe another month, he could cut ties with Missy and never have to think about her ever again.

Bree came out onto the porch behind him, her camera equipment slung over her arms to load into her SUV. There was the other woman that would plague his thoughts. If Ian was smart, he would cut ties and not think about Bree again, either, but that wasn't going to happen. When it came to his college love, he was the dumbest man in the world.

"I can help you with that," he said, stepping into the driveway and scooping a heavy bag off her shoulder.

"I've got it, but thank you," she said with a smile. "I'm used to hauling all this stuff around on my own, you know."

"Is there any more?"

"Just my backpack and the tripod. They're in the living room."

"I'll go get them." Ian went inside, climbing up the stairs two at a time. He found her bag and the tripod and picked them up. He gave a quick scan over the house and didn't see anything else that belonged to her. He went back outside and handed her the last items to put in her car.

"I guess that's it," she said, stepping back to slam the hatch closed. Bree swayed nervously in her Converse, her hands buried in her back pockets.

Her hair was braided again today, the same way it had been when they'd played in the snow. He felt the memory threaten to ignite a fire in him, but now was not the time. He'd had all day yesterday to get his fill of Bree. Now, he would have to wait until Thursday, at least. Even if he wanted to see her, it would take days to manage the mess he'd been ignoring when he unplugged.

"It's been a wild couple of days, hasn't it?"

Ian stepped forward, wrapping his arms around her waist and tugging her against him. "It's certainly not what I expected when I came up here. My life is completely different driving down the mountain than it was driving up it."

She looked at him with a smile that showcased her full pink lips and straight snow-white teeth. "Life doesn't always turn out the way you plan. Sometimes, it turns out even better than you can imagine."

"This is way, way better." Ian leaned in to capture her lips with his own. Bree melted into him, every soft curve pressing against his hard angles. He wanted to pin her body to the SUV, strip off every inch of her clothing and make love to her one last time. "Can you stay just one more hour?" he murmured against her lips.

She shook her head, reluctantly pulling away. "No, I've got to get on the road. Yesterday I told Natalie I'd get back in time to help them break down and clean up the rest of the Conner wedding."

"You gain an hour going back with the time change."

Bree smiled, kissing him softly, then disentangling from his arms. "I've already factored that in. Sorry."

Ian nodded. "I tried. Have fun cleaning up the reception hall."

"I'll see you on Thursday," she said with a bright, encouraging smile that seemed a little forced. She didn't seem to want to leave any more than he did.

"That's right," he said, nodding. "I'll pick you up about seven Thursday night."

"I'll be ready. Don't forget to take your guitar home with you," she added. "After that party Thursday night, I want you to play for me again. This time, naked."

Her words were meant to be a promise of a seductive night to come, but Ian felt every muscle in his body involuntarily stiffen at her words. He didn't respond, he just smiled tightly. "Drive safely."

Bree hugged him, then pulled away to climb into her car. He moved back to the porch, watching as she backed out and then headed down the winding road to the highway. The minute her taillights disappeared around the bend, the ache of anxiety started pooling in his stomach.

What, exactly, was he doing?

He was living in a fantasyland. Ignoring all the signs that his pleasant river cruise was about to go straight over a waterfall.

This should've been the end. He'd told himself he

could handle this. That it was just going to be physical and everything would be fine. But now it was anything but fine. He should've waved goodbye to Bree and put their relationship back on the shelf where it belonged. Instead, he'd asked her to go to that party with him. He wanted her to go. He thought she'd have a good time. He was excited about the idea of seeing Bree in a slinky dress and extending this relationship beyond their time here in the mountains.

But that wasn't the problem. The problem was that he was just delaying the inevitable.

They weren't going to work out. He knew that the minute he'd laid eyes on her again. Things might seem okay when they were here in Gatlinburg, but back in Nashville it would fall apart. Because Bree didn't want Ian Lawson, record producer. She wanted Ian Lawson, the musician. She wanted to roll the clocks back nine years and pretend that SpinTrax and everything else he'd done in his life didn't matter.

Bree had pushed too hard. Harder than just a well-meaning person would. She'd pushed him to play. Pushed him to sing. Pushed to photograph him while he did. She'd asked him to write new songs. A moment ago, she'd asked him to play for her again on Thursday night. It was abundantly clear that Bree didn't want *him* with his contracts, business meetings and A-list musical roster. She wanted the fantasy that didn't exist, and she would do whatever she could to change and mold Ian into what she wanted.

That wouldn't work. The ship had sailed and Ian could never return to being the idealistic musician he'd been back in school. He had been young, ignorant of the world and so excited by the potential of his future. Once all those things come crashing down around you,

there's no going back. He had grown up. He wished
Bree would do the same.

With a sigh, Ian went inside and started closing up
the house. He turned down the thermostat, shut doors,
pulled curtains and checked locks. He quickly cleaned
out the refrigerator of anything perishable and gathered
up the trash in the garage so Rick could take it down
to the dump later. Finally, he ran through his bedroom
and bath, looking for anything left behind and then
carried his bag into the entryway. He paused, looking
at the guitar leaning against the wall by the front door.

Now he had to make a choice. He'd come to a fork
in the road. If Bree were still here, she would needle
him until it was loaded into his car. With her gone, it
was only up to him. It was a tougher decision than he'd
expected.

Ian was fighting with himself over wanting that same
fantasy she did. It was easy to ignore his dreams when
they were buried in the closet along with his guitar. At
the same time, Bree spoke about his potential and his
music so passionately that it made him want to believe
that he could have his musical dream and his company.
She insisted there was no reason he couldn't have both.

With her miles ahead of him on the highway, the
realm of possibilities was starting to crumble. It sounded
like a good idea. A perfectly nice idea. Yet he knew it
was impossible. His company took up so much of his
time, he could barely date. Before Missy crashed into
his life, he hadn't had a date in months.

How could he possibly manage working at SpinTrax,
dating Bree and rebooting his musical career? It was
impossible. At least one of the three things would suffer
and he was pretty sure he couldn't let it be his record
label. A hundred people depended on that succeeding.

What would that mean for his future with Bree? She wouldn't tolerate being anything but number one on his priority list. That shoved his future in music to the bottom rung. Could he stand to play knowing it wouldn't lead anywhere?

As if the universe were answering his question, his phone rang. It startled him, having been off for the past few days, but he'd turned it back on as they were getting ready to go. He looked down to see his talent manager's name and number on the screen.

"Hey, Keith."

"Looks who's back in the land of the living. Did you enjoy losing contact with the modern world?"

Ian chuckled. He didn't think he would, but it had been easy to pass the time with a naked, willing Bree beneath him. Who needed Candy Crush when you had that? "I needed a break and I got one. Now I'm ready to jump back into the fray."

"Good because the fray has been anxiously waiting for your return. I don't know if I'm a talent manager or your public relations officer. Several magazines have called looking for exclusives on your side of the Missy story. Ryan Seacrest and Howard Stern both want you to call in to their radio shows. If I were you, I'd go with Seacrest. Stern would ask a bunch of creepy questions about Missy's sex life. I'd feel like I had to listen to support you, and I really don't want to know."

Ian sighed into the phone. "Anything important happen? Anything aside from the mess with Missy?"

"All your other artists seem to be doing fine. The only calls I've gotten in the past few days have been from Missy's manager. Big surprise. He's trying to push for a new contract because her numbers have improved."

"Not for all the tea in China," Ian said. "If she's such a hot commodity, let her jump to a new label. There's got to be someone out there that will take her on her numbers alone. They're not stellar, but she's not going to play the fair circuit anytime soon, either."

He bent down, grabbing the handle of his bag and carrying it into the garage to throw in the back of his Escalade.

"I'll pass that along," Keith said. "In the appropriate legal speak," he added.

"Thanks. I'm hitting the road in about five minutes and I'll come straight to the office. I need to make a few quick pit stops, but I'll see you in a few hours."

"Can't wait for you to come back," Keith said. "See you soon."

Ian hung up and went back into the house. Talking to Keith made him feel normal again. His business was what drove his life and he was ready to get back to it.

In the living room, he glanced once more at the guitar. There was no room in his life for it, but he couldn't bear to leave it behind. Just like with Bree.

In the end, the guitar went in the back of the car with everything else.

Nine

"Wow." It was all Ian could say.

Bree arched an eyebrow at Ian. "Wow? Really?" She looked down at her outfit in confusion.

"Yeah, wow," he repeated. She looked incredible. How did she not know that? He'd expected her to choose something black, slinky but conservative. It was red. Fire-engine red. And lace. The dress had a conservative collar, long sleeves and a hemline just above the knee. Even then, it was the sexiest thing he'd ever seen. To start, it fit like a glove. It was also sheer. Except for the appropriately placed red fabric panels that ran down the front and back, the rest was see-through. He could see her pale skin peeking through everywhere else, including along each side. Panties…were an impossibility. And his mouth went bone-dry with the revelation.

"It's new," Bree said with a shy shrug. "The girls took me shopping and helped me pick it out. Will it be okay for the party? I know you said sparkly, but sparkles aren't really my thing."

Ian shook his head furiously. This was way better than sparkles. "This is fine. It's great. Amazing. You look incredible in it. Actually, we can even skip the party and stay home, you look so good."

Bree smiled, her bright red lipstick a shock of color against her pale, flawless skin. Her blond waves were pinned back into a chignon at her neck, a few loose strands along her face. She was wearing nude pumps and no jewelry. She didn't need anything else. She shined like a jewel all on her own.

"You're not that lucky," she said. "You promised me a party with rock stars and I intend to have it."

"If you insist. Are you ready to go?" If she was, they needed to go now, before he changed his mind and ravished her on the gray leather sofa he could see over her shoulder.

"I am." Bree reached to pick up a nude beaded clutch and stepped out onto her porch. She locked the door and he escorted her to the Escalade.

The party was being held in a Brentwood mansion ten miles outside of the city center. It was the home of former country music star and music producer Luke Chisholm. Luke had made his millions, burned out and dropped out of the music scene for several years. He'd reappeared four years ago, starting his own record label, like Ian. They would've been rivals if they didn't target different artists. Ian was after rock and pop music, a rarity in Nashville. Luke, like so many others, specialized in country and bluegrass music. Because of that, they had developed a friendship, always talking about collaborating with their artists but never getting around to it.

It didn't take long to get to the party and Ian was

glad. Just sitting beside him in the car, Bree was a distraction. The hem of her dress crept higher when she sat in the Escalade, tempting him with creamy thigh for one mile after the next. He almost missed his exit from sneaking peeks of her as he drove.

As they pulled up into the circular driveway of the mansion, they were greeted by a valet. Ian got out of the car, turned over his key, opened Bree's door and took her arm. They started up the stairs to the entrance.

"So, is this party for something in particular?" Bree asked as they approached the front door.

"Not really. Luke usually throws a party once or twice a year, no occasion. I always try to make it to his. It's for social mingling, mostly. A little business. There will be a mix of business guys like me, some artists, other industry people..."

"Interesting," she said, although she didn't look impressed. "Any drunk karaoke singing?"

Ian chuckled. "No. But with half the music stars of Nashville in attendance, it would be one hell of a performance, drunk or not."

A man in a tuxedo greeted them at the door and directed them through the marble foyer into the backyard.

"It's outdoors?" Bree asked with worry furrowing her delicate brow. "I didn't bring a coat. Or much of a dress, for that matter. Who holds an outdoor party in the winter? This isn't California."

Ian leaned in to Bree's ear. "I'm sure Luke has it under control. He takes care of every detail. Look," he said pointing at a few women just outside the glass. "Those ladies don't look cold."

A set of French doors opened up to a pool complex. A large semicircular pool sprawled out in front of them, crowds of people milling around it and standing on

Plexiglas platforms hovering over it. Scattered around the area were tall gas space heaters. As they stepped outside it almost felt warmer than it did inside the house.

"This is beautiful," Bree said, her gaze moving over the twinkling lights in the trees, the tables draped with rich fabrics and the floral arrangements that seemed to reach for the sky. "Don't be offended, but I'd much rather be here as a photographer than a guest. I really want to take some pictures of this setup. And the flowers. Gretchen would just love it. It makes me wonder what florist they're working with. But…I won't," she added with a shy smile. "I'll be cool. I don't want to embarrass you."

That made Ian chuckle. His Bree was many things, but cool wasn't how he'd describe her. She was much more comfortable behind the lens than strutting around in front of it, but he wanted to change that. A quick glance around was enough to prove that she was easily the most beautiful woman at the party. She should be as comfortable in front of the lens as behind it. "You didn't smuggle that big camera of yours in that tiny purse, did you?"

She smiled. "I wish I had, but I'm no Mary Poppins."

"Too bad. Without it, you'll just have to play my hot date tonight." He slipped an arm around her waist, pulling her close enough to kiss. Instead, he leaned in and whispered into her ear. "And if I find you in a corner talking to a photographer, I'll find a…creative…way to punish you later."

"Yes, sir," Bree said with a smile that indicated she wouldn't mind.

They stepped into the crowd, melting into the throng of well-dressed and powerful people. When he first got into the business, he'd been starstruck. Now it was just another day at work. On the far left, he spotted the nearest bar. "Would you like me to get you a drink?"

"Sure. Bring me a white wine. Chardonnay if they have it."

"You got it." Ian leaned in to press a quick kiss to her cheek and pulled away. There were several people in front of him in line, including Luke, the man throwing the party.

"If you're picking up the bar tab, shouldn't you be able to skip the line?"

Luke turned, a smile crossing his face when he saw Ian. They shook hands. "You'd think so. But I'm okay with waiting. It let me run into you, for one thing." The smile faded for a moment. "How are you, Ian?"

Ugh. That. Ian had tried to avoid the topic of the Missy debacle, but it was inevitable that it would pop up at an event like this. The music industry in Nashville was a small world. Everyone knew everyone's business. "I'm fine, really. The whole thing seems sort of surreal at this point."

"I knew Missy was a handful, but I never expected she could do something like that." Luke shook his head. "You know, she's been sniffing around my label this week. Her manager called the other day wanting to talk about Missy branching out into country music. I laughed at him."

Ian winced. "I'm sure you're not the only place she's called. I keep waiting to bump into her here. It's the perfect hunting grounds for an artist in need of a contract."

"Oh, she's here somewhere." Luke stepped up to get his drinks, then waited as the bartender poured two for Ian. "I saw you come in with a pretty lady. You'd better hope Missy didn't see you."

Ian shrugged. "I don't care what Missy thinks. After

the week I've had, I deserve to have a beautiful lady on my arm who isn't crazy."

"Right you are." Luke laughed. "But watch out for Missy. She will make it out of this scandal one way or another. Hopefully it won't be by climbing over you to get there."

"I will." Ian was glad he wasn't the only one who could see Missy for who she really was.

"Listen, call me next week and we can chat. I've got to get this drink back to Mrs. Chisholm."

Ian nodded, waving at Luke before picking up his drinks and turning in the direction he'd come. His eyes found Bree in the crowd, then he froze. A feeling of dread washed over him. Luke was right. Missy was not only here, but she had Bree cornered.

The two women were talking, but he could tell it wasn't idle chatter. Missy looked like she was on the verge of losing it. Taking her rage out on Ian's date wouldn't be out of character for her. They were far too close to the edge of the pool for any sort of squabbling. One or both would end up in the frigid, illuminated water.

As fast as his feet could move him through the crowd, he arrived at Bree's side. "Missy!" he said, interrupting whatever conversation they were having. Ian handed Bree her glass of wine and then wrapped his arm around her waist. He took two giant steps backward, putting some breathing room between them and Missy and moving that much farther away from the water's edge just in case. "I didn't expect to see you here tonight."

Missy crossed her arms over her chest, pushing her breasts up to the point of indecency. She was wearing red, too, although her dress was lacking the elegance of Bree's. It was satin, tight and short, with a plunging neckline. "You didn't think I was just going to tuck my tail in and run, did you?"

He wasn't that lucky. "Of course not. Why should you be ashamed of lying and manipulating everyone in your life, especially me? Now, if you'll excuse us…" Ian tried shifting them away from Missy.

"You can walk away from me, but this isn't over, Ian," Missy said ominously.

He sighed, turning back to face her. "Yes, it is. And there's nothing you can do about it, at least not here if you want a new record deal from anyone at the party. Goodbye, Missy."

Before she could say anything else, he propelled Bree in the opposite direction, following closely on her heels. They were on the other side of the party before they stopped.

"Thank you for rescuing me," Bree leaned in and whispered against his neck. "I thought she was going to throw me in the pool. This dress cost me way too much to get ruined the first time I wore it."

"Don't thank me. It's my fault she came after you." Ian took a deep breath. Less than ten minutes into the party and things were going downhill fast. "What did she say to you?"

"Eh." She shrugged. "The usual jealous woman stuff. Who am I? What am I doing coming to this party with you? Do I know who she is? Nothing very original. You interrupted before I could say something ugly to her."

Ian was glad he got there in time. Missy had a short fuse and no shame. He didn't want her ruining this night for Bree. He could already tell the party was going to be a lot of fun with her by his side. He usually spent most of his time conducting business and checking his phone. Tonight, he didn't have the urge to do either. He wanted to take Bree for a turn on the dance floor and introduce her to everyone. He wanted to feed her a chocolate-covered strawberry from the dessert table and snuggle with her by the fire pit.

"I'm sorry about Missy, Bree. I promised you a fun night, and after that scene, you're never going to want to come with me to another one of these things."

"Missy hasn't scared me off yet. And actually," Bree said with a smile, "all you promised me was a chance to meet Jack Wheeler."

He had said that, hadn't he? "You're right." He looked up, scanning the crowd, and found Jack sitting nearby with a group of other musicians she would probably be equally excited to meet. "Come with me," he said, taking her hand. "I'm going to do my part and introduce you to Jack."

"And then what?" she asked.

"And then I'm taking you home and slowly peeling you out of that dress."

Ian kept his word. They spent another hour or so at the party, chatting with enough stars to make Bree's head spin. And then they made a quick exit.

She expected Ian to take her back to her town house, but instead, he drove back into the city and the center of the music district. "Where are we going?"

"To my place."

They eventually pulled into the parking garage of a tall residential building. Ian pulled into his reserved space and escorted her to the elevator that took them up to his penthouse.

"Now it's my turn to say 'wow,'" she said as they stepped into the marble foyer. There was a stone compass star on the floor of the round entry and a sparkling chandelier overhead. "This is amazing."

Ian led her into the modern kitchen with black cabinets and gray, concrete countertops. "Thanks. I'll give your regards to my decorator. She fretted over it and almost no one ever sees it but Winnie and me. Hell, I barely see it."

Bree approached the kitchen, running her fingertips along the counter. "Is Winnie here?"

Ian shook his head. "She's not a live-in employee, although she has a room in case she needs to stay over. She'll be back in the morning, so no stumbling into the kitchen naked for a cup of coffee."

"Hmm…" Bree said thoughtfully. "You think you're going to keep me here all night, do you?"

"Yep," he said, reaching into the wine chiller to pull out a bottle. "I'm certain of it. Because I'm not driving you home until I leave for work in the morning." He poured two glasses of chardonnay and handed one to her.

"In that case, I'm losing the heels." Bree kicked out of the stilettos, sighing with bliss to be flat on the ground once again. The shoes were hot, no doubt, but she really just preferred her Converse. She even had red ones that would've matched the dress, but she didn't need Amelia freaking out over her major fashion faux pas.

"That's better for the tour, anyway." Ian started through the house, pointing out details as they walked. He had the entire top floor to himself, with an unnecessary number of bedrooms and bathrooms in addition to an office, a gym and a movie theater.

"Ian, why such a big penthouse? You could have someone secretly living here and you wouldn't ever know it."

Ian shrugged. "I didn't want a house. I wanted to be in the city, close to the studio. I liked the features. And I guess I figured that someday I might need the other rooms for a wife and family."

"Or Missy and all her assistants?"

Ian looked at her with a pinched, irritated expression that quickly faded to a smile. "Or *that*. Dodged a bullet there." At the end of a corridor, Ian opened a door and let her step in ahead of him. "This is the master suite," he said, slipping out of his suit coat and tossing it across the back of a chair.

It was another beautiful space. After being at his rustic cabin for several days, it was interesting to see how modern his apartment was. Glass, chrome, polished stone and leather. The stark-white king-size bed was on a raised black marble platform. It had a tall white suede headboard and another chandelier hanging over the bed. There was a sitting room with a television and a fireplace, and beyond that, she could make out the master bath. It was larger than her living room and she had what she thought was a pretty spacious town house.

Bree stepped onto the raised platform and sat on the edge of the bed to sip her wine. "Pretty impressive," she said. "A far cry from your dorm room and that lumpy twin bed."

"Thank goodness." Ian sat beside her as she sipped the last of her wine and placed the empty glass on the platform by her feet. Together, they looked out through the wall of windows to the skyline of downtown Nashville. The glowing twin spires of the Batman Building and the bright red L&C sign on the top of the Life and Causality Building made for quite a view.

She was lost in the twinkling lights of downtown when she felt Ian's hand at her neck. He found the snap and the zipper and ran it down the long curve of her back. She closed her eyes, relishing the feel as his fingertips followed the same trail, caressing her skin down to the hollow at the base of her spine. She shivered, his touch sending a wave of goose bumps across her arms and legs. Those same goose bumps immediately vanished when Ian pushed her sleeves off her shoulders and placed a searing kiss on her bare skin.

Ian kept pushing until the dress was peeled down to her waist, exposing her breasts. She slipped her arms out of the sleeves and arched her back to lean against his chest. His hands immediately moved over her breasts. She gasped as his fingertips teased the hard pebbles of her nipples.

"You look amazing tonight," he whispered, letting the tip of his tongue graze her earlobe. "I've never wanted a woman as much as I want you right now."

"Oh, yeah?" she purred, letting her hand slip in between his thighs to confirm it.

Ian groaned loudly, his hand moving quickly to her wrist to tug her away. "Not yet." He stood up, looking down on her as she sat on the edge of the bed. He placed his hands on her shoulders and pushed until she was lying back on the bed. His hands quickly went to her hips, gripping the bunched fabric there to tug it down her legs.

He stood back up, looking at her completely nude body with a blazing heat of desire in his eyes. Slowly, he pulled off his tie and unbuttoned his dress shirt.

Bree slid back on the bed until she reached the pillows. "Don't make me wait any longer," she said. She was immediately joined by a naked and sheathed Ian, his body covering every inch of hers. She didn't hesitate to part her thighs and allow him to slip between them. He surged forward until he was buried deep inside her.

She closed her eyes and savored the feeling. Not just the distinctly feminine experience of sex, but the intimacy it built between them. It was something she had lacked with other partners but never with Ian. And especially not now. She had never felt closer to a man in her life than she felt to Ian at this moment.

They moved together like they were one. He tasted her mouth, her breasts, her throat, drawing soft cries from her lips. She clung to him, tensing her muscles around him as she felt her release build up inside her.

"Ian!" she gasped.

"Let go," he whispered against the soft line of her jaw. "Just let go."

Bree felt herself giving in. Not just to his request to let go, but to the thoughts that were racing through her own head. She'd resisted. She had good reason to. But in the moment, she didn't want to hold back anymore.

Bree wanted her relationship with Ian to last beyond tonight, beyond her gallery showing this weekend. She wanted to give this a real try, and Ian's actions had encouraged her to think it was a possibility. He really seemed to enjoy the time he spent with her away from work. She'd spied the guitar in his bedroom when she walked in, so perhaps he was getting some pleasure from embracing his music again. He seemed happier. His smile was enough to make her heart ache and her chest tighten.

She could really lose her heart to Ian. Just a little life balance for them both could make all the difference in the success of their second chance.

And she wanted this to be their second chance. Not just a fun fling. It meant too much to her for that. And if she was honest with herself, she had already lost the fight. Bree loved Ian and she had since she was eighteen years old. Seeing him again had brought everything back to the surface and she was tired of fighting her feelings.

As Bree unraveled the protective wrappings around her heart, she felt her body start to unravel also. The swell of emotion and pleasure built up inside of her so quickly, she could barely react before it was upon her.

"Yes, Ian," she whispered, clinging to his shoulders as the spasms of her release rocked through her body. "Love me!" she cried again and again until it was over. A moment later, Ian found his own release, shouting her name into the delicate crystal fixture overhead.

He was too wrapped up to understand her pleas. Love me, she'd begged, but it had nothing to do with his physical touch and everything to do with his heart.

Love me.

Ian woke early the next morning, as usual. Any other morning, he would reach for his phone to check the time, read over his email and then hit the ground running. His routine rarely varied—shower, coffee then out the door by seven and in the office by seven-thirty.

But not today.

Today, when he opened his eyes, he wasn't propelled out of bed by the cold sheets beside him and the peek of sunlight through the windows. All he could see was golden-blond hair. Bree was curled against him, comfortable and warm. Her soft, rhythmic breathing was soothing, tempting him to fall back asleep with her in his arms. And he wanted to. He had zero interest in getting up and starting his day. He wanted to stay right where he was for as long as possible.

Propped up on his elbow, he watched her sleep for a few moments. She had the same serene expression he'd tried to catch with her camera in the mountains. The soft, pouted lips...the rose-tinted cheeks...the dark blond lashes against her peach skin... Ian wanted to memorialize the moment so he could have it with him always.

Of course, there was another way.

Ian's chest constricted when he thought about it. Having Bree here, waking up with him every morning, was exactly what he wanted. That was better than a picture any day. He wanted her right here when he woke up and in his arms when he fell asleep. Knowing she would be at his apartment each evening was a powerful driver for him to go home when the normal workday was at an end. He desperately needed balance in his life, but for years, he'd had no reason to go home.

She might drive him mad at times, but no one else challenged him like Bree did. No one understood him, cared for him and maybe even loved him the way Bree did. She had touched him in a way no other woman had before. They may have spent far longer apart than they'd spent together, but he wanted to change that.

He was overwhelmed with the sudden urge to shake her shoulder and wake her up. When her blue eyes opened and looked up at him, he knew exactly what he wanted to say. It might be crazy, but he wanted to tell her that he loved her and ask her to marry him. It wasn't very romantic. He didn't have a ring or flowers or, hell, pants on, but the words were on the tip of his tongue, begging to leap out of his mouth.

When he'd proposed to Missy, there had been an ache of worry in his gut. He hadn't wanted to do it. Every nerve in his brain was screaming for him not to do it. But now, there was only excitement. He was at peace with his decision. All he had to do was wake her up and say the words.

Bree made a soft cooing sound in his arms and rolled onto her back. A moment later, her eyes fluttered open and slowly came to focus on his face. Her nose wrinkled in sleepy confusion. "Hi," she said. "What's the matter?"

"Nothing is the matter." His heart started racing in his chest as the adrenalin surged through his veins. "I just wanted to ask you a question."

Bree rubbed her fists into her eyes and yawned. "What?"

"Bree, I…" he began, and then, in that moment, he lost his nerve. Ian hadn't changed his mind, but he knew Bree deserved better. Thirty years from now when she told this story to their grandchildren, he didn't want it to be embarrassing. He didn't want Bree to have to leave out the details about how they were naked in bed and she was half-asleep. He needed to do this right. The ring, the flowers, the perfect moment…

Her show.

That would be perfect. She'd worked so hard on it. What better way to wrap up her big night than to propose in the middle of the gallery?

"Ian?" Bree roused him from his plans with a delicate hand to his cheek. "You *what*?"

He smiled, picking up her hand and placing a soft kiss against the palm. "I want pancakes for breakfast."

She chuckled and shook her head. "Pancakes, huh? You made it sound like you were about to propose marriage or something. So serious looking. Well, how about you and I climb into that gigantic shower of yours and, afterward, I will make you pancakes."

"Sounds great," Ian agreed. And it did. If he could start every day like this for the rest of his life, things would be just about perfect.

Ten

He was late. This was not how he needed to start off tonight.

Ian shut down his laptop and slipped his phone into the holster at his hip. He was putting his suit coat on when he caught movement out of the corner of his eye.

Missy.

She was standing in the doorway looking like she'd walked right out of a music video. She had on leather pants, a red-and-black corset top and five-inch heels. Her makeup and platinum-blond hair were camera-ready. It was a little much for a Monday night, but Missy lived by a policy of go big or go home.

Even then, with her fake breasts nearly spilling over the top of her corset and her pouty moist lips, Ian had a hard time imagining he'd ever slept with Missy, much less nearly married her. After spending time with Bree, a more natural beauty, Missy looked overdone. Forced. She was trying too hard.

He wasn't sure why she'd gone to so much trouble. Judging by the strained, angry expression on her face, she wasn't here to win him back. Ian knew this moment was coming, eventually, but why did it have to come right now?

Ian silently cursed and rounded his desk. He did not have time for this. He was already late for Bree's gallery show. He couldn't miss it. Not only was it super-important to her, but he knew it meant more than that. Bree was waiting, just waiting, for the other shoe to drop. For him to blow off something for work. She had been holding her breath since they had gotten back together. He couldn't screw this up.

"Ian," Missy said, strolling leisurely into his office. "Now that you're home, we need to talk."

Ian sat on the edge of his desk, his arms crossed over his chest. "There's nothing to talk about, Missy. I told you on the phone it was over."

Missy laughed, a low sultry sound that was a trademark of her albums. It was extremely unnerving to Ian.

"Ian, do you really think I'm here to win you back?"

He swallowed. "I really don't know why you're here, Missy."

"Well, you can stop worrying your little head about that. I'm not about to get on my knees and beg you to love me. Our relationship was nothing more than a fantasy I concocted to sell records. And it worked."

She was right. Even despite the scandal, her sales numbers had climbed to near historic highs for her at SpinTrax. Ian would never understand the public. He didn't know if her fans just didn't care about the way Missy lived her life or if the train wreck was part of the appeal. A part of him had hoped she'd just check into rehab and fall off the radar for a while, but no such luck. She was soaking up the publicity, both good and bad.

"What's your point, Missy?"

"My point is that I am still a valuable commodity. I'm not going to let you cast me aside, Ian."

He frowned at her. He should've known this was about business. It always was with her. "If you're so valuable, why don't you go to another label? Certainly there's someone else out there willing to put up with your antics for the money. Or—" he hesitated "—are you not worth the aggravation? Will no one else take you on, Missy?"

He could tell that he was right by the way her eyes narrowed angrily at him. She'd probably spent the past week with her manager trying to hunt down a new deal. If she'd been successful, she wouldn't be here right now.

Missy's face tightened, an unattractive red mottling her airbrushed face. Her bloodred fingernails were digging into her palms. He wouldn't be surprised if she scratched him with those claws. He slipped his phone out and set it beside him on the desk. If he needed to dial security quickly, he could.

"You're going to re-sign me, Ian."

At that, he had to laugh. It wasn't the smartest move, considering how close Missy was to the edge, but he couldn't help it. She couldn't make him do anything, and the last thing on Earth he was going to do was sign Missy to his label again.

"If you don't, I'm going to get a lawyer and sue you."

Ian's brow furrowed into a frown. "Sue me for what?"

"Sexual harassment."

Ian almost choked. It wasn't true. Not even remotely, but once a charge like that was thrown out there, it was hard to overcome in the court of popular opinion. "Please tell me, Missy, how I sexually harassed you. As I recall, you're the one who came to me, plying me with alcohol in your seduction plot. You're the one who pretended to be pregnant so we would get married. How is that me harassing you?"

"Well, you see," she said with a sly smile, "I didn't really want anything to do with you. I brought you that dinner as a peace offering. I never expected you to demand sex in exchange for another record contract. I didn't know what to do, so I gave into your insatiable sexual appetite."

"That's a lie."

Missy shrugged. "Only you and I were there. Prove which version of events is fact."

"How will you explain the fake pregnancy scandal?"

"You threatened me." Missy's dark eyes were wide and innocent, putting on a show for his benefit. "Even after I gave myself to you, it wasn't enough. You were still going to drop me from the label. You even said you'd ruin my career so I'd never work anywhere again. So I did what I had to do."

Ian shook his head. "Because marrying the guy who harasses you is always the best plan."

"People make dumb choices under duress. My lawyer will produce specialist after specialist who will get on the stand and tell everyone how I was being terrorized."

"Terrorized?" Ian could hardly believe this. Missy didn't have a stitch of evidence to back up her outrageous story, but with enough lawyers and enough money, it wouldn't matter. Either in court or out, she could destroy him. Destroy SpinTrax.

He took a deep breath to collect himself. He couldn't let himself get emotional. This was business and he was first and foremost a businessman. He wasn't going to let Missy manipulate him. She was threatening him because she expected him to lie down and take it. She figured she would get her way, just like she always did. But that would end here.

"Okay," he said calmly.

"What do you mean 'okay'? You're going to sign me to a new deal?"

He shook his head. "Absolutely not. There's no way in hell you're getting another contract from SpinTrax, Missy. Go ahead. Take me to court. Drag my name through the mud. I don't care. All you'll do is destroy the record label and put a lot of hardworking people out of a job. Either way, you'll end up without a record deal. You think you're a hard sell now? Just wait until the president of every record label sees what you did to me. Their lawyers won't let them touch you with a ten-foot pole. You might take me down, but you'll destroy us both in the process. Is that what you want?"

Missy's lips twisted as she tried to decide what to do. He'd called her bluff. He didn't want to lose his record company. He didn't want all of his employees to lose their jobs. But if it happened, it wouldn't be the end of the world. He'd make sure every one of his employees got placed at another label. They were all talented, dedicated people and it wouldn't be hard to find them another contract. The only person who would be out of work was Ian. And Missy. He was okay with that.

Two weeks ago, he wouldn't have felt the same way, but today, he just didn't care. Being with Bree had taught him that he wanted more from his life than just a successful business. He wanted a musical career of his own, even if he never achieved the level of success he dreamed of. Playing for others made him happy, be it for an audience of two or two thousand. He wanted a family and he wanted Bree to be a part of it. The engagement ring in his coat pocket was evidence of that.

That didn't mean he wanted to lose everything he'd built, but it wouldn't destroy him. He wouldn't let it. He'd done this once, so he could do it again. This time, he would have Bree at his side. The idea of it made him feel invincible. Let Missy just try to ruin him.

As calmly as he could, he looked down at his watch and realized how late he was for Bree's show. By the time he got there, it would nearly be over. He tried to maintain a bored countenance as he looked down. He didn't want Missy to mistake his anxiety over being late for concern about her threat.

"So, I'm glad we talked, Missy. It's been enlightening on several levels." He slid his phone back into the holster, stood and made his way toward the door to usher her out. "Have your lawyer call my lawyer and we'll move forward with this if that's what you want to do. Either way, this discussion is now over. I have somewhere to go and I'm already late."

"Meeting the wedding photographer?"

"Not that it's any of your business, but yes."

Missy flung her blond hair over her shoulder, lifting her defiant chin to look him in the eye. "I can't believe you brought her to that party the other night. You can point fingers all you want, but sleeping with the woman there to take our engagement portraits is pretty low."

"I'm not arguing with you about this, Missy. Our relationship is over. What I chose to do after that is none of your concern."

"From an international pop star to a lowly wedding photographer," she mocked. "Sounds pretty desperate to me."

Ian snorted. Even with half the male population lusting after her, Missy was incredibly insecure. And she should be. She couldn't hold a candle to Bree. "You'd know desperation when you saw it, wouldn't you, Missy?"

Missy's face scrunched up in anger. "You go to hell, Ian!" She spun on her expensive heels and marched out of his office.

"Good riddance," he said, stepping out into the hallway and closing the door behind him. He had to get across town to Bree's show and now.

Bree was a fool. She'd suspected it for a while now, but standing in the middle of the Whitman Gallery with a half-empty glass of champagne and Ian nowhere in sight, she was certain.

She hadn't noticed his absence at first. She'd figured he wouldn't be there on the dot anyway, and she'd been busy when the event had first started. The gallery owner had introduced her to the waiting crowd and she had spoken for a few moments about her collection and its inspiration. Then she'd made her way through the room, meeting people and chatting about her work. Before she knew it, nearly two hours had passed and there was no sign of him.

She pulled her flip phone out of the pocket of her dress, but it was just as she expected. No calls. No texts. No surprises. The show was almost over and he had stood her up once again.

Bree slammed the phone shut and shoved it back in her pocket. She was trying not to let this ruin her night. She had worked long and hard to get to this point. A lot of important and influential people in the industry were here tonight to see her work. Big things could be on the horizon for her if she played her cards right. That meant she had to focus, smile and schmooze with the people strolling through the gallery. And she had. But as the night went on, it was getting harder to keep a smile on her face.

It helped that so many of her friends had come to support her. All her coworkers and even some of the couples who had appreciated the work she'd done for their weddings were in attendance. Both her parents had come, which was a miracle on its own. She'd figured her mother would show, but her dad's arrival had caught her off guard. He'd torn himself away from his construction business for Bree's big night. He knew how important it was to her. How could Ian not see that?

"Oh, Bree, this one is wonderful."

Bree pulled herself out of her funk to see Amelia beside her. Her eyes were focused on the large black-and-white photo in front of them. No wonder her thoughts had gotten so dark. She didn't realize she'd stopped in front of that particular portrait until that moment.

It was the photo she'd taken of Ian in the mountains. She hadn't planned on adding additional pieces to her collection this late, but once she saw the shot of him playing his guitar, she knew she had to include it. It might very well be one of her best pieces in the gallery tonight. She'd been proud of that shot. Now she was looking at having her most well-received piece being a photo of her ex. Of course.

"I've never seen this photo before," Amelia said. "I thought I'd seen all your work."

"It's a new one." Her tone was noncommittal, trying to keep Amelia from pushing the subject. In addition to this portrait, she'd also printed out the picture Ian had taken of her in bed that morning in Gatlinburg.

It was a beautiful shot with the morning sun giving a golden aura to her shape. Because she hadn't taken it, it couldn't be in her collection, but she was going to hang it in her apartment somewhere. He'd been right. There weren't enough photos of her.

"I really love it. Is that Ian playing the guitar? *The* Ian?"

Bree took a deep breath. "Yes, that's him. Soak it in. It might be all you ever see of him."

Amelia turned to look at her with a frown. "Why? What's going on? I thought he was supposed to be here tonight. I was looking forward to meeting him."

"I was looking forward to introducing you to him." Bree could feel unwanted tears start to form beneath her eyelids. She wasn't going to cry at her showing. She wouldn't. She could hold it together until she got home and could mope privately.

Amelia wrapped a comforting arm around her shoulder. The caterer and pastry chef of From This Moment was big on the power of love. She was a true believer, unlike Natalie, who thought the whole concept was bunk. Bree fell in the middle of the spectrum. She believed in love; she just didn't think that love alone could solve all her problems.

Bree hadn't mentioned how she felt about Ian to her, or anyone for that matter. If she had, Amelia would be telling Bree she had no doubt that Ian would charge in on his white steed and sweep her off her feet.

"He'll be here," Amelia reassured her. "I'm sure he got caught up in something, but he still has time."

He had fifteen minutes. Even if he showed up, it wouldn't matter. He would have missed the whole thing.

"I'll be fine, Amelia. Don't worry about me. Enjoy yourself. Drink more wine before the bar closes. I've got to go wrap up a few things with the gallery management before we're done."

Amelia departed reluctantly. The look on her face made it obvious that she knew Bree was just making excuses to be alone. The crowds were starting to dwindle and it was a cue for everyone to go home. Bree thanked the last folks as they made their way out, then sat down on the bench in the center of the room.

This part of the gallery was a white-walled rectangle with track lighting to illuminate the art. Bree was facing four pictures, each showcasing a part of Nashville that she loved. She had never been more proud of her work than she was tonight. Yet her heart was heavy. She'd wanted to believe that Ian meant what he'd said when he told her he'd be here come hell or high water. Just like she'd wanted to believe him back in school. But the results were just the same. She was alone. Forgotten. Discarded.

"Bree!"

She looked up to see Ian burst into the room. He looked panicked. Frantic. And he should. There were only five other guests in the gallery. Catering was breaking down. The party was over. And here he was. She supposed she should be pleased that he arrived at all, but at the moment, she just couldn't make herself appreciate that fact.

Bree stood slowly. She turned toward him as he approached her, but she didn't go to him the way he expected her to. She knew that by the way he stopped short of pulling her into his arms.

He stood awkwardly a few feet away, a bundle of white daisies in his hands. They were her favorite flower, but she didn't know if he remembered that or if it was just a good guess. Either way, a couple of flowers couldn't make up for what he'd missed.

"These are for you," he said, holding out the bouquet.

"Thanks." Bree accepted them, but it didn't do much to soften the hard, armored exterior she'd built up waiting for him to arrive.

"I'm so sorry I'm late. I can explain," he began, but Bree didn't want to hear it.

"You don't have to explain, Ian. I was expecting this," she said with a sad shake of her head. "I didn't want to be right. I hoped I was mistaken, but I knew how this night would end."

He looked mildly stunned by her cold response. Apparently he thought flowers and a good excuse would get him off the hook. "How does it end?"

"It ends with you going your way and me going mine. Just the way it should have when we left the mountains. You and I both know we were putting off the inevitable by trying to make things work between us."

"No," Ian argued, reaching out to touch her shoulder, but she pulled away. "Bree, listen to me. I was on my way here when Missy barged into my office and threatened to sue me. I dealt with her as quickly as I could and rushed over here. I didn't want to miss this. Tonight was supposed to be special. I wouldn't have deliberately ruined it."

Bree shrugged. It sounded like a pretty fantastic story, but the truth was it didn't matter why he'd missed the show. A pileup on the expressway. An emergency with one of his artists. A flat tire in the rain. There was always something and there always would be. That was just the kind of man he was.

"I'm sorry to hear you're having more trouble with Missy," she said. "But I'm not interested in excuses, Ian.

My father was always full of excuses and apologies. He never blew off school programs or special events on purpose. He wanted to come, but time and time again, his work interfered and he'd promise to make it up to me next time. I don't blame you for being late. At the same time, I don't have to tolerate it, either."

Bree watched a parade of emotions move across Ian's face. Each of them lasted only a second, every one different from the next, leaving her unsure of what he was thinking or feeling. At least until he spoke.

"*Tolerate* it? You don't have to tolerate it?" Ian repeated her words with incredulity. He took a deep breath and ran his fingers through his hair. "You know, that's funny you should say that considering what I've tolerated with you over the past week and a half."

Bree was taken aback by the unexpected assault of words. What had she forced him to tolerate? Her cooking? An unwanted photo session? "With me? Like what?"

"Like your constant needling to change me. You act like you want to be with me, Bree, but you really don't. You want to be with that coffee-shop musician from nine years ago. You practically shoved that guitar into my hands, nagging me until I had no choice but to play or listen to you go on about it. You didn't give a damn how I felt about the whole thing. I had good reasons for not playing that guitar, but you didn't care. When you looked at me, all you saw was this fantasy musician you lost and were desperate to get back. Never mind what I wanted. Never mind what was healthy for me. You wanted what you wanted and you were determined to get your way."

"How dare you! You're acting like I forced you into a life of crime instead of convincing you to face the fact that you're unhappy with your life. You miss your music, but you just won't admit it to yourself because you're afraid to play and fail again. Don't pin your insecurities on me just because I've been successful. I told you the other night that I didn't love you just because of your music. I love you for you and I just wanted you to be happy again. I'm sorry if that makes me into some kind of harpy."

Ian flinched at her words, his gaze narrowing at her. "Yeah, Bree," he said at last with a mocking bitterness underlying his words. "I'm sure you're only interested in my mental health and well-being."

Bree could feel her entire face flush in anger. Her heart pumped furiously in her chest, making the sound of her blood racing in her ears almost deafening. She glanced around the room and noticed that everyone was gone now. She didn't know if they'd left on their own or the scene she was causing with Ian had made them uncomfortable and driven them away. She supposed it didn't matter at this point. It was better not to have an audience for this, anyway.

"You know, my father made it tonight," she said. "The King of Emergencies. The Duke of Last-Minute Meetings. He was here for once in his life. On time. He sat through the entire introduction of me and my work, staying around to look at every picture. When he left tonight, he told me he was so glad he could be here and how proud he was of me."

Ian didn't respond to that. He just stood there, watching her with a tightly clenched jaw.

"And sitting here, alone, I realized how pathetic it was that I was so pleased he came. Somehow it negated the twenty-eight years he missed. And it shouldn't have, but I wanted his approval so badly. I wanted him here for my big showing. That's all I wanted from you."

Ian swallowed hard, considering her words. "I'm sorry I couldn't be here for you tonight. I'm here now. I brought you flowers. I was prepared to…" His voice trailed off and he shook his head. "It doesn't matter. Apparently that's just not good enough. You know, all I ever wanted from you was to be accepted the way I am. Most people would be pleased with a wealthy, successful businessman, but not you. No matter what I do, I'm never good enough. I got enough of that from my father and my college advisors. I certainly don't need it from you."

Bree felt a momentary hitch in her chest. "You are good enough, Ian. You're more than good enough. You are an exceptional person. The only person who doesn't believe it is you, but how can I convince you of that when all you hear are criticisms?"

"So you're saying it's my own fault I feel like a loser? Thanks, Bree. That really helps."

"No! I would never—"

Ian held up his hand to interrupt her. "No. It's okay. You're allowed to feel however you want to feel. But know that we're adults now. We're not kids anymore. And adults have responsibilities. *I* have responsibilities. I would've loved to have been here with you tonight, but it just didn't happen. I had to do what I could to protect my employees, my artists and their families. Instead of standing here looking at some amazing pictures, I was being threatened by a woman who wants to take away everything I've worked years to build. I'm sorry if you don't agree with my priorities, but I had to make a decision and that's what I chose."

For a moment, Bree wanted to stop the fight and

find out what happened with Missy. This had obviously been more than her usual diva hissy fit. But she didn't get the chance.

Ian gestured toward his throat. "I've had it up to here with criticism today. We're obviously fighting an uphill battle. I don't have the time or the energy to waste on this…because I'm so busy," he said, bitterly mocking her criticisms. "You can't accept me the way I am, so I guess you're right about us going our separate ways tonight. There's no point in this relationship going any further."

Bree felt a sharp pain in her chest, as though he'd finally driven the dagger into her heart. It knocked the wind out of her, took away whatever fight she had left. Despite what she said, she didn't want to lose him, even if it was for the best. She was broken. "Fine," she said quietly, her lips nearly trembling with the tears she was struggling to hold back.

Ian nodded, his expression solemn, his green eyes moving over her face without really seeing anything. "Congratulations on your showing tonight. I'm sure it was well received. Good luck with your future endeavors."

At that, Ian turned and walked out.

Bree watched him go, then slumped back down onto the bench. This night was good and truly ruined.

Eleven

"Are you just going to sit around the house all day?"

Ian looked up from his long-standing perch on the couch to see his housekeeper, Winnie, glaring at him through the doorway. She had a vacuum at her side and a look of disgust on her face. That wasn't good. He was obviously cramping her style.

"Maybe," he said, being honest. He didn't have plans to get off this couch anytime soon. He was just going to sit here until he figured out what do to. So far, no luck. Perhaps he should have taken off more than two days from work. "Why?"

The older woman walked into the room and crossed her arms over her chest. "Well, I have things to do and for once you're actually underfoot. You don't pay me to just sit around and watch you mope."

Ian's brow went up at Winnie's sharp tone. "I'm not stopping you from working. Just vacuum around me.

Or clean the other four-thousand square feet I'm not occupying. And I'm *not* moping," he added.

"Sure you're not. You're home in your pajamas instead of at work in a suit. You're strumming your guitar and playing moody songs instead of guiding the careers of your artists. Not to mention that I found *fifteen* candy bar wrappers in the trash can this morning. Tell me you're not moping."

Ian looked at Winnie and frowned. Had he really eaten that many? So maybe he *was* moping. So what? "I've had a rough couple of weeks. Am I not allowed to take a little time to deal with all of it?"

Winnie came over to the couch and sat beside him. "Of course you are, Ian. I can't imagine what you've been through with Missy and then, so soon after, with Bree. I'm just worried because I've never seen you like this. Not in the five years I've worked for you. Not even after you found out Missy was pregnant—and don't bother trying to tell me you were happy about that because I know you weren't.

"You've been as precise as Swiss clockwork for the past five years and it wasn't until now that you've gotten me worried." Winnie gestured toward the guitar. "I didn't even know you played the guitar, Ian. I've been cleaning this place all these years and have never run across one. Or sheet music. Or a picture or anything that would make me think you even played an instrument. Where did this one come from?"

"From the mountain house. I brought it home with me. This is the guitar I bought myself when I was thirteen."

"Why haven't you ever played music around here before?"

"I gave it up when I dropped out of school and started working for the record company."

"Why?"

Ian sighed. He'd just been through all this with Bree. He didn't really want to rehash it, especially because now he realized it had been the wrong choice and justifying his actions was more difficult. "Because I wasn't any good."

"That's funny," Winnie noted. "You've sounded pretty good to me."

"Thanks, Winnie." Ian wasn't fishing for a compliment, but he appreciated it, anyway. It made him feel good to have someone other than Bree tell him that, even though Winnie's praise felt more like that of a mother.

"So what's changed that you're playing again all of a sudden? Wait," she said, "let me guess. It's about Bree."

He nodded. "She encouraged me to start up again. I used to play when we were dating in college."

"Well, she was right," Winnie said. "You're good. You should play more often."

Ian sighed. "I just don't have the time, Winnie. You know I'm always working. I'm either at the studio or working here in my office."

"What about when you were snowed in all that time? Did the world unravel?"

"No," he admitted.

"Did your well-trained employees handle everything while you were away?"

"Yes." Keith had gone above and beyond, as had several others at the studio. He'd already put in some paperwork with payroll to give them bonuses. They deserved it.

"So why do you have to do everything?"

That made Ian frown. It was his company. Why wouldn't he? "What do you mean?"

"You have worked yourself to the bone for years building this label. You've achieved success. Things are going well. You don't have to work as hard anymore. You've just admitted that you have competent staff. Why not take a step back? Let them take on greater responsibility?"

"I'm not just going to sit back—"

"I'm not suggesting you stop going in to the office," Winnie interrupted. "I'm suggesting that you don't have to be responsible for everything. You always put work first because you think that's the only way to be successful. But you're allowed to have a life outside of the office. If that life includes music or a family, great. And even if you just spend all your free time in the bathtub playing with rubber duckies, it's up to you. But don't waste any more time telling yourself you can't do it."

She was right. He paid her to help run his life, to almost fill the role of a wife, and she did it well. She was an incredible cook, she was well organized and she was an excellent sounding board. He didn't know how many times he'd solved a problem by talking it over with Winnie while she cooked or ironed clothes. He needed to give Winnie a raise, too. He'd get his accountant on that immediately.

Winnie patted him on knee. "I've seen you work miracles with your business over the years, Ian. You can do anything you want. Why can't you do this?"

At that, Winnie leaned in to give him a peck on the cheek, then stood. "Okay, enough with the pep talk. This very special episode of *Blossom* is over. Now, get out of the living room so I can clean."

"Thanks, Winnie," he said with a chuckle. Ian got off

the couch and grabbed the neck of his guitar. He carried it with him into his office. Once inside, he stopped, not quite sure why he'd come in here. He didn't want to open his laptop and get sucked into work. He'd taken today off deliberately. So, then what?

He walked over to his leather executive chair and settled into it. With the guitar across his lap, he strummed it gently and tried to think about what he wanted to do next. He liked his office. For whatever reason, it had good energy and he was able to come up with great ideas when he worked from this space. Perhaps it would shake out some plans today, too.

What he knew was that he had made a mistake with Bree. A critical one. That was what had trapped him on the couch in a state of suspended activity while he tried to figure out what to do about it. He'd relived it in his mind. How he could've changed it. What he could've said to make Bree smile instead of going for the jugular when he was pushed.

The drama with Missy couldn't have been foreseen, but it just as easily could've been one of a dozen different emergencies that cropped up from time to time. The truth was that he could've handled it better.

Now he found himself in a quandary. If it was anyone but Bree, he would bury himself in his work and forget about her. But doing that would just prove her right. And it would leave him alone with nothing to show for his time with her but an old guitar, a broken heart and a diamond engagement ring.

It seemed crazy to have bought her a ring so quickly, but it didn't feel quick with Bree. It felt as though they'd been together forever.

Ian opened his nearest desk drawer and reached inside. He pulled out the small velvet box and opened it to look at the ring. The three-carat oval diamond was encircled with a halo of micro-pavé diamonds and set in a platinum band inset with more micro-pavé diamonds. He'd known it was perfect for Bree the moment he saw it. It was elegant yet playful, a ring that would go just as well with a gown as a pair of jeans and sneakers.

It belonged to her, even though he hadn't given it to her yet. He wanted Bree to have it. And he wanted her to know how much he truly loved her. The problem was that Bree would never feel like she was important. He had to show her how much he cared. How sorry he was about their fight and missing her show. Flashing a diamond wouldn't be enough. She'd look at that as the same kind of bribes her father had always offered.

But words wouldn't do, either. Bree had spent her whole life hearing platitudes and excuses from her father and from Ian back when they dated in school. He could promise her the sun, moon and stars, but it wouldn't mean a damn to her until he handed her a planetary body. Especially after the blowup Sunday night. He'd proved to her that his promises meant nothing, even when he had the best of intentions.

Bree would only believe his actions. So action he would take.

Briana Harper has done what few artists in Nashville have been able to do—capture the heart and soul of a town and its people.

Gretchen held the newspaper in her hand and read Bree's long-awaited review aloud at the Monday-morning business meeting.

Armed with a camera, she was able to see beyond

the rhinestone-studded facade to the indomitable spirit that has long characterized the people and the ideals of Nashville. I predict this is just the beginning of a long and successful career for Ms. Harper.

It had been a week since the showing. The review had been published in the Sunday paper, but Bree hadn't been able to read it. She'd brought it into the office for someone else to read it first. As it turned out, she had chewed her fingernails to the quick for no reason. The show had been very well received. Apparently the art critic had left before Ian showed up and their shouting match outshined the photography.

Bree's three business partners applauded, making her cheeks flush with embarrassment.

"An excellent show, my dear," Amelia said. "We should have champagne instead of Starbucks this morning."

"Champagne at nine in the morning?" Natalie asked, looking mildly scandalized in her sensible black cashmere sweater.

Amelia just shrugged. She wasn't as bothered by breaking social norms. "Why not? We have a massive stock of wines in the other room."

"A celebratory latte is just fine. Thank you for picking them up, Natalie."

"Of course," Natalie said with a polite smile. "It's Monday."

Routines were routines. As such, Bree set aside the newspaper and fired up her tablet. It was time to discuss the Williams wedding and talk about upcoming events. The Williams event had been large and for that, Bree was thankful. She'd been a wreck the first few days after her show and her fight with Ian. The wedding had forced her to pull herself together and focus on the intricacies of her work.

She'd like to return to that focus now. Talking about the show would just make her think of how it had ended. She accepted the folded newspaper from Gretchen and laid it on top of her notebook.

"You don't seem very happy with your review, Bree." Amelia was frowning at her.

Bree glanced down at the glowing review and pasted a smile on her face. "Of course I'm happy. I'm thrilled. I couldn't have asked for a better write-up. The Whitman Gallery has already called and asked to keep the collection on display for another week. This could lead to another, possibly bigger, show. And this review should bring in more business for From This Moment, too. It's great promotion."

"We don't need more business," Gretchen noted. "We're booked solid for the next year and a half. We really should've scheduled ourselves a vacation or two in there."

"We get the week between Christmas and New Year's Eve off," Natalie pointed out.

Gretchen nodded. "I'll try to remember that the other fifty-one weeks a year."

"We can take vacations," Natalie argued. "We just have to stagger them. Amelia is going to her high school reunion soon. You could take time off if you wanted to. We just can't all go at once."

Gretchen and Natalie started bickering about the intricacies of their corporate leave policy. Bree tuned out, opening up a digital sticky note and making a list of things she needed to do today. By the time she was done, they'd stopped arguing and the attention shifted to business at last.

They finished up the details about an hour later and Bree was the first to dismiss herself. She needed to get the pictures from the weekend downloaded and start going through them. At the reception alone, she often took five hundred photos, not to mention everything else the day of the ceremony and the rehearsal and dinner the night before.

She was about halfway through the photographs when she heard a gentle knock at her door.

"Come in."

She turned in time to see Amelia with the mail. Bree expected her to just leave anything on her desk, but instead, she shut the door and sat down in her guest chair.

Bree groaned inwardly and spun in her chair to face her. "What do you need? When I get done with these pictures I can help with some sugar flowers if that's it."

Amelia shook her head. "I'm not here because of sugar flowers, Bree, and you know it."

She had avoided any kind of serious discussions with her friends and coworkers since the show. They knew that Ian had finally shown up and they'd broken up, but that was it. She'd been hoping she would make it to her Tuesday-Wednesday weekend without talking about it, but that wasn't going to happen. "So what, then?"

Amelia focused her dark eyes on Bree and started twirling her auburn hair around her index finger. "I don't know the details of what happened last week, but don't think I haven't noticed you avoiding me."

"I haven't been avoiding you," Bree said, but they both knew she was lying. "I've been avoiding…talking about *it*. Not you."

"Well, let's cut to the chase, then. Why didn't you tell me you're in love with Ian?"

"What?" Bree shot up in her chair, nearly spilling the half-consumed latte in her hand.

Amelia put the mail in her lap and crossed her arms over her chest. "Don't play dumb with me. You've had that lovesick look in your eye since you got home from the mountains. And after your show—the tremor from your heart breaking probably registered on the Richter scale."

Bree winced at her words. She thought she'd hidden her pain pretty well and kept up an appropriate level of professionalism at the office, but apparently not. "Is it that obvious?"

"Not necessarily. I just know you well enough to see the turmoil you're trying to hide."

"I'll be fine. Just give me a few days. By the Campbell rehearsal on Friday, I should be right as rain."

"You're not going to get over a broken heart in three days. You're in love. Even if you're hurt, it's going to take time. Tell me what happened."

Bree didn't want to recount the scene, but she did it. It had played over and over in her mind during the past week, so it was easy to retell. "When it's all said and done, I trusted him and gave him my heart and I shouldn't have. I was a fool because he did exactly what I knew he would. It's my own fault. I marched myself up the steps to the gallows and put the noose around my neck. I can't get mad at the hangman for doing his job."

Amelia nodded sadly. She sat quietly for a moment. "So where does that leave you two?"

"We're finished. Over. There's obviously no room for anything in his life but his work, and that must be the way he likes it despite his protests and promises.

If that's his choice, then that's just the way it is. I'm not going to waste energy fighting to be a priority in his life."

"But you still love him," Amelia stated.

Her words made tears threaten in Bree's eyes. She took a deep, cleansing breath, looking up at the ceiling and blinking frantically to keep them from spilling down her cheeks.

"I don't know that I ever stopped. And that's what scares me the most. If I was in love with him for nine years while we were apart, how long will I be in love with him going forward? I can't afford to lose another nine years pining for him. I want to be able to find a healthy romance with someone who thinks I'm important. I want to have a family. I don't want to wake up and be forty with nothing to show for my life but pictures of other people's relationships."

There was a sadness in Amelia's eyes as Bree spoke, convincing her that her friend understood how she felt. For a bridal company, they were four women completely miserable at relationships. Bree had apparently been in love with Ian all these years, so her attempts at dating were failures. Amelia was always searching for the big sweeping romance that might not even exist. Gretchen was more comfortable with her art than with men. And Natalie…she didn't even believe in love. They were a sad group.

"Well, I'm sorry everything went down that way. I promise we won't end up forty and alone. What do you say you and I go out on Wednesday night? We might even be able to talk Gretchen into coming. It might cheer you up to get your mind off things."

Bree's eyes widened. Natalie, Gretchen and Amelia had been her friends long before they were business partners, but over the years, the work had taken over their free time. They hadn't gone out for anything more than a working lunch or vendor meeting for a very long time. To go out for drinks in the evening, just for fun, was almost unheard of anymore. Amelia must really be worried about her.

She sighed. Maybe Amelia was right to be worried. "Okay. That sounds fun," she agreed, although her tone was flat and unconvinced. She would make sure it was fun, whether it took too much wine or the dreaded tequila to loosen her up.

"Great," Amelia said with a bright smile. "I'll let you get back to work. Here's your mail." She dropped a couple items onto her desk and slipped back into the hallway.

After all that, Bree wasn't quite ready to return to shot after shot of someone else's happy, romantic day. Instead, she picked up her mail and sorted through it. There was a thank-you note from a recently married couple who adored their wedding photos, a catalog for a photography supply website where she liked to shop and some junk mail.

The last piece of junk mail caught her eye before she tossed it into the trash. It was a postcard for a bar downtown. She'd never even been to that bar before, so she couldn't imagine how she'd gotten on their mailing list.

Frowning, she flipped over the card. It was advertising a special event on Wednesday. For a moment, her eyes flicked over the words without processing them. Then her heart leaped in her chest and she read it again.

Dollar-beer Wednesdays. No cover charge. Musical entertainment from seven to nine by singer/songwriter Ian Lawson.

That was interesting. She stared at the card for several moments, waiting for her vision to clear and the words to change. When they didn't, she had to come to terms with what it meant. Ian had found a way to make room in his life for his music. It seemed it was easier than making room in his life for her.

With a sigh, she held the postcard out over the trash can and dropped it in with the rest of the junk mail.

Good for him.

Twelve

"**S**he's not coming."

"Relax," Keith assured him and handed him his guitar. "The set doesn't start for ten more minutes. She's coming, even if just out of morbid curiosity."

Ian's talent manager at SpinTrax had stepped in to help Ian kick off his new musical career. At the moment, he was serving as his manager, agent, roadie and moral supporter, and all out of the goodness of his heart. Tonight they were playing for fifty bucks and free beer.

So maybe not entirely out of the goodness of his heart. Keith really liked beer.

"No. She's not going to come," Ian insisted, voicing his fears. "She's too angry with me."

He hadn't gone out on a limb and booked this show *for* her. He'd done it for himself, but if she wasn't here to witness it, it wouldn't feel as important. She was the reason he was here. She planted the seed in his mind, pushed him to think outside of the box he'd forced himself into. She was right, of course. He needed to do this. He couldn't suppress the music inside of him any longer.

His future was full of possibilities tonight. There wasn't a fork in the road; there was a starburst. This show might lead to other bookings or it might be his last performance. He might end up only playing for personal enjoyment. He might land his own record deal. Maybe he'd try focusing on songwriting and see if he could sell his songs for other people to sing. It didn't matter. The point was that he was trying. He was putting himself out there, making time in his life for something other than work.

He thought for certain that no matter how she felt about their relationship, she would come to support his music. Or at the very least, come just to rub it in that she was right. Or outright heckle him from the crowd.

And there was a crowd. More than he'd expected to see. It was a good thing he'd done nothing but practice all week. A few tables were scattered throughout with some people at the bar and others standing near the back. Even with all those people, he knew Bree wasn't here. He'd know the moment she arrived. He could feel it when she was near to him. And right now, all he could feel was sick to his stomach.

"Maybe she'll do what you did and show up three minutes before it's over. It would serve you right," Keith noted.

Ian narrowed his gaze at him. "Whose side are you on?"

Keith smiled. "Yours. I'm trying to distract you from your nerves."

Ian opened his mouth to argue that he wasn't nervous, but that wasn't true. He hadn't performed for more than one person at a time for almost a decade. To go from that to a bar packed with one hundred drunk critics was a little unnerving. More than a little. He was a mess.

Doubts pounded at him from all directions. What was he doing here? He was a record executive. He had no business playing at a bar. He had no business playing *anywhere*. This was going to be a disaster, but he still had a chance to avert it. Would anyone notice if he slipped out the back?

"Maybe this was a mistake."

"The only mistake would be you walking out and pissing off a bunch of people who came for some good music." Keith leaned in and patted him on the shoulder. "You're good. I wouldn't tell you that if it wasn't true."

Ian knew that. He'd personally witnessed Keith destroy the dreams of countless wannabe musicians. If you weren't good enough, he would tell you. That was why he'd gone straight to Keith when he decided to give his music another shot. If he was delusional and Bree was just coddling him, Keith would say as much. Instead, his talent manager had crossed his arms over his chest and narrowed his eyes and when the song was done—he'd smiled. It had been damn stressful, but Keith had liked it.

And now, here Ian was. The small platform in the corner of the bar had a stool, a microphone and an amplifier to plug into his new electric acoustic guitar. They'd done a sound check before most people came into the bar and everything was ready to go.

"It's time. Knock 'em dead," Keith said.

Ian nodded and went up onto the platform. Adjusting his guitar, he scanned the crowd again but still no Bree. He tried not to let that get him down. There were a hundred other people in the bar who expected a good show, whether his ex-girlfriend showed up or not.

Leaning into the microphone, Ian introduced himself and thanked everyone for coming. There were a few rowdy "whoops" from the crowd, but they settled down as soon as he started to play. He opened with his acoustic version of "Layla" to get the crowd warmed up.

Five songs into the set, he looked up and saw a group of women pushing their way over to an empty table near the back. He finished his song and watched them settle in as the crowd applauded. There was a shorter girl with curly dark hair, a fiery redhead, a brunette with a sleek ponytail and a blonde whose face he couldn't see.

It was Bree. In that moment, she turned to look at him, her eyes widening with surprise. Her gaze flicked from him to the redhead. She smacked her friend on the shoulder, her lips moving rapidly with angry words. She tried standing up again, but a woman on each side grabbed her arms and tugged her back into the chair.

Apparently she had not planned to come see him tonight. The redhead had lured her here. He'd have to buy Bree's friend a drink later.

Taking a deep breath, Ian decided to play "I'll Love You Forever" for his next song. It was a risk. If she truly didn't want to sit through his show, this song would push her out the door. If she stayed, she might be receptive to the other tune he had in store for later tonight.

He started in on the song he'd written for her all those years ago. His gaze flicked over her, noting a stiffness in her posture, but she hadn't left. She was listening intently, a drink in her hand. He sang as sincerely as he could, and by the end of the song, she had relaxed with a small smile curling her lips.

The applause for that song was bigger than any other

one so far. Given it was an original they'd never heard before, he felt a boost of confidence surge through him.

"That song," Ian said into the microphone, "was written for my college sweetheart. I promised her that I would love her forever. As many of us know, life can get in the way of our plans. We didn't stay together, but I kept my promise. I have never, ever stopped loving her. Even years later, no other woman has touched my heart the way she does."

Bree's wary blue gaze was focused on him the entire time he spoke. Her expression was painfully neutral, not allowing him insight into what she was thinking or feeling about his words. All he could do was charge forward.

"That lovely lady," Ian continued, "is here tonight. I won't embarrass her by pointing her out, but I wanted everyone to know because this next song is about her, too. It's a new song, one I wrote over the past few weeks that we've been apart. You see, I was an idiot, as the male of the species tends to be, and I screwed up my second chance with her."

In response to his confession there was a rumble in the crowd, punctuated by a woman's loud shout of "Men suck!" from the bar.

Ian laughed, thankful it wasn't Bree who'd shouted it. "Sometimes we do. I won't argue that. Being miserable and alone inspired me to write this song." His gaze traveled back to Bree. "I wrote it in the hopes that she would hear it, realize how much I love her and give me another chance."

Bree's pink lips parted slightly as though she were sucking in a gasp of air. He wasn't quite sure what to think of it. She hadn't rushed into his arms, but she hadn't left. She seemed receptive, even though he'd hurt her. That's all he could ask for.

"If she doesn't, you can come home with me!" another woman shouted from a table on the right.

Ian smiled at her and started strumming his guitar. "Well, thank you, sweetheart. It's always good to have a backup plan," he replied to a chorus of laughter from the crowd. "The song I wrote for her is called 'Love Me Anyway.'"

This was the moment that counted. How Bree received this song would determine how the rest of the night would play out. There were several possible outcomes, the best being walking out of here with Bree forgiving him and agreeing to marry him. The worst, with Bree leaving with her girlfriends and Ian getting drunk and going home with the mouthy brunette.

The song was fast-paced and humorous. It wasn't like any song he'd written before. The lyrics were nothing more than a laundry list of his flaws set to a catchy melody. He was certain Bree was aware of each of them, even if she had been too polite to point them out. He knew he worked too much. He needed help prioritizing his life. He needed to have more fun and less stress. He ate too much junk food. He snored louder than a rabid badger during allergy season. He had weirdly shaped toes. Nobody was perfect. But he loved her more than anything else in the world. The chorus announced that he was a work in progress and then asked her to love him despite all that.

That part earned him a round of applause from the crowd and a smile from Bree. The second verse was more of a risk. It was a list of *her* flaws. She was an emotional live wire. She hogged the covers. She owned a cell phone that had previously belonged to Fred Flintstone. She cheated at Scrabble. She always thought she was right. She was pushy and could nag a man into his grave. Last, she had the ability to see right through him, making him absolutely insane.

But he loved her, anyway.

They were *both* works in progress and he wanted to spend the rest of his life with her no matter how long their lists of flaws became. If they improved over the years and ended up polished like diamonds when they were older, great. But if they just got fat together and bickered over the little things twenty-four hours a day, that was great, too. He just wanted to be with her, just as she was, and he hoped she felt the same way.

Every word was true. As he finished playing the last few chords of the song, he looked up to find Bree smiling through her tears. Bingo.

The crowd stood to applaud the song, blocking his view of her. Shouts of "forgive him" could be heard over the roar. Ian didn't wait for the applause to stop before he left the stage. He unplugged his guitar and stepped down into the sea of people and tables.

His chest was tight with excitement and his brain swirled with scenarios as he finally reached her table. Suddenly, he realized something wasn't right. He was in the right place, but there was no tearful, smiling blonde waiting for him with open arms.

Bree was gone.

Bree had to get out of there. She couldn't breathe. The rush of emotions and the swell of the applause had combined to press against her chest like an anvil. She'd bolted before the other girls could stop her, hitting an emergency exit door and dashing into the alley behind the bar.

The air was cold and stung as it rushed in and out of her lungs, but she didn't care. It was better than being in there. Listening to him tell her how much he loved her and asking if she would do the same. She didn't know what to say. She did love him, despite his weird toes and his workaholic tendencies. She wished she didn't, but she did.

She sagged back against the brick facade of the building, her burgundy leather jacket protecting her from the rough surface. All the energy she had was sucked out by the emotional upheaval, leaving her legs feeling like quivering gelatin as the building held her up. She needed to pull herself together. One of the girls would follow her out here eventually. Standing in an alley sobbing was not healthy.

Bree wiped away her tears and dropped her face into her hands. How had this happened? This was supposed to be a night on the town with her friends to *forget* about Ian. Instead, Amelia had tricked her into coming here, saying she wanted to try this new place she'd seen but with a name she couldn't remember. Bree didn't even realize they were at the same place on the same night until she heard him playing on the small stage. The snoop had read her mail.

Betrayal. She was calling Amelia "Brutus" from now on. A wicked, redheaded meddler! Bree had tried to leave the moment she'd figured out what was going on, hopefully before Ian saw her, but it was no use. Amelia and Gretchen had grabbed her and tugged her into the chair. Gretchen had driven so Bree would have had to call a cab to leave. She'd also have to listen to them complain about her being a coward every day for the next year or so if she'd left.

So she'd stayed. And look what came of it! He'd

bared his heart and soul to a room full of strangers. He'd made her laugh, made her cry and made her question everything. Just when she'd finally seemed to pull herself out of the doldrums.

The emergency exit door opened. Bree expected Natalie or Amelia to step out, but instead, it was Ian.

He was looking amazingly handsome yet casual for his musical debut. His expensive suits were nice, but her heart fluttered at the sight of him in a tight pair of jeans. Tonight, he'd paired dark denim with a black T-shirt that fit every muscle of his ripped upper body like liquid latex had been poured over him.

That thought made her mouth go dry in an instant. She'd already sucked down two drinks since she'd arrived for the same reason. Now, more than ever, she needed to be able to talk, but her tongue was like a dry wad of cotton balls in her mouth.

"Your friends told me you ran out this way." He watched her with curious eyes. "I guess you didn't like the new song."

Bree couldn't speak, but she shook her head. "It… was great," she managed. And it was. The content was poignant. The melody was memorable. The accompaniment was inspired. It was a great song, even if it announced to the world that she was a cover hog and a know-it-all. She supposed that was better than telling everyone she was a world-class belcher.

Ian took a few steps closer, a wary expression lining his face. He looked concerned that she might bolt at any moment. He needn't worry about that. Even if her legs would work, she had no idea where she was and her ancient cell phone couldn't look up a cab company in its Yellow Pages app. She was at Gretchen's mercy.

"But it didn't change anything." His soft words were

defeated. She hated that. Ian was a powerful business-man, master of his universe, yet she felt like she could crush him with the slightest inclination. His words weren't a question. He just assumed that she couldn't forgive him.

"No, it didn't."

Ian's gaze fell to the alley pavement, his shoulders slumping slightly in defeat.

"I still love you just as much as I did before I heard it."

Ian's head shot up, a lock of dark hair falling into his eyes. "What? You love me?"

Bree nodded.

His hands dropped to his sides in aggravation. "Then why the hell did you run? You're giving me heart pal-pitations."

She shook her head. "I don't know. It was all too much at once. I needed fresh air. Space. I needed room to think."

Ian stepped closer, placing his hands at her waist. "Have you had enough time to think?" he asked.

She nodded. "I'm much better now that you're here." Bree rested her hands on his forearms and looked up into the green eyes she'd dreamed about the past few days. There was a difference in his face tonight. Less tightness in his jaw. Less stress drawing lines into his forehead and around his eyes. Even without his phone and his computer in the mountains, his mind had been burdened with the worries of his work and his life.

Tonight there was none of that. He looked…happy. Something had changed in his life since she'd seen him last. Big changes. "What's going on with you, Ian? This isn't the same man from a week ago."

"I've treated myself like one of my artists and given myself a makeover. A *life* makeover."

Bree's brow shot up curiously. "What does a life makeover entail?"

Ian smiled. "Everything. When Missy threatened the label the night of your showing, I realized my business isn't my whole world. I've made it the center of my life, but in the end it didn't matter nearly as much to me as you do. Or my music. Or my mental health. So I hired a business manager to offload a lot from my plate. He's handling the business details while Keith handles the artists. I'm still involved, I still make the big decisions, but I'm not bogged down with the little stuff. It's cut my hours in half."

Bree was stunned by the confession. That was a huge step, one she'd never expected him to make. No wonder he looked as though he didn't have a care in the world. "Are you going into withdrawal yet?"

He shrugged. "I have my moments. I've tried to fill my extra time with my music to keep from getting sucked back in. I've bought some new instruments. I got a baby grand piano and blank sheet music to work on some songs. Keith is acting as my agent for now, but I think I'm going to try to get a full-time agent and see where I can get this to go, if anywhere. I'm just happy to be playing again. I had no idea how badly I missed it in my life until I let it back in. So thank you for that."

Bree didn't know what to say. She'd thought perhaps that tonight was just a little pet project he'd do on the side. Open mic nights every other weekend. Playing his guitar as they sat by the fireplace at his penthouse. She never expected him to try pursuing it professionally again. "That's amazing, Ian. I'm so proud of you for taking the leap. I know it's scary, but you're really talented."

He smiled. "Thank you. That show wasn't the scariest thing I did tonight, though."

Bree's brow furrowed in confusion. "What could be scarier than singing to a hundred rowdy drunks?"

"Doing this."

Bree watched as Ian slipped one hand into his pocket and then dropped down onto one knee. Her eyes widened with surprise and realization as the pieces came together in her mind. He was proposing. *Proposing!* Her heart started racing madly in her chest. He looked up at her with dark green eyes so overflowing with love, she felt herself start to choke up.

"Briana Harper, you are the love of my life. I've spent years trying to catch lightning in a bottle again, but no one can compare to you. I want to spend every day of the rest of my life with you. Not with my employees. Not with my money or my fancy, empty apartment. None of that matters if you're not with me.

"If I'm playing music, I want you there to hear it. When you take pictures, I want to be in your wake, hauling all of your equipment. I don't just want you to be my wife—I want you to be an integral part of my life. That means I will try my hardest to make sure you always feel like you're the most important thing in the world to me. Will you do me the honor of marrying me?"

Ian opened up the small velvet box to display the ring he'd chosen for her. She gasped when the streetlights hit the giant diamond inside. It was massive, bigger than anything she could've imagined and nothing like she'd ever seen. Considering she took a lot of engagement ring and wedding ring portraits, that was saying a lot. It was oval and surrounded by tiny diamonds that continued around the band.

It was the most beautiful thing she'd ever seen. And even then, the ring couldn't touch the words that went with it. The man she loved had just promised her everything she'd ever wanted. Not just love, but a lifetime of companionship. Of feeling important, never cast aside when work and other priorities interfered.

"Yes," she whispered through the tears that suddenly started streaming down her cheeks. "I will marry you."

Ian slipped the ring onto her hand with fingers that shook almost imperceptibly. With it placed snugly, he stood and scooped her into his arms. He smiled a wide, contented smile before leaning in to capture her lips with his own.

Bree melted into him, the world suddenly feeling more right than it had in a very long time. Being in his arms, knowing she was an integral part of Ian's future, she could forget anything else happening around them. She even forgot they were in an alley behind a bar until an employee came out and threw a sack of trash into the Dumpster a couple yards away.

That brought them both back to reality. Ian took her hand and led her toward the door so they could share the good news with their hundred new friends. Bree was certain the dark-haired woman in the front would be highly disappointed to know Ian had been snatched up before she got her chance.

"Do you mind if I announce our engagement to the crowd? I think it will get them amped up for the second set."

Bree nodded and leaned in to give him a good-luck kiss. "One condition, though," she added.

His brows went up. "What's that?"

"I want a disclaimer. I don't cheat at Scrabble. You're just a poor loser with a limited vocabulary."

"Fair enough," he said with a smile. "If you'll still marry me, I'll get up there and tell them anything you'd like."

Epilogue

"What about this dress?" Gretchen slid a bridal magazine across the meeting-room table to Bree. "I like the giant silk rosettes at the bottom."

Bree glanced at the picture and wrinkled her nose. "That's a little fussy for me. I want something more simple and timeless. I was thinking more along the lines of this one." She tapped the page and slid her magazine back to Gretchen. "It's ruched ivory organza with a small crystal embellishment at the hip. I'm definitely not in the market for a ball gown. Please keep in mind that I'm wearing sparkly silver Converse under whatever dress I choose."

She expected Amelia to lodge a complaint about her bridal footwear, but her fashionable coworker didn't seem to be listening. She was lost in her own bridal magazine, flipping slowly through the pages but not seeing anything. She seemed like she was a million miles away, a slight frown pulling down the corners of her mouth.

Amelia had been like this since she'd gotten back from her high school reunion nearly a month ago. She'd been excited to go, but she'd returned from her hometown a little quiet and more pensive than usual. Bree thought that graduating in Las Vegas would make for a more exciting reunion, but Amelia hadn't come home excited. She also hadn't come home wanting to talk about it much.

Bree's wedding was a year off at least, so dress shopping wasn't critical, but she thought it might perk up Amelia to look at dresses with her. She'd brought in a stack of magazines for everyone to look over today before their weekly meeting. Amelia loved fashion, and bridal gowns were the epitome of that to her. She couldn't wait to sneak out of the kitchen to see the bride's dress each Saturday.

But Bree's plan hadn't worked. Amelia hadn't said a word all morning as she mindlessly flipped through the pages of the massive bridal magazine.

Bree knew that what happened in Vegas was supposed to stay there, but this was getting ridiculous. "Amelia?"

The redhead snapped her head up, her thoughts finally on the here and now. "What?"

Gretchen and Bree looked at each other and they both frowned. There was something going on and she was going to get to the bottom of it right now. "What is going on with you?"

Amelia's dark eyes widened and she shook her head dismissively. "There's nothing going on with me. I just didn't sleep very well last night."

"Liar," Gretchen accused and crossed her arms

over her chest. "You've been acting funny since you got home from Las Vegas. What happened at your reunion? When I went to mine, all the cheerleaders had gotten fat and all the nerds were rich. I was still the artistic one with the name no one recalled. I had a few drinks, a few laughs with people who didn't remember who I was and I went home. Nothing to lose sleep over."

Amelia twisted her lips in thought but didn't say anything. Whatever it was that had happened, she didn't want to talk about it. That was just too damn bad, Bree decided. She hadn't wanted to go to that bar and hear Ian sing, either. Amelia had forced her, and look how it had turned out. She was getting married. It was time for Amelia to spill about what was bothering her.

"What's the big deal? What could you have possibly done there that's so bad? It's not like you eloped in one of those tacky wedding chapels," Bree argued.

Amelia looked up at her, her eyes suddenly wide with panic. Her mouth dropped open, her lips moving in argument without making any sound.

"Amelia…" Gretchen pressed, "tell me you didn't elope in a Las Vegas wedding chapel."

She took a deep breath and slowly nodded. "I did. The details are a little blurry, but I woke up married to my best friend."

* * * * *

"I'm not going anywhere. I want to help you out and make things easier for you and Seth."

"I don't think you being around will do anything but make things more difficult for us," she said honestly.

T.J. cupped her cheek with his palm and held her gaze with his. "There's something going on between us, Heather. I know you're as frightened for yourself by whatever it is drawing us together as you are afraid of Seth being hurt. And to tell you the truth, I'm unsettled by it, too. But I gave it a lot of thought last night and I don't think we can ignore it like it doesn't exist. I give you my word that I'll walk through hell before I hurt you or Seth."

"We can try to ignore it," she insisted, unable to sound as convincing as she would have liked. She didn't even try to deny there was a definite chemistry between them. They'd both know she was lying.

"I'm not willing to do that," he said firmly as he lowered his head.

The moment his lips settled over hers, Heather gave up trying to fight with herself...

* * *

The Cowboy's Way
is part of the No.1 bestselling series from Mills & Boon® Desire™—Billionaires & Babies: Powerful men...wrapped around their babies' little fingers.

THE COWBOY'S WAY

BY
KATHIE DeNOSKY

MILLS & BOON

Published in Great Britain 2015
by Mills & Boon, an imprint of Harlequin (UK) Limited,
Eton House, 18-24 Paradise Road, Richmond, Surrey, TW9 1SR

© 2015 Kathie DeNosky

ISBN: 978-0-263-25245-3

51-0115

Kathie DeNosky lives in her native southern Illinois on the land her family settled in 1839. She writes highly sensual stories with a generous amount of humor. Her books have appeared on the *USA TODAY* bestseller list and received numerous awards, including two National Readers' Choice Awards. Kathie enjoys going to rodeos, traveling to research settings for her books and listening to country music. Readers may contact her by e-mailing kathie@kathiedenosky.com. They can also visit her website, www.kathiedenosky.com, or find her on Facebook.

This book is dedicated to all of the single parents who work so hard each and every day to meet the many challenges of raising a child alone.

One

As he sat at Sam and Bria Rafferty's dining room table after a delicious Christmas dinner prepared by his sisters-in-law, T. J. Malloy couldn't help but smile. He listened to his foster brothers and their wives talk about what they had planned for the week leading up to the family's annual New Year's Eve party, which T.J. hosted at his ranch. And, as always, there was the usual good-natured ribbing and the laughter that always followed, as well as everyone making faces and funny noises to get a smile or a giggle out of the babies. Life was good and he was one grateful son-of-a-gun for the way everything had turned out.

Thanks to their foster father, Hank Calvert, T.J. and the other five men who had been placed in the man's care when they were teenagers had straightened out their lives. In the process, they had bonded and become a family T.J. loved with all his heart. Now, he owned his own ranch, where he raised champion reining horses—a dream he'd had for most of his thirty-two years. And because he'd made several wise investments, he had more money in the bank than he could spend in three or four lifetimes.

Yup, he truly was a blessed man and he had the good sense to know it.

"Your turn, T.J.," Bria said, smiling as she dished up slices of homemade red velvet cake. "What are your plans for the week?"

"Same as every year," he said, smiling back at his sister-in-law. "I'll spend the week training my horses and waiting for you all to show up on New Year's Eve afternoon."

Four years ago when he bought the Dusty Diamond Ranch and built his seven-bedroom house, everyone had decided that he would host the family's New Year's Eve gatherings. He had enough bedrooms to accommodate the entire family, and they could all bring in the New Year together without having to be out on the roads after celebrating with a few drinks. His brothers brought their wives or a date and once the kids had been tucked in for the night, they sat around and talked or watched a movie. It had become a tradition and one that T.J. looked forward to every year.

"Do you have a lady in your life who will be joining us this year?" Nate Rafferty asked, grinning from ear to ear.

Nate and Sam were the only biological brothers of

the bunch, but they couldn't have been more different if they had tried. While Sam was a happily married family man, Nate was wilder than a range-raised colt. He loved the ladies and seemed to have made it his mission in life to date every single woman in the entire southwest. But as rowdy as he was, Nate had the same sense of loyalty that had been instilled in all of Hank's foster sons. Come hell or high water, Nate would be there for any one of them—the same as they would be there for him.

"T.J. does have a woman in his life, Nate," Lane Donaldson said, laughing as he put his arm around his wife, Taylor. "But for some reason he won't break down and ask his neighbor to join us."

"You just had to go there, didn't you, Freud?" T.J. replied, shaking his head in disgust. He should have known Lane would feel the need to comment. Having earned a master's degree in psychology, the man knew exactly which buttons to push to get a rise out of any one of them. "She and her stallion are on one side of the fence and I'm on the other. And that's the way it's going to stay."

That Wilson woman had been T.J.'s neighbor for close to two years, and he'd seen her only a handful of times. But his brothers constantly teased him about his "interest" in his ornery neighbor, even though all he knew about her was how careless she was with her horse. Hell, he didn't even know her first name. And furthermore, he didn't want to know it.

"You haven't seen her since we put up that six-foot fence between your ranch and hers this past spring?"

Sam asked, trying to dodge the glob of mashed potatoes his ten-month-old son had scooped off the high-chair tray and tried to throw at him.

"Nope. I haven't seen her or her stallion and that suits me just fine." T.J. couldn't help but laugh when little Hank landed the mashed potatoes right square on the end of Sam's nose.

"Now that you have solved the problem of her stallion jumping the fence, what are you going to complain about?" Ryder McClain asked, laughing. His laughter immediately turned to a groan when his baby daughter, Katie, missed the burp cloth on his shoulder and "christened" the back of his clean shirt.

"Thank you, Katie," T.J. said, grinning as he reached over to take the baby from his brother while Ryder's wife, Summer, wiped off the back of his shoulder. "That shut your daddy up real quick."

"You'd better watch out, T.J.," Ryder said, grinning back at him. "You could be next. The smell of a clean shirt always seems to make my daughter nauseous."

The most easygoing of the band of brothers, Ryder was also the most courageous. A rodeo bullfighter, he used to save bull riders from serious injury, or worse, on a regular basis. But since he'd married Summer and they had little Katie, Ryder had cut way back on his schedule and only worked the rodeos Nate and their brother Jaron Lambert competed in. T.J. suspected it was because Ryder wanted to make sure his brothers were well protected from the dangerous bulls they rode in their quest to become national champions. T.J. also knew Ryder would never admit that was the reason he hadn't completely quit being a bullfighter.

"Will you be at the party, Mariah?" Lane's wife, Taylor, asked Bria's younger sister.

"Probably not," Mariah said slowly. She paused as she glanced across the table at Jaron. "I've met someone and he's asked me to go to a New Year's Eve party with him at one of the clubs up in Dallas."

Everyone looked at Jaron to see how he would react to Mariah's news. The entire family knew the two had been attracted to each other practically from the moment they'd met. But Mariah had only been eighteen at the time and at twenty-six, Jaron had decided—and rightly so—that he was too old for her. Unfortunately, in the seven years since, Jaron hadn't changed his stance and Mariah had apparently become tired of waiting on him and decided to move on.

"Congratulations on the new guy," Jaron said tightly, breaking the awkward silence. "Have a good time."

To the outward eye, his brother looked sincere, but T.J. knew better. By nature, Jaron was more reserved and quieter than the rest of the men, making it hard to figure out what he was thinking. But when he was pissed off, his voice took on an edge that was rock-hard, ice-cold and impossible to ignore. That edge was present now and T.J. knew Jaron was warning the rest of the men that he wasn't in the mood for their affectionate teasing about Mariah, now or later. T.J. also knew every one of his brothers would respect Jaron's need for silence on the matter.

"What about you, Nate?" T.J. asked, counting on the

man to ease some of the sudden tension in the room. "Are you bringing someone this year?"

Nate shook his head. "I bought the Twin Oaks Ranch over by Beaver Dam a few weeks ago," Nate stated proudly. "I've been too busy lately to think about anything but what I'm going to do with the place."

"When did this happen?" T.J. asked, astounded. "I don't recall you mentioning it when we were together at Thanksgiving."

"I didn't want to jinx it in case the deal fell through," Nate said as he shoveled a big bite of red velvet cake into his mouth.

Nate's superstition didn't surprise T.J. one bit. Every rodeo rider he knew was superstitious about something. Even he'd had certain rituals he went through before he climbed on the back of a rank bucking horse when he competed.

"You're finally putting down roots?" Sam asked, looking like he couldn't quite believe Nate was serious.

"Don't take this the wrong way, bro, but I never thought I'd see the day you settled down," Ryder said, shaking his head.

"I just bought a ranch," Nate said, grinning. "I never said I was settling down."

"When do you move into your new den of iniquity?" T.J. asked, handing baby Katie to Summer for the rest of her bottle.

"I won't be moving in for a while," Nate said, taking another bite of the red velvet cake in front of him. He shrugged. "I've got some work I need to do on it first. I'm going to knock down a couple of walls to make a great room and the plumbing and wiring need to be upgraded. I also need to make a few repairs to the fences and maybe build a couple of new barns before I bring in livestock."

"Just let us know when and how we can help and we'll be there," Lane said, speaking for all of them.

"I'll do that." Nate smiled at the women seated around the table. "And I'm counting on these lovely ladies to help out when it comes to decorating the house."

T.J. raised an eyebrow. "Even the master suite?"

Nate shook his head as his grin turned suggestive. "I've got my own ideas for that."

"I'll bet you do," Ryder said, voicing what the rest of the men were thinking.

"We can skip the details on your choice of decor for your bedroom," Bria said, handing T.J. a slice of cake.

Everyone nodded their agreement and the rest of the evening was filled with talk about renovating Nate's ranch house, causing T.J. to breathe a sigh of relief. If they were talking about something else, they weren't teasing him about his neighbor. And that was just fine with him. The less he was reminded of the woman, the better.

Several hours later, after finalizing plans for when everyone would arrive for the New Year's Eve party, T.J. left Sam and Bria's for the hour's drive back to his ranch. It had been raining all day, and by the time he reached the turn-off leading up to the Dusty Diamond's ranch house, it had become an outright downpour.

He started to turn his truck onto the lane, but then stopped when he noticed a faint glow of red about a hundred yards up ahead. The best he could tell, it was the taillights of a car and he knew without a shadow of doubt that the creek had flooded out again, blocking the road. It only happened three or four times a year, but whenever there was a significant amount of rain, the slow-moving stream that bordered his ranch to the east turned into a raging river. With as much water as had fallen over the course of the day, the creek was probably a good twenty feet or so out of its banks on either side of the ravine.

Unable to ignore the fact that whoever was in the vehicle might need help, T.J. drove on until he reached the compact gray sedan sitting in the middle of the road. He could tell someone was still inside, and from what he could see of the slim form, that someone was female. Cursing the nasty weather, T.J. got out of his truck and jogged up to the driver's side door.

"Is there anything I can do to help, ma'am?" T.J. asked as the woman inside lowered the window. She stopped halfway, and he wasn't certain if it was to keep out the rain, or because he was the one offering her assistance. But he almost groaned aloud when he realized the driver was his archenemy, that Wilson woman from the neighboring ranch.

He hadn't seen her since the last time her horse jumped the fence, back in the spring, when he'd had to take the stallion back over to the Circle W. It had been about the tenth time the horse had trespassed on Dusty Diamond land, and T.J.'s patience with the situation had come to a swift end. That's when he'd had his brothers help him put up the six-foot fence between the two properties. The fence had eliminated the problem of her horse romancing T.J.'s mares and he had thought he wouldn't have to deal with her again. Apparently, he'd been wrong.

"I was afraid of this," she said, not looking any happier to see him than he was to see her.

T.J. wasn't sure if she meant she had been afraid of not being able to get across the creek or she'd been afraid that he would be her only source of help. Either way, she wasn't in the position of being choosy, and he wouldn't walk away and leave her to solve the problem on her own. His foster father would probably come back from the dead to haunt him if Hank knew one of the boys he had raised had left a lady in distress to fend for herself.

"Even if it stops raining now, you won't be able to get back to your ranch until morning," T.J. pointed out. As he stood in the downpour, chilling water dripped off the back of his wide brimmed hat and ran down his neck. It was damned uncomfortable and he wasn't inclined to mince words. "You'll have to follow me to the Dusty Diamond. You can stay there tonight."

She stubbornly shook her head. "We may be neighbors, but I don't really know you and from our past run-ins, I'm not interested in getting acquainted."

"Believe me, lady, I'm not, either," T.J. stated flatly. "But there's no way you'll make it across forty feet of rushing water without stalling out or being swept down into the ravine. Then I'd be obligated to jump in and try to fish you out before you drowned. I'd really like to avoid that if possible." He took a deep breath and tried to hold on to his temper. "Do you have anywhere else you can go?"

As she stared at him, she caught her lower lip between her teeth as if she was trying to think of somewhere—anywhere—she could spend the night other than at his place. She finally shook her head. "No."

"Well, I'm not going to let you stay here in your car all night," he said impatiently.

"You're not going to *let* me stay in my car?"

From the tone of her voice, he could tell he had ruffled more than a couple of feathers.

"Look, I'm just trying to keep you from having to spend a damp, uncomfortable night in your car," he stated. "But it's your choice. If you want to sit out here instead of sleeping in a warm, dry bed, that's your choice."

When it dawned on him that she might be frightened of him, he felt a little guilty for being so blunt. He could even understand her reluctance to take him up on his offer. The few times they had come face-to-face, he had been angry. She probably thought he was an ill-tempered bastard. Unfortunately, he wasn't doing anything now to correct that impression.

"Hey, I'm sorry," he said, making a conscious effort to remove the impatience from his tone. "It's dark, cold and I'm getting soaked to the bone out here." He hoped the friendly smile he gave her helped to alleviate some of her fears. "It's warm and dry at my place and I've got plenty of room." As an afterthought, he added, "And all of the bedrooms have locks on the doors."

She glanced in the rearview mirror at something

in the backseat, then hesitated a few seconds longer before she shook her head. She sounded tired and utterly defeated when she finally murmured, "I don't have a choice."

"When we get to the house, you can park in the garage," he offered. "There's plenty of room and you'll be able to stay dry getting inside the house."

"All right. I'll follow you," she said, rolling up the driver's side window.

He jogged back to his truck and started it up. Once he had it turned around and checked to make sure she wasn't having any trouble doing the same, T.J. drove back to the lane leading up to his home. When he steered the truck around the ranch house to the attached three-car garage, he pressed the remote to raise two of the wide doors and parked inside. By the time he got out, the woman had stopped her older Toyota between his truck and the Mercedes sedan he rarely drove.

He walked over and opened her door. When she got out of the car, his breath caught. The times he had taken her errant horse back to her and knocked on her door to demand she keep the horse on her ranch, as well as during their conversation a few minutes ago in the dark, cold rain, he had been so frustrated, he hadn't paid much attention to his neighbor's looks. But he sure as hell noticed them now.

A few inches over six feet tall, T.J. didn't meet many women who could look him square in the eye without having to tilt their heads back. But the Wilson woman was only four or five inches shorter than him. When their gazes met, he felt like he had been kicked in the gut.

She had the bluest eyes he'd ever seen and for reasons that baffled him, he wanted to take her long, strawberry blond hair down from her ponytail and run his fingers through the soft-looking, wavy strands. The woman wasn't just pretty, she was heart-stoppingly gorgeous. He couldn't believe he had missed seeing that before.

When she turned to open the back door of her car and reached inside, he briefly wondered if she carried an overnight bag around just on the outside chance she got stranded somewhere. But when she straightened and turned to face him, T.J. barely managed to keep his jaw from dropping. She held a blanket-covered child to her shoulder with one arm, while she tried to keep her grasp on her purse and a diaper bag with the other.

In the course of about three seconds several questions ran through his mind. First, he remembered that when he'd stopped to see if she needed help, she had been sitting in her car contemplating how she was going to get back to her ranch. Surely she wouldn't have tried to cross the flooded road with her kid in the backseat? The realization of what might have happened if she had tried such a thing caused a tight knot to form in the pit of his stomach. Second, when he'd asked her if there was anywhere else she could go, she had told him there wasn't. What would she have done if he hadn't come along and offered her shelter for the night? Would she have tried to tough it out all night in the car with a child?

"Let me help you," T.J. said now, stepping forward to take her purse and the diaper bag. Aside from the fact that it was just good manners for a man to help a woman carry things, the dark smudges beneath her eyes were testament to the fact that she was extremely tired.

"Thank you…Malloy." She shook her head as she closed the car door. "I don't know your first name."

When he stepped back for her to precede him through the door leading into the mudroom, he did his best to give her a friendly smile. "The name's T.J., Ms. Wilson."

He suddenly realized that in the four years since he'd bought the ranch, he'd been so busy starting his breeding program and getting settled in, that he hadn't bothered to get acquainted with more than one or two of the other ranchers in the immediate area. And the few times he had met up with Ms. Wilson, it hadn't been under the best of circumstances. He had been pissed off about her stallion impregnating his mares and hadn't bothered to introduce himself and, understandably, she hadn't been inclined to give him her name or exchange pleasantries when he had put her on the defensive.

He felt a little guilty about that. Oh, who was he kidding? He felt downright ashamed of himself. No matter if he had been angry or not, he had better manners than that and shouldn't have been so demanding.

"My name's Heather," she said as they walked into the kitchen. When he turned on the lights, she stopped and looked around. "Your home is very nice."

"Thanks." He set her purse and the diaper bag on the kitchen island, then shrugged out of his wet jacket before helping her out of hers. "Would you like something to eat or drink, Heather?" he asked, doing his best to be cordial.

"Thank you, but it's late and if you don't mind, I'd rather get my son settled down for the night," she said, sounding as if she was ready to drop in her tracks.

"No problem." Hanging their coats in the mudroom, he picked up the two bags and led the way down the hall to the stairs in the foyer. "Do you need to call someone to let them know where you are and that you and your little boy are all right?"

T.J. wondered where her significant other was and why he wasn't with her. Any man worth a damn wouldn't have let his woman go out alone on a night like this. In T.J.'s opinion, there was no excuse for the man not being on the cell phone at that very moment checking to see that she and their little boy were safe and going to be all right.

Climbing the steps, she shook her head. "No. There's no one. It's just me and Seth."

When T.J. stopped and opened the door to the first bedroom on the second floor, he stepped back for her to enter. "Ladies first." Following her into the room, he added, "If this isn't to your liking, I've got five more bedrooms to choose from."

"This is fine, thank you," she said, reaching for her purse and the diaper bag as if she would like for him to leave.

When her hand brushed his, he felt a tingling sensation along his skin and quickly reasoned that it was probably a charge of static electricity. But he couldn't dismiss the heat he felt radiating from her quite so easily.

Frowning, he asked, "Are you feeling all right?"

"I've felt better," she admitted as she set the two bags on the bench at the end of the bed.

Without a second thought about the invasion of her space, T.J. walked over and placed his palm on her forehead. "You've got a fever." Lifting the edge of the blanket, he noticed the sleeping baby's flushed cheeks. "Both of you are sick."

"We'll be fine," she said, placing the little boy on the bed. "I had to take my son to the emergency room. I was on my way back home when you stopped to see if we needed help."

"What was the diagnosis?" T.J. asked, hoping the little guy was going to be okay.

"He has an ear infection." She reached for the diaper bag. "They gave me an antibiotic for him, as well as something to give him if his fever spikes."

"What about you?" he asked. "Did you see a doctor while you were there?"

She shook her head. "I'll be all right. I'm just getting over the flu."

"You should have seen a doctor as well," he said, unable to keep the disapproval from his voice.

"Well, I didn't," she retorted as if she resented his observation. "Now, if you'll excuse me—"

"While you get him settled in bed, I'll go get something for you to sleep in," he interrupted, leaving the room before she could protest.

When he entered the master suite, T.J. walked straight to the medicine cabinet in his adjoining bathroom. Taking a bottle of Tylenol from one of the shelves, he went back into his bedroom and looked around. What could he give her to wear to bed? He preferred sleeping in the buff and didn't even own a pair of pajamas. Deciding that one of his flannel shirts would have to do, he took one from the walk-in closet and headed back to the room Heather and her son would be using.

"Will this be okay?" he asked, holding up the soft shirt for her inspection. "I'm sorry I don't have something more comfortable."

"I could have just slept in my clothes," she said, covering the baby with the comforter. Turning to face him, she took the garment he offered. "But thank you for...everything."

"Here's something to take for your fever," he said, handing her the bottle of Tylenol. He went into the adjoining bathroom for a glass of water, then handed it to her as he pointed to the bottle. "Take a couple of these and if you need anything else, my room is down at the other end of the hall."

"We'll be fine," she said, removing two of the tablets from the bottle.

He stared at her for a moment, wondering for the second time since finding her stranded on the road how he could have missed how beautiful she was all those times he took her horse back to her. Even with dark smudges under her eyes, she was striking and the kind of woman a man couldn't help but wonder—

"Was there something else?" she asked, snapping him back to reality.

Deciding the rain must have washed away some of his good sense, he shook his head. "Good night."

When he left the room and closed the door, he heard the quiet snick of the lock being set behind him as he started down the hall to his bedroom. Under the circumstances, he could understand her caution. A woman alone couldn't be too careful these days. She didn't know him and until tonight, he hadn't given her a reason to think she might want to change that fact.

"You're one sorry excuse for a man," he muttered to himself.

He'd had his mind made up that she was just a defiant, uncaring female who arrogantly ignored his pleas to keep her horse at home. It had never occurred to him that she was every bit as vulnerable and overworked as any other single mother. Of course, he hadn't known about the kid until tonight. But that was no excuse for jumping to conclusions about her the way he had.

As T.J. took off his damp clothes and headed for the shower to wash away the uncomfortable chill of the cold rain, he couldn't stop thinking about his guests down the hall. He didn't know what the story was with Heather and her little boy, but it really didn't matter. Whether she wanted to accept his help or not, right now she needed it. She and her kid were both sick, and since there didn't seem to be anyone else to see to their welfare, T.J. was going to have to step up to the plate.

One of the first things Hank Calvert had taught him and his brothers was that when they saw someone in need, it was only right to pitch in and lend a hand. He had told them that life could be an obstacle and sometimes it took teamwork to get through it. And if anyone ever needed a helping hand it was Heather Wilson.

Of course, T.J. didn't think Hank had ever run into anyone with as much stubborn pride as Heather. The woman wore that pride like a suit of armor and was a little too independent for her own good. He toweled himself dry, walked into the bedroom and got into bed. He lay there for several long minutes, staring up at the ceiling as he listened to the rain pelt the roof. Heather's situation was a lot like his own mother's.

Delia Malloy had been a single mother with all the responsibilities that entailed. She had done a great job of holding down a job and providing for their family of two while she raised him. T.J. would always be grateful for the sacrifices she had made. But when he was ten years old, they both came down with the flu. That was when his life changed forever.

His mother had taken good care of him and made sure he recovered with no problems, but what she hadn't done was take care of herself. Physically rundown, she developed a case of pneumonia and hadn't been able to fight off the infection. She died a week later and T.J. had been sent to live with his elderly great-grandmother.

That's when all hell broke loose and started him on a downward spiral that ended up sending him to the Last Chance Ranch. His great-grandmother had really been too old to oversee what he was up to and who he was with. And he had been too hurt and angry about losing his mother to listen to her anyway. Looking back, he had been ripe for falling in with the wrong crowd and by the time he was thirteen, he had been arrested five times for vandalism and criminal mischief. Shortly after that his great-grandmother passed away and his case worker had decided that placing him with a set of normal foster parents would be more of the same, so he had been placed under the care of Hank Calvert. And even though it had been the luckiest break of his life, he was determined to see that Heather's little boy didn't go down the same path he had taken.

Her little boy was counting on his mother to be there for him throughout the rest of his childhood, and for the kid's sake, T.J. would try to make sure that happened— at least this time. Whether she liked it or not, he was going to take care of Heather and her son while they were sick and flooded out of returning to their home. In the bargain, he'd make sure that her little boy didn't suffer the same motherless childhood that T.J. had.

Around dawn the morning after she followed T.J. Malloy home, Heather lay in bed, feeling as if she had been run over by a truck. Assessing her symptoms, she realized that although her muscles weren't as achy as they had been for the past couple of days, they were extremely weak. Just lifting her head from the pillow took monumental effort. Thankfully her headache was gone, but one minute she was hot and the next she was shivering—indicating that her temperature was still elevated. Thank heavens she had been able to scrape up the money to get Seth to the doctor a couple of months earlier for a flu shot. At least she wouldn't have to worry about him catching the illness from her.

"Mom-mom," Seth said, sitting up to pat her arm.

She could tell from the tremor in his voice that he was about to cry and she knew why. For an almost two-year-old, he was a sound sleeper and had slept through the night since he was three months old. But he wasn't used to sleeping anywhere but his own bed, in his own room, and he was probably disoriented by the strange surroundings.

"It's all right, sweetie."

Rubbing his back, she hoped he would settle back down and sleep for a little while longer before he insisted they get up for breakfast. Since coming down with the flu, it had been a real struggle to take care of a toddler, as well as a barn full of horses by herself, and she couldn't help but want to get a little more sleep while she could. Fortunately, it had been a mild case of the illness or she would have never been able to manage on her own. But without being able to get enough rest, it was taking her twice as long to get over it.

Just as Seth closed his eyes and seemed to be drifting back to sleep, a tap on the door caused him to jerk awake and start to cry.

Shivering from the chills and feeling as if her legs were made of lead, Heather picked up her crying son and got out of bed. Without thinking about the fact that she was wearing nothing more than Malloy's flannel shirt and her panties, she walked over to unlock and open the door. "What?"

"I thought you and your little boy might like something to eat," Malloy said, holding out a tray of food.

If she had felt better, she might have tried not to sound so impatient. She might have acknowledged his thoughtfulness. At the moment, just the thought of food made her stomach queasy and she wished he hadn't disturbed her son.

"Th-thank you, but…" Her voice trailed off when she noticed his expression. "Is s-something wrong?"

"Let me help you back to bed," he said, brushing past her to set the tray on the dresser. "I'd ask if you still have a fever, but I already know the answer."

"H-how?" She wished her teeth would stop chattering like a cheap pair of castanets.

Turning back, he took Seth from her, then put his arm around her shoulders and guided her back to the bed. "Just a hunch," he answered, smiling.

Once she was back in bed, she noticed that Seth had stopped crying and was staring at the tray of food Malloy had set on the dresser. "Mom-mom, eat."

Groaning, she started to get up, but Malloy stopped her. "I'm assuming that means he's hungry?" When she nodded, he pointed to the tray. "I've got toast and scrambled eggs. Do you think he'll let me feed him while you rest?"

She barely managed to nod before she pulled the comforter around herself and closed her eyes. If she felt better, she would have asked why he was being so nice to her, instead of thinking about how handsome he was. Her breath caught. Where had that come from?

If she was thinking T. J. Malloy was good-looking, her fever had to have made her delirious. That was the only explanation. If she could just rest for a moment, she'd be able to get up and take over feeding her son, as well as return to her senses.

Two

When Heather opened her eyes again, she noticed that the sun was shining through a part in the curtain and Seth was sound asleep on the bed beside her. Looking a little closer, she noticed he was wearing a pair of pajamas she had never seen before and his copper-red hair had been neatly combed to the side.

How long had she been asleep and where had the clothes her son was wearing come from?

Glancing at the clock on the nightstand, Heather couldn't believe that it was already midafternoon. She had slept for eight straight hours. She couldn't remember getting that much sleep at one stretch since before Seth was born.

Her heart stalled. Had T. J. Malloy taken care of her son?

She vaguely remembered a knock waking Seth and her opening the door to find Malloy standing on the other side with a tray of food. Had she dreamed that he had helped her back to bed?

When she realized that all she had on was his shirt and her panties, Heather closed her eyes and hoped when she opened them she would somehow be transported to her own bed in the Circle W ranch house and that the past twenty-four hours would prove to be nothing more than a dream. But aside from her embarrassment over a stranger seeing her wearing so little, she wasn't entirely comfortable with the fact that Malloy had taken care of Seth. She didn't really know her neighbor and from the previous run-ins she'd had with him, she wasn't sure he was someone she wanted around her son. When Malloy had brought her stallion back the few times Magic Dancer had jumped the fence between their properties, the man had been the biggest grouch she had ever met.

"The horses," she murmured suddenly, remembering that she had livestock to feed. Hopefully the water blocking the road had receded. She needed to get home to tend to the horses, as well as make sure the buckets she had left in the utility room to catch the drips from the leaking roof hadn't overflowed.

As she sat up, Heather realized she felt a lot better than she had that morning. Her fever was gone. Maybe she had turned the corner and was over the worst of the flu. Sleeping all night and most of the day had probably been a tremendous help. It was a shame she hadn't had the opportunity when she'd first come down with the illness. Her recovery time would have been a lot shorter.

But she hadn't had that luxury in so long, it was hard to remember what it was like to have help with anything. After she had Seth, she'd had no choice but to let go of the men who had worked for her late father because she couldn't afford to pay them. It was the only way she had been able to make ends meet on the Circle W. That meant she had to take care of feeding the horses, mucking out stalls and trying to keep up the endless other chores on a working horse ranch, as well as take care of a baby.

Careful not to wake Seth, she started to get up, then immediately sat back down on the side of the bed when her knees began to shake. She might be feeling better, but she was still extremely weak. It was going to be a real test of her fortitude to lift heavy buckets of water and bales of hay while she was in this state.

She tried again, and had just managed to walk over to the rocking chair where she had draped her clothes the night before, when the door opened.

"You shouldn't be up yet," Malloy said, entering the room and walking over to her.

She supposed he had the right to just waltz right in without asking if she minded. After all, he did own the place. But she wasn't happy about it.

She grabbed her jeans and sweatshirt and held them in front of her. "Don't you believe in knocking?"

"I was just checking on your little boy and didn't expect you to be awake yet." He shrugged as if he wasn't the least bit concerned about it. "How are you feeling?"

"I'm much better and as soon as I get dressed, Seth and I will go home and leave you alone." She wished he would leave the room so she could take a quick shower before Seth woke up.

"Don't worry about getting back home," he said, his deep voice wrapping around her like a comforting cloak. "You really should stay until there's no danger of a setback."

Heather shook her head as much to stop the lulling effect of his voice as in refusal. "I appreciate everything you've done, but I don't want to impose." Feeling her knees start to shake again, she sat down on the rocking chair. "Besides, I need to get my livestock fed."

"All you have to do is rest and get better," he said, smiling. "I had one of my crew go over to your place when the water receded around noon to let your men know you and the little guy were okay. Since no one was around, my man took care of feeding your horses for you."

She looked up at him and was hit with an unexpected observation. T. J. Malloy wasn't just handsome, he was knock-your-socks-off good-looking. Her breath caught.

The few times that he had brought her horse home, she hadn't noticed anything beyond his dark scowl and formidable stance as he threatened to take legal action against her if she didn't keep her horse on her side of the fence. But without his wide-brimmed, black Resistol pulled down low on his brow, she could see a kindness in his striking hazel eyes that she would never have expected. And for some reason she found his brown hair, which curled around his ears and over the nape of his neck, sexy and rather endearing.

She frowned. Where had that come from? And why did she find anything about the man attractive?

It had to be some kind of residual effect of the fever. It was causing her to see Malloy in a different light. Surely as soon as she recovered her strength, she would come to her senses, regain her perspective and see that T. J. Malloy was just as unpleasant and unappealing as ever.

"Are you feeling all right?" he asked, looking concerned.

"Uh, yes," she said, nodding. "I'm just a little weak." As an afterthought, she added, "Thank you for having one of your hired hands tend to my horses."

"No problem." He gave her the same smile that had caused the illusion of him being amiable. "I assume you gave your men the rest of the holiday weekend off?"

"Since you sent one of yours over to take care of my horses, I assume you didn't?" she asked instead of answering his question.

She didn't want to tell him that she'd had to lay off the two men. For one thing, it was a matter of pride. She didn't want Malloy realizing that the Circle W had fallen on such hard times. And for another, she didn't like anyone knowing that she and her child lived alone on the ranch. Not that it made a lot of difference, but she felt a little safer with people thinking the hired men were still in residence.

"I did offer to let them off, but they preferred me paying them double time for working this weekend," he said, unaware of her thoughts. "So don't worry about the horses until your men get back on Monday. I'll have one of mine go over there again tomorrow and Sunday to take care of them."

"That isn't necessary," she insisted. "I'll do it."

He stubbornly folded his arms across his broad chest and shook his head. "You need to take it easy for a couple more days and make sure you're completely over the flu before you start doing anything too strenuous. You won't be doing yourself or your little boy any favors if you're in the hospital with pneumonia." Something in his tone, as well as his body language, told her than he was determined to have his way in the matter.

Just as determined to have her own way, she shook her head. "Don't worry about me. I'll be fine."

"That's what you said last night and this morning," he remarked. "I wouldn't consider barely having enough strength to stand doing all that great."

He probably had a point, but she hated to admit that he was right, almost as much as she hated that she found him so darned good-looking.

"Why do you care?" she asked bluntly. Apparently the flu had removed some kind of filter in her brain. She was unable to keep from blurting out whatever she was thinking.

His easy expression changed to the dark scowl she was more used to seeing from him. "Having the flu isn't something you should take lightly. It can have serious complications. I'm just trying to make sure you're around to raise your little boy, lady."

She knew he was only doing what he thought was

right, but it had been a very long time since anyone had cared to lend her their assistance or show they were concerned for her well-being. Even her late fiancé's parents had severed all ties with her when their son died. And they hadn't bothered contacting her since, even knowing she had been pregnant with their grand-child. That's when she had decided she didn't need them or anyone else. She was a strong, capable woman and could do whatever had to be done on her own.

Shrugging, she stared down at the clothes in her lap. "I'm sorry if I sound ungrateful," she said, mean-ing it. "There's no excuse for my being rude. I do ap-preciate your help. But I've taken care of Seth since I came down with the flu and I'm doing a lot better now. I know I'll be fine." She looked up into his hazel eyes. "Really."

"I respect your need for independence," he said, his tone less harsh. "All I'm trying to do is help you out for a couple more days. Rest up here, at least until to-morrow. I'll have one of my men go over to your place, then all you'll have to do when you get home is take care of yourself and your little boy."

It was obvious he wasn't going to give up and she wasn't up to a full-scale verbal battle. And honestly, it would be nice to not have to take on everything all by herself for once.

"All right," she finally conceded. "One of your men can take care of the horses for me tomorrow, but now that the road is clear there's no reason for us to stay here and inconvenience you any longer." She pointed toward the bathroom door. "Now if you'll excuse me,

I'd like to take a shower and get dressed so we can go on home. Seth and I have taken up enough of your time and generosity. Besides, we'll both rest better in our own beds."

She could tell Malloy wanted to say something about her insistence on going home, but Seth chose that moment to rouse up and start crying. Normally a sound sleeper, he could snooze through just about anything at home. But now that he was unfamiliar with the surroundings, their arguing had obviously disturbed him.

"It's all right, sweetie," she said, getting out of the chair. When she walked over to the bed to pick him up, she discovered that it took more effort than usual.

"Here, let me help," Malloy said, stepping forward to pick up her son.

To her surprise when Seth recognized who held him, the little traitor laid his head on the man's shoulder and smiled at her.

"Did you give him his medication?" she asked, feeling like a complete failure as a mother. She had slept while a total stranger fed, changed and apparently bonded with her child.

Malloy nodded. "I read the dosage on the bottle's label and gave the antibiotic to him right after breakfast and then again after lunch."

"You seem to know a lot about taking care of a child," she commented, wondering if he might have one of his own. She felt a little let down that he might have a significant other somewhere, but she couldn't for the life of her figure out why.

"I have a ten-month-old nephew and a six-month-old niece," he answered, as if reading her mind. "But other than watching their parents take care of them, I'm a trial-and-error kind of guy. That's why I had to change this little guy's sleeper and my shirt after lunch." Malloy grinned. "I *tried* to let him feed himself and quickly learned that was an *error.*"

Heather smiled at the visual image as an unfamiliar emotion spread throughout her chest. There was something about a man being unafraid to hold and nurture a child that was heartwarming.

Not at all comfortable with the fact that the man drawing that emotion from her was T. J. Malloy, she asked, "Would you mind watching him for a few minutes while I take a quick shower?"

"Not at all," he said, shaking his head. "Take your time. You'll probably feel a lot better."

"I'll feel better when we get home." She stared down at the jeans and sweatshirt she still held. "Seth is going to need diapers and we both need clean clothes."

"Not a problem," Malloy answered. "I had one of my men drive up to Stephenville this morning to pick up a few things I thought you would need. I had him get both of you a change of clothes, as well as diapers and some kind of little kid food."

"How did he know what sizes to get?" That explained where Seth's new pajamas came from.

"I told Dan to take his wife along for the ride." Malloy looked quite pleased with himself. "They have three kids under the age of five and I figured if anyone would know what you both needed, it would be Jane Ann."

He pointed toward the dresser. "Your clothes are over there in the shopping bag."

"I'll reimburse you for everything," she said, thankful to have clean clothes to put on after her shower. "Do you still have the sales slip?"

"No, I don't and no, you won't pay me back," he said, firmly.

"Yes, I will." She didn't have a lot in reserve and hoped it didn't cost much, but she did have her pride. She wasn't the gold digger her fiancé's parents had once accused her of being when she'd called to let them know about Seth's birth. And besides, considering her past with Malloy, she wasn't inclined to have him complaining about some other way she'd been negligent.

Malloy released a frustrated sigh. "We'll discuss it later."

"You can bet we will," she vowed.

Deciding there was no reasoning with the man at the moment, Heather tugged at the shirt she was wearing to make sure it covered her backside as she got the bag of clothes from the dresser, then walked into the bathroom and shut the door.

When she looked in the mirror, she groaned. Her long hair resembled a limp mop and other than the few freckles sprinkled across her nose and cheekbones, she was the color of a ghost—and a sickly one at that.

But as she continued to stare in the mirror, the weight of reality began to settle across her shoulders like a leaden yoke. A shower and clean clothes could make her feel a little better physically and T. J. Malloy could offer as much neighborly help as he wanted, but nothing could wash away the worry or the hopelessness she faced when she returned home.

Unless something miraculous happened between now and the end of the January, she and her son were going to be homeless. And there didn't seem to be a thing she could do to stop it from happening.

When Heather went into the adjoining bathroom and closed the door, T.J. sat down on the rocking chair with Seth and released the breath he had been holding.

What the hell was wrong with him? The woman looked thoroughly exhausted, was just getting over the flu and, without a shadow of doubt, was as irritable as a bull in a herd full of steers. So why was he thinking about how sexy she looked wearing his shirt? Or how long and shapely her legs were?

Earlier that morning, he had damned near dropped the breakfast tray he had been carrying when she opened the door. She hadn't bothered with the top couple of buttons on the flannel shirt he'd given her to sleep in and he'd noticed the valley between her breasts. What was worse, she had been too ill to even try to be enticing and she had still managed to tie him into a knot the size of his fist.

"You're one sick SOB, Malloy," he muttered, shaking his head.

As he sat there trying to figure out what it was about her that he found so damned alluring, he frowned. He wanted her out of his hair as much as she wanted to leave. So why did he keep insisting that Heather needed to stay another night? Why couldn't he keep his mouth shut, help her get her son buckled into his car seat and wave goodbye as they drove away?

Looking down at the little boy sitting on his lap, T.J. shook his head. "Be glad you're too young to notice anything about girls. They'll make you completely crazy with little or no effort."

When Seth looked up at him and grinned, T.J. suddenly knew exactly why he was being overly cautious about them leaving. He couldn't stop comparing Seth's situation with T.J.'s own as a kid. Every child deserved to have their mother with them for as long as possible, and although Heather was clearly over the worst of her illness and thought she was ready to go home, he wanted to make sure there was no possibility of a serious complication. If she had her hands full taking care of a kid and a ranch while she continued to recover that would increase the chances of her having a relapse—or worse.

"I'm just trying to keep your momma upright and mobile for you, little guy," T.J. said, smiling back at the child.

The little copper-haired boy on his lap gave him a big grin and patted T.J.'s cheek as he babbled something T.J. didn't understand. He figured Seth was thanking him for taking care of his mother and an unfamiliar tightening filled T.J.'s chest. As kids went, Heather's was awesome. Friendly and well-behaved, Seth was no problem to watch and if he ever had a kid, T.J. wanted one just like him.

He gave Seth a hug. "I'll make sure to see that you're

both taken care of so that you can be together a long time."

He had a sneaking suspicion there was more to his interference than that, but he wasn't going to delve too deeply into his own motivation. He wasn't sure he would be overly comfortable with what he discovered. Hell, he still wasn't comfortable with the fact that he found his nemesis even remotely attractive.

The sudden crack of thunder followed closely by the sound of rain beating hard against the roof caused T.J.'s smile to turn into an outright grin. "It looks like Mother Nature agrees with me about the two of you staying put," he said, drawing a giggle from Seth.

A few minutes later, when Heather walked back into the bedroom after her shower, T.J. noticed she wore the new set of gray sweats Jane Ann had picked out for her. He wouldn't have thought it was possible, but damned if the woman didn't manage to make baggy fleece look good.

His lower body twitched and he had to swallow around the cotton coating his throat. Heather was as prickly as a cactus patch and tried to reject everything he did to help her, but that didn't keep him from wanting to take her in his arms and kiss her senseless.

Unsettled by the wayward thought, he focused on telling her about how the nasty weather would change her plans. "You don't have a choice now. You're going to have to stay here until tomorrow."

Her vivid blue eyes narrowed. "Are you telling me that you won't allow me to leave?"

"Nope. I'm not telling you anything of the sort,"

he said, quickly deciding that he needed to watch the
way he phrased things. He had seen that warning look
in his sisters-in-law's eyes when his brothers made a
verbal blunder and he wasn't fool enough to ignore it.
"I'm just making an observation."

Heather frowned. "Would you care to explain that?"

"Listen." He pointed toward the ceiling and knew
the moment the sound of rain pounding on the roof
registered with her from the defeated expression on
her face. "It's coming down like somebody's pouring
it out of a bucket. With as much rain as we had yesterday, the creek is full and it's a good bet the road is
already starting to flood again."

Groaning, she sank down on the side of the bed. "I
have things I need to do at home."

T.J. shrugged. "The livestock are already taken care
of. I'm sure whatever else there is you need to tend to
will keep until tomorrow."

As soon as the words were out, he could tell he had
pissed her off again. "Do you dismiss what you need
to get done as unimportant?" she asked, spearing him
with her sharp blue gaze.

"It depends," he answered, wondering why she had
taken offense to his comment and why he found her
spitfire temper a little exciting. "If it needs my attention right away, I take care of it."

"Then what makes you think the things I need to get
done are different?" She stood up to fold the clothes
she had worn the day before and stuffed them into the
shopping bag. "You don't have any idea what I have
to do or what might need my immediate attention."

He felt as if he had stepped into a minefield—any way he went could prove explosive. "I didn't mean to imply that your concerns are less important than mine." Suddenly irritated with her short temper, he set her little boy on his feet and watched Seth walk over to his mother, then he rose from the rocking chair. "I just meant that whatever you need to do will have to wait until after the water recedes again. And before this escalates into something that could make the remainder of your stay a pain in my..." Pausing, he looked down at the toddler gazing up at him. He wasn't about to add a word to the kid's vocabulary that she could take him to task over. "Make the remainder of your stay difficult, I think I'll go see what I can rustle up for our supper." Walking out into the hall, he turned back. "I'll be up later to help you and Seth downstairs. And don't even think about trying it on your own. A broken neck won't help you get away from here any faster."

Before she had a chance to tie into him over something else, he closed the door. He descended the stairs and went into the kitchen to see what he could find for them to eat.

"So much for trying to be a nice guy," he muttered as he opened the refrigerator to remove packages of deli meats and condiments. Slamming the food down onto the kitchen island, he turned to get a loaf of bread from the bread box on the counter. "If she fell down the stairs she'd probably find a way to blame me and then sue my ass off."

"Do you need me to help with dinner, Malloy?"

When he turned back, Heather and her son stood

just inside the doorway. Closing his eyes for a moment, T.J. tried to shore up his patience.

"You didn't listen to a dam…dang thing I said, did you?" he asked, opening his eyes to look directly at her. "As weak as you are you shouldn't have tried the stairs on your own. Did you even consider that you or your little boy could have fallen and been seriously hurt?"

"I'm not a hothouse flower. I can do things on my own. I *have* been doing things on my own. Besides, we took it slow and I held on to the railing," she said, shrugging one slender shoulder. "As you can see, Seth and I made it to the bottom without incident."

He shook his head at her stubbornness. "Do me a favor and don't try it on your own again. I'd rather you didn't tempt fate."

"I'll think about it." She was silent for a minute before she asked bluntly, "Why are you being so nice to me and my son? Why do you care what happens to us?"

T.J. stared at her for a moment. He supposed he could understand her wariness. Before last night the only times she had seen him were under less than favorable circumstances. He had been returning her errant stallion—the one who had covered his mares and ruined his breeding program for more than a year—and hadn't really cared to be overly polite.

"I think before we go any further, I need to explain something," he said seriously. "All those times I had to bring your horse back to you, I was angry that he'd covered several of my mares. I raise and train reining horses and having them bred by a rogue stallion set my breeding program back by at least a year." He shook his head. "But I could have been more civil when I asked you to keep him confined, instead of making demands and threatening to get the law involved."

She stared at him for several long moments and just when he thought she was going to reject his apology and explanation, she nodded. "I can understand your frustration and I'm sorry about him causing a delay in your breeding program. I did try to keep him on the Circle W, but I think Magic tries to live up to his name. He can be a regular Houdini when it comes to getting out of his stall or around a fence."

"Some horses are like that," T.J. admitted. "Especially studs when there's a harem of mares waiting for them."

They were both silent for several long seconds before she spoke again. "As long as we're clearing the air, I owe you another apology. You've been very accommodating and I really do appreciate all of your help. Earlier I was frustrated that Seth and I weren't going to be able to go home, but that's no excuse for taking it out on you. I'm sorry."

"I'll accept your apology if you'll accept mine," he said, meaning it. "I should have been more understanding about your horse getting out."

A hint of a smile appeared as she led her little boy over to the opposite side of the kitchen island, where T.J. stood. "And just to put your mind at ease, if I had fallen down the stairs, I wouldn't have sued you, Malloy."

He couldn't help but grin as he opened one of the cabinets above the counter and reached for a couple of sandwich plates. "The name's T.J. and I'm glad I won't have to be calling my lawyer." As he started making their sandwiches, he added, "So what do you say we start over and try being a little more neighborly with each other from now on?"

When he noticed the twinkle in her blue eyes and the dimples on either side of her mouth as she smiled at him, he felt like he'd taken a sucker punch to the gut. He had to have been as blind as a damned bat not to have noticed how pretty she was before.

"I suppose being more congenial is better than wanting to shoot you on sight," she said, oblivious to his thoughts.

T.J. laughed, releasing some of the tension suddenly gripping him. "Yeah, being friendly is preferable to dodging lead." He pointed to the slices of meat and cheese in front of him. "My housekeeper is up in Dallas with her family until after the first of the year and I'm not very good at cooking. I hope you don't mind sandwiches for supper."

"A sandwich is fine for me." She shook her head. "I still don't have much of an appetite anyway. But if you don't mind, I'd like to find something else for Seth. I try to make sure he gets his veggies every day."

"When I sent Dan and his wife to Stephenville, Jane Ann got a few frozen dinners she said were especially for little kids." T.J. nodded toward the refrigerator. "She said they weren't her first choice for feeding toddlers, but they would be better for Seth than some of the things I'd probably try to feed him." He couldn't help but laugh. "I zapped one of them in the microwave for lunch and I can honestly say, he really enjoyed flinging the macaroni and mini meatballs at me."

"He behaves pretty well for being almost two, but he still has his moments," she said, laughing as she and the kid walked over to open the freezer door on the side-by-side refrigerator.

The sound of Heather's laughter caused a warm feeling to spread throughout his chest. He didn't have a clue why, but for some reason it felt good to make her laugh.

T.J. frowned as he finished the sandwiches and set them on the table. He and Heather were little more than strangers and he still wasn't convinced they could be friends. Why did he care one way or the other that he had made her laugh?

He wasn't sure what his problem was, but he decided that some things were better left unexplored. He was already having enough trouble with the fact that Heather and her son hadn't been on the Dusty Diamond a full twenty-four hours and he'd noticed—even when she was at her worst with the flu and wearing a baggy set of sweats—that she was sexy as sin. If that wasn't proof enough that he was one extremely disturbed hombre, he didn't know what was.

"This is a very interesting family room," Heather said when T.J. showed her and Seth around his house after they finished dinner. "But I think this would come closer to qualifying as a man cave than a place where a family gathers."

He chuckled. "That's what I usually call it, but I

thought it might sound a little more inviting if I referred to it as the family room."

One wall of the huge space was dominated by an antique bar that looked as if it had come straight from a saloon in an old Western movie. Made of dark mahogany, the intricate carvings on the front were complemented by the marble inlayed top and the highly polished brass boot rail attached along the bottom a few inches above the floor. A large mirror in an ornate gold frame hung on the wall behind the bar Shelves on both sides were filled with expensive-looking whiskey, rum and tequila bottles. Several feet from the end of the bar an old-fashioned billiard table with hand-tied leather strip pockets stood, waiting for someone to send the racked, brightly colored balls rolling across its green felt top. All that was missing from that side of the room was a saloon girl with rosy red rouge on her cheeks and a come-hither look in her eyes.

"Would you like to watch a movie?" he asked, motioning toward the biggest flat-screen television she had ever seen. It graced the wall at the far end of the room. It wasn't surprising to see that speakers had been hung on the walls surrounding the area, guaranteeing the viewer an audio experience that was sure to make him or her feel as if they were part of the action.

"I've got all the satellite movie channels, as well as pay-per-view," he added. "I'm sure we could find something to watch that you'd like."

The huge, comfortable-looking, brown leather sectional sofa in front of the television looked extremely inviting and Heather was tempted. "Maybe another time," she said, hiding a yawn behind her hand. "I'm afraid I'm still pretty tired and it won't be long before I'll have to get Seth in bed for the night."

"It's understandable that you're tired. You haven't regained all of your strength." When Seth walked past him toward a basket of toys beside the sofa, T.J. grinned. "And before you ask if those are mine, I keep them around for my niece and nephew."

"Do you babysit often?" she asked. He certainly seemed to know more about watching children than most bachelors.

He shook his head. "I don't get to watch them all that much because of the rotation. But once in a while one of my brothers and sisters-in-law will ask me to keep one of them when they want to go catch a movie or have a kid-free dinner."

She frowned. "The rotation?"

"I have five brothers," he said, shrugging. "Three of them are married and unless they all want to go out together, my other two brothers and I have to take turns with Mariah."

"Is she your sister?" Heather asked, wondering what it would be like to have that many siblings.

He shook his head. "She's our sister-in-law's sister."

"What happens when the couples go out together?" she asked.

He grinned. "That's when we bachelors get together and become a babysitting tag team."

"That sounds…effective." Laughing, Heather shook her head. "I still can't get over six boys. Your poor parents. I can only imagine the chaos."

"Actually, they're my foster brothers," he said, smiling. "We met as teenagers and finished growing up together on the Last Chance Ranch."

"Oh, I'm sorry," she said, wondering if growing up a foster child was a painful subject for him.

He shook his head. "Don't apologize. Thanks to our foster father, Hank Calvert, moving to his ranch was the best thing that ever happened to all of us. We've become a real family and there's nothing we wouldn't do for each other."

"That's wonderful," she said, meaning it. She had never known that kind of closeness with her sister. If they had been close, Heather wouldn't have had such a struggle the past couple of years.

They were silent for a moment before he asked, "What about you? Do you have brothers and sisters?"

"I have an older sister," she answered, nodding. "But Stephanie and her husband live in Japan and I haven't seen or heard much from her in several years."

"That must be tough," he said, his tone sympathetic.

"I would like to say that it is," she confessed, feeling a twinge of regret. "But my sister and I never really had anything in common, nor were we ever all that close. I always loved growing up on the Circle W and couldn't imagine moving so far away that I wouldn't be able to come back whenever I wanted to ride my horse. But she couldn't wait to grow up and leave it and our family as far behind as her Prada knockoffs could take her." Heather paused as a wave of emotion swept over her. "She didn't even bother to come home for our father's funeral two years ago."

T.J. put his arm around her shoulders and pulled her to his side in a comforting gesture. "It's never too late, Heather. Maybe one day you and your sister can find some common ground."

His companionable hug not only startled her, but when she glanced up to meet his warm hazel gaze, she could tell it had also surprised him. An awkward silence followed the physical connection and neither of them seemed to know what to say. Deciding to put some distance between them, she took a step away from him and started toward her son to take him upstairs.

"I think I should probably go ahead and get Seth settled down for the night," she said, feeling a little breathless.

"I'll help the two of you get upstairs," T.J. said, lifting her baby so that Seth was sitting on T.J.'s forearm.

"Thank you, but I can make it on my own," she said, holding out her arms to take Seth.

But her little boy had other ideas. Shaking his head, he placed his little arm around T.J.'s neck and smiled at her as if to say she didn't have a choice in the matter. He wanted T.J. to carry him and that was that.

As they walked down the hall and up the stairs, Heather couldn't help but wonder if it might not be wise to get a boat for the next time the road flooded. Under normal conditions, it wouldn't be an issue. She, and her parents before her, had always kept plenty of supplies on hand to get them through whenever the creek flooded. But last night she had no choice but to risk being caught on the wrong side of the creek. Seth needed to see a doctor and a trip to the ER had been her only option. But if she had a boat, she would be able to get them home and not have to rely on the generosity of a man who threw her off-guard and caused her son to turn into a deserter.

Of course, getting a boat to cross the floodwaters would be contingent on them still living on the Circle W. And unless a miracle happened, enabling her to pay the back taxes on the ranch, she was going to lose her home and she and her son would have to live elsewhere.

Just the thought of losing the place her family had owned for several generations was more than she could bear, and she decided to wait until she returned home to consider her options. At the moment, the feel of T.J.'s hand at the small of her back, guiding her as they climbed the steps, was distracting and every bit as disconcerting as him giving her a companionable hug.

Heather wasn't the least bit comfortable with what she was feeling. She already had too many things on her plate to worry about an unwanted attraction to her sexy neighbor.

Her heart skipped several beats. She thought T.J. Malloy was sexy? Dear lord, she needed to get home and regain her perspective.

When they reached the room she and her son were sharing, Heather reached to take Seth from T.J. "Thank you again for all you've done for us."

"I'm just doing what any good neighbor would do," he said, shrugging.

T.J. placed Seth in her arms and as T.J.'s eyes locked with hers, she felt as if she could easily become lost in the compassion she detected in his hazel gaze. But as they continued to stare at each other, the air seemed to fill with a charged tension that she hadn't felt in a very long time—not since her fiancé had been killed in an industrial accident shortly after they discovered she was pregnant with Seth.

As the moment stretched into an awkward silence, she cleared her throat and reached for the doorknob. "I'll, um, see you in the morning."

He continued to stare at her for several seconds before he nodded and reached up to trace his finger down her jawline. "Sleep well, Heather."

His deep baritone saying her name and the feel of his feather-light touch caused her heart to flutter wildly and it took everything she had to stop herself from leaning closer. "G-good night, T.J."

Before she made a complete fool of herself, Heather quickly carried her son into the bedroom and closed the door behind them. Had she lost her mind? She still wasn't entirely certain she could trust the man. Why was she feeling flustered and breathless from staring into his mesmerizing hazel eyes? And why hadn't she protested when he touched her?

She wasn't looking for a man to add one more complication to her already difficult life. She had a child to raise and a ranch to try to hold on to. The last thing she needed was any kind of distraction. And that included a seemingly well-meaning cowboy with a hypnotic gaze and the unsettling ability to remind her she was a woman who hadn't been held by a man in quite some time.

Three

The following afternoon, T.J. stood in his driveway and watched Heather's gray sedan drive down the lane toward the main road. Stuffing his hands in the front pockets of his jeans, he sighed heavily. She was almost completely recovered from having the flu and at this point, he was pretty sure there wasn't any danger of her becoming ill again. So why wasn't he all that happy to see her leave?

He still wasn't sure he even liked her. She seemed to take offense to just about everything he said and trying to get her to accept his help when she clearly needed it was like trying to convince birds not to roost in the trees at night. And although they had established a truce of sorts, it was an uneasy one at best.

After last night, when he hugged her in the family

room, then touched her cheek as they said good-night at her bedroom door, things had turned awkward between them. This morning they had both seemed grateful to have Seth to focus on over breakfast and in the hours before she left to go home. Heather read a book to him that she'd had in the diaper bag and T.J. had gotten down on his hands and knees to give the little guy rides around the man cave. So why did he feel let down that she and her kid were leaving?

But as T.J. stood there gazing at the taillights of her car, he had to be honest with himself. He suspected he knew the reason behind her haste to leave the Dusty Diamond and his reluctance to see her go.

And it had nothing whatsoever to do with her wanting to check on her horses or his concern about her having a setback.

Last night he had seen the same awareness in her expressive blue eyes that he was sure she had seen in his. The slight sway of her body when he touched her cheek told him that she'd felt the magnetic pull between them as strongly as he had.

When he watched her car reach the end of the lane and turn onto the main road, he shook his head at his own foolishness and headed toward the barn. Just because Heather Wilson revved his engine didn't mean a damned thing. She was an extremely attractive, single woman who had been staying with him in close quarters and he was a man who had been neglecting his libido for longer than he cared to admit. Naturally he was going to notice how long her legs were and wonder about how they would feel wrapped around him as he sank himself deep inside of her.

T.J. cussed a blue streak when he felt his body start to tighten. Had he lost his mind? Heather Wilson was the last woman he should be getting all hot and bothered about. She wanted to argue with him over everything and just trying to use good manners around her proved to be a powerful struggle. Hell, he didn't really know the woman beyond the fact that she lived on the ranch next to his, she had a horse that was an escape artist and her little boy was cute as a button.

"Hey, boss? You got a minute?"

When T.J. looked up, one of his men was walking toward him from the far end of the barn.

"Sure," he answered, thankful that the sandy-haired cowboy had interrupted his train of thought. "What's on your mind, Tommy Lee?"

"Didn't you tell me Ms. Wilson's men had the weekend off?" the man asked as he strolled up to him.

T.J. nodded. "They should be back on Monday. Why?"

"I don't know if this means anything," the man said. "But earlier, when I was over at the Wilson place feeding the horses, I noticed something that didn't seem quite right."

"What's that?" T.J. queried, frowning. "When I sent Harry over there yesterday, he didn't mention seeing anything out of the ordinary. What did you see that he didn't?"

"I probably wouldn't have noticed myself, but last night when it stormed the wind blew kind of hard and must have blown Ms. Wilson's bunkhouse door open. When I went to pull it shut, I got a look inside." Tommy Lee shook his head. "There weren't any signs of it being lived in and it didn't look like it had been used in quite a while. Everything was real dusty and it had that stale smell like when a place is closed up for a long time."

T.J. frowned. Heather's men might live elsewhere, but that was unlikely. The area was comprised of large ranches and since a working cowboy's day started well before dawn, it was a matter of convenience for the men to live on the outfit where they worked, or at least nearby. Even T.J.'s foreman, Dan, and his family lived in one of the two small houses T.J. had built on the property when he bought the Dusty Diamond, in anticipation of some of the men he hired being married.

"Anyway, I just thought I'd let you know," Tommy Lee continued, shrugging.

"Thanks for passing along the information," T.J. answered. "I appreciate it, Tommy Lee."

"Do you want me to go over there again tomorrow mornin' to do the feedin'?" the man asked as he started back toward the end of the barn where he had been repairing a stall door.

"No, I'll go over there first thing in the morning to take care of her horses and check things out for myself," T.J. said as he entered the tack room.

He knew he should probably let one of his men take care of going over to Heather's tomorrow. It was really none of his business about her men and he was certain she would tell him as much. But he wanted to check on her and Seth anyway and he refused to delve too deeply into the reasons why.

Taking one of the lead ropes hanging on a hook on the wall, he couldn't stop thinking about what he had just learned. As he walked to one of the stalls to get the sorrel gelding he'd been training he wondered why Heather had let on like she had given her men the weekend off if she didn't have anyone working for her. Did that mean she was trying to run the Circle W by herself? With a kid and a case of the flu?

He led the horse back to the tack room to saddle him. T.J. wasn't sure what the deal was with Heather Wilson. But he had every intention of finding out.

If, as he suspected, she was trying to run her ranch on her own—without *any* help—it would explain a lot.

Whenever her stallion had gotten onto his property, he'd wondered why she hadn't immediately instructed her men to make the needed repairs to the fence to keep it from happening again. It was not only the mark of a good rancher to keep his fences in decent condition, but it was also the neighborly thing to do to keep your animals from being a nuisance. But if there was no one working for her, there wasn't any way Heather could have mended her fences with a baby in her arms.

The guilt he had experienced after she explained that she had tried to keep the stallion confined increased tenfold. She had either been too stubborn or too proud to explain things and ask for his help. From being around her the past couple of days, he suspected it was a combination of both.

Shaking his head at her obstinacy, he finished saddling the gelding. Just as he secured the cinch his cell phone rang. "What's up, Nate?" he asked when he recognized his brother's number on the caller ID.

"When we got to talking about my new place the other night, I forgot to ask what you want me to bring to the New Year's Eve party." Nate paused a moment before adding, "And keep in mind that I don't know beans from buckshot about cooking so it will have to be something I can buy that's already prepared."

"Don't worry about it," T.J. answered. "Taylor volunteered herself and Bria to handle the food." Taylor had been a personal chef before she married Lane and the woman was as passionate about food as she was about their brother—and Bria was the best home cook in central Texas.

"You know we really lucked out in the sisters-in-law department," Nate commented. "Bria and Taylor are the best cooks in the whole damned state and Summer loves to plan all the other details for our get-togethers. We don't have to do a thing but show up."

T.J. chuckled. "Like you'd do anything even if they didn't."

"Hey, like I told you. I could buy food that's already cooked to bring to the parties," Nate answered, sounding quite pleased with himself about that contribution.

"What are you going to do when you move to Twin Oaks Ranch?" T.J. asked, laughing. "You'll eventually get tired of slapping a piece of meat between two slices of bread or zapping something in the microwave."

"I'll do the same as you, smart-ass," Nate retorted. "I'll hire a housekeeper who cooks."

"Touché, Romeo." T.J. laughed out loud. "I didn't think you'd made any plans past fixing up your ranch house into a pleasure palace." He couldn't help but grin. "Maybe you're finally starting to grow up."

"Nah." Nate laughed. "Then I'd be too much like your sorry hide."

"What's wrong with that?" T.J. asked, going along with his brother's good-natured ribbing.

"If I was like you, I'd strike out every time I tried to talk to a woman." Nate grunted. "You know as much about women as I know about cooking."

"Oh, really?" T.J. knew better, but asked anyway. "What makes you say that?"

"Take your neighbor lady for example. Instead of showing her your ornery side when you took her horse back to her, you should have turned on the charm," Nate said as if he was an expert on the subject of the fairer sex. "You should have smiled and had a friendly little chat with her about something like the weather or that new steakhouse up in Stephenville—anything other than the real reason you were there. By the time you got around to leaving, I'm betting she'd have offered to have her hired hands fix that fence without you even having to bring up the subject. You would have gotten what you wanted and she'd have thought it was her idea to take care of it for you."

T.J.'s good humor suddenly drained away like water running through a sieve. Heather and his run-ins with her had been a touchy subject with him before, but after getting to know her a little better over the past couple of days and learning that she might be trying to run the

Circle W without any kind of help, he felt too guilty to discuss the matter with anyone, and especially not with his skirt-chasing brother.

Of course, Nate had no way of knowing any of the details about the past forty-eight hours and T.J. had no intention of enlightening him. But Nate's comments were hitting a little too close to what T.J. had already figured out for himself—he'd been a prized jackass in his handling of the situation.

Deciding it was definitely time for a change in the direction of their conversation, he knew exactly what to say to distract Nate. "So how's that kind of thinking working out for you with that little blonde over in Waco?" T.J. asked.

She was the only woman Nate had ever returned to after moving on to other conquests, and their on-again, off-again relationship had the entire family speculating if she was the one who would finally cure Nate of his wild ways.

There was a long pause and T.J. wasn't sure his brother hadn't hung up on him.

"Jessica and I aren't seeing each other anymore," Nate finally said, sounding a little less sure of himself.

"Again? Want to talk about it?" T.J. asked.

"There's nothing much to say," Nate said, his tone quiet. "She wants one thing and I want another."

They were both silent for several long moments before T.J. offered, "You know any one of us will listen if you change your mind."

"Hey, you know me. I'm just fine." Nate's laughter sounded a bit forced. "I like keeping my options open."

They talked a few more minutes before ending the call, then T.J. clipped his cell phone to his belt and led the sorrel gelding from the barn into the adjoining indoor arena. Mounting the horse, he used the reins to guide it into the series of moves that would be expected of the animal and its rider during competition. But as the horse executed the patterns flawlessly, T.J.'s mind was on other things.

Nate clearly wasn't as good with women as he let on, not if the blonde was breaking things off between them. Unfortunately, there wasn't anything T.J. could do about his brother's situation. But there was, however, something he could do about the situation with Heather and her son.

First thing tomorrow morning, he fully intended to go over to the Circle W and assess the situation for himself. If it turned out that she was indeed on her own over there, as he strongly suspected, she could talk until she was blue in the face but he wasn't going to take no for an answer.

He was going to help Heather. And in the bargain, assuage his conscience for being such a jerk about her horse.

Heather yawned and finished putting Seth's coat and hat on him, then lifted him into the strap-on baby carrier she was wearing.

"As soon as we feed the horses and muck out the stalls, you can take a nap while I see if I can find a few extra dollars in the budget to fix the roof over the utility room."

In answer, her son smiled at her and sleepily laid his head against her breast. While she fed the horses and mucked out stalls, Seth would doze on and off and babble to her about the horses, which he loved. Then he'd sleep for another half hour or so after they returned to the house. It wasn't easy working with a toddler strapped to her chest and the chores took almost twice the amount of time that they would have taken otherwise, but after almost a year and a half of having to do it this way, she and Seth were both used to the routine.

As she left the house, Heather noticed a pickup truck with the Dusty Diamond logo painted on the side parked beside her ancient Toyota. Why wasn't she surprised that T.J. had again sent one of his men over to take care of the chores? She'd never met a man more determined to have his way. He had decided that she didn't need to be out doing the chores and he was doing everything he could to make sure she wasn't.

But when she started across the yard, she looked up to find that it was T.J. himself standing in the barn's wide doorway. Her heart skipped a beat. As much as she would like to ignore her reaction, just the sight of the man caused her to catch her breath. Leaning one shoulder against the door, he had his arms folded across his broad chest and his long blue-jean-clad legs crossed casually at the ankles. But his wide-brimmed, black hat was pulled down low on his forehead and he wore the same dark scowl that she had seen each time he'd brought her stallion back.

A twinge of disappointment ran through her. Just

when she had started to think he really was one of the good guys, he had apparently returned to being the disapproving, judgmental neighbor.

"What are you doing here, Malloy?" she asked, aggravated with herself for giving his rugged good looks and the return of his ornery disposition a second thought.

"I came to take care of your horses and check to see if you and Seth are all right," he said, his tone flat.

"As you can see we're both doing fine and I'm perfectly capable of taking care of my own horses," she answered, stopping in front of him. "Now if you'll excuse me, I need to get that done."

Uncrossing his big booted feet, he straightened, blocking her entry into the barn. "I've already fed them and after I turned them out into the pasture for some exercise, I mucked out the stalls and put down fresh straw. They're already back in their stalls and should be good until tomorrow."

"How long have you been here?" she asked, disturbed by the fact that he had been on the property for at least a couple of hours without her realizing he was even there.

What if he'd been someone else? Someone who was up to no good? A thief would have been able to take anything he wanted and she would have been none the wiser. Or worse yet, someone could have broken into the house before she'd had the chance to retrieve her father's old shotgun that hung above the fireplace mantel in the living room.

Not that retrieving the shotgun would have done

a lot of good. It had a broken trigger and hadn't been capable of firing in more than twenty years. Not to mention the fact that she wasn't even sure how to load it. But just the sight of the gun might be enough to intimidate someone into leaving her and her son alone.

"I got here around dawn and it was long enough to know that you haven't been completely honest with me, Heather." He nodded toward the house. "It's still pretty damp and chilly. Why don't we go inside? We can talk there."

"There's nothing to discuss," Heather said, standing her ground. "I haven't been dishonest with you."

At least, technically she hadn't been. She'd just omitted a few facts.

His frown darkened and a muscle twitched along his lean jaw when it started to rain. "*Please* could we go inside the house to talk before we all get drenched? That wouldn't be good for you or Seth."

"I really need to take inventory of my supplies," she hedged. "I'll be going into town to the feed store tomorrow and I want to make sure I get everything."

She could tell from his determined expression that T.J. wasn't going to give up.

"You need oats, hay and straw," he said, placing his arm around her shoulders to turn her and Seth back toward the house. "But I think you already knew that."

Heather didn't protest further as they crossed the yard and entered the house. For one thing, she needed to get her son out of the weather. And for another, she was too distracted by the comforting feel of T.J.'s arm holding her close to his side.

She knew he was only trying to shield her and Seth from the rain, but that did little to lessen the effect his nearness was having on her. His clean masculine scent, combined with the rich smell of leather and the heat from his body, seemed to warm her all the way to her soul.

"Let me hold him while you take off your coat," T.J. said as they entered the house. Shrugging out of his leather jacket, he draped it over one of the kitchen chairs as she unfastened the sides of the toddler carrier. He smiled as he turned to lift her son. "Hey there, little guy. Did you miss me?"

Seth jabbered a sleepy greeting before laying his head on T.J.'s shoulder.

While she hung her jacket in the laundry room to dry, T.J. took off Seth's hat and coat. When she returned to the kitchen her chest tightened at the sight of T.J. swaying back and forth with her son snuggled against his broad chest. How many times over the past two years had she regretted that Seth and her late fiancé had been cheated out of a father-and-son relationship?

Heather frowned. She would have expected to resent any man except her fiancé having that special time with her son. But she didn't. She found it endearing and that bothered her.

Of all the men to be tender and caring with her son, she would have never expected it from T. J. Malloy, nor was she sure she was comfortable with it. She didn't want to see Seth start to care for T.J. and then be disappointed or hurt when the man lost interest in them.

"He's asleep," T.J. said quietly. "Where do you want me to lay him down?"

She showed T.J. down the hall to Seth's small bedroom. He got Seth settled in his bed and she and T.J. walked back into the kitchen before Heather spoke. "I assume by now you've figured out that I'm operating the Circle W on a shoestring," she said, resigned to the fact that T.J. wasn't going to leave without an explanation.

Nodding, he pulled out a chair at the round oak table, sat down and causally rested the ankle of one leg on the knee of the other as if he didn't have a care in the world. "How long have you been trying to run things without help?"

She sighed. At this point, there was no sense in being evasive. He'd been in the barn and she was certain he'd observed how many repairs needed to be made, as well as how little she kept on hand in the way of supplies. He probably even knew that the bunk house hadn't seen a hired hand in more than a year.

"After my father died, I managed to keep the two men who worked for him until Seth was about four months old."

"So the better part of two years," he said, frowning.

"Yes."

"Why didn't you tell me you were alone over here with a baby whenever I brought your horse back?" he demanded.

"The first time you had to bring Magic back, I wasn't even home," she answered defensively. "You put him in the corral and left a note fastened to the gate, asking me to keep him off your land."

"You could have told me one of the other times when you were at home," he said pointedly. "I would have been more understanding if you had. I could have helped you."

"Oh, give me a break, Malloy." She shook her head. "You were too angry to listen even if I had tried to explain." Suddenly irritated by his tone and the accusatory expression on his handsome face, she added, "Besides, it wasn't any of your business then and to tell you the truth, it's none of your concern now."

"I would have helped you out," he repeated, apparently choosing to ignore the warning in her voice. "I could have at least had my men take care of repairing your fences for you."

"I'm not a charity case." Her anger grew with each passing second when she detected the sympathy in his hazel gaze. She didn't want anyone feeling sorry for her or thinking that she was incapable of doing things herself. And especially not T. J. Malloy. She wasn't sure why, but she couldn't stand him thinking that she was a helpless wimp. "And I certainly don't need or want your pity."

"I never said you were a charity case," he said gently as he rose to his feet. The tone of his voice caused an unfamiliar softening deep inside of her. "But there's nothing wrong with neighbors helping each other out. It doesn't mean that I feel sorry for you. I'm just trying to do what I feel is right."

"You've performed your neighborly duty for the

past few days," she said, her heart skipping a beat as he approached. "And I really appreciate your assistance, but…"

Her voice trailed off as he stopped within inches of her. Tipping up her chin with his index finger, he lifted her head until their gazes met. "Heather, I'm really sorry for being a jerk about your horse. But honestly, I'm not an unreasonable man. I swear I would have listened and understood if you'd only explained the situation."

His deep voice had a soothing effect on her and when he put his arms loosely around her waist and leaned forward, she couldn't have stopped him if her life depended on it. Brushing her lips with his, the kiss was soft and brief, and wasn't meant to excite. Unfortunately, she found the caress to be one of the sexiest she could ever remember and she responded by swaying closer to him.

As his mouth settled over hers, his arms tightened around her. Heather tried to remind herself why allowing T.J. to kiss her wasn't a good idea. But as he traced her lips with his tongue, her eyes drifted shut and she couldn't think of one single reason to call a halt to the caress.

Without a thought to what she was doing, she raised her arms to his shoulders and tangled her fingers in the soft brown curls at the nape of his neck. Her heart sped up when he coaxed her mouth to open for him. Slipping his tongue inside, he deepened the kiss. As he explored her with tender care, a warmth she hadn't felt in a very long time began to flow through every part of her. Her knees felt as if they would give way as he lightly stroked her inner recesses.

The sudden sound of thunder rumbling, followed closely by rain pounding on the roof in what could only be described as another Texas gully washer, helped to clear the haze from her obviously foggy brain. She pushed away from him as her senses returned.

"I'm sorry," he said, releasing her immediately. "I was out of line."

"No. I mean, yes." She shook her head as she tried to gather her thoughts. She hurried into the laundry room to escape. "There's something I have to do."

Finding the buckets she used when it rained, she placed one under the drip coming from the ceiling between the clothes dryer and the water heater. When she turned around, T.J. was standing in the doorway, watching her.

"A leaky roof was one of the reasons you were so anxious to leave the Dusty Diamond, wasn't it?" he asked. "You needed to make sure the buckets didn't overflow."

She nodded as she placed another one of the pails next to the furnace. "I haven't had time to make the repairs."

"When did it start leaking?" he asked, his gaze holding hers as she straightened and turned to face him.

"This past summer." She shrugged. "One of the really severe storms blew off several shingles and I haven't had the opportunity to replace them."

"That was in the spring," he said, folding his arms across his broad chest.

His stance and the tone of his voice were unmistakably disapproving and it not only erased any lingering traces of warmth she felt from his kiss, but it also reignited her anger. It was easy for him to pass judgment. He wasn't the one struggling to make ends meet while trying to raise a child alone and find the extra funds needed for the innumerable things around the Circle W in need of repair or replacement. Nor was he the one who would seem vulnerable if he reached out for help.

"Thank you for stopping by to take care of my horses, but you won't have to bother with helping me again," she said, brushing past him as she walked into the kitchen to retrieve his jacket. She handed it to him and moved to the back door. "I'm sure you have more important things to do with your time than to take me to task over things that are absolutely none of your business."

T.J. stared at her for a moment as if he wanted to argue the point. Then he pulled on his coat. "If you need help with anything don't hesitate to give me a call."

"I'll keep that in mind," she said as she opened the door. "But don't worry about us. Seth and I will be just fine."

T.J. had no sooner cleared the entrance than the door was forcefully shut behind him. Hearing the distinct sound of the dead bolt being set, he shook his head.

"So much for being a good neighbor," he muttered as he pulled his hat down low to shield his face from the rain and jogged the short distance to his truck.

She was pissed off again and unless he missed his guess, it was more a matter of her stinging pride than anything he had said. It was crystal clear she needed help—both with the work around the ranch and repairs to the house. But if there was one thing he had learned in the past several days, Heather Wilson was way too proud for her own good.

Why did she feel the need to prove herself? Why was she scared to death that someone would see her situation and look down on her for having such a struggle?

And he had no doubt that she was having a tough time of things. Although the horses were well taken care of, the amount of supplies she had told him better than anything else that she was hurting financially. Most ranchers tried to keep enough feed and bedding on hand to last for a couple of weeks, at the very least. Heather barely had enough for the next couple of days. And if her flimsy excuse about needing to take inventory of her supplies hadn't been enough to convince him of how embarrassed she was by her circumstances, the heightened color on her cheeks as she tried to explain about her leaking roof was.

Cursing the woman's stubborn pride, he started the truck and drove down the lane to the main road, turning toward the Dusty Diamond. If she would let him, he could make things a hell of a lot easier for her. But he had a feeling they would be passing out ice water in hell before that happened.

As he stared out the windshield he had to concentrate hard on the road ahead. The wipers were on the fastest setting, but couldn't keep up with the amount of rain falling. He suddenly brought the truck to a stop and uttered a string of cuss words that would have raised a sailor's eyebrows. He had been so distracted by Heather and what he'd observed of her ranch that he had forgotten all about the swollen creek and the inevitable flooding. Fortunately, the water always receded quickly once it stopped raining, but it didn't appear that the rain was going to ease up anytime soon.

Staring through the sheets of water running down the windshield, T.J. decided he only had two options. He could either sit in his truck in the middle of the road for what could turn out to be the rest of the day and night or he could turn it around and go back to the Circle W.

Given the choices, there was really only one thing he could do. Heather wasn't going to be overly happy about it—and for that matter neither was he—but there wasn't any way around it. He was going to have to stay at her place until the road cleared.

A few minutes later, he parked the truck in front of her house, got out and jogged across the yard. He took the back porch steps two at a time. Drawing in a deep breath, he raised his arm to knock.

"The road is flooded out," he said when Heather opened the door.

She stared past him at the heavy rain just beyond the porch, then, sighing audibly, she stepped back for him to enter the house.

"I'll set another place for lunch," she said, sounding resigned. "You're going to be here a while."

Four

After an uncomfortably silent lunch with her unexpected guest, Heather was glad when T.J. took Seth into the living room to play while she washed the dishes and cleaned up the kitchen. She needed the distance between them to figure out why she seemed to lose all common sense whenever she was around him.

Normally, she was a very even-tempered, rational woman. Maybe she had a little more pride than was good for her and she was pretty stubborn about some things, but she didn't know anyone who didn't have a few flaws. But there was nothing about her behavior when she was near T.J. that made a bit of sense. He seemed to have the ability to anger her beyond words one minute, then turn around and have her melting into his arms without a thought about why she shouldn't, the next.

But as she thought about her irritation with him earlier this morning, she had to admit to herself that part of the problem was her overwhelming embarrassment about her situation. It was humiliating to let anyone see how run-down the Circle W had become in the two and a half years since her father had passed away. Especially a man like T.J., who had family and more money to spare than most people saw in their entire lives. At one time the ranch had been one of the finest in the county, raising registered quarter horses for competition in the pleasure class at horse shows, as well as supplying a couple of dude ranches over in New Mexico with horses for their trail rides. But now? Seeing the Circle W through the eyes of a stranger, she was certain that it just looked shabby and sad.

When her father had been alive and well, he had at least half a dozen hired hands working for him, close to a hundred horses grazing in the pastures and the barns and outbuildings had been painted a striking red with white trim. The board fences and house had always been kept a pristine white, the trees and shrubs were always neatly trimmed and everything was in excellent repair. But in the years following his death, Heather hadn't had the time or the money to keep up with everything. The roof leaked, fences needed mending, paint was peeling and the trees and shrubs were overgrown and shapeless.

Her breath caught on a sob as she thought about the assurance she had given her dying father as he lay sick in the hospital with end-stage cancer. He had begged her to hang on to the ranch that had been in his family for over a hundred and fifty years and she had given him her word that she would. But that promise was quickly becoming one she was finding almost impossible to keep.

That hurt more than anything else. Not being able to honor his last wish was going to be one of the biggest disappointments of her life.

She and her father had always been extremely close. He had been her best friend and taught her everything she knew about ranching. She often thought that closeness had played a part in why there was an emotional distance between her and her sister.

Stephanie was actually her half sister—her mother's daughter from a previous marriage. From what Heather had learned over the years, her father had doted on Stephanie until Heather was born. After that, he didn't seem to have as much time for his stepdaughter and Stephanie clearly resented Heather for that.

"Heather, do you need help?" T.J. asked, from behind her.

"No, I just finished up in here," she said, shaking her head.

She had been so lost in her disturbing thoughts that she hadn't noticed his approach. But she noticed it now. He was so close, she could feel the delightful heat from his body. A shiver of awareness coursed through her and, making sure she kept her back to him, she quickly swiped away the moisture that had gathered in her eyes before she turned to face him.

"Where's Seth?"

"In his bed." T.J. laughed. "I think I wore him out. We played for quite a while with a little barn that mooed every time the door was opened. Then he yawned a couple of times, crawled up in my lap and went to sleep."

"Thank you for watching him while I got things cleared away from lunch," she said as she turned to start the coffeemaker. "It isn't always easy trying to get things done while watching him, too."

T.J. smiled. "Seth's a great little kid. I enjoy spending time with him."

Heather took a deep breath and released the last of her lingering anger. It wasn't T.J.'s fault her ranch was so run-down and it was past time that she stopped taking her frustration out on him.

"It's still raining and it looks like you'll be here awhile." She reached in the cabinet for two mugs. "Would you like some coffee?"

"Sure." He was silent for several long moments before he commented, "We've had more rain in the past couple of days than I can ever remember at this time of year."

"It has been unusual," she agreed, walking over to set a mug of coffee in front of him.

As they stared at each other she was reminded of how comforting it was to have another adult to talk to. She had been so busy taking care of Seth and the ranch, she hadn't had time to think about how truly alone she had been.

The moment stretched into awkwardness and she

knew of only one way to ease the tension. When she lowered herself onto the chair across from him, they stared silently at each other a few seconds longer before she finally took a deep breath. "I'm sorry for the way I reacted earlier today when I discovered you fed the horses and then later when you asked me about the leaking roof."

He eyed her over the rim of the raised coffee cup in his hand before he responded. "I just wanted to help." Shaking his head, he added, "But like you said, what you do on your ranch really isn't any of my business."

"That isn't an excuse for my being hostile toward you," she said, feeling worse about her behavior by the minute. He had done nothing but try to help her and she'd been nothing but ungrateful. Of course, she had been sick and thoroughly worn-out. But she suspected it had more to do with not being used to confiding in anyone for longer than she cared to remember.

Sighing, she admitted, "I was…embarrassed."

Setting his mug on the table, he nodded. "I thought that might be the case. But I swear, I wasn't being judgmental when I asked how long the roof had been leaking."

"The Circle W hasn't always looked like this or been in this bad of shape," she said, staring at the hot, black liquid in the cup in front of her. "It used to be the nicest horse ranch in the county." She took a deep breath to chase away the sense of regret that always came over her when she thought about how things used to be, and what she'd lost. "It's just been hard for me to keep up with everything the past couple of years."

"Since you had Seth?" he mused.

"The money problems actually started a few months before that—when my father passed away," she admitted. She wasn't certain why it was important to her that T.J. understand her circumstances. It just was. "Insurance took care of most of Dad's treatment, but it didn't cover everything." Holding her coffee mug with both hands in an attempt to stop them from trembling, she added, "After I used what money my dad had in savings to pay off the medical bills, I managed to keep the only two men left who worked for him until after I had Seth. Once he was old enough to stay in a baby carrier, so I could take him with me to do the chores, I had to let the men go."

Raising her gaze to meet his, her chest tightened at the compassion she saw in his eyes.

"That's when your stallion started getting out to come over to my place?" he asked.

She nodded. "Between trying to take care of a baby and run the whole ranch by myself, I didn't have the time to repair the fences and there was no one to help me do it."

"So you've been here by yourself for a year and a half?" T.J. frowned. "What about Seth's daddy? Couldn't he have helped you?"

"Seth's father was killed in an industrial accident shortly after we found out I was pregnant," she said, shaking her head.

"I'm sorry, Heather."

Her chest tightened with emotion at the sincerity

in his voice. It felt good to finally be able to talk to someone about it.

"Thank you, T.J." She swallowed around the lump clogging her throat. "I won't pretend that it wasn't one of the toughest times of my life—losing my fiancé and my father within a few months of each other—but I got through it. I have a beautiful son and although we don't have much of a family left, we have each other."

They were silent for a few moments before he spoke again. "I know it's none of my business, but how have you been making ends meet?"

She paused for a moment. The concern she detected and the gentle tone of his voice made her feel that he actually did care. The feeling was unexpected and coupled with how attractive she found him, it could prove to be a disastrous combination for her.

Maybe telling him a little more about her situation would help to cool some of those feelings. She shrugged. "I get a small check each month from an annuity my fiancé set up shortly before he was killed and although I don't like it, when I have to, I sell one of the brood mares."

He looked taken aback. "I didn't realize—"

"You're not the only one with a breeding program," she interrupted, smiling. "Magic Dancer is an American Quarter Horse Association world-champion pleasure horse and before my dad retired him from competition, that stallion won in several different age classes." She rose to refill their coffee cups. "Quite a few of his colts have won world championships in their classes and even my brood mares come from champion bloodlines."

"In other words, your stallion didn't spoil my mares, he may have improved my program." T.J. frowned as he sat forward. "I knew his confirmation was outstanding, but I didn't realize he was a registered quarter horse. Why didn't you tell me that instead of letting me rant about keeping him on your property and how he had spoiled my mares?"

Heather laughed as she set his refilled cup on the table. "If you had stopped to take a breath when you were reading me the riot act, I might have."

When she started to return to the opposite side of the table T.J. caught her hand in his. "Why don't we start over and forget about what's happened before I found you and Seth stranded on my side of the creek?" he asked as he pulled her down to sit on his lap.

Instead of her confessions pushing him away, he seemed even more eager to explore this attraction between them.

Unsure of what he was up to, Heather merely nodded as she stared into his incredible hazel eyes. A deep forest green with a halo of brown around the pupils, they seemed to have a hypnotic effect on her. She couldn't work up so much as a hint of a protest.

"Wh-why not make the fresh start now instead of three days ago?" she asked when she finally found her voice.

His slow smile sent her pulse racing and caused a flutter deep in the pit of her stomach. "If we did that, I would be obligated to forget how cute you looked wearing my flannel shirt and how long and shapely your legs are." With one arm around her waist, he held her securely against him as he reached up to cup her cheek with his other hand. "That's something that I just can't do." His eyes darkened. "And as long as we're clearing the air, I have my own confession to make." —

Her heart skipped a beat. "What would that be, T.J.?"

"I may have been out of line when I kissed you, but I don't regret it one damned bit," he said, his tone low and intimate. "In fact, I'd really like to kiss you again."

"That probably wouldn't be…a good idea," she said, finding it hard to draw in enough air.

"Why not, Heather?" he asked as he slowly stroked her cheek with the pad of his thumb.

She was sure there were some very good reasons why kissing him again would be unwise. At the moment she couldn't think of a single one. His touch was making her feel warm all over, and her ability to think rationally was all but impossible.

"Did you like when I kissed you earlier?" he persisted.

Heaven help her, but she couldn't have lied to him if she had tried. "Yes. I liked it very much."

"Then why don't I go ahead and kiss you now?" he asked, his smile so darned sexy she was certain he could charm the birds right out of the trees. "We can discuss why it wasn't a good idea later."

Before she had a chance to respond, his firm lips settled over hers. Closing her eyes, Heather gave up trying to remember why she should call a halt to the caress. As he traced the seam of her mouth with his tongue, it suddenly didn't matter anymore. The mingled scents of expensive leather and warm, virile male surrounded her and she opened for him, her body asking him to deepen the kiss, and she didn't give her submission a second thought.

Exploring her with soft gentle strokes of his tongue, he sent heat flowing through her body as he slid his hand from her cheek down to her collarbone. But when he continued down the slope of her breast to cup her fullness with his large palm, he created a longing deep within her that she had almost forgotten existed. She knew without a doubt that she could easily lose herself in the feelings T.J. was creating.

The hardness of his building arousal against her hip should have been enough warning to bring her to her senses, but his desire only heightened the need swirling deep inside of her. As more ribbons of heat threaded their way throughout her entire body, Heather remembered that it had been over two and a half years since she'd experienced even the slightest stirrings of passion. She had been so busy being a caregiver, a single mother and the owner and manager of a ranch in deep financial crisis that she had forgotten what it felt like to be a woman in the arms of a man who desired her.

A tiny moan escaped her when T.J. slowly slid his hand down her side to her hip, then to her knee and back up along the inside of her thigh. Even through her jeans his touch caused her to tingle all over. Unable to sit still, she moved her own hands to unfasten the first few snaps on his chambray shirt. When she rested her palms on his bare chest, the feel of his hard muscles and the steady beating of his heart caused a yearning inside of her that robbed her of breath.

As he eased away from the kiss, T.J. nibbled his way along her jaw to whisper in her ear, "I think I'm going to go out to the barn for a little while, sweetheart."

His warm breath sent goose bumps shimmering over her skin, and Heather blinked as her hazy brain tried to grasp what he had said. "B-but you've already taken care of the horses. There really isn't anything left to do out there until tomorrow."

His low chuckle caused a delicious shiver to slide up her spine as he set her on her feet then rose from the chair only to pull her back into his arms.

"Yes, but if I don't go somewhere to cool off for a while, one of two things is going to happen right now. We'll either end up doing something you're not ready for or I'll end up losing my sanity." He kissed the tip of her nose. "I'll be back in time to babysit Seth while you make supper."

As she watched T.J. step back to fasten the snaps on his shirt, then shrug into his jacket and leave the house, Heather swallowed hard. Although need still ran through her veins, she had to thank the stars above that he'd had the presence of mind to end the kiss.

What had she been thinking? Getting involved with T. J. Malloy—or any other man—at this point in her life would be insane. She had a ranch she was trying to hold on to. She had her son's welfare to think about and the last thing she needed was to add to her stress by entering into any kind of emotional or physical involvement.

Of course, she could be overreacting to the situation. Just because there was an undeniable chemistry drawing them together didn't mean anything. All most men needed to become aroused was a warm, willing woman.

Her cheeks heated as she thought about her reaction to him. She certainly hadn't shown even the slightest bit of reluctance. He probably thought she was an easy conquest. Or worse yet, desperate for the attention of a man.

Shaking her head at her behavior, she put their coffee cups in the sink and walked down the hall to check on her son. T.J. was most likely only looking for a good time, and although she hadn't exactly shown him differently, she wasn't a no-strings kind of woman. She had a little boy who was counting on her to protect him—from homelessness *and* from men with no intention of getting serious about a family—and that was exactly what she intended to do.

As she looked in on Seth, she made a silent vow to be stronger and wiser than she'd been before. She wasn't going to allow T.J. to get too close and risk her son becoming too attached to him only to have T.J. move on when he'd had his fill of her. Her suffering the disappointment of being rejected by a man was one thing, but she'd walk through fire before she allowed it to happen to her son.

* * *

"Do 'gain," Seth said, laughing.

"Again?" T.J. let loose with an exaggerated groan. "Wouldn't you rather play with the barn that moos when you open the door?"

"No," the toddler said, giggling happily. "Wide hossy."

He knew that when he gave Seth another ride around the living room perched atop his back, the little boy would want more. But the kid seemed to enjoy listening to T.J. groan about it and Seth thought it was extremely funny when T.J. gave in. Knowing the toddler was having fun was all it took to keep T.J. on his hands and knees and crawling around on the floor.

"The two of you seem to be getting along pretty well in here," Heather commented as she walked into the living room from the kitchen.

"Hossy," Seth said, patting T.J. on the back of the head.

Nodding, she looked from T.J. to Seth. "He's a great horsey, but it's time for you to have a bath, little man, and get ready for bed."

"No," Seth insisted. "Wide hossy."

"Seth." There was a warning in Heather's voice that T.J. new wouldn't be wise for either him or Seth to ignore.

"Would it be all right for me to give him one last ride?" T.J. asked, mindful that it was Heather's call. He didn't want to disappoint the kid, but he didn't want to piss off the boy's mother by interfering with her parenting, either.

"Pease?" Seth begged from T.J.'s back.

"Please?" T.J. echoed, grinning.

"Ganging up on me is not fair," she warned. "But all right. One more ride then it's time for your bath and bed, Seth."

"Otay," Seth said happily as he tugged on the back of T.J.'s shirt. "Go hossy."

Groaning, T.J. got the giggle out of Seth he was looking for and made another trip around the living room, stopping in front of Heather.

"Okay, partner," T.J. said, straightening when she lifted the little boy from his back. "Time for you to take a bath and me to chill out for a little while in front of the TV."

"I'll be back in few minutes," she said, carrying Seth down the hall.

While Heather gave her son a bath and got him ready for bed, T.J. sat down on the couch and used the remote to turn on the television. He really wasn't interested in watching a show, but when Heather returned a distraction might help ease the awkwardness that had developed between them since he'd left the house to go out to the barn earlier that afternoon.

When he'd fed her horses that morning, he had noticed several stalls in need of repair. So, this afternoon, when he'd had enough adrenaline flowing through his veins to bench-press a dump truck, he'd hammered nails into every loose board he could find. By the time he returned to the house an hour or so later, Heather hadn't had a lot to say to him and he was pretty sure he knew why.

He was willing to bet everything he had that while he'd been trying to expend his pent-up energy, she had been thinking about the chemistry between them and how fast it had threatened to flare out of control. He'd seen the heat in her eyes after that kiss and, knowing the way women had of stewing on things, she had probably talked herself out of letting it happen again.

He frowned. He'd realized there was a mutual attraction between them when she'd first stepped out of her car the night she and Seth stayed at his place. Hell, he would have to be nine kinds of a fool not to have noticed the spark. But he hadn't anticipated the pull to be so intense and he knew beyond a shadow of doubt that Heather hadn't, either. Their chemistry had scared her and, to tell the truth, he wasn't overly comfortable with it himself. He liked his life the way it was. He wasn't looking for anything long-term. He came and went as he pleased and didn't have anyone he had to answer to. But he wasn't sure it was going to be possible to ignore whatever this was that was happening with them.

When he'd pulled her down onto his lap after their conversation over coffee, he had only meant to offer his compassion for all she'd been through. Losing both her fiancé and her father within such a short time, then facing single motherhood without any kind of support system, had to have been extremely hard for her. That kind of heartbreak on top of heartbreak would have destroyed a lot of women. And on top of that, she'd been running the whole Circle W outfit by herself. He honestly didn't know how she'd managed.

Heather was a survivor and he wanted her to know how much he admired her. But the minute he had her in his arms, his good sense seemed to desert him completely. All he had ended up doing was showing her that he had about as much control over his hormones as a teenaged boy on prom night.

Disgusted with himself and too restless to sit still, T.J. shook his head and got up to look out the window. It had stopped raining, but it would be some time tomorrow before the road cleared. At least he would be able to tend to her horses in the morning before he had to go back to his ranch.

As he stood there wondering what else he could do to help Heather, Seth ran up beside him, grinning. The little boy patted T.J.'s thigh to get his full attention. Jabbering something T.J. couldn't understand, Seth reached up and took T.J. by the hand to tug him along.

"Seth," Heather said firmly, hurrying into the room. There was no denying the irritation in her tone. "It's time for bed."

Reaching down, T.J. picked up the toddler then turned to face Heather. "Was he telling me good-night?"

She hesitated a moment before she shook her head. "No, he wants you to tuck him into bed."

"I think that can be arranged," T.J. said, laughing as he ruffled the little boy's copper-colored hair. "I like your pajamas, partner. I wish I had a pair with horses on them."

To his surprise Seth wrapped his arms around T.J.'s

neck and hugged him, then gave him a rather juicy kiss on the cheek. "Go bed now."

Heather didn't look happy as he carried Seth down the hall to his room and T.J. couldn't help but wonder what he'd done to upset her this time. He couldn't think of anything, but he had every intention of finding out what was wrong once they had Seth settled down for the night.

"Good night, partner," T.J. said, when he placed the toddler in his tiny bed. "I'll see you in the morning."

"'Tory," the little boy said, yawning.

"I'll only be a few minutes," Heather said, picking up a book.

When T.J. started to leave the room, Seth sat up in bed and shook his head. "'Tory."

"I'm not real good with toddler-speak," T.J. said, frowning. "What does he want?"

"He wants you to stay for the story," she said, sighing heavily.

T.J. could tell Heather didn't want him hanging around for their nightly ritual, but he had a feeling that whether he left or he stayed, either way he was going to upset one of them. "Would you rather I go on into the living room to watch TV, Heather?"

She stared at him for a long moment before she shook her head. Then she sat down on a small chair beside the bed. "No, it's fine for you to stay." Opening the book, she added, "It won't take more than a couple of pages and he'll be asleep."

As she started reading about a little train named Thomas, T.J. watched her expressions and listened to

the tone of her voice. Heather was a great mom and
Seth was lucky to have her. She listened to her son,
cared about what he wanted and tried to accommodate
his wishes within reason. She was the kind of mother
that any man would want for his children. The kind of
mother T.J. would want for his kids.

His heart stalled. What the hell? He'd never even
thought about having kids before. Was he actually
thinking about that now?

When he noticed Seth's eyelids drift lower and lower
until they closed completely, T.J. breathed a little easier.
The sooner the little boy was sound asleep, the sooner
he and Heather could go into the living room and he
could regain his perspective.

Heather continued reading for another minute or
two before she closed the book, stood up and turned
off the lamp on the dresser. She followed T.J. from the
room and closed the door behind them.

When they entered the living room, T.J. turned and
put his hands on her shoulders. "What's wrong? And
don't tell me nothing. You weren't this quiet when you
were sick."

"Let's go into the kitchen," she suggested. "We can
talk in there without disturbing Seth."

Nodding, he waited until they were both seated at
the kitchen table before he asked, "What's going on,
Heather?"

He watched her take a deep breath before she looked
him square in the eye. "After the road clears and you're
able to get back to your ranch, I'd rather you not come
over here anymore."

"Why? Was it because of that kiss this afternoon?" He had figured they would get around to discussing it sooner or later. But he had hoped that talking about it would lead to more kisses. If the determined expression on her pretty face was any indication, it didn't appear it was headed that way.

"Yes and no," she said slowly.

"Would you care to explain that?" Besides the kiss, he couldn't think of anything else he'd done that could have upset her to this degree.

"I don't want you to take offense to what I'm about to tell you," she said, choosing her words carefully. "But I don't want you around Seth anymore."

Of all the grievances he might have expected her to have with him, not wanting him to interact with her son wasn't among them.

"Why don't you tell me how I'm supposed to take it?" he demanded, suddenly angry. "As far as I know, Seth and I have been getting along just fine. I've even made sure to watch my language around him because I didn't want him picking up words you'd rather he didn't learn."

She nodded. "And I appreciate your vigilance on that."

T.J. folded his arms and leaned back in his chair. "Then what's the deal, Heather? Why am I good enough to look after him one minute, but not the next?"

"I'm trying to protect my son from becoming too attached to you," she explained. "I don't want to see him get hurt."

T.J.'s anger hit the boiling point. Unfolding his arms,

he sat forward and pointed his finger at her. "Let's get one thing straight right here and now, Heather Wilson. I would never do or say anything to cause you or Seth any kind of harm—physically or emotionally. I'm not that kind of guy and I never will be."

"I know you wouldn't mean to," she said, shaking her head. She looked vulnerable and upset. "But children hold nothing back. When they care for someone, they give their love and trust unconditionally because they don't know any other way. They don't realize that because someone is in their life now that the person might not always be there. I can see he likes you and he wants you around, but I'm afraid he'll start to depend on you to be there for him. Then when you aren't, when you get tired of us, he won't understand."

T.J. stared at her for several long moments. Seth wasn't the only one she was trying to protect. She might not realize it, but Heather was afraid of being hurt emotionally, as well. Given all that she had lost, he could understand her caution. But he could tell by the stubborn set of her chin that she had her mind made up. Trying to convince her of the flaw in her reasoning at this point in time would be nothing more than wasted energy.

Even though he hated to give in, he said, "It's your call." He shrugged as he rose from the chair. He motioned toward the living room. "If you don't mind, I think I'll watch the news and turn in. I assume it's all right for me to stretch out on the couch?"

A shadow of disappointment briefly crossed her pretty face, verifying what he suspected. She was afraid she would start to count on him, to want him to be around. What she didn't realize—and what he wasn't going to point out—was that she had already started depending on him. She already wanted him to be a part of her and Seth's lives. Otherwise she wouldn't have been let down when T.J. hadn't argued with her about her decision.

"I'm sorry about you having to sleep on the couch," she said in apology, straightening her shoulders as she rose to her feet. "I closed off the upstairs to save on the heating bills, as well as wear and tear on a furnace that's older than I am."

"No problem," he said, following her to the hall closet. When she handed him a pillow and blanket their hands brushed and a jolt of yearning ran straight up his arm to settle in the middle of his chest. He did his best to ignore it.

"I'll see you tomorrow."

"Good night."

T.J. turned and walked into the living room, tossed the blanket and pillow on the couch, then sat down in one of the armchairs to stare blindly at some cop show on TV.

What the hell was going on? He wasn't looking to get tangled up with a woman, was he? So why the hell did Heather telling him to buzz off matter to him?

He should be relieved. Instead he was pissed off by her stubbornness and by what he believed to be her unreasonable fear that he would somehow cause her or Seth some kind of emotional pain.

As he stared at the TV, he pondered their conversation. He knew her reluctance stemmed from having lost the two most important men in her life in a relatively short period of time. She had to have felt completely abandoned and although she might not realize it, her current resistance to getting close to anyone was due to her fear that she could lose any new person in her life the way she had lost her father and fiancé.

Was he open to taking on that kind of emotional baggage?

They certainly had an abundance of chemistry between them. They couldn't be within ten feet of each other without him wanting to take her in his arms. And if her reaction to him was any indication, she wanted to be there.

So what did he intend to do about it?

He really didn't think he had ever been in a real relationship. There were women he'd dated, but he had been so focused on his goal of winning world championships in bronc riding events and then buying a ranch and building his breeding program that he hadn't been serious about any of them.

In his rodeo days, he'd spent time with some of the buckle bunnies who hung around hoping to add another rider's name to the list of cowboys they'd bedded who had earned championship belt buckles. He wasn't overly proud of his past, but his name had been added to several of those bunnies' lists. And, of course, whenever he had an overwhelming urge for female companionship, he'd made his share of trips over to the Broken Spoke in Beaver Dam to find a warm, willing woman who didn't want anything more from him than one night and a real good time. But he had never committed himself to any kind of exclusive or serious relationship with a woman, especially not a woman with a child in tow.

Heather wasn't the type of woman a man took to bed and then walked away from the following morning without so much as a backward glance. She was part of a package deal. She had a cute little kid. Any man who entered into a relationship with her would be in a relationship with her little boy, as well. Was T.J. even thinking about trying to make that kind of connection with Heather? What if things didn't work out? He certainly didn't want to hurt Seth if they didn't.

T.J. turned off the television and removed his boots, got up from the chair and stretched out on the couch. As he lay there, trying to ignore the obviously broken spring poking him in the middle of his back, he knew exactly what he was going to do and why he was so damned frustrated.

Heather was more than just a single mother who was barely making ends meet and had no one to turn to for help. She was the only woman who had piqued his interest this much in a very long time—maybe ever. He just couldn't walk away from that. If he did, he had a feeling he would regret it for the rest of his life. His instincts had served him well over the years and he wasn't about to start questioning them now.

Whether she liked it or not, she would have to get used to the fact that he wasn't going anywhere. She needed someone to turn to if things got rough or slipped out of her control. And T.J. intended to be there for both her and Seth.

Now all he had to do was convince her to give him a chance. And he intended to get started on that first thing in the morning.

Five

The following morning, Heather woke up to find the pillow and blanket she had given T.J. the night before stacked neatly on the end of the couch, but he was nowhere in sight. As she continued on into the kitchen, she looked out the window over the sink to see if his truck was still parked next to her car. It wasn't.

When a keen sense of disappointment washed over her, she tried to remind herself that this was the way she wanted it—the way it had to be. She should be happy that he hadn't argued with her, that he'd done what she'd asked.

But she wasn't.

She had spent a miserable night going over all of the reasons why she'd asked T.J. to stay away from her and her son. Surely that was the only way to ensure that Seth didn't get hurt.

But reasoning with herself didn't do a thing to stop the abject loneliness that seemed to go all the way to her soul.

Sighing, she turned to get a mug from the cabinet. That's when she noticed a note on the counter in front of a freshly made pot of coffee. T.J. let her know that he had tended to the horses. He'd thanked her for giving him a place to stay for the night and told her to get in touch with him if she needed anything.

"Well, it looks like you accomplished what you set out to do," she muttered to herself as she poured a cup of coffee and started a pan of oatmeal for her son's breakfast.

So why didn't she feel better about it?

"Mom-mom, hungee," Seth said sleepily as he toddled into the room.

"I'm making your favorite, sweetie. Oatmeal with cinnamon and a sprinkle of brown sugar," she said, picking him up.

"Hossy?" he asked, looking around the kitchen.

"T.J. had to go home," she said gently.

"No!" Seth shook his little head. "My hossy."

"Maybe we'll see T.J. another time," she offered, hoping the thought would be enough to keep Seth from becoming more upset.

Luckily, it did seem to pacify him for a while, but he did ask about T.J. periodically throughout the morning and by the time she got Seth down for his nap after lunch, Heather felt as if she could cry. It was clear that

Seth missed T.J. and if she was honest with herself, she did, too.

How could the man have integrated himself into their lives in such a short amount of time? And what was there about him that was so darned compelling?

He wasn't the first man who had shown her attention since she'd found herself on her own.

One of the ranchers from the next county over had bought one of her brood mares last year. Several months ago, he had come by to take her and Seth for ice cream on the pretense of discussing the purchase of another horse. It had quickly become apparent that he considered the outing a date. Although he was nice enough, the kiss he'd given her when he'd brought them home had done nothing to encourage her to go anywhere else with him. She compared that to the first time T.J. had kissed her. That had felt as if time stood still. It had left her wanting him to do it again, and soon.

She rubbed at the tension building between her eyes. Why him? Why did T. J. Malloy have to be the one to awaken a need in her that she had all but forgotten?

When she'd told him that she was concerned for Seth, concerned about the bond she could see growing between them, she had deliberately omitted the fact that she was frightened by the way he made her feel, as well. T.J. reminded her of how much she missed being in a relationship, of how lonely life was without someone to share it with.

Of course, he had talked about being a good neighbor and wanting to help her with the ranch, but beyond kissing her a few times he hadn't mentioned anything about a relationship. And she wasn't interested in one, either.

Was she?

As she sat at the kitchen table, wondering if the stress had finally gotten to her and she'd lost what little sense she had left, Heather heard a vehicle coming up the driveway. When she glanced out the window, two white trucks with the Dusty Diamond logo painted on the sides, followed by T.J.'s black truck, parked close to the barn. The beds of the trucks were all piled high with bales of hay, straw and sacks of grain.

She wasn't certain whether she was happy to see T.J. or angry that he had ignored her request not to stop by again. A mixture of emotions coursed through her when he got out of his truck. Even from a distance he was so darned good-looking it was almost sinful, but he apparently had ignored everything she'd told him.

She started to go outside to see what he thought he was doing, but when she glanced at the clock she realized Seth would be waking up soon. Not wanting to get him up before his nap was over and unwilling to leave him alone in the house, she stepped out onto the porch to call out to T.J. "Would you please come up to the house for a few minutes?"

When he walked across the ranch yard and up the steps, just the sight of him was enough to take her breath away, which seemed to happen too frequently around him. But when he stopped in front of her and gave her a brief kiss on the lips, she wondered if she would ever breathe again.

"What's up, sweetheart?"

His easy smile sent a shiver of longing straight up her spine and she forgot all about admonishing him for kissing her and for not staying away liked she'd asked.

"Wh-where did all that come from?" she asked, pointing to the supplies his men were unloading and carrying into her barn. It was much easier to focus on what he had done than on the man himself. "I can't pay for it. I only buy what I can afford."

He shook his head. "Don't worry about it. I had some extra hay and straw taking up space in my loft. The other day when my foreman ordered oats, he ordered several dozen extra bags. I thought you might as well have them. It'll save you from having to make a trip to town in the next day or so."

"I told you I'm not a charity case," she said, shaking her head.

He had the audacity to ignore her. "Where's the little cowboy?"

"He's taking a nap," she answered automatically. "Tell your men to stop unloading those supplies and take them back to your place."

Cupping her elbow in one hand, he turned her, opened the door and escorted her into the house. "That's not going to happen, Heather. I owe you and I've let this debt go long enough."

She frowned. "What are you talking about? You don't owe me anything."

He nodded. "Yes, I do. You have a champion stallion that bred at least eight of my mares over the past couple of years. I never paid the stud fees."

"Have you lost your mind?" she demanded. "Up until yesterday, you thought Magic Dancer was an unregistered rogue stallion who had done serious damage to your breeding program."

"I found out differently," he said, shrugging. He removed his jean jacket and pulled out a chair. Then he sat down at the table as if it was his right. He motioned for her to join him at the table.

"Have a seat. We need to talk."

She remained standing. "About?"

"Sit and I'll tell you," he answered.

"Do you always have to have your way?" she asked as she took the chair across from him. "I thought I made myself clear last night about—"

"We'll discuss your edict a little later." She had seen that look of determination on his handsome face before—the evening when he'd insisted she and Seth spend another night at his ranch. "Right now, I want to tell you something and I want you to promise that you'll wait until I'm finished before you comment."

Heather wasn't certain remaining silent would be in her best interest, but it was apparent he wasn't going to tell her what he had on his mind until she gave her word she wouldn't interrupt.

She sighed heavily. "All right."

"After I take care of your horses tomorrow—"

"I told you I would take care of my own horses from now on," she insisted.

Instead of reminding her of her promise not to interrupt, he simply tilted his head slightly and gave her a smile that clearly stated he had known she couldn't keep her comments to herself.

"Oh, all right," she said, folding her arms beneath her breasts. "Finish what you were going to tell me."

"Like I was saying, after I tend to the horses tomorrow, one of my men and I are going to go up on the roof and check to see what it will take to keep it from leaking." When she started to tell him she wouldn't allow it, he held up his hand. "Hear me out. We'll only do a patch job that will hopefully get you through until spring. Is that the only area that's been leaking?"

"Yes, but—"

"Okay, we'll give it a quick fix to get you through the rest of the winter, then you can see about having that section reroofed when the weather warms up."

He sat back in the chair as if he was quite proud of himself.

"Are you finished?" she asked. When he nodded, she shook her head. "I can't let you climb on top of my house and run the risk of falling off."

To her surprise he threw back his head and laughed. "Sweetheart, I appreciate your concern for my safety, but I know what I'm doing when it comes to roofing houses. From the time I graduated high school until I graduated from college, I spent every summer roofing houses during the week while I rode rodeo on the weekends to earn money for school."

"I don't care. I'm not going to let you do that," she insisted. "I wouldn't feel right about you fixing my roof without compensation and right now I can't pay for it. And while we're talking about things I can't pay for, you might as well tell your men to load those supplies back on your trucks and return them to the Dusty Diamond because I can't pay for those, either."

"I thought we already had that settled," he said, getting up to walk around the table. Before she knew what he was up to, he scooped her up, sat down in her chair and settled her on his lap. "The supplies are for the stud fees I owe you for your horse breeding my mares. End of discussion." He kissed the side of her neck. "And my men and I *will* be fixing your roof tomorrow. If you want to make lunch for us, we'll call it even. Once again, end of discussion."

How was she supposed to protest when she couldn't even think with him holding her, kissing her? And why was she unable to resist when he picked her up to set her on his lap?

She wasn't sure. But every time he held her like this, she not only felt the chemistry between them, but a calm also came over her, as if she'd found a safe haven from all the responsibilities she'd faced for the past two and a half years.

"And just so you know, last night when you told me you didn't want me around, you misunderstood my silence as agreeing that I would do what you wanted," he said, nibbling kisses from her neck to the hollow beneath her ear. "That wasn't the case, sweetheart. I'm not going anywhere. I want to help you out. I want to make things easier for you and Seth."

"I don't think you being around will do anything but make things more difficult and complicated for us," she said honestly.

He cupped her cheek with his palm and held her gaze with his. "There's something going on between you and me, Heather. Whatever is drawing us together—I know it makes you as frightened for yourself as you are afraid of Seth being hurt. And to tell you the truth, I'm unsettled by this pull between us, too. But I gave it a lot of thought last night and I decided we can't ignore it. It exists, whether we like it or not. But I give you my word that I'll walk through hell before I hurt you or Seth."

"We should try to ignore it," she insisted, unable to sound as convincing as she would have liked, even to herself. She didn't try to deny that there was a definite chemistry between them. They'd both know she was lying.

"I'm not willing to do that," he said firmly as he lowered his head.

The moment his lips settled over hers, Heather gave up trying to fight with herself and closed her eyes. She might not be the least bit comfortable with it, but she wanted T.J.'s kiss. She wanted him to make her feel that she was more than just a single mom, struggling to make ends meet on a ranch that was quickly slipping through her grasp. She wanted him to make her feel like a woman again.

When he coaxed her mouth to open for him, he slipped his tongue inside to tease her into playing a game of advance and retreat. Heat flowed from the top of her head all the way to the soles of her feet. She felt a strong sense of feminine power course through her when he encouraged her to take control and explore him the way he had explored her.

She brought her hand up so she could tangle her fingers in the soft curls at the nape of his neck. His arms tightened around her. When her nails lightly chafed his skin, a groan rumbled up from deep in his chest. That's when she became aware of his rapidly growing arousal pressing against her hip. Her own body responded with a delicious warmth that gathered in the most feminine part of her, and she couldn't stop herself from melting against him.

"Hossy!" she heard Seth squeal as he ran into the kitchen.

The warmth flowing through her veins quickly cooled. Pulling back, she looked at T.J. to see if he was angered that the kiss had been called to such an abrupt halt. His understanding smile surprised her. A lot of men would have resented someone else's child interrupting a passionate embrace. But T.J. seemed to be taking it in stride.

"We'll continue this later," he promised Heather, kissing the tip of her nose. Turning his attention to Seth, T.J. grinned as he reached down with one arm to pick up her son. "Hey there, little partner. Did you have a nice nap?"

"Yesh," Seth said, throwing his arms around T.J.'s neck to hug him. "Wide hossy."

"You'll have to ask your mom," T.J. said, laughing.

"Pease, Mom-mom?"

Her son looked so hopeful she couldn't say no.

"Just one and then we'll have to let T.J. get back to helping his men," she said as she got up from T.J.'s lap.

"Otay." Seth's little grin melted her heart.

Her little boy meant everything to her, but T.J. was right. Whatever this was between the two of them couldn't be ignored. She just hoped she wasn't setting up Seth—or herself—for an emotional fall.

But as she watched T.J. get down on his hands and knees to give Seth a ride around the kitchen, she realized that whatever force of nature was drawing her and T.J. together, it included her son, too. Seth wasn't a child who easily warmed up to strangers, but he had immediately gravitated toward T.J. And T.J. didn't seem to mind in the least. In fact, watching the two together was like watching a father playing with his son.

Her breath caught in her throat and she had to force herself not to panic. She had always heard that it took a special man to accept another man's child as his own. Was T.J. really that kind of man?

Thus far, he had been extraordinary. He hadn't hesitated one bit to help her with Seth and if he saw that she needed something, whether she wanted him to or not, he did his best to take care of it for her. He was the kind of man she would want to be a father to her son.

She shook her head to dispel the thought that he could be a father to Seth and reminded herself to take things one day at a time. Nothing had been said about a relationship and T.J. had promised that he wouldn't cause Seth any kind of harm, not even emotionally. But could she take it on faith that T.J. wasn't just telling her what she wanted to hear? She'd had so many disappointments in the past couple of years, it was hard for her to trust that everything would work out.

"Okay, partner, time for me to go see if my crew has everything unloaded and put away in the barn," T.J. said, stopping to let Heather lift Seth from his back.

"What do you say, Seth?" Heather prompted.

"Tank 'ou," he said, smiling.

"You're welcome, partner," T.J. said as he rose to his feet.

Holding her son with one arm, Heather reached for T.J.'s jacket with the other. "I'm still not comfortable with all of this," she said quietly as she handed him the jacket.

"We've already settled everything, sweetheart." He took his jacket from her, pulled it on and wrapped his arms around both her and Seth. "We'll take things one day at a time and see where each day takes us." He checked his watch. "I wish I could hang around, but I got a call from one of my brothers after I got home this morning. I'm supposed to meet him over in Beaver Dam for supper."

"You don't owe me any kind of explanation," she said, shaking her head. "I wasn't even expecting you to come by today."

"I just wanted you to know where I'd be in case you need me for anything," he said, kissing her forehead as he handed her a business card with the Dusty Diamond logo printed on it, along with his cell number.

"Seth and I will be just fine," she assured him, tucking the card into her jeans pocket.

"Then I'll see you tomorrow," he said, stepping back to head for the door.

As she watched T.J. leave the house, Heather felt as if she had just jumped off into the deep end of a pool with no idea how to swim. Was she really going to let T.J. help her? Was she really going to go along with his idea that they needed to explore their attraction?

Watching him from the kitchen, she saw him talk to his men then turn to wave to her as he got into his truck. Heather's heart skipped a beat and she nibbled nervously on her lower lip. Just the thought of becoming involved with anyone scared her beyond words.

Her child deserved a father—a man who would love him, play with him and teach him things. But could a man still care for another man's child once he had one of his own? Did that kind of man even exist?

Her father had been one of the finest men she had ever known and he hadn't been able to do it. Her older sister had been the child of their mother's first marriage and from what she had discerned from Stephanie's comments, everything had been fine until Heather was born. After that, her father doted on Heather and no longer seemed to have enough time for her sister. She didn't want to see the same thing happen to her son.

But whether it was smart or not, it appeared that she had already become involved with T.J., and her son had started looking to him as a father figure, even if he was too young to realize it.

When T.J. spotted Lane at the back of the Broken Spoke, he stopped at the bar for a bottle of beer before walking over to slide into the seat on the opposite side of the wide booth. Taking off his hat, he hung it on one of the pegs on the wall.

"What did you do to piss off Taylor this time?" he asked, unable to keep from grinning.

Lane frowned. "What makes you think my wife is mad at me?"

"Since the two of you got married last spring, I can count on one hand the number of times you've gone anywhere without her," T.J. replied. "And if my memory serves me right, both of those times you had done something that caused her to pitch a hissy fit and you wanted to give her the time and space to cool off."

T.J. had decided as soon as he met Taylor that the fiery redhead was perfect for Lane. Her passion and enthusiasm for life tempered Lane's tendency to be overly serious and analytical, while his calm lessened her propensity to overreact.

"Well, I didn't do anything this time," his brother said, shaking his head. "She's not been feeling very well the past couple of days."

"Does she have the flu?" T.J. asked, hoping that wasn't the case. "That's what Hea—" He coughed to cover his blunder. "That's what I've heard is going around."

"No, she's got some kind of stomach bug," Lane said, obviously missing T.J.'s slip of the tongue. "Since she doesn't feel like cooking and doesn't want to do anything but sleep, I figured I'd let her rest and see if you and the other guys wanted to grab a steak."

"Who else is coming?" T.J. asked.

"I think Ryder and Sam are headed this way." Lane took a swig of his beer, then laughed. "Sam said, after Bria gets little Hank down for the night, she and Mariah are going to experiment with hairstyles for Mariah's big night in Dallas with her new boyfriend. And Ryder said that Summer told him if he didn't stop hovering over her and the baby, she was going to bop him."

T.J. laughed. "I can't say I blame Sam for not wanting to hang around for the hairstyling. And as protective as Ryder is, I'm surprised he hasn't covered both Summer and the baby in bubble wrap."

Grinning, Lane nodded. "Can you imagine what Ryder will eventually put some poor, pimple-faced boy through when the kid comes around trying to date Katie?"

"What do you want to bet Ryder makes sure he's cleaning one of his guns when the kid comes to pick her up?" T.J. asked, feeling sorry for whoever dared to ask out his niece.

"Yeah, he'll intimidate the stuffing out of the kid," Lane agreed.

"But you'll have to admit, the boy will think twice before trying anything out of line with Katie," T.J. added. "By the way, have you talked to Jaron since Mariah made her announcement Christmas night?" he asked, knowing their brother hadn't been happy to hear the news that she was seeing someone.

"When I called to ask him to join us tonight, I tried to talk to him about it." Lane shrugged. "He told me to mind my own business and said he had something else he had to do."

T.J. nodded. "You know how he is. He's not much on talking about his troubles. He tends to brood about things that are bothering him more than the rest of us do."

"Yeah," Lane agreed. "But until he's ready, it doesn't do any good to try to draw him out."

"Nope." T.J. took a long draw of his beer. "Jaron knows where to find us when he's ready to talk."

"There's Sam and Ryder," Lane said, pointing toward the bar's front door.

As T.J. watched his brothers make their way to the booth, he slid to the far side for one of them to sit down. When Sam and Ryder joined them, T.J. asked, "What about Nate? Is he going to be here?"

Lane shrugged. "He said he was heading to Waco this evening."

"He really needs to marry that girl and get it over with." Ryder was only saying what they were all thinking.

"He told me the other night that they broke up again," T.J. commented. "Right before he tried to give me advice on women."

They all laughed.

"And who was he trying to give you advice about?" Sam asked. "The only woman I know of that you've been seeing on a semi-regular basis is that neighbor of yours with the stallion."

T.J. almost choked on his beer. He knew that if his brothers got wind that he had been over at Heather's more than he'd been home for the past couple of days, they would never let him hear the end of it. But he wasn't sure how he could answer Sam without lying to him. And that's one thing he refused to do. He had never been dishonest with his brothers about anything and he wasn't going to start now.

Shrugging, he tried to be evasive. "He was telling me that I mishandled the situation with Hea—that Wilson woman about her horse."

"Whoa!" Ryder exclaimed.

Lane raised an eyebrow and slowly set his beer bottle on the table. "When did this come about, T.J.?"

He knew feigning ignorance wasn't going to stop the coming interrogation, but he tried anyway. "What?"

"You seeing your neighbor," Sam answered.

"Who said I've been seeing her?" he asked defensively. It was the first time he had been in the hot seat with his brothers over a woman and he suddenly knew how Sam, Ryder and Lane felt when they were the ones being counseled about their relationships.

"Any time we've mentioned her before you've always gone ballistic about her and her horse," Ryder stated flatly.

"I've let that go," T.J. said.

Sam shook his head. "I'm not buying it. The other night over at my place your reaction was as strong as ever. What's happened in the past few days that's changed your mind about her?"

"What makes you think something happened?" T.J. asked, knowing that he was only delaying the inevitable. His brothers weren't going to give up until they found out what was going on with him and Heather.

"The fact that you're answering every question we

ask with one of your own is a pretty good clue," Lane said, his smile about as irritating as any T.J. had ever seen.

"Is that your expert opinion, Freud?" T.J. retorted.

Lane laughed. "Yup."

"Fess up, bro," Ryder said, grinning like a damned jackass.

Blowing out a frustrated breath, T.J. gave in and explained about finding Heather and Seth stranded on his side of the creek Christmas night.

"They were both sick and I couldn't leave them sitting along the side of the road to fend for themselves," T.J. said, shaking his head. "Hank would come back from the grave to haunt me."

His three brothers nodded their agreement. Their foster father had instilled a keen sense of what was right and what wasn't. Leaving a woman in distress without helping her out of whatever situation she found herself in was an unforgivable sin. No exceptions.

"Did you know she had a kid when you were giving her such a hard time about that horse?" Ryder demanded.

"No." T.J. shook his head. "I wouldn't have been so demanding if I'd known she was trying to juggle taking care of a baby and running the Circle W by herself."

"Where's the little boy's daddy?" Sam asked. "Can't he lend a hand?"

Filling them in on what Heather had told him about losing her father and her fiancé just a few months apart, T.J. left out how much she was struggling. His brothers didn't need to know how hard she was finding it to make ends meet. For one thing, he had to consider her pride. She hadn't liked having to tell *him* and he didn't figure she would appreciate him discussing her business with his brothers. And for another, they had probably already figured it out for themselves.

"You're going to continue helping her out, aren't you?" Sam asked, his know-it-all smile almost as irritating as Lane's.

"I owe her," T.J. said, nodding. "It turns out that stud of hers is a registered quarter horse and a multi-champion horse in the pleasure class."

"And you thought he'd screwed up your breeding program," Lane said thoughtfully. "While in fact, he might have improved it."

Ryder laughed. "Funny how jumping to conclusions can come back to bite you in the butt."

"Shut up, smart-ass," T.J. muttered, wishing he'd skipped having supper with his brothers.

"What can I get for you guys?" a young, ponytailed waitress asked as she walked up to the booth. Snapping her chewing gum, she smiled as she added, "Our special tonight is a T-bone steak smothered in onions and green peppers with sides of French fries and coleslaw."

"Sounds good to me," Sam said.

"Make that two of the specials," Ryder agreed.

"How about you, T.J.?" Lane asked. When he nodded, Lane turned back to the girl. "Looks like we'll all have tonight's special, medium rare and add another round of beer to that order."

The girl nodded. "I'll be back with your beer in just a minute."

T.J. was relieved that once she left, the conversation turned to other things. By the time they finished dinner and got ready to leave, they all agreed they needed to get together for a brothers' night out more often.

"I guess I'll see all of you in a couple of days at the Dusty Diamond," T.J. said, reaching for his hat.

"We'll be there. Be prepared to help me carry in all the baby stuff we'll have to bring for Katie." Ryder laughed. "Going anywhere with a baby is like moving."

Sam nodded. "You got that right. It is getting a little better now that little Hank is almost a year old. But damn, even a trip to town can be a major undertaking."

"We'll be there if Taylor feels up to it," Lane said, nodding.

"She called Bria this afternoon and asked if Bria could handle making the dinner and the snacks they'd planned for our New Year's Eve party by herself," Sam said, looking concerned. "Have you taken Taylor to the doctor?"

"She has an appointment tomorrow afternoon," Lane said as they all stood up.

"Maybe he can give her something to get rid of whatever's making her feel bad," T.J. offered when they stopped to pay their checks at the bar.

"Let us know what the doctor has to say," Ryder added. As they walked out to the parking lot, he asked, "So are you going to invite your neighbor to the party, T.J.?"

"You really should," Sam said, grinning. "If you two are going to continue seeing each other, she might as well meet us now and see what she's up against."

"I'll think about it," T.J. muttered as he waved good-bye to his brothers and got into his truck.

On the drive home, he thought about what his brothers had said. He had entertained the idea of asking Heather and Seth to join the annual New Year's Eve party, but he hadn't had a chance to weigh the pros and cons of having her meet his family.

It wasn't that he thought they wouldn't welcome her or that she wouldn't fit in. He knew for a fact they would accept her and Seth with open arms and he was pretty sure Heather would become instant friends with all of his sisters-in-law. So why was he holding back?

He had talked to Heather about exploring what was drawing them together, but beyond that he hadn't mentioned anything about pursuing a relationship. Would it even be wise to introduce her to his family before they were even dating? What if nothing came of their seeing each other?

Turning his truck onto the lane leading up to his house, T.J. knew what he was going to do. Besides the fact that he wanted to spend time with her, he couldn't stand the thought of Heather and Seth sitting over in the Circle W ranch house by themselves while he and his family had a good old time seeing in the New Year together. But he knew it wouldn't be easy to convince her to join them.

He couldn't help but smile as he drove the truck into the garage. Fortunately he was up for the challenge.

Six

T.J. positioned the extension ladder he had brought from his ranch against the side of Heather's house, then walked back to his truck for one of the buckets of roof patch he'd had his foreman pick up at the local hardware store the day before. As soon as Tommy Lee finished taking care of Heather's horses, he would work with T.J. to fix the roof. Then T.J. intended to talk to her about the New Year's Eve party at his place the following night.

"T.J.?" Heather called from the porch. When he stepped around the corner of the house to see what she wanted, she was coming down the steps holding Seth's hand. "I'm sorry to bother you, but when Seth found out you were outside he insisted he had to see you."

T.J. grinned. "Hey there, partner."

"Hi!" Seth said, grinning from ear to ear. As soon as they stepped off the bottom step, Seth pulled his hand from Heather's and ran toward T.J.

Bending, T.J. caught the toddler in his arms. "How are you today?"

Seth's excited rapid-fire answer and the waving of his hands had T.J. looking to Heather for an interpretation.

"He's trying to tell you about helping me make lunch for you and your hired hand," she said, walking up to them.

"I'll bet you were a big help for your mom," T.J. said, smiling. "What did you help her fix up for us?"

"Scetti balls," Seth said proudly.

T.J. glanced at Heather. "Spaghetti and meatballs?" When she nodded, he tickled Seth's stomach, causing the toddler to burst into a fit of giggles. "We've had that before, haven't we, partner?"

Seth nodded. "You house."

"That's right," T.J. agreed, laughing. "You ate almost as much as I ended up wearing." When he spotted Tommy Lee walking out of the barn, T.J. set the little boy on his feet. "Time for me to fix the roof, but I'll be in as soon as I'm finished to eat lunch with you and give you another ride. How does that sound?"

"Please be careful," Heather said as she took Seth by the hand.

"Hey, where do you think you're going?" T.J. asked, stepping forward to wrap his arms around her waist.

She looked confused. "I thought you were going up on the roof."

"Not without a kiss," he said as he pressed his lips to hers. With Seth hanging around nearby, T.J. made sure to keep the kiss brief. When he lifted his head, he stared at Heather for several long seconds. She was so damned beautiful, it was all he could do to keep from kissing her until they both collapsed from lack of oxygen. "To be continued in the very near future."

"We'll be inside," she replied softly. "Come on in when you two get done."

As he watched her turn and lead Seth back into the house, he took a deep breath and waited for Tommy Lee. "Once I get up on the roof, all you have to do is hand me the bucket of roof patch."

"Fair enough, boss," the man said, looking relieved. "I'm not all that gung ho on heights."

"You climb up in the barn loft all the time," T.J. said as they walked around to the side of the house where he had put the ladder.

"I never said it didn't bother me," Tommy Lee admitted.

"I'll tell Dan to send Harry up there from now on," T.J. said, starting to climb up the ladder. When he reached the roof, he turned for the bucket. "You don't have any kind of problem with needles do you?"

"Nope." Tommy Lee handed T.J. the patching material. "Why?"

"Because Harry breaks out in a cold sweat every time he thinks about having to help the veterinarian," T.J. answered. "From now on you can help inoculate the horses."

"Sounds good to me," Tommy Lee said as he

climbed back down the ladder. "Funny that Harry never mentioned that."

"Did you tell him about your problem with heights?" T.J. asked, opening the bucket.

"Not on your life," Tommy Lee said. There was a pause before the young cowboy spoke again. "Oh, I get it."

T.J. couldn't help but grin as he started smearing the black, tar-like substance over the damaged spots on the roof. Tommy Lee's naiveté came more from being a twenty-year-old kid and out on his own for the first time than from anything else.

Just as T.J. finished with the last spot showing signs of damage, Tommy Lee let loose with a curse that raised even T.J.'s eyebrows.

"Get down here now, boss," the young man shouted. "Ms. Wilson's house is on fire."

Making his way across the roof to the ladder, T.J. could see thick gray smoke coming from the open window below. He repeated Tommy Lee's creative combination of cuss words and added a few of his own as he came down the ladder in what had to be record time. He ran around to the back of the house, followed closely by the younger cowboy. T.J. threw open the door and they met Heather carrying Seth as she ran through the kitchen to get out.

"I turned it off, but I think the furnace is on fire," she said.

"Get them out of here," he ordered Tommy Lee.

While his hired hand got Heather and Seth to safety, T.J. grabbed the fire extinguisher he had seen in a utility closet the night he'd stayed with Heather and entered the laundry room. He pulled the lever on top, sprayed foam on the furnace's smoldering motor and didn't stop until the small cylinder was empty. He wanted to make sure there was no chance of flames flaring up again before he went outside to see that Heather and Seth were all right.

"What happened?" he asked when he exited the house. He walked across the yard to where Heather stood, cradling Seth, and took them both into his arms.

"I-I'm not sure," she said, shivering against him. "I heard a pop and then smelled smoke. When I went to see what happened, smoke was coming from the furnace. I turned it off and opened the window, but the smoke just kept getting worse."

"Well, it's out now," he said, hugging her and Seth to him. "But I'm afraid your furnace motor is most likely a lost cause."

"That's…it. This…is the last…straw," she said haltingly. He could tell she was a hair's breadth away from dissolving into tears, and knowing how proud she was, he didn't think she would appreciate having an audience witnessing it.

"Tommy Lee, why don't you go ahead and put the bucket of roof patch in the tool shed, then take the ladder and go on back to the Dusty Diamond," T.J suggested. He'd intended to stay after lunch to talk to Heather about attending the family's New Year's Eve party, and now he was glad he had the young cowboy follow him over to Heather's in one of the ranch trucks.

"Will do, boss," Tommy Lee said, looking relieved to be escaping the coming waterworks.

"Why don't we get you and Seth out of this chilly air?" he asked, turning her toward the house. He lifted Seth from her and put his free arm around her shoulders to guide her up the steps and through the open back door.

Once they were inside, Heather turned into him and he held her while she sobbed against his chest. He'd rather climb a barbed-wire fence buck-naked than to see a woman cry, but Heather's tears made him feel worse than any he'd ever witnessed. He wanted to help, but he wasn't sure she would let him. He had barely convinced her to allow him to tend to her horses and fix her roof. Getting her to let him replace the furnace, or even just get it repaired, would be next to impossible.

"M-Mom-mom?" Seth said, his little voice wobbling.

Great! T.J. was going to have a sobbing woman and a crying toddler all at the same time.

"Your mom is going to be okay, Seth," he said, hoping to soothe the little boy. "I'll take good care of both of you. How does that sound?"

The child stared at him for a moment before he finally nodded. "O-tay."

When Heather's crying ran its course, T.J. reached for a soft cotton dish towel to dry her eyes. "Can you take Seth?" he asked. "I'm going to make a call to see if I can get a repairman out here right away."

"I-I'm so…sorry," she said, reaching for her son. "I never…cry."

"It's all right, sweetheart. This is just a little bump in the road and you're not going to face it alone." Cupping her face with his palms, he kissed her forehead. "Since it's supposed to be cold tonight, why don't you go ahead and start gathering some things for you and Seth to spend the night at my place? This late in the day, it's doubtful the furnace people will be able to get out here until tomorrow."

She stared at him for several long seconds before she drew in a deep breath. "Thank you, T.J."

He shook his head. "There's nothing to thank me for, Heather. I told you that I wanted to help you and make your life easier." He kissed her again. "And that's just what I'm going to do, sweetheart."

After dinner, Heather turned on the dishwasher and finished cleaning up T.J.'s kitchen before she started down the hall to join him and Seth in the game room. Fortunately, she'd had the presence of mind to bring the spaghetti and meatballs with them when she and Seth followed T.J. to the Dusty Diamond. Since it was already cooked, all she'd had to do was reheat it and she owed him at least one meal for patching her roof, making sure the burnt-out furnace motor hadn't caught the rest of the house on fire and the number of other things T.J. had done for her over the past several days.

A sudden wave of emotion threatened to overtake her, and she passed by the door to the game room and continued on to the powder room just a few feet away. Closing the door behind her, she took several deep breaths in an effort to chase away the tears she was trying desperately not to shed. It was bad enough that T.J. had witnessed her nerves getting the better of her earlier in the day, she refused to allow him to see her break down again.

What on earth was wrong with her? She hadn't been this weepy since she was pregnant with Seth. That could be blamed on hormonal changes and all that she had lost during the pregnancy. But today?

Over the past two years, she had worked hard to keep a positive attitude and not allow the stress to get to her. And for the most part she had been successful.

She might have been able to deal with the furnace issues if she didn't also have the worry of finding money for the real estate taxes due at the end of the next month. She had been over her meager budget time and again. Short of a miracle, it looked hopeless. She could sell the rest of her brood mares to pay for everything, but if she did that she wouldn't have a breeding program left. She needed what money the horses brought in to help keep everything else running around the ranch.

When she told T.J. that the furnace breaking down was the last straw, she had meant it. She couldn't afford to replace it and if she couldn't pay the back taxes there wouldn't be a reason to replace it anyway. The county would seize the property and she and Seth would have to find somewhere else to live.

Of course, if the furnace could be repaired, instead of replaced, she might catch a bit of a break. When T.J. called, the repairman had told him that he couldn't come out to the Circle W until tomorrow morning to assess the damage. But she didn't hold out a lot of hope that the solution would be that simple. The furnace was more than thirty years old and had been repaired so many times, it was probably a lost cause. But all the worry in the world wasn't going to change the outcome of the repairman's findings and she wasn't doing anyone any good making herself crazy over it.

She knew if she asked T.J. for help with her dilemma, he would be more than happy to do it. But there was no way her pride would allow her to do that. When she and her late fiancé first started dating, his parents had looked down on her because she was the daughter of a horse rancher, even though her parents had been far from destitute. They had gone so far as to accuse her of being more interested in the money their son would one day inherit than she was in him. She had vowed after that she would do without before she ever accepted help from anyone for anything. And although at times it had been extremely hard for her, she'd stuck to that vow. She saw no reason to go back on it now.

Taking a deep breath to calm herself, she splashed cold water on her face to erase some of the evidence of her panic then patted her skin dry. She left the powder room to join T.J. and Seth. She would just have to cling to the hope that things would work out.

"Why am I not surprised to see the two of you down on the floor again?" she asked, walking into the huge game room.

"Hossy," Seth said, happily patting T.J. on the top of the head.

T.J. laughed good-naturedly. "I think he's going to be a cowboy for sure."

"Why don't we let your horsey rest for a while?" Heather suggested, lifting Seth from T.J.'s back. "I'm sure his knees are getting sore from all the rides he's been giving you lately."

"Would you like something to drink?" T.J. asked, getting to his feet. He reached out to lightly run his finger along her cheek, sending shivers of anticipation coursing through her. "I've got soft drinks, beer and if you'd like, I could try to mix up one of those fruity drinks like a piña colada or a margarita." He grinned. "But I can't guarantee it will be any good. I'm a lot better at just opening a can or a bottle than I am at mixing up stuff."

Smiling, she had to catch her breath before she was able to speak. "Thank you, I'm fine. I need to let Seth play a little bit more, then give him a bath and get him settled down for the night."

"While you do that, I'll set up that little portable bed you brought with you," he offered as he pulled her to him for a quick kiss. "If you're not too tired, I'd like to talk to you about something after we get him in bed."

"All right," she said cautiously. "What do you want to discuss?"

"We'll talk about it later," he said, giving her a smile that caused her toes to curl inside her cross-trainers. Stepping back, he picked up Seth and headed toward the basket of toys he had mentioned keeping for his niece and nephew's visits. "Right now, I'm going to occupy my little partner here, while you put your feet up and relax for a while."

"You don't mind?" she asked.

He shook his head as he walked back over to her to brush her lips with his, then whispered close to her ear. "You need the break, sweetheart."

Tingles of excitement raced through her as Heather stared at him for a moment longer before she wandered over to the huge sectional sofa at the end of the room and sat down. Having help with Seth was a unique experience for her. Over the past two years, she had been so used to taking care of him on her own, she wasn't sure she even remembered how to relax.

As she sat there watching T.J. play with her son, she briefly wondered if this was the way it would have been if Seth's father had lived. Would he have been as helpful with their child as T.J. had been? Somehow, she doubted it. Although she knew Mike Hansen had loved her and would have adored Seth, he just hadn't been the thoughtful type.

A few minutes later, when she saw Seth yawn, she rose from the couch. "Time for a bath, sweetie."

"No," Seth said, frowning. "Wanna pway."

"I think we better listen to your mom," T.J. said, smiling. "She knows what's best."

Seth rubbed his eyes with both fists and shook his head. "Wanna pway."

"Tell you what, little partner." T.J. picked up her son and tickled his tummy. "I'll carry you upstairs for your bath and I promise we'll play again tomorrow. How does that sound?"

Heather's chest swelled with emotion when Seth threw his arms around T.J.'s neck to hug him. "Otay."

Although it frightened her to think that she might be setting them up for a tremendous amount of disappointment, she couldn't keep from being grateful for the attention T.J. had given Seth. In the past several days, it had been like watching a flower bloom. With T.J., Seth had opened up and become more talkative and outgoing than she could ever remember him being with anyone but her.

"Thank you," she said as they walked down the hall to the stairs.

T.J. put his free arm around her shoulders and drew her close. "For what?"

"For watching Seth and being so good with him," she answered.

"You've had a pretty rough day and I thought you could use a few minutes to catch your breath." His grin warmed her entire body. "And to tell you the truth, I'm having as much fun as he is. He's a great kid." As they entered the bedroom, T.J. handed her son to her and picked up the folded play yard she had brought for Seth to sleep in. "Now, while you give him a bath, I'll get this set up." T.J. leaned forward to kiss her. "I'll meet you in the man cave in about an hour for our little talk."

She had no idea what T.J. thought they needed to discuss and she wasn't entirely sure she wanted to know. What she was focused on—and what was far more unsettling than anything he could possibly say—was the excitement building inside of her at the thought of spending a little time alone with one of the sexiest, most remarkable men she had ever met.

While he waited for Heather to finish getting Seth to sleep, T.J. sat at the bar in his man cave drinking a beer and pondering how he could have gotten in so deep so damned fast. Whenever he was around Heather he couldn't seem to keep his hands off of her. All he wanted to do was hold her, kiss her—and do a whole lot more. And when he was away from her, he couldn't wait until they were together again.

Then there was her little boy. The time he spent with Seth was more special than T.J. would have imagined. The kid could melt rock with that cute grin of his and a couple of times T.J. had caught himself thinking about all of the things he could teach Seth when the boy got a little older.

He shook his head. Although he had no idea where they were headed and it definitely had him questioning his sanity, T.J. knew he couldn't turn back now. Come hell or high water, he would see this relationship through to the end, whether that came two months down the line or lasted an entire lifetime. If he didn't, he had a feeling he would end up regretting it for the rest of his life.

Hearing Heather enter the room, he turned to watch her and his heart stalled. She was without a doubt the most desirable woman he had ever seen.

"Do you have any idea how beautiful you are, Heather?" he asked.

When she walked over to where he sat on one of

the high-backed stools at the bar he didn't think twice about wrapping his arms around her and pulling her to him.

"I…um, never really thought a lot about being attractive," she said, her cheeks coloring a pretty pink.

She was clearly unused to receiving compliments and that was an oversight he intended to remedy every chance he got. "You are, sweetheart. You're also damned amazing in others ways, too." He nuzzled his cheek against the soft waves of her long strawberry blond hair. "You're a great mom and one of the strongest, most intelligent women I've ever known."

"Thanks, but what brought this on?" she asked, sounding delightfully breathless.

Leaning back to look into her brilliant blue eyes, he smiled. "I'm just stating the obvious."

"Is that what you wanted to talk to me about?" she asked, frowning. "You wanted to tell me that you think I'm amazing?"

Smiling, he pressed a kiss to her forehead. "Nope. But I do think you're amazing."

He rose from the bar stool and, after walking behind the bar to throw his empty beer bottle away, he took her by the hand and led her over to the sofa. As soon as they sat down, he watched her place an electronic receiver with a small video screen on the coffee table. He hadn't noticed her holding it, and when he looked closer he realized it was a baby monitor like the kind he had seen his sisters-in-law use for his niece and nephew.

"Now are you going to tell me what you wanted to discuss with me?" she asked.

Pulling her close, he smiled when she automatically brought her arms up to his shoulders and tangled her fingers in the hair at his nape. "We can get to what I want to talk about later," he said, lowering his head. "Right now, I'm going to do what I've been wanting to do all evening."

When he covered her mouth with his, T.J. reacquainted himself with her perfect lips. Soft and sweet, they were the kind of lips that a man couldn't resist and he didn't even intend to try. Instead he coaxed her to open for him. Teasing and exploring her with a thoroughness that instantly had him shifting to relieve the pressure building in his jeans, he laid her back on the wide couch without breaking contact.

Thankful that the sectional was extra wide, he stretched out with her. He half covered her body and his thigh came to rest against her feminine warmth. The moist heat radiating through the layers of their clothing sent his own temperature soaring and without a second thought, T.J. slid his hand from her back to her chest, cupping her full breast with his palm.

Her mint green T-shirt and bra quickly became intolerable barriers. Slipping his hand beneath the hem of the garment, he slid it up her abdomen to the valley between her breasts and unfastened the front clasp of the scrap of lace holding her captive. When he took the weight of her breast in his hand, his body burned from the feel of her satiny skin and hardened nipple. As he chafed the tight tip with the pad of his thumb,

Heather moaned softly and arched into his touch. The movement sent fire racing through his veins and as impossible as it seemed, his body tightened further. No matter what she'd said, no matter how hard she'd tried to push him away, he knew she wanted him as much as he wanted her. The thought was almost enough to send him spiraling out of control.

Breaking the kiss, he nibbled his way along her cheek to her temple. "Heather, I swear I only meant to kiss you," he said, his voice raspy with passion. "But I need you more right now than I need my next breath." He paused to raise his head and stare into her pretty blue eyes. "If you don't need me just as much, tell me now. Otherwise, I can almost guarantee you that we're going to make love." He kissed her soft, warm lips. "And when we do, I don't want you regretting one moment of what we share."

She stared at him for what felt like an eternity. "There are a lot of decisions I've made lately that I'm not sure of and some that I know I'll regret. I don't want to add—"

"I understand, sweetheart," he said, wondering if dead-lifting a horse or two would take care of the abundance of adrenaline coursing through him.

Removing his hand from her breast, he started to get up and head for the barn, but when Heather's arms tightened around his neck to hold him in place, he looked down at her and his heart started thumping against his ribs like a bass drum in a marching band. The desire he saw in her blue gaze was electrifying.

"Heather?"

"If you had let me finish, I was about to tell you that I don't want to add *not* making love with you to the list of things I'll regret," she said softly. "Tonight I want to forget about broken furnaces and wondering if I'm going to make ends meet from one day to the next. I don't want to worry about the future. Tonight I just want to feel."

His breath lodged in his lungs and it took a moment for him to draw in enough air to speak. "Are you sure, sweetheart?"

Nodding, she pressed her lips to his. "Yes."

Seven

Gazing up at T.J., Heather knew that she could very well be making the biggest mistake of her life, but she had never really had a choice. From the moment T.J. had kissed her that very first time in her kitchen, it had been leading up to this moment.

When he got up from the couch, he picked up the baby monitor, then held out his hand to help her to her feet. "Let's go upstairs to my room," he said, putting his arm around her shoulders to lead her toward the stairs. "We'll be more comfortable."

As they reached the top of the stairs, they stopped at the room she shared with her son to check on him sleeping soundly in the play yard before she and T.J. continued down the hall to the master suite. When he opened the door and turned on the bedside lamp using a switch by the door, he stepped back for her to enter ahead of him. She barely had time to notice that the room had a huge king-size bed, a wall of windows that seemed to make the star-studded night sky part of the room and that it was decorated in a rustic Western décor before he took her back into his arms.

"Sweetheart, I'm going to do my damnedest to take things slow," he said, raining tiny kisses from her lips to the hollow beneath her ear. "And I want you to promise that you'll let me know what feels good, what brings you the most pleasure."

Her heart raced at his intimate tone and her breathing became shallow due to his warm breath feathering over her sensitive skin. "It's been…quite a while."

"Since your fiancé?" he asked, bending to remove her shoes and his boots.

"Y-yes," she answered breathlessly when he caressed her foot and ankle as he removed her socks.

Removing his own, he straightened to take her hands in his. "We'll learn together how to please each other." His promising smile warmed her all over as he placed her palms on the front of his chambray shirt. "Why don't we start with you taking this off of me?"

Tugging the tail of the garment from the waistband of his jeans, she slowly released the snaps, then slid her hands inside the cloth to ease it from his wide, heavily muscled shoulders and down his bulging biceps. As the shirt fell to the floor, a shiver of excitement coursed through her at the sight of his well-developed torso.

"You're beautiful," she said, lightly touching the

thick pads of pectoral muscle. "Your muscles are so defined."

He shrugged. "It's a remnant from my rodeo days."

"Let me guess, you rode the rough stock," she said, glancing at the size of his upper arms. Every cowboy she had ever known who competed in those events had biceps most men would kill for. "Horses or bulls?"

"Bareback and saddle broncs," he said, smiling. "I also did a little team roping with my brother Lane when I first started out."

His smile faded and a shudder ran through his big body as she used her finger to trace each ridge and valley of his exceptional abs. By the time she reached his navel, a groan was rumbling up from deep in his chest. "You have no idea how good it feels to have you touch me like this," he said, his voice gruff with need.

"Probably as good as it felt when you touched me earlier on the couch," she admitted, wondering if that sultry female voice had really come from her.

He reached for the hem of her T-shirt to lift it up and over her head. Then, when he brushed her bra straps over her shoulders, she realized he hadn't refastened the clasp. But the thought was fleeting as he covered her breasts with his hands. The feel of his calloused palms chafing her taut nipples caused her to tremble with longing and her knees to feel as if they would give way.

When he lowered his head to kiss his way from her collarbone down the slope of her breast to the tight peak, Heather felt heat race through her veins to gather into a pool in the most feminine part of her. But when

T.J. took her nipple into his mouth to tease her with his tongue, she thought she would surely burn to a cinder.

"Does that feel good?" he asked as he moved to do the same to her other breast.

"Y-yes," she said, bracing her hands at his waist to steady herself.

He held her gaze with his as he slid his hands down her sides to her waistband, then made quick work of unbuttoning her jeans and slowly easing down the zipper. She took a deep breath and nodded, and he slipped the denim from her hips and down her legs. When she stepped out of the jeans, he took her in his arms. The feel of her breasts crushed to his hard chest sent a tiny electrical current skipping over every nerve ending in her body. It had been so long since she'd been desired by a man, since she had felt the heat and yearning of undeniable passion, that she briefly wondered how she had managed to keep her hands off of him as long as she had.

"O-one of us…is overdressed," she managed to say when she finally found her voice.

Stepping back, T.J. grinned. "I'd let you take care of getting rid of my jeans, but I think it would be better for me to do it this time." When he unbuttoned the waistband, then gingerly pulled the zipper down over the large bulge straining at his fly, Heather fully understood the reason for his caution. "Sometimes an erection and a zipper can be a painful combination," he said as he shoved the jeans down his long legs, then kicked them to the side.

When he started to remove his boxer briefs, she

smiled as she reached out to run her index finger along the top of the elastic waistband. "If you'd like, I can do that for you," she offered.

She watched him swallow hard a moment before he placed his hand at the top of her panties. "Why don't we do it together?"

When they lowered the last barriers between them, T.J. took a step back. "You're even more beautiful than I imagined," he said as his gaze seemed to touch every part of her.

"I was thinking the same thing about you," she said, memorizing every detail of his magnificent male body.

"As good as you look, I want to feel you against me," he said as he wrapped his arms around her and pulled her to him.

When their bodies met, it felt as if every nerve in her body tingled to life. She delighted in the contrast of her smooth feminine skin pressed to his hair-roughened male flesh. But when she felt him shudder with the surge of desire coursing through him and she realized his hard arousal was nestled against her soft lower belly, her need for him was overwhelming. She had to cling to him for support.

"Why don't we get into bed before we both collapse right here on the floor?" he asked, guiding her toward his big king-size bed.

When she pulled back the comforter and lay down, she watched T.J. reach into the drawer of the nightstand to remove a small foil packet. After he tucked it under his pillow, he stretched out beside her and took her back into his arms.

"You are without a doubt the most exciting woman I've ever known," he said, lowering his head to kiss her with a passion that left her feeling light-headed.

Before she could tell T.J. she had similar thoughts about him, he slid his hand from her hip down to her knee, then back up along the inside of her thigh, rendering her completely speechless. Shivers of excitement coursed through her when he touched her with a feather-light caress, then parted her to stroke the tiny nub of intense sensation within.

Needing to touch him just as he was touching her, Heather moved her hand from his side. When she found his rigid length, his groan was deep and filled with pure male pleasure. "Sweetheart…if you keep doing that…we're both going to be mighty…disappointed," he said, sounding as if he was extremely short of breath.

"I want you, T.J.," she whispered. He tested her readiness for him with gentle strokes that were driving her wild. She wasn't sure how much more she could take without going insane. "Now!"

"I want to be inside of you, too," he said as he reached beneath his pillow for the foil packet.

When he arranged their protection, he took her back in his arms. Nudging her knees apart, he rose above her. Heather's eyes locked with his as she reached down to guide him into her. As he slowly made them one, she savored the exquisite sensations of being completely filled with him.

"You feel so damned good." She watched him close his eyes for a moment before he opened them again and smiled. "I need to love you now, Heather."

"P-please."

He slowly rocked against her and with each thrust of his body into hers, the thrilling tension within her built. The connection she felt with T.J. was unlike anything she had ever experienced with anyone. Though she'd tried to ignore it, that connection had been there from the beginning. It might have frightened her with its intensity if she'd been able to think. But all she could do was feel his body surrounding hers and the mind-blowing friction carrying them toward the pinnacle of fulfillment.

All too soon Heather felt the tightening deep in her lower body reached a crescendo, then set her free as wave after wave of pleasure coursed through her. Holding on to T.J. to keep from being swept away, she felt him surge into her one final time. Groaning, he rested his head against her shoulder and joined her in the satisfaction of sweet release.

Heather held his body to hers as she cherished the unbroken connection between them. That's when she knew for certain they were truly one—one heart and one soul.

Panic began to fill her. Had she done the unthinkable and fallen for T.J.?

After getting to know him, he had turned out to be entirely different from the man she'd first thought him to be. He was kind, caring and the most considerate man she had ever met. And her heart was telling her that she could trust him. When he told her that he would never do anything to cause her or Seth any kind of harm, one look in his eyes left no doubt that he was completely sincere. But it wasn't always that easy. Sometimes causing someone emotional pain was unintentional and unavoidable.

"Are you all right, sweetheart?" he asked, rolling to her side.

She nodded. "That was…"

Her voice trailed off as she stared at him. The caring she detected in his incredible hazel eyes was breathtaking. If she'd had any last traces of doubt about what she felt for T.J., the look in his eyes would have melted them. She *was* falling for him and it scared her as little else could.

"Incredible," he finished for her, unaware of her inner turmoil. Holding her close, he gave her a kiss so tender it brought tears to her eyes. "You're amazing, Heather."

She wanted to tell him what a remarkable man he was, how much she appreciated all he had done for her, but she hadn't yet fully come to terms with her feelings. If she hadn't already fallen in love with him, she was extremely close.

"That was wonderful," she said, meaning it. "But I really need to go back to the bedroom I'm sharing with Seth."

Smiling, he nodded. "I understand, sweetheart." When he got up from the bed, he didn't seem the least self-conscious as he retrieved their clothes from the floor and handed hers to her. "I'll walk you down the hall," he said, pulling on his jeans.

When she put her clothes on and started for the door, T.J. put his arm around her waist and held her against him as they walked to the room where her son was sleeping.

"You never did tell me what you wanted to talk about," she commented.

Stopping at the door, he reached out to tuck an errant strand of hair behind her ear. "It can wait until morning." He cupped her face with his palms and gave her a kiss that caused her toes to curl into the thick hall carpet. "Sleep well, Heather."

As she stepped into the room and closed the door behind her, she doubted she would get any sleep. She had a lot to think about and some decisions to make concerning the Circle W and how much she should tell him about her situation.

And if she didn't have enough on her plate, she had just added one more: the fact that she was falling hopelessly in love with T. J. Malloy.

When T.J. returned to his house after meeting with the furnace repairman out at the Circle W, he found the note he'd left Heather earlier that morning lying on the kitchen counter, indicating that she was still asleep. Smiling, he walked down the hall to his office. After putting the mail he had picked up from her mailbox on his desk to give to her later, he climbed the stairs and opened the door to her room to check on her and Seth.

"Hi!" Seth said, standing up in the play yard. Grinning, he motioned toward the bed across the room. "Mom-mom seep."

T.J. put his finger to his lips to silence the toddler and stepped into the room to pick up Seth and carry him out into the hall so he didn't disturb Heather. "How are you this morning, partner?"

The child babbled something that T.J. didn't even pretend to understand.

"How would you like to have breakfast with me while we let your mom get some rest?" he asked, carrying Seth downstairs to the kitchen. "Would you like to help me whip up a skillet full of scrambled eggs?"

"Otay," Seth said, nodding.

T.J. was thankful the kid liked eggs. Aside from making sandwiches, scrambling eggs and popping bread into the toaster were the only culinary skills T.J. possessed.

Gathering all the things he would need, T.J. pulled one of the kitchen chairs over to the counter, stood Seth in the seat and got a mixing bowl down from one of the cabinets. "You can help me scramble the eggs and milk together," he said, earning a big grin from the little boy. "But when it comes time to cook them on the stove, all you can do is watch. Understand?"

"Otay," Seth agreed.

Once he had the eggs cracked and put into the bowl, T.J. added a little milk to make them fluffy and smooth, then reached for a wire whisk. He handed it to Seth, then held the bowl and guided the toddler's hand in a circular motion.

It was going to take twice as long to get the eggs scrambled enough to put in the skillet, but T.J. wouldn't have missed the smile on Seth's face for anything in the world. The kid was having a ton of fun, and as far as T.J. was concerned, that made it worth the delay.

"Why didn't you wake me?" Heather asked, hurrying into the room. T.J. turned in time to see her glance at the clock. "I've missed the appointment with the furnace repairman."

"Don't worry about it," T.J. said, as he continued to help Seth mix the eggs. "I met him over at your place just a little while ago and he said the furnace needed a new motor, but that was the only damage. I told him to go ahead and repair it." He shrugged. "The only drawback is, the furnace is so old, he's going to have to order the replacement motor."

"Thank you, I appreciate your thoughtfulness, but you should have woke me up so I could meet with him," she said, setting her purse on the island. "It's my problem to take care of. Not yours."

He should have known she would take his trying to be helpful the wrong way. He'd thought that after the amazing connection they had made the night before, she might be more willing to let him help her. But he should have realized that letting go of her fierce pride was going to be a hard thing for her to do.

"You needed to rest," he said, turning back to see how Seth was doing with the scrambled eggs. "And you told me yesterday that you hoped the furnace could be repaired. All I did was tell the guy what you would have told him."

She sighed. "Did he say how soon the new motor will get here?"

"He told me that because of the holiday tomorrow, it won't be in until the first part of next week." Glancing over his shoulder at her, he added, "Looks like you're going to be extending your stay here." He smiled. "And that doesn't bother me one bit, sweetheart."

She rubbed her temples with both hands. "I can't take advantage of you like that."

"Believe me, I don't mind," T.J. assured her. "You've seen how big this house is. Most of the time, I rattle around in it like a lone bb in an empty boxcar."

"Then why did you build something this big?" she asked, frowning.

"I liked the design and I had the money," he said, shrugging.

He decided because she wasn't in the best of moods to wait until after breakfast to explain that his family spent New Year's Eve at his place every year. Which would lead to him telling her about his family descending on them tonight like a swarm of locusts. She might throw a plate of eggs at him for not mentioning it sooner.

"I suppose that's as good a reason as any," she commented.

Looking into the bowl, T.J. smiled at Seth. "Looks like the eggs are ready to go in the skillet, partner." Lifting the boy down from the chair, T.J. moved the bowl and the chair closer to the stove, but made sure the toddler was well away from any danger. "Ready to watch me cook the eggs?"

"Mom-mom, me hep," Seth said happily when T.J. lifted the toddler back onto the chair.

"I see that." Heather walked over to peer at the skillet. "I thought you said you didn't know how to do anything in the kitchen but make sandwiches."

"Eggs and sandwiches are it," he said, smiling at the most beautiful woman in the world.

After last night, he knew he was a goner. He had never felt a connection as strong or as right as the one he and Heather had shared, nor had he ever felt closer to a child than he did to Seth.

His heart pounded hard against his ribs. Was he really thinking long-term? Was he ready for that?

"Do you want me to take over?" she asked.

"Nope." Thankful for the interruption to his unexpected thoughts, he smiled as he looked at Seth. "We have this, don't we, partner?"

Grinning, Seth nodded and jabbered something that Heather seemed to understand.

"Would you like for me to set the table?" she asked.

"That's sounds like a winner." T.J. leaned over to give her a quick kiss. "And if you're of a mind to, a cup of coffee would be nice. I don't know why, but I woke up tired this morning," he teased. "I wonder why?"

Her cheeks colored a pretty pink. "I'm not going to dignify that with an answer," she said with a smile as she turned to set the table.

While he and Seth finished cooking the eggs, Heather made toast. By the time they sat down to eat, T.J. had a fairly good glimpse of what his life could be if he made things more permanent with Heather. Was that what he wanted?

It certainly wasn't unpleasant. Doing things with Seth—teaching him things—was pretty awesome. And just thinking about making love to Heather each night and waking up each morning with her in his arms had his body reacting in a very predictable way. But an instant family was a lot of responsibility.

He'd lain awake most of the night thinking about what he wanted and he still didn't have any firm answers. On one hand it scared the living hell out of him to make that kind of commitment—to be responsible for someone besides just himself. What if he came up lacking? What if he failed them in some way?

Other than Hank being his foster father during his time at the Last Chance Ranch, T.J. had never had a father. And he really hadn't had an example of what a husband was supposed to be. He'd watched his brothers as they learned what their wives expected of them, but that was only at family get-togethers. It might be different in their daily lives.

One thing that he didn't have to worry about was the financial aspect of being in a relationship. Because of wise investments, his grandkids' grandkids would never have to work a day in their lives if they didn't want to. It was being responsible for their emotional well-being that concerned him. He knew he would move heaven and earth to give Heather and Seth everything they could ever need or want. But was he enough to keep them both happy emotionally?

And then there was the problem of what his life would be like without them in it. Yes, it had happened quickly, but at this point, he didn't even want to think about not having them with him. Yet he wasn't sure that what he felt for Heather was love. He couldn't say he had ever loved a woman before. With nothing to

compare to his feelings for Heather, how was he supposed to know for sure?

"You look awfully serious all of a sudden," Heather
said, wiping Seth's hands after he finished eating. "Is
everything all right?"

"Sure." T.J. decided he could give their future more
thought later on. Right now, the time had come to warn
her about all of his family showing up later that afternoon. "I was just thinking about what I wanted to discuss with you last night."

"Okay, what's on your mind?" She rose from the
table to remove their empty plates, rinse them and put
them in the dishwasher. "I'm beginning to think this
is something you dread telling me and that means I
should dread hearing it."

"It's not anything bad," he assured her. "In fact, I'm
pretty sure you'll really enjoy yourself." He nodded at
Seth. "And I know my little partner is going to have
the time of his life."

"What is it?" she asked, looking suspicious.

He checked his watch. "In about five hours, my
family is going to start showing up for our annual New
Year's Eve party. I was going to ask you to join us, but
we kept getting distracted."

Her eyes widened. "I can't impose on your family
gathering," she said, shaking her head until her ponytail swung back and forth. "Seth and I have taken advantage of your generosity as it is. We'll go back home.
I'm sure we can stay warm enough if I—"

"Like hell," T.J. said, leaving the table to walk over
and take her in his arms. "It's supposed to be colder to-

night than it was last night. And while we're at it, let's get something straight right now. You haven't taken advantage of me. I want both of you here with me."

"I don't have anything with me that I can wear to a party," she said, looking distressed.

He frowned. "What's wrong with what you have on?"

She gave him a look like she thought he was being overly obtuse. "I'll be in jeans and a shirt while everyone else is—"

"Dressed just like you," he interrupted. "My sisters-in-law are going to be in jeans and sweaters or sweatshirts." He smiled. "Trust me, you'll fit right in, sweetheart." He kissed her until they both gasped for breath. "You and Seth are with me and I want you to meet my family. I'm betting by the time they leave after brunch tomorrow, you'll be wondering why you were so concerned."

Even as he said the words, he knew they were true. They were a part of his life now and meeting his family was the next step toward making it permanent.

When his brothers and sisters-in-law arrived late that day, Heather was relieved to see that T.J. had been right. She didn't feel out of place at all. The only awkward moment had been when his brother Nate asked if she had a stallion. When she told him yes, he grinned, wrapped her in a brotherly hug and welcomed her to the zoo. She had wondered what T.J. told them about his and her past run-ins, but whatever he'd said hadn't seemed to make a difference.

In fact, she was really enjoying herself. She had loved spending time in the kitchen with the women as they prepared dinner and snacks for the evening. Having other women to talk to was something she'd missed since moving back to the Circle W.

After graduating high school, she had moved two hours away to go to college, met Seth's father and lost touch with most of her girlfriends. Then, when she came back home to live after her fiancé was killed, she discovered that all of her friends had either moved away or they no longer had anything in common. But sitting in T.J.'s family room, she felt like one of the girls again.

"Heather, how old was your little boy when he started walking?" Bria Rafferty asked as she reached for another handful of homemade trail mix. "I've caught little Hank standing alone without holding on to anything several times, but he hasn't tried taking steps yet."

"Seth did the same thing for a few weeks," Heather said, smiling. "Then one day right after he turned eleven months old he just took off." She laughed when Seth ran around the sectional sofa where they were sitting, then ran back toward T.J. and his brothers gathered around the bar. "And he hasn't stopped since."

"He's adorable," Summer McClain commented as she rejoined the group after wiping off her husband's shirt because their daughter missed the burp cloth again. "I love his copper-colored hair. It reminds me of your hair, Taylor. Maybe one day you'll have a little red-haired boy or girl."

"Maybe." Taylor Donaldson smiled as she sipped her glass of ginger ale. "He really is a very sweet little boy, and so cute, Heather."

"Thank you," Heather answered, her chest swelling with pride.

When T.J. walked over to the couch with Seth perched atop his shoulders, Summer smiled. "T.J., you seem to be having fun this evening."

Heather looked around at a couple of the brothers, who were making faces as they tried to get the baby girl in Ryder McClain's arms to smile. The others were letting little Hank try on their wide-brimmed hats. "I think all of the men are having a good time with the kids."

"Of course they're having a good time," Bria agreed, laughing. "These guys are all just large children themselves."

"Hey, I resemble that remark," T.J. said, grinning.

"We know," all four women said in unison.

As their laughter died down, Taylor's husband, Lane, walked over to join them. "Are you ready, babe?"

"I suppose so," she said, smiling as she rose to her feet.

"You aren't leaving, are you?" Bria asked.

"Nope," Lane answered, grinning. "Hey, could you sorry excuses for cowboys stop propping up the bar and come over here for a minute," he called to his brothers.

"What's up now, Freud?" Sam asked, walking across the room with his giggling son wearing his hat.

"He's probably going to try to analyze all of us," Nate said, laughing.

"If he hasn't figured out by now that your elevator doesn't go all the way to the top floor, he might as well set fire to that psychology diploma of his," T.J. said dryly.

"So what's up, Lane?" Ryder asked, handing his baby daughter to his wife.

"Taylor and I wanted to let you all know that in a little less than eight months we're going to add another member to the family," Lane said, gazing lovingly at his wife.

"God help us," Ryder said, laughing. "Another little Freud." He stepped forward to shake Lane's hand, then hugged Taylor. "Just a word of advice. Get as much sleep between now and the baby's due date as you can."

"Yeah, after the baby gets here, sleep won't be much more than a fond memory," Sam said, tickling his giggling son.

"You know who to call for babysitting," Nate Rafferty said, raising his beer bottle in salute.

"Yeah, anybody but you," Jaron Lambert said, smiling. The most reserved of the brothers, Heather decided he could be the poster child for the phrase *the strong, silent type*.

Heather continued to watch the genuine joyful response of all the family members to the news of a new baby on the way and she couldn't help but envy them. As boys, the men had been brought together as strangers by the foster care system and sent to the Last Chance Ranch. But because of their shared experience and the memories they made together as adolescents, they had bonded and become a family that was closer than some who were related by blood.

As the evening wore on, Heather and the other women got their children down for the night, then returned to the game room to talk for a while before they turned on T.J.'s huge television to watch the colorful lighted ball drop at midnight in Times Square. Just before the big event, the men wandered over from the bar to join the ladies.

When T.J. sat down beside her on the sofa, he put his arm around her and drew her close. "Are you having a good time?" he whispered close to her ear.

"It's been a very nice evening," she said, smiling. "I love how relaxed and informal it's been. Thank you for including Seth and I in your family party."

With his arm still around her shoulders, he reached out to take her hand in his. "This is the first one of our family New Year's Eve parties that I've really looked forward to seeing the ball drop," he admitted.

"Why?"

"Because that means I get to kiss you," he said, his eyes filled with such promise it robbed her of breath. "And since there's an hour's difference between here and the east coast, I get to kiss you when it's midnight here, as well."

"I have a hard time believing this is the first time you've had a date on New Year's Eve," she said doubtfully.

"It's the first one since the family started ringing in the New Year together," he said, lifting her hand to his mouth to kiss the back of it.

The gesture made her feel warm all over. T.J. hadn't made any attempt to hide their relationship or whatever it was that was going on between them. From the moment his family began to arrive earlier in the day, he had taken every opportunity to show her affection.

"All right, guys," Nate said, standing up. "The ball has started dropping. On your mark, grab your girls... kiss!"

Heather might have laughed at the man's countdown, but T.J.'s mouth immediately covered hers in a kiss that caused her head to spin. When he lifted his head, he smiled.

"Happy New Year, sweetheart. I have a feeling this is going to be the best year ever—for both of us."

Looking into T.J.'s hypnotic hazel eyes, she hoped with all of her heart he was right.

Eight

The next morning, after the family finished the brunch Heather and his sisters-in-law had made, everyone took off to drive back to their ranches and T.J. breathed a sigh of relief as he glanced over to check on Seth, who was playing on the braided rug on the other side of his office desk. He loved his family—loved getting together with them—but for the first time since he'd started hosting the New Year's Eve parties, he was glad to see them leave.

He'd spent a miserable night in the master suite, knowing that the woman he wanted in his bed was just down the hall. Even the cold shower he had suffered through when everyone went upstairs to their rooms hadn't cooled off the burn he had for Heather.

He had asked her to sleep in his room, but she appar-

ently wasn't yet ready for his family to learn the extent
of their relationship. He was pretty sure his family had
already figured it out, but if Heather wasn't ready for
it to be common knowledge that they were sleeping
together, he wasn't going to push the issue.

"Did you send one of your men over to tend to my
horses or should I go over to feed them and muck out
the stalls?" Heather asked, walking into his office.

When she came around his desk, he turned his chair,
took her by the hand and pulled her down onto his
lap. "I sent Tommy Lee over there a couple of hours
ago," T.J. said, nodding. He gave her a peck on the lips.
"When he came back he said everything looked fine."

T.J. started to settle his mouth over hers to give her
the kiss he knew they both wanted. But Seth chose that
moment to get up from where he had been sitting to
walk over to them.

"Mom-mom," the little boy whined, rubbing his
eyes.

"I think somebody is still tired from having such
a big night," she said, picking up Seth. She smiled. "I
need to take him upstairs for a nap."

"You want me to carry him up there for you?" T.J.
asked, reaching up to stroke the little boy's copper hair.

She shook her head. "You go ahead and finish whatever you were doing. I'll probably only be a few minutes."

T.J. couldn't resist giving both of them a kiss on
each of their cheeks. "I'll be right here when you get
back."

As he watched Heather carry Seth from the room,

T.J. couldn't stop thinking about how quickly the two of them had become so important to him. From the time he had found them stranded on his side of the creek, all he'd been able to think about were ways to help them, to keep them with him.

He knew of only one way to do that permanently—with a ring, a preacher and a lifetime promise. Was he really thinking about taking that step this soon?

T.J frowned. Watching her with his family last night, he had come to the realization that he loved her—had probably loved her from the moment she stepped out of her car that night in his garage. And he couldn't care more for Seth if the little boy had been his own child. But was he ready to make that commitment? He was almost positive Heather's feelings for him went just as deep. Would she even consider becoming his wife?

He still wasn't sure that he could be everything Heather and Seth needed. But he could for damned sure try.

Right now, though, he just wanted to enjoy having Heather and Seth in his home for a few more days. He could give the future a lot more thought later. He shook his head and reached for his cup of coffee, accidently knocking off the pile of Heather's mail he had placed on his desk the day before. After he'd come home from the Circle W, he had gotten busy and forgotten all about it.

As he scooped up the pieces from the floor an envelope with Final Notice stamped on the front caught his eye. One look at the return address and he had a good idea he knew what it was. The letter had been sent from the county treasurer's office. He would bet every last dime he had that Heather was behind on her real estate taxes.

He placed the unopened envelope on top of the rest of her mail as the revelation sank in. Knowing what a struggle it was for her to keep the Circle W going, he really wasn't all that surprised. What did alarm him was the fact that she might lose the ranch.

He sat back in his desk chair, trying to think of how he could find out what was going on. She was prickly enough about her circumstances that he doubted she'd confide in him on her own. Asking her straight up was out of the question. She would no doubt tell him where to go and how to go about getting there.

But he needed to know what he could do to help her.

A sudden thought had him breathing a sigh of relief as he turned on his laptop. There was one way he could find out what she was up against and not run the risk of pissing her off. Delinquent taxes, court reports and other records were posted on the county's website. All he had to do was go online and check the public records. If, as he suspected, there was a problem, then he would figure out what he could do to help her.

Fifteen minutes later, T.J. closed the browser on his laptop and blew out a frustrated breath. Taxes hadn't been paid on the Circle W property in three years and the ranch was due to be seized by the county the first of next month. It would be put up for auction after that.

Of course, if the debt was satisfied, along with all the penalties and interest charges, Heather could keep the ranch. But he knew for certain she didn't have that kind of money. If she did, she wouldn't have had to sell off some of her brood mares to make ends meet.

He could offer to pay the taxes for her, but hell would freeze over before she'd let him do that. Or he could offer to lend her the money. But he knew her pride wouldn't allow her to go for that option either. So what was he supposed to do?

Sitting back and doing nothing while she lost her ranch wasn't in his DNA. The Circle W had been in her family for generations and should be there for Seth to take over when he came of age. As long as T.J. had breath in his body and the money to rectify the situation, he would see that it was.

He would help first, and ask permission after. He'd had no trouble winning her over to his way of doing things with all her other ranch problems. This one would be no different.

Picking up the letter from the county clerk, he opened his desk drawer, placed the envelope inside, then slid it shut. Heather had already dealt with more than her share of stress the past few days. He wasn't going to give her the notice and add to it. Besides, he already knew how he was going to take care of the matter. And as long as she didn't know about it first, she couldn't stop him. But he had every intention of giving her the security of the ranch being there for Seth.

"You're looking serious again," Heather said, walking back into his office.

"Just pondering the mysteries of the universe," he said, smiling. "Did you get my little partner settled down for a nap?"

She nodded. "He had the time of his life last night, but he's completely worn-out."

Looking down at the pile of her mail minus the upsetting letter, he handed her the bundle. "I forgot to tell you that I picked up your mail yesterday when I went over to meet the furnace repairman."

"Thanks," she said, taking it from him. "I was just thinking that I should drive over to the ranch and pick it up after Seth wakes up."

As he watched her thumb through the envelopes he felt a little guilty about hiding the letter from her, but he was certain she already knew about the situation and he had already made up his mind about handling it for her. Unfortunately, he couldn't put his plans into motion until the first of next week when the courthouse reopened.

"Heather, I have a horse I need to work with," he said, leaving his desk chair to wrap his arms around her. He had one more decision to make and he needed a little alone time to think it through and decide what he was going to do.

Kissing her, his body hardened so fast it left him a little dizzy. It always seemed to be this way with her. He took a deep breath and tried to focus. If he didn't already know what he was going to do before, he did now. But he still needed time to make some plans and the sooner he got started on them the better.

"Why don't you bring Seth out to the arena when he wakes up and I'll give him a real horseback ride?" he suggested.

"He'd love that," she said, smiling.

When he looked into her crystalline blue eyes, the emotion he saw there convinced him that everything was going to work out to his satisfaction. He was not only going to pay her back taxes, but he was also going to take that leap of faith and ask her to become his wife.

When Heather paid the furnace repairman with the last of her reserves and closed the door behind him, she sighed heavily. Her and her son's fate had just been sealed. They were going to be looking for somewhere else to live at the end of the month, but at least they would be warm until then.

"Hossy?" Seth asked, looking at the door.

"You've got a one-track mind, sweetie." Scooping him up into her arms, she kissed his smooth baby-soft cheek. They had only been home a few hours and she already missed T.J. terribly. It seemed Seth did, too. "Maybe we'll see him when he gets back from Stephenville."

Her son looked at the door again before he shook his head. "Hossy," he said stubbornly.

"You're as determined to have your way as T.J. is," she said, laughing.

When she finally got Seth distracted with the barn that mooed when the door was opened, she made a pot of coffee. Fighting tears, she took the local newspaper and started looking at what was available for rent in the area. For one reason or another, she found fault with all of the places in her price range and she was pretty sure she knew why. None of them were the Circle W or the Dusty Diamond.

Propping her elbow on the table, she rested her chin on the heel of her hand. She could understand feeling this way about her own ranch. It was home. But she really hadn't expected to feel that way about the Dusty Diamond. Of course, it didn't take a genius to figure out why she felt so at home there. That's where T.J. was.

Lost in thought, it took a moment for her to realize that someone was knocking on the door. But apparently her son had heard the sound because when she started to get up from the table, he raced past her.

"Hossy! Hossy!" he shouted, turning back to give her a look that was meant to urge her to hurry up and open the door. "Hossy!"

Before she could reach for the knob, the door opened and T.J. walked in to pick up Seth. "Hey there, partner!"

As she watched, her son threw his little arms around T.J.'s neck and hugged him with all the exuberance an almost two-year-old could possess. "Mine hossy!"

Heather laughed. "I really need to work on him learning how to say T.J."

He tickled her son's tummy. "I'm fine with whatever he wants to call me."

The smile T.J. gave her caused her heart to race and when he put his arm around her shoulders and pulled her to him, Heather's chest tightened with emotion. She realized now that she had been wrong in her assumption that no man could love another man's child as much as he would his own. Just seeing T.J. and Seth together was all the proof she needed to dispel that misconception.

"Would you like some coffee?" she asked, needing a moment to shore up her composure.

"That sounds good." Kissing her, his gaze caught hers. "There's something we need to talk over."

"Oh, dear heavens," she said, laughing as she walked over to pour him a cup of coffee. "The last time we went through this, I ended up meeting your family and they were wonderful."

"Yeah, but you have to admit I had good reason to be nervous about that." He grinned as he sat down at the table with Seth in his lap. "Having all of them together in one place is a lot like trying to keep up with what's going on at a wild horse race," he said, referring to the rodeo event where a team of three cowboys attempted to catch, saddle and ride a wild horse.

"There were times it was a bit of a free-for-all," she admitted, setting his coffee on the table in front of him. Smiling as she sat in the chair across from him, she added, "But in a really good way."

As she watched, he started to pick up his coffee mug, but then stopped with it halfway to his mouth. "Looking for somewhere else to live?" he asked, nodding toward the open newspaper still lying on the table.

Heather's cheeks burned with humiliation as she stared at him. There was no sense in trying to be evasive or lying about it. He would eventually find out anyway. But that didn't make her loss any easier to put into words.

"S-Seth and I are…going to be evicted at the first of

next month." She trained her eyes on her tightly clasped hands on the top of the table. "The taxes haven't been paid since my father got sick."

When T.J. set his coffee cup down, he reached out to cover her hands with his and she had to fight to keep her tears in check. Keeping her gaze fixed on their hands, she refused to look at him. Her pride was taking a direct hit as it was, and she didn't think she could stand to see his eyes filled with pity.

"Sweetheart, that's not going to happen," he said gently.

"Yes, it is," she said, nodding. "Just before Christmas I received a notice from the county telling me they were starting the proceedings to seize all of my assets to satisfy the debt."

"Heather, look at me," he commanded. When she looked up, instead of sympathy his hazel eyes were filled with determination. "I'm telling you that you aren't going to lose the Circle W."

Something in his tone and confident expression caused a cold feeling to spread throughout her chest. "How can you be so sure?"

"I didn't intend to tell you like this," he said slowly. "But the other day when I got your mail there was a final notice from the county about the ranch."

"You opened my mail?" she asked as anger began to replace the dread that had filled her.

He shook his head. "I didn't have to."

"Then how—"

"When I noticed the return address, I went online to the county government's website. It's a matter of public record, sweetheart." He gently squeezed her hands with his a moment before he reached into the inside pocket of his jacket to remove some folded papers. Laying them on the table in front of her, he added, "But as of this morning, the debt has been settled and you're no longer in danger of losing your ranch."

She stared at him for endless seconds as his words settled in. Then jerking her hands from beneath his, she jumped to her feet. "You didn't!"

"Yes, I did," he said firmly.

"Have you listened to anything I've told you these past two weeks?" she demanded.

"I've listened to everything," he said, nodding.

"You couldn't have." His calm demeanor infuriated her even more. "If you had, you would know that I don't want anyone—and especially you—feeling sorry for me. I'm not a charity case. I pay my own bills."

"I don't feel sorry for you," he insisted. "This is not charity. I just want to take care of you and Seth and make your lives easier."

"Do you even hear yourself?" She shook her head. "If that isn't pity, I don't know what is."

"M-Mom-mom," Seth said uncertainly, his little chin wobbling as he looked from her to T.J. Their raised voices were upsetting her baby and she walked over to take her son from T.J.

"I'd appreciate it if you would leave now," she said as she hugged Seth close. "You're upsetting my son."

T.J. slowly stood up. "This isn't over, Heather."

"Yes…it is." She took a deep breath to keep her voice from shaking. "You can't always have your way,

T.J. When you care about someone, you have to listen to what they want. But since you didn't, the Circle W and everything here, with the exception of our personal effects, is yours now."

"Like hell," he said angrily. "I paid the back taxes so that you can hang on to this place for Seth, not because I wanted it. I've got my own place. I don't want yours."

"Well, whether you wanted it or not, it's yours." When Seth started to cry, she pointed toward the door. "Now please leave so that I can take care of my son."

"This isn't over," T.J. said angrily.

"Yes, it is."

Walking over to the door, he turned back. "Don't let your stubborn pride do this to us, Heather."

She stiffened her spine and straightened her shoulders. "There is no *us*, T.J. If there had been, you would have discussed what you intended to do with me before the fact, not after you'd already done it."

He looked as if he wanted to say more, but instead he just shook his head, opened the door and left. She heard him rev his truck's engine a moment before gravel spun and the truck sped down the driveway toward the main road.

"Hossy!" Seth cried, reaching his little hand toward the door as if he knew he'd lost his best friend.

"He's gone, sweetie," she finally said, feeling as if her heart had shattered into a million pieces.

"Hossy," Seth repeated as he buried his face in the side of her neck. His tears wet her shirt and, unable to bear her son's distress, she didn't even try to hold back her own tears.

When her son finally cried himself to sleep, she put him in his bed and wandered back into the kitchen to stare at the legal papers T.J. had left on the table. She'd never felt more lonely in her entire life. Not even losing her fiancé and her father so close together, having a baby by herself and struggling to keep the ranch running had left her feeling as desolate as she felt at this moment. Her breath caught on a sob. She knew now beyond a shadow of doubt that her worst fears had just been realized. She and Seth had both fallen hopelessly in love with T.J. and he had broken both of their hearts.

T.J. sat in his man cave with his second bottle of beer, staring at his reflection in the big mirror above the bar. He'd chugged the first beer in one continuous gulp and he just might do the same with the bottle he held now. Why did he have to fall in love with a woman who had more stubborn pride in her little finger than most people had in their whole damned bodies?

Taking a long draw from the bottle in his hand, he had to admit that part of her reaction was his own damned fault. If he hadn't asked her about the rental ads she'd been looking at in the newspaper, he wouldn't have gotten the cart before the horse.

He reached into the front pocket of his jeans and withdrew the small black velvet box he had been carrying around all day. Setting it on the bar, he opened the lid to stare at the three-carat princess-cut diamond engagement ring he had intended to give her when he asked her to be his wife. His intention had been to ask her to marry him first, then give her the document for the paid taxes as an engagement present.

"Way to go, jackass," he muttered to the man staring back at him from the mirror. "You just might have screwed up any chance you had with her."

Restless, he snapped the lid on the box shut, then got up to toss the empty beer bottle into the trash can behind the bar. Wandering into the kitchen, he found his housekeeper, Theresa, standing at the counter cutting up vegetables for his dinner.

"I hope that whatever you're making freezes well," he said, walking over to look out the French doors leading to his patio. "I'm not hungry and probably won't be eating supper."

"You don't look like you feel well, T.J.," she said with concern in her eyes. "Is everything all right?"

He shrugged. "Things have been better."

"Is there anything I can do to help?" she asked.

"Not unless you can turn back time a few hours," he admitted.

"Sorry," she said, shaking her head. "But it might help if you wait a couple of days before you go talk to the young lady and tell her you're sorry for whatever you've done."

"How did you—"

"I've seen that same look on more than one young cowboy's face when he's done something to anger his woman," she said wisely. "So tell me about this young lady who's stolen your heart."

For the next half hour, T.J. told the older woman

about Heather and Seth and what he had done to fall out of his woman's good graces.

When he finished, she nodded. "You're right. You really messed up. Big-time. But I don't think all is lost."

"You don't?"

"No." She smiled. "As long as you're willing to give her a little time to calm down, I think she'll realize that you meant well, even if you did do something that you knew deep down she was going to take offense to."

"That's it?" he asked incredulously. "That's all I have to do?"

"Well, that and be willing to do a fair amount of groveling," Theresa said, laughing as she put the casserole she had been making into the oven.

"Thanks, Theresa," he said, kissing her wrinkled cheek.

She laughed. "Just remember our little talk the next time I hit you up for a raise."

"Will do," he said, smiling for the first time since he'd left Heather's.

As he walked back into the man cave, T.J. felt more hopeful. He just had to wait the few days Theresa had suggested before he went over to try to talk things through with Heather.

The way he saw it, he had one shot left. He loved her and Seth more than life itself and now that he'd figured that out, he wasn't about to do anything else that might screw up things. Even if he had to wear out the knees on a pair of jeans, he was going to beg Heather to understand and accept that he had only had the best of intentions.

The rest of his life depended on it.

Nine

Heather sniffed back tears as she finished packing the rest of the kitchen items into a carton, then taped it shut. She only had a few more of Seth's clothes and hers to pack and they would be ready to finish loading the small trailer she had rented.

Looking around, her breath hitched on a sob. The Circle W had always been home and she couldn't believe that when she drove away later that afternoon, she would never again be able to walk through the house where she had grown up. Nor would she be able to take Seth fishing along the creek bank or watch him ride his first horse around the feed lot.

But as much as not being able to do those things bothered her, it was never again seeing the man she loved that filled her with sorrow—a pain deeper than she could have ever imagined. She realized that she should have handled the situation a little differently when he'd confessed what he'd done. But why couldn't T.J. understand that by choosing not to talk to her about what he wanted to do, he had cut her out of the decisions about her own family's ranch? He'd made her feel ashamed that she had been unable to do more to save her legacy. He had completely missed, or possibly ignored, her need to be independent and prove herself capable of providing for herself and her son.

"Mom-mom, hossy?" Seth asked, walking into the room.

It tore her apart every time her little boy asked about T.J. She had failed to protect her son from becoming emotionally attached to T.J. and in the end he was suffering as much, if not more, heartache than she was. She was an adult and could understand the choices she had to make. But Seth was too young to realize what had happened.

"No, sweetie," she said, picking him up. "We won't be seeing T.J. anymore."

She had no sooner made the statement than the back door opened and the man in question walked right in. Of course, she supposed he could do that now. After all, he owned the place.

"Good morning," he said, smiling.

Seth immediately held out his arms and leaned toward T.J. for him to hold him. "Hossy!"

"How's my partner doing today?" T.J. asked, smiling. He gave Heather a questioning look as if to ask if he could hold her son.

Not wanting to make the situation any more stressful for Seth, she nodded. Her son immediately wrapped his arms around T.J.'s neck and held on to him as if he was a lifeline. It made her feel worse than ever.

"In a way, I'm glad you stopped by," she said, walking over to the counter for the large envelope with his name on it. Handing it to him, she added, "It will save me having to send you the keys to all of the buildings, as well as the papers you'll need for transferring ownership of the horses and the deed to the property."

"Where are you going to go?" he asked. His expression gave nothing away as to what he might be thinking.

"I thought we might go up to Oklahoma," she answered. "I heard on the news there are several job openings in the Tulsa area."

He looked so good in his black Western-cut suit jacket, white oxford cloth shirt and dark blue jeans, it brought tears to her eyes. She turned away to keep him from seeing her pain.

"There are a few things we need to get settled before you go," he said, pulling out one of the chairs at the table.

"Everything you'll need is in the envelope," she answered. Noticing that Seth had laid his head on T.J.'s shoulder and gone to sleep, she reached for him. "I'll put him in the play yard."

"I'll do it," T.J. said, standing to walk into the living room where she had set up the portable bed. "You've already got Seth's bed taken apart and put into the trailer?" he asked when he returned.

She nodded. "All I have left are a few boxes and the play yard to put in the trunk of my car."

"I'll carry them out for you when we get ready to leave." He motioned toward the chair he had pulled out from the table. "Sit down. There's something I need to tell you."

"I can't imagine there's anything left to say."

He gave her an indulgent smile. "Will you please sit, Heather?"

Sighing, she walked over and sat down in the chair. It was clear he wasn't going to tell her what he thought needed saying until she did as he asked.

"There's something you need to know about me," he said, leaning back against the counter. He folded his arms across his wide chest and casually crossed his legs at the ankles. "It might help you see my side of things and explain my need to take care of you and Seth."

"I don't see how—"

He held up one hand to stop her. "Just hear me out."

"All right."

"My mom was a single mother," he said, meeting her gaze head-on. "I know now how hard she struggled to work, pay bills and take care of me. And believe me, she did a hell of a job and made a lot of sacrifices just to keep me from finding out that we didn't have it as good as everyone else." He shook his head. "When I look back, I realize now that all those times she said she wasn't all that hungry were really times that she was leaving the food for me so that I had plenty to eat."

She watched a shadow of sadness briefly cross his

handsome face and knew that what he was about to tell her next was something that had caused him a lot of emotional pain.

"What happened?" she asked softly.

"My mom and I both got the flu when I was ten," he said, giving her a meaningful look. "There wasn't enough money for both of us to see a doctor, so she made sure I was taken care of, but she neglected herself. I got better. She didn't. She died of pneumonia a week or so later."

"Oh, T.J., I'm so sorry," she said, realizing why he had been so insistent that she stay at the Dusty Diamond when he learned that she had the flu.

"Me, too," he said gruffly. He seemed to take a sudden interest in the tops of his expensive alligator-skin boots. Then he raised his head to look directly at her. "The night I found you and Seth stranded by the flooded-out road, I made a vow that I wouldn't let the same thing happen to your son."

"I—I had no idea," she stammered.

"Just like my mom, you didn't have anyone to take care of you. You didn't have anyone to see that you got better." He shrugged. "I couldn't walk away from that."

"I don't know what to say." She was completely stunned.

"I didn't want you to know," he said, shaking his head. "I didn't insist on taking care of you so that you would feel sorry about me losing my mom when I was ten years old." He pointed toward the hall. "I did it for that little boy in there. I didn't want him going through life without his mother."

Tears filled her eyes. How could she have ever thought that T.J. wouldn't love her son as much as his own father would have?

"Is that when you went into the foster system? After your mom passed away?" she asked.

"No, I was sent to live with my great-grandmother," he said, shaking his head. "But she was elderly and didn't have the energy to chase a preadolescent boy who had a knack for getting himself into trouble every time he turned around." He reached up to rub the back of his neck as if he was trying to decide how much to tell her. "I was put into the system when I was fourteen. She passed away a couple of months later."

"You were in trouble?" she asked, completely shocked.

He nodded. "I fell in with a bad crowd and landed in juvenile detention more than once for vandalism. For whatever reason, my case worker decided that I was a candidate for this new foster home run by an ex-rodeo champion."

"That's why it was called the Last Chance Ranch?" she asked.

"Yup, and it was the best thing that ever happened to me," he said, smiling fondly. "Hank Calvert made me face the anger I'd felt at losing my mom. He made me realize that instead of blaming everyone else for it, I should accept that's just the way things go sometimes. He also believed in me and after a while, I started believing in myself."

"So all of your brothers were in trouble, too?" she asked, marveling at the men they had all become.

"We were all hell-raisers," he said, laughing. "But with Hank Calvert's help, we all straightened up our acts and became honest, upstanding citizens."

"I would have never guessed," she admitted.

"He saw to it that we all went to college, too." T.J. grinned. "You could never tell it by looking at me, but I'm more than just a rodeo cowboy who won a couple of world championship belt buckles. I graduated from Texas State with a master's degree in business."

"Hank sounds like a wonderful man," she said, meaning it. "Sam and Bria's son is named after him, isn't he?"

"Yes." T.J. shoved away from the counter and walked over to her. Kneeling down in front of her, he took her hands in his. "Heather, I know you think I was being high-handed when I paid your taxes, but I only wanted to do something that would help relieve the stress I know you've been under for far too long." He kissed each one of her palms. "I don't ever want to see callouses on these hands again from where you've had to work like three men just to keep this ranch running."

"I don't think you have to worry." His kind words were causing her heart to break all over again. "Remember, you own the Circle W now."

"Sweetheart, did you bother looking at the documents I left here the other day after I paid the taxes?" he asked, smiling.

She shook her head. "No. I didn't have the heart."

"I never said I bought the ranch for back taxes," he said, his tone indulgent. "I said I paid the taxes. And if you had bothered to look at those papers, you would have seen that I paid them in your name."

"But it wasn't your responsibility," she insisted. "It was my debt. I couldn't pay them and I—"

"I understand that, sweetheart," he said, kissing her. "But I was going to give you the papers as a gift after I asked you something."

A bubble of hope began to form inside of her, but she tried to tamp it down. "What were you going to ask me, T.J.?"

As she watched, he pulled a small black velvet box from his jacket pocket. "I was going to ask you if you would consider making me the happiest man on earth by becoming my wife. Then I had planned to give you those papers as an engagement present." He flipped open the box. Resting inside was one of the biggest diamonds she had ever seen.

"Oh, my God!" she said, covering her mouth with her hand. "I never... I mean, I didn't know... I never dreamed..." She let her voice trail off when she realized she wasn't capable of coherent speech.

"I love you, Heather," he said, his expression quite serious. "I will always love you. And if you'll let me, I'd like to take care of you for the rest of my life."

Tears trickled down her cheeks as she looked at the man she loved with all her heart. How could she have been so stubborn and let her pride get in the way of the happiness she could have with this wonderful man?

"T.J., I'm so...sorry," she said haltingly. "I know I'm stubborn and—"

"You don't have to apologize, sweetheart." He shook

his head. "I knew you weren't going to be overly happy about it. But if my plan to give the paid tax receipt to you as an engagement present had worked out, it would have probably saved both of us a lot of heartache."

When a fresh wave of tears began to roll down her cheeks, he set the ring box on the table, stood up and lifted her from the chair. Then he sat down with her on his lap. "I hope like hell those are happy tears," he said, holding her close.

"Y-yes," she said, putting her arms around his neck. "I love you with all my heart, T.J."

"Yes, they're happy tears or yes, you'll marry me?" he asked, grinning like he already knew.

"B-both."

"Thank God!" He removed the ring from the box to slip it on her finger. He kissed her then and the warmth of his love lit the darkest corners of her soul. When he lifted his head to gaze at her with more love shining in his eyes than she would ever deserve, he smiled. "There's one more thing that I would like to ask you."

"What's that?" she asked, wiping the tears from her cheeks.

"If you don't mind, I'd like to adopt Seth," he said seriously. "I love that little boy and I swear I'll be the best dad I can possibly be."

"I'd like that," she said, knowing he would be a wonderful father to her son.

T.J. smiled. "He's actually another reason I wanted to pay the taxes on this place. I wanted to make things easier for you, but I also wanted to make sure it was here for him when he gets old enough to take it over.

It's been in your family for generations and I didn't want him to lose that."

"Thank you," she whispered as more tears threatened.

They were silent for several minutes as they enjoyed being in each other's arms again.

"When do you want to get married, Heather?" He chuckled. "And please don't make this a long engagement. I want to start our lives together as soon as possible."

"How does Valentine's Day sound?" she asked, happy to give him his way on this particular issue.

"Better than the Fourth of July, but still further off than I'd like," he said, kissing her again.

Happier than she ever dreamed it was possible to be, she smiled. "Since I'm going to be your wife, could I ask you something I've been wondering about?"

"Sweetheart, you can ask me anything," he answered.

"What does T.J. stand for?"

Groaning, he rested his forehead against hers. "I guess you'll find out anyway when we get our marriage license."

"It can't be that bad," she said, shaking her head.

"Believe me, it's not that good," he replied.

She cupped his lean cheek with her palm as she gazed into his eyes. "Why don't you tell me and let me decide?"

"Tobias Jerome," he said, rolling his eyes. "I don't know what my mom was thinking when she hung that name on an innocent little baby."

"It's not bad at all," she said, wondering why he didn't like it.

"Do I look like a Toby or a Jerry?" he asked, raising one dark eyebrow.

"Well, not really," she admitted. "You do look more like a T.J. than either one of those two names.

"That's why when we have kids there won't be any of them named Tobias Jerome," he said, laughing.

"How many children do you want?" she asked, loving the idea of Seth having a brother or sister and no longer worried at all that T.J. wouldn't have enough love for all his children, biological or adopted.

"I've got a big house with lots of bedrooms," he said, grinning. "How does seven sound?"

"We'll revisit that subject later," she said, laughing.

His expression turned serious. "I love you, Heather."

"And I love you, T.J. With every breath I take."

Epilogue

"Well, we're down to two unmarried brothers now," T.J. said as he and his brothers stood at the bar in his man cave-turned-family room, celebrating his and Heather's wedding.

They had decided on a small intimate ceremony, with only his family in attendance, and that suited him just fine. The fewer guests they had, the sooner he could whisk Heather away for their honeymoon.

"Who do you think will be next?" Sam asked.

"Well, it isn't going to be me," Nate said. "I'm about ready to swear off women for good."

"And if you believe that, I've got some prime real estate in Death Valley to sell you," Ryder said, laughing.

T.J. looked lovingly over at his beautiful wife, who was talking with his sisters-in-law and Bria's sister,

Mariah. "That's what I said, Nate. And look at me now. I couldn't be happier."

"Yeah, but Heather is a great woman," Nate retorted. "She's not as unreasonable as you once thought and she's definitely not as unreasonable as most women."

T.J. couldn't help but smile. None of his brothers had any idea about what he and Heather had worked through to get to where they were now. And he wasn't going to enlighten them.

"It could be Jaron," Lane suggested.

When Jaron didn't protest immediately, they all turned to catch him staring at Mariah again.

"What?" he asked, clearly unaware of Lane's comment.

"We were just speculating on whether you or Nate will be the next to take a trip down the aisle," Lane said, grinning.

Jaron shook his head. "You better bet on Nate," he said emphatically. "If you're betting on me, you'll lose."

"I've got Nate," T.J. said, plunking down a hundred-dollar bill on top of the bar.

"Who's going to hold the pot this time?" Ryder asked.

"I'll do it," Sam said.

As T.J. watched his brothers each place their bets on who they thought would be the next to get married, Seth ran up and threw his arms around T.J.'s leg. "Mine daddy!"

Laughing, T.J. picked up his son. He and Heather had told Seth that T.J. would be adopting him and would be his daddy. That was all it had taken for the kid to abandon calling T.J. *Hossy* and to start calling him *Daddy*.

While the brothers continued to speculate on Nate's and Jaron's prospects, T.J. carried Seth over to the woman they both loved with all their hearts.

"I don't know about you, but I'm about ready to start our honeymoon," he whispered in her ear.

Her smile robbed him of breath. "Me, too."

"Did you get Seth's things together for Sam and Bria to watch him while we're gone?" T.J. asked, setting Seth on his feet to go play with his new cousin, little Hank.

Heather nodded. "Bria had Sam put Seth's suitcase and car seat in their car just before the ceremony."

T.J. pulled her close for a kiss that left them both breathless. "Then let's get out of here, sweetheart."

"You never did tell me where we're going," she said, giving him a smile that had him burning to get her alone. "Can you at least tell me which direction it's in?"

"Does it matter?" he asked, laughing.

She shook her head and when she put her hand in his, T.J. felt like the luckiest man alive.

"Whatever way you go, cowboy, I'll be right by your side."

"I love you, Mrs. Malloy," he said, kissing her again.

She lightly touched his cheek. "And I love you, T.J. With all my heart."

* * * * *

15_INSHIP

MILLS & BOON®

Need more New Year reading?

We've got just the thing for you!
We're giving you 10% off your next eBook or
paperback book purchase on the Mills & Boon
website. So hurry, visit the website today and type
SAVE10 in at the checkout for your exclusive

10% DISCOUNT

www.millsandboon.co.uk/save10

Ts and Cs: Offer expires 31st March 2015.
This discount cannot be used on bundles or sale items.

MILLS & BOON®
Desire™

PASSIONATE AND DRAMATIC LOVE STORIES

A sneak peek at next month's titles…

In stores from 16th January 2015:

- **His Lost and Found Family** – Sarah M. Anderson
  and **Terms of a Texas Marriage** – Lauren Canan

- **Thirty Days to Win His Wife** – Andrea Laurence
  and **The Texan's Royal M.D.** – Merline Lovelace

- **Her Forbidden Cowboy** – Charlene Sands
  and **The Blackstone Heir** – Dani Wade

Available at WHSmith, Tesco, Asda, Eason, Amazon and Apple

Just can't wait?
Buy our books online a month before they hit the shops!
visit www.millsandboon.co.uk

These books are also available in eBook format!

MILLS & BOON®

Why shop at millsandboon.co.uk?

Each year, thousands of romance readers find their perfect read at millsandboon.co.uk. That's because we're passionate about bringing you the very best romantic fiction. Here are some of the advantages of shopping at www.millsandboon.co.uk:

* **Get new books first**—you'll be able to buy your favourite books one month before they hit the shops

* **Get exclusive discounts**—you'll also be able to buy our specially created monthly collections, with up to 50% off the RRP

* **Find your favourite authors**—latest news, interviews and new releases for all your favourite authors and series on our website, plus ideas for what to try next

* **Join in**—once you've bought your favourite books, don't forget to register with us to rate, review and join in the discussions

Visit **www.millsandboon.co.uk**
for all this and more today!

LLS_WEB